JODI PICOULT

Lone Wolf

First published in Great Britain in 2012 by Hodder and Stoughton
An Hachette UK company
First published in America in 2012 by Atria Books
An imprint of Simon & Schuster, Inc.

This paperback edition published in 2013

9

A CIP catalogue record for this title is available from the British Library

ISBN 978 1 444 75456 8

Typeset in by Palimpsest Book Production Limited, Falkirk, Stirlingshire

Printed and bound by CPI Group (UK) Ltd, Croydon, CR0 4YY

Hodder and Stoughton policy is to use papers that are natural, renewable
and recyclable products and made from wood grown in sustainable forests.
The logging and manufacturing processes are expected to conform to
the environmental regulations of the country of origin.

Hodder and Stoughton Ltd
A division of Hodder Headline PLC
338 Euston Road
London NW1 3BH

www.hodder.co.uk

For Josh, Alex, and Matthew Picoult
Your aunt loves you. Lots.

ACKNOWLEDGMENTS

I'm fortunate to be surrounded by people who make me look much smarter than I am, all of whom contributed to the research for this book. In the medical field, I am indebted to Dr. James Bernat, who spent hours with me discussing potential traumatic brain injuries and was always available to field an email with yet more questions from me. Thanks to social workers Nancy Trottier and Jane Stephenson, as well as Sean Fitzpatrick and Karen Lord of the New England Organ Bank. Jon Skinner provided me with detailed medical care costs in New Hampshire. Lise Iwon, Lise Gescheidt, Maureen McBrien, and Janet Gilligan are my legal wizards; Jennifer Sargent not only found wonderful legal wrinkles for me to iron out but connected me with people like Elizabeth Stanton, who could help me navigate them. Thanks to Doug Irwin for letting me use the line about the difference between dreams and goals.

If we're counting blessings, I have to give credit to the publishing company that has been my home for over a decade (mostly because the people inside it are amazing): Carolyn Reidy, Judith Curr, Sarah Branham, Kate Cetrulo, Caroline Porter, Chris Lloreda, Jeanne Lee, Gary Urda, Lisa Keim, Rachel Zugschwert, Michael Selleck, and the many others who have quite literally made me the author I am. The publicity machine behind me is a force to be reckoned with: David Brown, Ariele Fredman, Camille McDuffie, and Kathleen Carter Zrelak – wow. Just wow. And Emily Bestler – after all this time I hardly know how to thank you for all you've done. Luckily we have reached the point where we can read each other's minds.

Laura Gross is the second longest relationship in my life, after my husband. As an agent, she's formidable. As a friend, she's unforgettable. Thanks for letting me steal your line about the table and the stool.

To my mom, Jane Picoult: maybe all moms feel under-appreciated (God knows I do sometimes). But here is public proof that you're not. If we had our choice of moms, I would have picked you. Thanks for being my first reader, my unflaggable cheerleader, and for telling me that Dad couldn't put down the wolf sections on the plane.

A special thanks goes out to Shaun Ellis. When I created the character of Luke Warren, a man who lives among wolves in order to know them better, I didn't realize that someone like that already existed in the real world. Shaun has written a memoir, *The Man Who Lives with Wolves*, which I encourage you all to read. He and his assistant, Dr. Isla Fishburn, welcomed me to Devon to meet his captive packs, to very kindly share his life experience and his vast knowledge of these amazing animals, and to let me borrow bits and pieces of the incredible life he has led to flesh out my fictional character. Kerry Hood, my British publicist, kindly chauffeured my son Jake and me to Combe Martin. I will never forget how Shaun taught the three of us to howl . . . and what it sounded like when the other packs answered our call. He is a wonderful human spokesman for his wolf brethren, and more information about his charitable foundation is included at the end of this book.

Finally, as always, I have to thank my own pack: my husband Tim, my children Kyle, Jake, and Samantha. As is the case with wolves – I'd be nothing without all of you.

PROLOGUE

All stories are about wolves. All worth repeating, that is. Anything else is sentimental drivel . . . Think about it. There's escaping from the wolves, fighting the wolves, capturing the wolves, taming the wolves. Being thrown to the wolves, or throwing others to the wolves so the wolves will eat them instead of you. Running with the wolf pack. Turning into a wolf. Best of all, turning into the head wolf. No other decent stories exist.

– Margaret Atwood, *The Blind Assassin* (2000)

Luke

*I*n retrospect, maybe I shouldn't have freed the tiger.

The others were easy enough: the lumbering, grateful pair of elephants; the angry capuchin monkey that spit at my feet when I jimmied the lock; the snowy Arabian horses whose breath hung in the space between us like unanswered questions. Nobody gives animals enough credit, least of all circus trainers, but I knew the minute they saw me in the shadows outside their cages they would understand, which is why even the noisiest bunch – the parrots that had been bullied into riding on the ridiculous cumulus-cloud heads of poodles – beat their wings like a single heart while making their escape.

I was nine years old, and Vladistav's Amazing Tent of Wonders had come to Beresford, New Hampshire – which was a miracle in its own right, since nothing ever came to Beresford, New Hampshire, except for skiers who were lost, and reporters during presidential primaries who stopped off to get coffee at Ham's General Store or to take a leak at the Gas'n'Go. Almost every kid I knew had tried to squeeze through the holes in the temporary fencing that had been erected by the circus carnies so that we could watch the show without having to pay for a ticket. And in fact that was how

1

I first saw the circus, hiding underneath the bleachers and peering through the feet of paying customers with my best friend, Louis.

The inside of the tent was painted with stars. It seemed like something city people would do, because they hadn't realized that if they just took down the tent, they could see real stars instead. Me, I'd grown up with the outdoors. You couldn't live where I did – on the edge of the White Mountain National Forest – and not have spent your fair share of nights camping and looking up at the night sky. If you let your eyes adjust, it looked like a bowl of glitter that had been turned over, like the view from inside a snow globe. It made me feel sorry for these circus folks, who had to improvise with stencils instead.

I will admit that, at first, I couldn't tear my eyes away from the red sequined topcoat of the ringmaster and the endless legs of the girl on the tightrope. When she did a split in the air and landed with her legs veed around the wire, Louis let out the breath he'd been holding. Lucky rope, he said.

Then they started to bring out the animals. The horses were first, rolling their angry eyes. Then the monkey, in a silly bellman's outfit, which climbed onto the saddle of the lead horse and bared his teeth at the audience as he rode around and around. The dogs that jumped through hoops, the elephants that danced as if they were in a different time zone, the rainbow fluster of birds.

Then came the tiger.

There was a lot of hype, of course. About how dangerous a beast he was, about how we shouldn't try this at home. The trainer, who had a doughy, freckled face like a cinnamon roll, stood in the middle of the ring as the hatch on the tiger's cage was lifted. The tiger roared and, even as far away as I was, I smelled his bouillon breath.

He leaped onto a metal stand and swiped at the air. He stood on his hind legs on command. He turned in a circle.

I knew a thing or two about tigers. Like: If you shaved one, its skin would still be striped. And every tiger had a white mark on the back of each ear, so that it seemed like it was keeping an eye on you even when it was walking away.

Like: They belonged in the wild. Not here, in Beresford, while the crowd shouted and clapped.

In that instant two things happened. First, I realized I didn't much like the circus anymore. Second, the tiger stared right at me, as if he had searched out my seat number before-hand.

I knew exactly what he wanted me to do.

After the evening show, the performers went down to the lake behind the elementary school to drink and play poker and swim. It meant that most of their trailers, parked behind the big top, were empty. There was a guard – an Everest of a man with a shaved head and a hoop ring piercing his nose – but he was snoring to beat the band, with an empty bottle of vodka beside him. I slipped inside the fence.

Even in retrospect, I can't tell you why I did it. It was something between that tiger and me; that knowledge that I was free, and he wasn't. The fact that his unpredictable, raw life had been reduced to a sideshow at three and seven.

The trickiest cage to unlatch was the monkey's. Most, though, I could open with an ice pick I'd stolen from my grandfather's liquor cabinet. I let out the animals swiftly and quietly, watching them slip into the folds of the night. They seemed to understand that discretion was in order; not even the parrots made a sound as they disappeared.

The last one I freed was the tiger. I figured the other animals ought to have a good fifteen minutes of lead time to get away before I released a predator on their heels. So I crouched down in front of the cage and drew in the soft dirt with a pebble, marking time on my wristwatch. I was sitting there, waiting, when the Bearded Lady walked by.

She saw me right away. 'Well, well,' she said, although I couldn't see her mouth in the mess of the whiskers. But she didn't ask me what I was doing, and she didn't tell me to leave. 'Watch out,' she said. 'He sprays.' She must have noticed the other animals were gone – I hadn't bothered to try to disguise the open, empty cages and pens – but she just stared at me for a long moment, and then walked up the steps to her trailer. I held my breath, expecting her to call the cops, but instead I heard a radio. Violins. When she sang along, she had a deep baritone voice.

I will tell you that, even after all this time, I remember the sound of metal teeth grinding against each other as I opened the tiger's cage. How he rubbed up against me like a house cat before leaping the fence in a single bound. How I could actually taste fear, like almond sponge cake, when I realized I was bound to get caught.

Except . . . I didn't. The Bearded Lady never told anyone about me, and the circus roadies who cleaned up elephant dung were blamed instead. Besides, the town was too busy the next morning restoring order and apprehending the loose animals. The elephants were found splashing in the town fountain after knocking down a marble statue of Franklin Pierce. The monkey had made its way into the pie case at the *local diner and was devouring a chocolate dream silk torte when he was caught. The dogs were Dumpster diving behind the movie theater, and the horses had scattered. One was found galloping down Main Street. One made its way to a local farmer's pasture to graze with cattle. One traveled over ten miles to a ski hill, where it was spotted by a trauma helicopter. Of the three parrots, two were permanently lost, and one was found roosting in the belfry of the Shantuck Congregational Church.*

The tiger, of course, was long gone. And that presented a problem, because a renegade parrot is one thing, but a loose carnivore is another. The National Guard was dispersed into the White Mountain National Forest and for three days, schools in New Hampshire stayed closed. Louis came to my house on his bike and told me rumors he'd heard: that the tiger had slaughtered Mr. Wolzman's prize heifer, a toddler, our principal.

I didn't like to think about the tiger eating anything at all. I pictured him sleeping high in a tree during the day; and at night, navigating by the stars.

Six days after I freed the circus animals, a National Guardsman named Hopper McPhee, who had only just joined up a week earlier, found the tiger. The big cat was swimming in the Ammonoosuc River, its face and paws still bloody from feeding on a deer. According to Hopper McPhee, the tiger came flying at him with intent to kill, which is why he had to shoot.

I doubt that highly. The tiger was probably half asleep after a meal like that, and certainly not hungry. I do, however, believe that the tiger rushed Hopper McPhee. Because like I said, nobody gives animals enough credit. And as soon as

that tiger saw a gun pointed at him, he would have under-
stood.

   That he was going to have to give up the night sky.
   That he'd be imprisoned again.
   So, that tiger? He made a choice.

Part One

If you live among wolves you have to act like a wolf.

– Nikita Khrushchev, Soviet premier,
Quoted in *Observer*, London, September 26, 1971

Cara

Seconds before our truck slams into the tree, I remember the first time I tried to save a life.

I was thirteen, and I'd just moved back in with my father. Or, more accurately, my clothes were once again hanging in my former bedroom, but I was living out of a backpack in a trailer on the north end of Redmond's Trading Post & Dinosaur World. That's where my father's captive wolf packs were housed, along with gibbons, falcons, an overweight lion, and the animatronic *T. rex* that roared on the hour. Since that was where my father spent 99 percent of his time, it was expected that I follow.

I thought this alternative beat living with my mom and Joe and the miracle twins, but it hadn't been the smooth transition I'd hoped for. I guess I'd pictured my dad and me making pancakes together on Sunday morning, or playing hearts, or taking walks in the woods. Well, my dad did take walks in the woods, but they were inside the pens he'd built for his packs, and he was busy *being* a wolf. He'd roll around in the mud with Sibo and Sobagw, the numbers wolves; he'd steer clear of Pekeda, the beta of the pack. He'd eat from the carcass of a calf with wolves on either side of him, his hands and his mouth bloody. My dad believed that infiltrating a pack was far more educational than observing from afar the way biologists did. By the time I moved in with him, he'd already gotten five packs to accept him as a bona fide member – worthy of living with, eating with, and hunting with them, in spite of the fact that he was human. Because of this, some people thought he was a genius. The rest thought he was insane.

On the day I left my mom and her brand-spanking-new family, my dad was not exactly waiting for me with open arms. He was down in one of the enclosures with Mestawe, who was pregnant for the first time, and he was trying to forge a relationship with her so she'd pick him as the nanny for the pups. He even slept there, with his wolf family, while I stayed up late and flicked through the TV channels. It was lonely in the trailer, but it was lonelier being landlocked at an empty house.

In the summers, the White Mountains region was packed with visitors who went from Santa's Village to Story Land to Redmond's Trading Post. In March, though, that stupid *T. rex* roared to an empty theme park. The only people who stayed on in the off-season were my dad, who looked after his wolves, and Walter, a caretaker who covered for my dad when he wasn't on-site. It felt like a ghost town, so I started hanging out at the enclosures after school – close enough that Bedagi, the tester wolf, would pace on the other side of the fence, getting used to my scent. I'd watch my father dig a birthing bowl for Mestawe in her den, and meanwhile, I'd tell him about the football captain who was caught cheating, or the oboe player in the school orchestra who had taken to wearing caftans, and was rumored to be pregnant.

In return, my dad told me why he was worried about

Mestawe: she was a young female, and instinct only went so far. She didn't have a role model who could teach her to be a good mother; she'd never had a litter before. Sometimes, a wolf would abandon her pups simply because she didn't know better.

The night Mestawe gave birth, she seemed to be doing everything by the book. My father celebrated by opening a bottle of champagne and letting me drink a glass. I wanted to see the babies, but my father said it would be weeks before they emerged. Even Mestawe would stay in the den for a full week, feeding the pups every two hours.

Only two nights later, though, my father shook me awake. 'Cara,' he said, 'I need your help.'

I threw on my winter coat and boots and followed him to the enclosure where Mestawe was in her den. Except, she wasn't. She was wandering around, as far from her babies as she could get. 'I've tried everything to get her back inside, but she won't go,' my father said matter-of-factly. 'If we don't save the pups now, we won't have a second chance.'

He burrowed into the den and came out holding two tiny, wrinkled rats. At least that's what they looked like, eyes squinched shut, wriggling in his hand. He passed these over to me; I tucked them inside my coat as he pulled out the last two pups. One looked worse off than the other three. It wasn't moving; instead of grunting, it let out tiny puffs every now and then.

I followed my dad to a toolshed that stood behind the trailer. While I was sleeping he'd tossed all the tools into the snow; now the floor inside was covered with hay. A blanket I recognized from the trailer – a fluffy red plaid – was inside a small cardboard box. 'Tuck them in,' my father instructed, and I did. A hot water bottle underneath the blanket made it feel warm like a belly; three of the babies immediately began to snuffle between the folds. The fourth pup was cold to the touch. Instead of putting her beside her brothers, I slipped her into my coat again, against my heart.

When my father returned, he was holding baby bottles full of Esbilac, which is like formula, but for animals. He reached for the little wolf in my arms, but I couldn't let her go. 'I'll feed the others,' he told me, and while I coaxed mine to drink a drop at a time, his three sucked down every last bottle.

Every two hours, we fed the babies. The next morning, I didn't get dressed for school and my father didn't act like he expected me to. It was an unspoken truth: what we were doing here was far more important than anything I could learn in a classroom.

On the third day, we named them. My father believed in using indigenous names for indigenous creatures, so all his wolf names came from the Abenaki language. Nodah, which meant *Hear me*, was the name we gave the biggest of the bunch, a noisy black ball of energy. Kina, or *Look here*, was the troublemaker who got tangled in shoelaces or stuck under the flaps of the cardboard box. And Kita, or *Listen*, hung back and watched us, his eyes never missing a thing.

Their little sister I named Miguen, *Feather*. There were times she'd drink as well as her brothers and I would believe she was out of the woods, but then she'd go limp in my grasp and I'd have to rub her and slip her inside my shirt to keep her warm again.

I was so tired from staying up round the clock that I

couldn't see straight. I sometimes slept on my feet, dozing for a few minutes before I snapped awake again. The whole time, I carried Miguen, until my arms felt empty without her in them. On the fourth night, when I opened my eyes after nodding off, my father was staring at me with an expression I'd never seen before on his face. 'When you were born,' he said, 'I wouldn't let go of you, either.'

Two hours later, Miguen started shaking uncontrollably. I begged my father to drive to a vet, to the hospital, to someone who could help. I cried so hard that he bundled the other pups into a box and carried them out to the battered truck he drove. The box sat between us in the front seat and Miguen shivered beneath my coat. I was shaking, too, although I'm not sure whether I was cold, or just afraid of what I knew was coming.

She was gone by the time we got to the parking lot of the vet's office. I knew the minute it happened; she grew lighter in my arms. Like a shell.

I started to scream. I couldn't stand the thought of Miguen, dead, being this close to me.

My father took her away and wrapped her in his flannel shirt. He slipped the body into the backseat, where I wouldn't have to see her. 'In the wild,' he told me, 'she never would have lasted a day. You're the only reason she stayed as long as she did.'

If that was supposed to make me feel better, it didn't. I burst into loud sobs.

Suddenly the box with the wolf pups was on the dashboard, and I was in my father's arms. He smelled of spearmint and snow. For the first time in my life, I understood why he couldn't break free from the drug that was the wolf community. Compared to issues like this, of life and death, did it really matter if the dry cleaning was picked up, or if he forgot the date of open-school night?

In the wild, my father told me, a mother wolf learns her lessons the hard way. But in captivity, where wolves are bred only once every three or four years, the rules are different. You can't stand by and just let a pup die. 'Nature knows what it wants,' my father said. 'But that doesn't make it any easier for the rest of us, does it?'

There is a tree outside my father's trailer at Redmond's, a red maple. We planted it the summer after Miguen died, to mark the spot where she is buried. It's the same type of tree that, four years later, I see rushing toward the windshield too fast. The same type of tree our truck hits, in that instant, head-on.

A woman is kneeling beside me. 'She's awake,' the woman says. There's rain in my eyes and I smell smoke and I can't see my father.

Dad? I say, but I can only hear it in my head.

My heart's beating in the wrong place. I look down at my shoulder, where I can feel it.

'Looks like a scapula fracture and maybe some broken ribs. Cara? Are you Cara?'

How does she know my name?

'You've been in an accident,' the woman tells me. 'We're going to take you to the hospital.'

'My . . . father . . . ,' I force out. Every word is a knife in my arm.

I turn my head to try to find him and see the firemen, spraying a hose at the ball of flames that used to be my dad's

14

truck. The rain on my face isn't rain, just mist from the stream of water.

Suddenly I remember: the web of shattered windshield; the fishtail of the truck skidding; the smell of gasoline. The way when I cried for my dad he didn't answer. I start shaking all over.

'You're incredibly brave,' the woman says to me. 'Dragging your father out of the car in your condition . . .'

I saw an interview once where a teenage girl lifted a refrigerator off her little cousin when it accidentally fell on him. It had something to do with adrenaline.

A fireman who has been blocking my view moves and I can see another knot of EMTs gathered around my father, who lies very still on the ground.

'If it weren't for you,' the woman adds, 'your dad might not be alive.'

Later, I will wonder if that comment is the reason I did everything I did. But right now, I just start to cry. Because I know her words couldn't be farther from the truth.

Luke

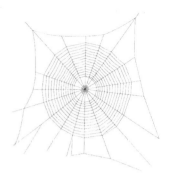

*W*hat I get asked all the time is: How could you do it? How could you possibly walk away from civilization, from a family, and go live in the forests of Canada with a pack of wild wolves? How could you give up hot showers, coffee, human contact, conversation, two years of your children's lives?

Well, you don't miss hot showers when all soap does is make it harder for your pack to recognize you by scent.

You don't miss coffee when your senses are on full alert all the time without it.

You don't miss human contact when you are huddled between the warmth of two of your animal brothers. You don't miss conversation when you learn their language.

You don't walk away from your family. You find yourself firmly lodged within a new one.

So you see, the real question isn't how I left this world to go into the woods.

It's how I made myself come back.

Georgie

I used to expect a phone call from the hospital, and just like I imagined, it comes in the middle of the night. 'Yes,' I say, sitting up, forgetting for a moment that I have a new life now, a new husband.

'Who is it?' Joe asks, rolling over.

But they aren't calling about Luke. 'I'm Cara's mother,' I confirm. 'Is she all right?'

'She's been in a motor vehicle accident,' the nurse says. 'She's got a severe shoulder fracture. She's stable, but she needs surgery—'

I am already out of bed, trying to find my jeans in the dark. 'I'm on my way,' I say.

By now Joe has the light on, and is sitting up. 'It's Cara,' I say. 'She's been in a car crash.'

He doesn't ask me why Luke hasn't been called, as her current custodial parent. Maybe he has been. But then again, it's likely Luke's gone off the grid. I pull a sweater over my head and stuff my feet into clogs, trying to focus on the practical so that I am not swallowed up by emotion. 'Elizabeth doesn't like pancakes for breakfast and Jackson needs to bring in his field trip permission slip . . .' My head snaps up. 'Don't you need to be in court tomorrow morning?'

'Don't worry about me,' Joe says gently. 'I'll take care of the twins and the judge and everything else. You just go take care of Cara.'

There are times that I cannot believe how lucky I am, to be married to this man. Sometimes I think it's because I deserve it, after all those years of living with Luke. But sometimes – like now – I am sure there's still a price I'll have to pay.

There are not many people in the emergency room when I run up to the front desk. 'Cara Warren,' I say, out of breath. 'She was brought in here by ambulance? She's my daughter?'

All my sentences rise at the ends, like helium balloons.

A nurse leads me through a door and into a hallway of glass rooms, shrouded with curtains. Some of the doors are open. I see an old woman in a hospital gown, sitting on a gurney. A man with his jeans cut open to the knee, his swollen ankle elevated. We move out of the way as a pregnant patient is wheeled past us, focused on her Lamaze breathing.

Luke is the one who taught Cara how to drive. For all his personal recklessness, he was a stickler when it came to the safety of his daughter. Instead of the forty hours she was supposed to log in before taking her driver's test, he made her do fifty. She's a safe driver, a cautious driver. But why was she out so late on a school night? Was she at fault? Was anyone else hurt?

Finally, the nurse steps into one of the cubicles. Cara lies on a bed, looking very small and very frightened. There's blood in her dark hair and on her face and her sweater. Her arm is bandaged tight against her body.

18

'Mommy,' she sobs. I cannot remember the last time she called me that.

She cries out when I put my arms around her. 'It's going to be all right,' I say.

Cara looks up at me, eyes red, nose running. 'Where's Dad?'

Those words shouldn't hurt me, but they do. 'I'm sure the hospital called him—'

All of a sudden, a resident steps into the room. 'You're Cara's mom? We need your consent before we can take her into surgery.' She says more – I vaguely hear the words *scapula* and *rotator cuff* – and hands me a clipboard for a signature.

'Where's Dad?' Cara shouts this time.

The doctor faces her. 'He's getting the best care possible,' she says, and that's when I realize Cara wasn't alone in that car.

'Luke was in the accident, too? Is he all right?'

'Are you his wife?'

'Ex,' I clarify.

'Then I can't really disclose anything about his condition. HIPAA rules. But yes,' she admits. 'He is a patient here, too.' She looks at me, speaking softly so Cara can't hear. 'We need to contact his next of kin. Does he have a spouse? Parents? Is there someone you can call?'

Luke doesn't have a new wife. He was raised by his grand-parents, who died years ago. If he could speak for himself, he'd tell me to phone the trading post to make sure Walter is there to feed the pack.

But maybe he can't speak for himself. Maybe this is what the doctor can't – or won't – tell me.

Before I can respond, two orderlies enter and begin to pull Cara's bed away from the wall. I feel like I'm sinking, like there are questions I should be asking or facts I should be confirming before my daughter is taken off to an operating suite, but I've never been good under pressure. I force a smile and squeeze Cara's free hand. 'I'll be right here when you get back!' I say, too brightly. A moment later, I'm alone in the room. It feels sterile, silent.

I reach into my purse for my cell phone, wondering what time it is in Bangkok.

Luke

A wolf pack is like the Mafia. Everyone has a position in
it; everyone's expected to pull his own weight.

*Everyone's heard of an alpha wolf – the leader of the pack.
This is the mob boss, the brains of the outfit, the protector,
the one who tells the other wolves where to go, when to hunt,
what to hunt. The alpha is the decision maker, the* capo di
tutti capi, *who, from ten feet away, can hear the change of
rhythm in a prey animal's heart rate. But the alpha is not
the stern disciplinarian that movies have made him out to
be. He's far too valuable, as the decision maker, to put himself
in harm's way.*

*Which is why in front of every alpha is a beta wolf, an
enforcer. The beta rank is the bold, big thug who is pure
aggression. He'll take you down before you get too close to the
boss. He's completely expendable. If he gets himself killed, no
one will really care, because there's always another brute to
take his place.*

*Then there's the tester wolf, who's very wary and suspicious,
who doesn't trust anyone he meets. He's always scouting for
change, for something new, and he'll be hiding out at every
corner to make sure that, when and if it happens, he's there
to alert the alpha. His skittishness is integral to the safety of*

the pack. And he's the quality-control guy, too. If someone in the pack doesn't seem to be pulling his weight, the tester will create a situation where the other wolf has to prove his mettle – like picking a fight with the enforcer, for example. If that beta can't knock him to the ground, he doesn't deserve to be the beta wolf anymore.

The diffuser wolf has been called many names through the years, from the Cinderella wolf to the omega. Though at first he was thought to be a scapegoat and at the bottom of the hierarchy, we know now that the diffuser plays a key role in the pack. Like the little, geeky lawyer to the mob who provides comic relief and knows how to keep all these other strong personalities calm, the diffuser throws himself headlong into all the intrapack bickering. If two animals are fighting, the diffuser will jump between them and will clown around, until suddenly the two angry wolves have taken their emotions down a notch. Everyone gets on with his job, and no one gets hurt. Far from being the Cinderella figure that always gets the short end of the stick, the diffuser holds the critical position of peacemaker. Without him the pack couldn't function; they'd be at war with each other all the time.

Say what you will about the Mafia, but it works because everyone has a specific role to play. They all do what they do for the greater good of the organization. They'd willingly die for each other.

The other reason a wolf pack is like the Mafia?

Because, for both groups, there is nothing more important than family.

Edward

You'd be surprised how easy it is to stand out in a city of nine million people. But then again, I'm a *farang*. You can see it in my unofficial teacher's uniform – shirt and tie – in my blond hair, which shines like a beacon in a sea of black.

Today I have my small group of students working on conversational English. They've been paired, and they are going to present a conversation between a shopkeeper and a customer. 'Do I have any volunteers?' I ask.

Crickets.

The Thai people are pathologically shy. Combine that with a reluctance to lose face by giving a wrong answer, and it makes for a painfully long class. Usually I ask the students to work on exercises in small groups, and then I move around and check their progress. But for days like today, when I'm grading on participation, speaking up in public is a necessary evil. 'Jao,' I say to a man in my class. 'You own a pet store, and you want to convince Jaidee to buy a pet.' I turn to a second man. 'Jaidee, you do not want to buy that pet. Let's hear your conversation.'

They stand up, clutching their papers. 'This dog is recommended,' Jao begins.

'I have one already,' Jaidee replies.

'Good job!' I encourage. 'Jao, give him a reason why he should buy your dog.'

'This dog is alive,' Jao adds.

Jaidee shrugs. 'Not everyone wants a pet that is alive.'

Well, not all days are successes.

I collect the homework from the students before they file out of the classroom, suddenly animated and chattering in a language I am still learning after six years. Apsara, a grand mother of four, hands me her assignment: a persuasive essay. I look down at the title: 'Eat Vegetarians for a Healthy Diet.'

'Sit on it, *Ajarn* Edward,' Apsara says happily. Before coming to language school, she tried to learn English from watching *Happy Days* episodes. I don't have the heart to tell her that's not a respectful expression.

I've been teaching English for six years now, in a language school that's in the center of the biggest mall I've ever seen in my life, about twenty minutes by taxi outside of Bangkok. I fell into the job by accident – after backpacking through Thailand and taking odd jobs to make enough *baht* to feed myself, I found myself tending bar at age eighteen, in Patpong. It was one of Thailand's famous ladyboy shows, with *katoeys* – transvestites who fooled even me – and I'd been trying to collect enough cash to leave the city. One of the other bartenders was an expat from Ireland, and he supplemented his income by teaching at the American Language Institute. They were always looking for qualified teachers, he said. When I told him I wasn't really qualified, he laughed. 'You speak English, don't you?' he said.

I make 45,000 *baht* teaching, now. I have my own apartment. I've had the obligatory flings with Thai natives and

I've gone out drinking with other expats at Nana Plaza. And I've learned a lot. You don't touch anyone on the head because it's the highest part of the body – literally, and spiritually. You don't cross your legs on the skytrain because doing so exposes the sole of your shoe to the person sitting across from you – and the bottoms of your feet are literally and spiritually unclean. You might as well be giving the other person the finger. You don't shake hands, you *wai* – by putting your hands in front of you like you're praying, with the tips of your index fingers touching your nose. The higher the hands are, and the lower your bow, the more respect you're showing. A *wai* can be used for greeting, apology, gratitude.

You've got to admire a culture that uses a single gesture to say both *thank you* and *I'm sorry*.

Every time I start to get sick of living here, or get the feeling that nothing ever changes, I take a step back and remind myself that I'm just visiting. That Thai culture and beliefs have been around a lot longer than I have. That what one person sees as a difference of opinion can be, to the other person, a sign of great disrespect.

I kind of wish I knew back then what I know now.

There really isn't an easy way to get to Koh Chang. It's 315 kilometers by bus from Bangkok, and even after you get to Trat, in the eastern provinces, you have to take a *songtaew* to one of the three piers. Ao Thammachat is the best one – it only takes twenty minutes by ferry to reach the island. Lam Ngob is the worst – the fishing boats that have been converted into ferries can take over an hour to make the crossing.

It may seem ridiculous to come all this distance when I

only have two days off from the language institute, but it's worth it. Sometimes Bangkok is suffocating, and I need to hang out in a place that isn't wall-to-wall people. I chalk it up to my upbringing in a part of New England that is still two hours away from the nearest mall. After sleeping last night at a cheap guesthouse, I've spent this morning trying to find my way to Khlong Nueng, the tallest waterfall on the island. And now, just when I am sweating and thirsty and ready to quit, the biggest boulder I've ever seen blocks the path. Gritting my teeth, I get a foothold and begin to climb over it. My boots slip on the rock, and I scrape my knee, and I'm already worried about how I'm going to climb back over from the other side – but I won't let myself give up.

With a grunt, I reach the top of the boulder and then slide down the far side. I land with a soft thud and glance up to see the most beautiful rush of water, frothing and sparkling and filling the ravine. I strip to my boxers and wade in, the clear pool lapping against my chest. I duck under the spray. Then I crawl out and lie on my back, letting the sun dry my skin.

Since I've come to Thailand, I've had hundreds of moments like this, when I run across something so incredible that I want to show it to someone else. The problem is, when you make the choice to be a loner, you lose that privilege. So I do what I've done for the past six years: I take out my cell phone, and I snap a picture of the waterfall. I'm never in these pictures, needless to say. And I don't know who I'll ever show them to, given that I've had cartons of milk that have lasted longer than most of my relationships. But I keep that digital album anyway – from the first spirit house I saw in Thailand, intricate and laden with offerings, to the arrangement of wooden penises at the Chao Mae Tuptim Shrine, to the creepy conjoined babies floating in formaldehyde in the Forensic Science Museum near Wat Arun.

I am holding the phone in my hand, looking at these pictures, when it starts to vibrate. I check the display to see who's calling – expecting a friend who wants to invite me out for a beer, or my boss at the institute asking me to cover for another teacher, or maybe the flight attendant I met last weekend at the Blue Ice Bar. It's always struck me as amusing that the cellular service in Nowhere, Thailand, is still better than in the White Mountains of New Hampshire.

Out of area.

'Hello?' I hold the phone up to my ear.

'Edward,' my mother says. 'You have to come home.'

It takes a full twenty-four hours to get back to the States and to rent a car (something I wasn't old enough to do when I left) and drive all the way to Beresford, NH. You'd think I'd be falling asleep, but I'm too nervous for that. In the first place, I haven't driven in six years, and that requires my full concentration. In the second place, I am replaying what I've already been told – by my mother, and by the neurosurgeon who did emergency surgery on my father.

His truck crashed into a tree.

He and Cara were found outside the vehicle.

Cara shattered her shoulder.

My father was unresponsive, with an enlarged right pupil. He wasn't breathing on his own very well. The EMTs called it a diffuse traumatic brain injury.

My mother called me when I first landed. Cara was out of her surgery; she was on painkillers and sleeping. The police had come by to interview Cara, but my mother had sent them away. She had stayed at the hospital last night. Her voice sounded like a string that was fraying.

I'm not going to lie: I've thought about what it would be like, if I ever came back. I imagined a party at our house, and my mom would bake my favorite cake (carrot ginger) and Cara would make me a sculpture out of Popsicle sticks with the words '#1 Bro' on the lid. Of course, my mom doesn't live there anymore, and Cara's way too old for Popsicle stick arts and crafts.

Probably you noticed that, in my fantasy victory lap, my father was not part of the picture.

After all this time in a city, Beresford feels like a ghost town. There are people around, for sure, but there's so much uninhabited space that it makes me dizzy. The tallest building here is three stories. From every angle, you can see mountains.

I park in the outside lot at the hospital and jog inside – I'm wearing jeans and a sweatshirt, which isn't really appropriate for a New England winter, but I don't even own those sorts of clothes anymore. The volunteer who's manning the front desk looks like a marshmallow – plump, soft, powdered. I ask for Cara Warren's room, for two reasons. First, it's where my mother will be. And second, I need a minute before I face my father again.

Cara's on the fourth floor, in room 430. I wait for the elevator doors to close (again, when was the last time I was ever *alone* in an elevator?) and take deep breaths. In the hallway, I walk past the nurses with my head ducked and push open the door that has Cara's name on a chart outside.

There's a woman sleeping in the hospital bed.

She has long, dark hair and a bruise on her temple, a butterfly bandage. Her arm is wrapped up in a cocoon against her body. She has one foot kicked out from the blanket, and there is purple polish on her toes.

She's not my little sister anymore. She's not little, period.

I'm so busy staring at her that at first I don't even notice my mother in the corner. She stands up, her hand covering her mouth. 'Edward?' she whispers.

When I left, I was already taller than my mother. But now, I have filled out. I'm bigger, stronger. Like *him*.

She folds me into an embrace. *Heart origami.* That's what she used to call it when we were small, and she'd open her arms and wait for us to run inside. The words feel like a splinter in my mind; I can feel them rubbing the wrong way even as I do what she is expecting and hug her back. It's a funny thing, how – no matter how much bigger I am than my mother – she still is the one holding me, instead of the other way around.

I feel like Gulliver on Lilliput, too overgrown for my own memories. My mother wipes at her eyes. 'I can't believe you're actually here.'

It doesn't seem right to mention that I wouldn't be here, not by a long shot, if my sister and father weren't in the hospital. 'How is she?' I ask, nodding toward Cara.

'In an OxyContin haze,' my mother says. 'She's still in a lot of pain after the surgery.'

'She looks . . . different.'

'So do you.'

We all do, I guess. There are lines on my mother's face I never noticed before, or maybe they weren't there. As for my father – well, it's hard for me to imagine him changing at all.

'I guess I should go find Dad,' I say.

My mother picks up her purse – a tote bag with the pictures of two half-Asian children on it. The twins, I guess. It's weird to think I have siblings I have never met. 'All right,' she says.

Right now, the last thing I want to do is be alone. To be the grown-up. But something makes me put my hand on her shoulder to stop her. 'You don't have to come with me,' I tell her. 'I'm not a kid anymore.'

'I can see that,' she says, staring at me. Her words are too soft, like they're wrapped in flannel.

I know what she's thinking: that she missed so much. Dropping me off at college. Attending my graduation. Hearing about my first job, my first love. Helping me decorate my first apartment.

'Cara might wake up and need you,' I say, to ease the blow.

My mother falters, but only for a moment. 'You'll come back?' she asks.

I nod. Even though that's exactly what I swore I'd never do.

At some point in my life, I thought about being a doctor. I liked the sterility of the profession, the order. The fact that if you could read the clues, you would be able to find the problem, and fix it.

Unfortunately, to be a doctor you also have to take biology, and the first time I held a scalpel to a fetal pig I fainted dead away.

The truth was, I wasn't much of a scientist. In high school I lost myself in books, which turned out to be a good thing, since that's how I furthered my studies once I left home. I've read more of the classics, I bet, than most college graduates. But I also know the stuff they never teach in lectures – like: avoid the upstairs bars on Patpong Road, because they're run by thugs; or pick a massage shop with a glass front where you can see the business inside, or you'll wind up with a 'happy ending' you weren't looking for. I may not have a degree, but I certainly got an education.

Yet, in the family waiting room with Dr. Saint-Clare, I feel stupid. Inadequate. As if I cannot string together all the information he's providing.

'Your father suffered a diffuse traumatic brain injury,' he tells me. 'When the paramedics brought him in here, he had an enlarged right pupil and was unresponsive. There was a laceration on his forehead, and he couldn't move his left side. His breathing was labored, so he'd been intubated by the EMTs. When I was called in, I saw that he had a bilateral periorbital edema—'

'A bi-what?'

'Swelling,' the surgeon translates. 'Around the eyes. We repeated the Glasgow Coma Scale test he'd been given at the site of the accident, and he scored a five. We performed an emergency CT scan and found a temporal lobe hematoma, a subarachnoid hemorrhage, and intraventricular hemorrhage.' He glances up at my face. 'Basically, we saw blood. All around the brain and in the ventricles of the brain – which is indicative of a serious trauma. We put him on Mannitol to reduce some of the pressure in the cranium, and immediately took him into surgery to remove the clot in the temporal lobe and the anterior part of the temporal lobe of his brain.'

My jaw drops. 'You took out some of his *brain*?'

'We relieved the pressure on the brain that would have otherwise killed him,' the doctor corrects. 'The temporal lobectomy will affect some of his memories, but not all. It doesn't affect the areas of speech or motor or personality.'

They had taken away some of my father's memories. Ones of his beloved wolves? Or ones of us? Which would he miss?

'So did it work? The surgery?'

'Your father's pupil is reactive again, and the clot's removed. However, the swelling and the hematoma produced an incipient herniation – basically, a shift of structures from one compartment of the brain to another, which put pressure on the brain stem and created little hemorrhages there.'

'I don't understand—'

'The pressure in his skull is down,' the doctor says, 'but he still hasn't awakened, there's no response to stimulation, and he isn't breathing on his own. We repeated a CT scan and can see that those hemorrhages in the medulla and the pons are a little larger than they were on the initial scan – and that's why he hasn't regained consciousness, and is still on a ventilator.'

I feel like I am swimming in corn syrup, like the words I want to use are rolling off my tongue in an indecipherable language. 'But is he going to be okay?' I ask, which is really the only question necessary.

The surgeon clasps his hands together. 'We're still letting the dust settle right now . . .'

But. There's a *but,* I can hear it.

'Those lesions we're seeing affect the part of the brain stem that controls breathing and consciousness. He may never get off that ventilator,' Dr. Saint-Clare says flatly. 'He may never wake up.'

When I was sixteen and had just gotten my driver's license,

I went to a party and stayed out past my curfew. I parked down the block and tiptoed across the grass, easing the door open in the hope that I could get away with this infraction. But as my eyes adjusted to the darkness, I saw my father sleeping in the recliner in the living room, and I knew I was doomed. My father always said that when he was out in the wild with the wolves, he never really slept. You had to stay semiconscious, one proverbial eye always open, to know if you were going to be attacked.

Sure enough, the minute I crossed the threshold he was out of that chair and in my face. He didn't say a word, just waited for me to speak for myself.

I know, I said. *I'm grounded.*

My father folded his arms. *A couple of hundred years ago, parents never let kids out of their sight*, he said. *If a pup disturbs his wolf father at two in the morning, he doesn't growl so the pup will leave him alone and let him go back to sleep. He sits up, alert, as if he's saying: What do you want to know? Where do you want to go?*

I was still a little drunk, and at the time I figured this was a lecture, his way of telling me he was mad at me. Now I wonder if he was just mad at *himself* – for giving in to his human side, so that he forgot to keep one eye open.

'Can I see him?' I ask Dr. Saint-Clare.

I'm led down the hall to an ICU room. A nurse is bent over the bed, suctioning something. 'You must be Mr. Warren's son,' she says. 'Spitting image.'

But I barely hear her. I'm staring at the patient in the hospital bed.

My first thought is: *There's been a terrible mistake. This isn't my father.*

Because this broken man, with the partially shaved head and the white bandage wrapped around his skull, with the tube going down his throat and the IV running into the crook of his arm . . .

This man with the Frankenstein's monster stitches on his temple and the black-and-blue mask of bruises around his eyes . . .

This man looks nothing like the one who ruined my life.

Luke

*R*ed *Riding Hood should be flogged.*
Single-handedly, that little girl and her grand-mother have managed to spread enough lies about wolves to get them poisoned, trapped, and shot into near extinction. Many of the myths about wolves originated in the Middle Ages, in Paris – where children were dragged off by wolves. Now it's believed that the animals in question were hybrid wolf-dogs. A pure-bred wolf, on the other hand, is more afraid of you than you are of him. He won't attack, unless something makes him feel that his safety has been threatened.

Some people believe that wolves kill everything they encounter.

In reality, they only kill to eat. Even when they attack a herd, they don't slaughter every animal. The alpha wolf very specifically directs which member of the herd should be brought down.

Some people believe that wolves will decimate the deer population.

In reality, for every ten times they hunt, they'll make a single kill.

Some people believe they infiltrate farms and kill livestock.

In reality, this happens so infrequently, biologists don't even count them as a category of predatorial risk.

Some people believe wolves are harmful to humans.

In reality, of the twenty or so recorded cases, the encounter between wolf and man was brought on by the person. And there's not a single documented case of a healthy, wild wolf killing a human.

You can imagine that I'm not too fond of the three little pigs, either.

Cara

I'm sitting at one of the outdoor tables at the trading post, wrapped up in my down jacket and a woolly blanket. There's no one here because it's February and the park is officially closed, but the signature attraction – the animatronic dinosaurs that you can't miss the minute you walk through the gates – runs year-round. It's some weird computerized wiring glitch – you can't turn off the *T. rex* without cutting power to the whole facility, and that of course would affect the skeleton crew that manages the animal habitats on the off-season. So every now and then, when I need to get away, I come to the part of the park that's a ghost town and watch the triceratops shake his plastic head every hour on the hour, dislodging last night's snowfall. I watch the raptor get into a mock fight with the *T. rex*, both of them thigh-high in drifts. It's creepy. It feels like I'm watching the end of the world. Sometimes, because it's so quiet, their canned roars get the gibbons all riled up, and they start hollering, too.

It's because of the gibbons, actually, that I don't hear my father calling my name until he's nearly standing right in front of me. 'Cara? Cara!' He is wearing his winter coveralls – the ones that hang outside the trailer on a tree branch and never get washed because the wolves recognize him by scent.

I can tell he's been in with the pack sharing a meal, because there's a little bit of blood on the ends of the long hair framing his face. He usually plays the diffuser, which means he gets right between the beta and the alpha rank on the carcass. It's crazy to watch, actually. Feeding time, for the pack, is like a gladiator sport. Everyone's got a set position around the carcass and feeds at a specific time on a specific part of the animal. There's growling and snarling and gnashing as each wolf – my dad included – protects his piece of the kill. He used to eat the raw meat, like the wolves, but when it started messing too much with his digestive system, he began to cook up bits of kidney and liver and hide it inside his coveralls, in a little plastic bag. He somehow manages to transfer this into the slit belly of the calf and eat like the wolves without them noticing anything's been doctored.

My father's face collapses with relief. 'Cara,' he says again. 'I thought I'd lost you.'

I try to stand up, to tell him that I've been here the whole time, but I can't move. The blanket's gotten caught, and my arms are trapped. Then I realize it's not a blanket, it's a bandage. And it's not my father who's been calling my name, it's my mother. 'You're awake,' she says. She's looking down at me, trying to smile.

My shoulder feels like there's an elephant sitting on it. There's something I want to ask, but the words taste like they're covered in clouds. Suddenly there's another face, a woman's face, soft as dough. 'When it hurts,' she says, 'press this.' She curls my hand around a little button. My thumb pushes down.

I want to ask where my father is, but I'm already falling asleep.

*   *   *

I am dreaming again, and this is how I know:

My father's in the room, but it's not my father. This is someone I've only seen in photographs – three pictures, actually, that my mother keeps inside her underwear drawer, beneath the velvet liner of the box that holds her grand-mother's pearls. In all three pictures, he's got his arm around my mother. He looks younger, leaner, short-haired.

This current version of my father is staring at me as if he's just as surprised to see me looking this way as I am to see him. 'Don't leave,' I say, but my voice is barely a voice.

That makes him smile.

This is the second reason I know I am dreaming. In those old photographs, my dad always looks happy. In fact, he and my mother *both* always look happy, which is again something I've only seen in pictures.

I'm awake, but I'm pretending not to be. The two police officers that are standing at the foot of the bed are talking to my mother. 'It's critical that we speak to your daughter,' the taller one says, 'to piece together what happened.'

I wonder what my father has told them. My mouth goes dry.

'Clearly Cara isn't fit for interrogation.' My mother's voice is stiff. I can feel the eyes of all three of them touching me like flame on paper.

'Ma'am, we understand that her health is the primary concern.'

'If you understood, then you wouldn't be here,' my mother says.

I watch *Law & Order.* I know all about how a microscopic paint chip can put away a lying criminal for life. Is their visit a routine one, part of every car crash? Or do they know something?

I break out in a sweat, and my heart starts beating harder. And then I realize that's something I can't hide. My pulse is right there on a monitor next to the headboard for everyone to see. Knowing that just makes it worse. I imagine the numbers rising, everyone staring.

'Do you really believe her father was trying intentionally to crash the car?' my mother asks.

There is a pause. 'No,' one policeman replies.

My heart's hammering so hard that, any minute now, a nurse is going to burst in and call a code blue.

'Then why are you even here?' my mother asks.

I hear one of the policemen rustle through his clothing. Through slitted eyes I see him give my mother a card. 'If you could just give us a call when she's awake?'

Their footsteps echo on the floor.

I count to fifty. Slowly, with a *Mississippi* after each number. And then I open my eyes. 'Mom?' I say. My voice is full of scrapes and angles.

She immediately sits next to me on the bed. 'How do you feel?'

There's still pain in my shoulder, but it's not what it was before. I touch my forehead with my free hand and feel swelling, stitches. 'Sore,' I say.

My mother reaches for that hand. There's a little clip on one of my fingers, with a red light glowing through the flesh. Like E.T. 'You fractured your shoulder blade in the car accident,' she tells me. 'You had surgery on Thursday night.'

'What day is it now?'

'Saturday,' she tells me.

I have entirely lost Friday.

I struggle to sit up, but that turns out to be impossible with one arm wrapped up mummy-tight against my body. 'Where's Dad?'

Something flickers across her face. 'I should tell the nurse that you're awake . . .'

'Is he okay?' My eyes fill with tears. 'I saw the paramedics with him, and then they . . . then they . . .' I can't finish the sentence, because I am starting to put together all the secrecy and the look on my mother's face and that hallucination I had of my father as a much younger man. 'He's dead,' I whisper. 'You just don't want to tell me.'

She grips my hand more tightly. 'Your father is *not* dead.'

'Then I want to see him,' I demand.

'Cara, you're in no condition to—'

'*Goddammit, let me see him!*' I scream.

That, at least, gets some attention. A woman wearing hospital ID – but not nurse whites – hurries into the room. 'Cara, you've got to relax—'

She is small and bird-boned, with black ringlets that bounce with every syllable. 'Who are you?'

'My name is Trina. I'm the social worker assigned to your case. I understand that you've got some questions—'

'Yeah, like how about this one: I'm wrapped up like King Tut and I've got Frankenstein stitches on my head and my father's probably in the morgue so how am I supposed to relax?'

My mother and Trina exchange a look, some secret code that lets me know in that instant they've been talking about me the whole time I've been drugged unconscious. Here's what I know: If they don't want to help me get to my dad, wherever he is, then I will walk there myself. Crawl, if I have to.

'Your father's suffered a very severe brain trauma,' Trina says, the same way you'd say, *I heard it's going to be a very cold winter* or *I think I need to take the car in to get the tires rotated.* She says it as if a severe brain trauma is a hangnail.

'I don't understand what that means.'

'He had surgery to remove swelling in the brain. He's not breathing on his own. And he's unconscious.'

'Five minutes ago, so was I,' I say, but the whole time I am thinking: *This is all my fault.*

'I'll take you to see your father, Cara,' Trina says, 'but you have to understand that when you see him, it's going to be a shock.'

Why? Because he's in a hospital bed? Because he's got stitches, like me, and tubes down his throat? My father is the kind of man who never rests, who's rarely indoors. Seeing him fall asleep in a chair is enough of a shock.

She calls in a nurse and an orderly to get me into a wheelchair, which requires moving my IV and gritting my teeth as I'm relocated. The hallway smells like industrial cleaner and that plastic hospital smell that's always freaked me out.

The last time I was in this hospital was a year ago. My dad and I were doing outreach with Zazi, one of the wolves we sometimes bring to elementary schools to teach about wolf conservation. My dad always goes through a mini-training session with the kids to teach them how to behave around a wild animal – don't hold out your fingers, don't approach too fast, let the animal catch your scent. And that day, the kids were being great, as was Zazi. But some idiot delinquent in another part of the building had pulled the fire alarm as a prank, and the loud noise startled the wolf. He tried to get away, and the nearest exit was a plate-glass window. My dad wrapped his arms around Zazi to protect him, so that he was the one who wound up going through the window instead of the wolf. Sure enough, when I got Zazi back into his travel cage, he didn't have a scratch on him. My father, on the other hand, had a cut so deep on his arm that I could see bone.

Needless to say my father refused to go to the hospital until Zazi was safely back home in his enclosure. By then, the dish towel he'd used as a makeshift bandage was a bloody mess, and the frantic school principal – who'd driven back to the trading post with us – insisted that my father go to the emergency room. There – *here* – he had to get fifteen stitches. But no sooner had we returned home than my dad headed down to the enclosure that housed Nodah, Kina, and Kita – the three wolves he'd had to raise from pups, the pack where he now functioned as a diffuser wolf.

I stood at the chain-link fence, watching Nodah bound up to my dad. Immediately he ripped off the white bandage with his teeth. Then Kina started licking the wound. I was sure he'd tear the stitches, and I was just as sure my father was hoping for that very thing. He'd told me about his time in the wild; how sometimes during a hunt he'd be injured because his skin didn't have the same protective fur covering that his brother and sister wolves had. When that happened, the animals would lick the gash until it reopened. My father had come to believe that something in their saliva functioned medicinally. Even though he was sleeping in dirt and had no access to antibiotics, in the nearly two years he spent in the woods, he never had a single infection and every wound healed twice as fast. As Kina dug deep, my dad winced a few times, but eventually the cut stopped bleeding and he left the enclosure. We started walking up the hill toward the trailer. *I freaking hate hospitals*, he said, an explanation.

Now as Trina wheels me down the hallway – my mother trailing behind – we pass people in casts, or shuffling with walkers or crutches. My room is in orthopedics, but my father is somewhere else. We have to get into the elevator, and go down to the third floor.

The sign next to the double doors we enter says ICU.

In this hallway, nobody's walking around except the doctors.

Trina stops pushing the chair and crouches down in front of me. 'Are you still feeling up to this?'

I nod.

Trina backs into my father's hospital room, pulling the wheelchair, and then turns me to face the bed.

My dad looks like a statue. Like one of those marble warriors you see in the ancient Greece section of a museum – strong, intense, and completely expressionless. I reach for his hand and touch it with one finger. He doesn't move. The only reason I know he's still alive is because the machines he's hooked up to are making quiet noises.

I did this to him.

I bite my lip because I know I'm going to cry and I don't want Trina and my mother watching.

'Is he going to be all right?' I whisper.

My mother puts her hand on my shoulder. 'The doctors don't know,' she says, her voice breaking.

Tears are running down my face now. 'Daddy? It's me. Cara. Wake up. You have to wake up.'

I'm thinking about all those stories you always hear on

the news, the miraculous ones, where people who were never supposed to be able to walk get out of bed and start sprinting. Where people who were blind can suddenly see.

Where fathers with brain injuries suddenly open their eyes and smile and forgive you.

I hear the sound of water running, and a door opens – one that leads to the bathroom. The younger version of my dad that I hallucinated yesterday walks out, still drying his hands on his sweatpants. He looks at my mother, and then at me. 'Cara,' he says. 'Wow. You're awake?'

That's the moment I understand that he was never a figment of my imagination. It's a voice I recognize, now housed in a different, adult body.

'What is he doing here?' I whisper.

'I called him,' my mother says. 'Cara, just—'

I shake my head. 'I was wrong. I can't do this.'

Immediately, Trina whirls the chair around, so that I am staring at the door again. 'That's all right,' she says, not judgmental at all. 'It's hard to see someone you love in that condition. You'll come back when you're feeling stronger.'

I pretend to agree. But it isn't just facing my father, unconscious in a hospital bed, that has made the floor drop out of my world.

It is seeing my brother, who's been dead to me for years.

I can't say that Edward and I were ever close. Seven years is a lot, when you're young, and there just isn't all that much that a high school kid will have in common with a kid sister who is still using her Easy-Bake oven. But I idolized my big brother. I would pick up the books he sometimes left on the kitchen table and pretend that I understood the words inside;

I'd sneak into his room when he went out and would lie on his bed and listen to his iPod, something he would have murdered me for if he knew I was doing it.

The elementary school was a distance away from the high school, which meant that Edward had to drop me off in the morning. It was part of a negotiated deal that included my parents paying for half of the eight-hundred-dollar beater he found at a garage, so he'd have his own wheels. In return, my mother insisted that my brother physically deposit me on the steps of my school before going on to his.

Edward took this direction literally.

I was eleven years old – plenty grown-up enough to navigate a traffic light's walk signal alone. But my brother never let me. Every day he parked the car and waited with me. When that signal changed and we stepped off the curb together, he'd grab my hand or my arm and hold on to it until we reached the other side. It was such a habit, I'm pretty sure he wasn't even aware he was doing it.

I could have pulled away, or told him to let go, but I never did.

The first day after he left us, the first day I had to go to school and cross alone, I was positive the street had grown twice as wide.

Logically, I understand that it wasn't Edward's fault my family fell apart after he left. But when you're eleven years old, you don't give a fuck about logic. You just really miss holding your big brother's hand.

'I *had* to call him,' my mother says. 'He's still your father's son. And the hospital needed someone who could make medical decisions for Luke.'

As if it's not bad enough that my father is in some kind of coma, the only person who seems to have information about his condition is, against all odds, my long-lost brother. The thought that *he's* the one who's been sitting next to my dad, waiting for him to open his eyes – well, it makes me furious.

'Why couldn't *you* do it?'

'Because I'm not married to him anymore.'

'Then why didn't anyone ask me?'

My mother sits down on the edge of the hospital bed. 'You weren't in any condition to be making decisions when you were brought in. And even if you had been – you're a minor. The hospital needed someone who's over eighteen.'

'He *left*,' I say, the obvious. 'He doesn't deserve to be here.'

'Cara,' my mother replies, rubbing her hand over her face. 'You can't blame Edward for everything.'

What she is careful *not* to say is that this was my father's fault – the breakdown of the marriage, and Edward's departure. She knows better than to bitch about my dad in front of me, though, because that's partly what made me move out of her house four years ago.

I had left my mother's house because I didn't fit into her new family, but I had wound up *staying* with my dad because he seemed to parent me in a way my mom never could. It's hard to explain, really. It didn't really matter to me if my bedsheets were washed weekly or only once every few months when someone remembered to do it. Instead, my dad taught me the name of every tree in the woods, knowledge I didn't even realize I was accumulating. He showed me that a summer storm isn't an inconvenience but a great time to work outside without being swarmed by mosquitoes or sweltering in the heat.

Once, when we were in one of the enclosures, a badger had the bad luck to wander inside. We usually let the wolves kill whatever small prey wound up in their pen, but this time, one of the adult wolves chased down the badger and, instead of killing it, bit the backbone so it was dragging its rear legs. Then he backed away, so that the two young pups in the pack could make the kill. It was, basically, a training session. That's what life with my father was like. With my dad, it didn't matter that Edward had left. With my dad I was worthy enough to be the only other member of his pack, the one he taught everything he knew, the one he depended on as much as I depended on him.

If my father doesn't wake up, I realize, I will have to go back to living with my mother.

Suddenly the door to my hospital room opens and the two policemen who were here yesterday walk in. 'Cara,' the tall one says. 'Glad to see you're awake. I'm Officer Dumont, and this is Officer Whigby. We'd like to talk to you for a few minutes—'

My mother steps between them and the hospital bed. 'Cara's barely out of surgery. She needs to rest.'

'With all due respect, ma'am, we aren't leaving this time without speaking to your daughter.' Officer Dumont sits down in the chair beside the bed. 'Cara, do you mind answering a few questions about the car accident?'

I look at my mother, and then at the cop. 'I guess . . .'

'Do you remember the crash?'

I remember every second of it. 'Not so much,' I murmur.

'Who was driving the truck?'

'My father,' I say.

'Your father.'

'That's right.'

'Where were you headed?'

'Home – he picked me up from a friend's house.'

My mother folds her arms. 'I'm sorry . . . but when did a car accident become a criminal offense?'

The officer looks up over his notepad at her. 'Ma'am, we're just trying to piece together what happened.' He turns to me. 'How come the truck swerved off the road?'

'There was a deer,' I say. 'It ran out in front of us.'

This is true, actually. I'm just leaving out what happened before that.

'Had your father been drinking?'

'My father never drinks,' I say. 'The wolves can smell alcohol in your system.'

'How about you? Were *you* drinking?'

My face goes red. '*No.*'

Officer Whigby, who's been pretty quiet, takes a step forward. 'You know, Cara, if you just tell us the truth, this will be a lot easier.'

'My daughter doesn't drink,' my mom says, angry. 'She's only seventeen.'

'Unfortunately, ma'am, the two aren't mutually exclusive.' Whigby pulls out a piece of paper and hands it to her. It's a lab report.

'Your daughter's blood alcohol content was .20 when she was admitted,' Officer Whigby says. 'And unlike your daughter, blood tests don't lie.' He turns to me. 'So, Cara . . . what else are you hiding?'

Luke

*M*y adopted brothers in the Abenaki tribe believe that
their lives are inextricably tied to those of wolves. Years
ago, when I first went to Canada to study the way Native
American naturalists tracked the wild wolves along the St.
Lawrence corridor, I learned that they see the wolf as a teacher
– in the way he hunts, raises his children, and defends his
family. In the past it was not unheard of for Abenaki shamans
to slip into the body of a wolf, and vice versa. The French
called the Eastern Abenaki in Maine and New Hampshire
the Natio Luporem, *the Wolf Nation.*

The Abenaki also believe that there are some people who
live between the animal world and the human world, never
fully belonging to either one.

Joseph Obomsawin, the elder I lived with there, says that
those who turn to animals do so because humans have let
them down.

That would fit for me, I suppose. I grew up with parents who
were so much older than my friends' parents that I would never
think of inviting a friend home from school; I would purposely
forget to tell my parents about open houses or basketball games
because I was always embarrassed to find kids staring openly
at my dad's white hair, my mother's soft wrinkles.

Since I didn't have a thriving social network as a kid, I spent a great deal of time alone in the woods. My father had taught me the name of every indigenous tree; what was poisonous, what was edible. He took me hunting for ducks when the moon was still high in the sky and our breath turned silver in front of us as we waited. It was there I learned to be so still that the deer would come into the clearing to feed, even if I were sitting on its edge. And it was there that I started to be able to tell the deer apart, to know which ones traveled together and which ones returned the next year with their offspring.

I cannot remember a time I didn't feel connected to animals – from watching a fox play with her kits to tracking a porcupine to letting the circus animals out of captivity. But the most amazing animal encounter I have ever had came when I was twelve years old, just moments before the most disappointing human interaction of my life. I was in the woods behind our home when I saw a female moose lying beneath the ferns with a newborn calf. I knew the cow; I'd seen her once or twice. I backed away – my dad had taught me never to get near a new mother and its young – but to my surprise the moose stood up and nudged her calf forward, until it settled, skin and bones, in my lap.

I sat there for an hour with the calf until the most majestic moose I'd ever seen entered the clearing. His rack was colossal, and he stood like a statue until the cow moose got to her feet, too, and the calf. Then the three of them disappeared silently into the woods behind me.

Amazed, I ran back home to tell my parents what had happened – certain they wouldn't believe me – and found them sitting in the kitchen at the table with a woman I didn't recognize. But when she turned around, I could see myself written all over her features.

'Luke,' my dad said. 'This is Kiera. Your real mother.'

He was not my dad but my grandfather. The woman I'd called Mom my whole life was my grandmother. My biological mother was their child – who, at seventeen, had been thrown in jail for selling heroin with her then-boyfriend. She found out two months later that she was pregnant.

When she gave birth to me at the local hospital, she'd been shackled to the bed.

It was decided that my grandparents would raise me. And that, rather than my having to grow up with the stigma of having an incarcerated mother, they'd move from Minnesota to New Hampshire, where nobody knew them. They'd start fresh, saying I was their miracle baby.

When the prison term ended, Kiera postponed reuniting with her family, deciding instead to get herself employed and settled. Now, four years later, she was the front desk manager at a hotel in Cleveland. She was ready to pick up the pieces of her life that she had left behind. Including me.

I don't remember much of that day, except that I didn't want to hug her, and that when she started talking about Cleveland I stood up and ran out the kitchen door into the woods again. The moose were gone, but I had learned from animals how to make myself scarce when necessary, how to blend in with the surroundings. So when my grandfather came looking for me, calling my name, he walked right past the copse of brush where I was hiding, where I stayed until I fell asleep.

The next morning, when I went back home, stiff and damp with cold, Kiera the impostor was gone. My parents, who were now my grandparents, were sitting at the table eating fried eggs. My grandmother offered me a plate with two eggs sunny-side up and a slice of toast. We did not talk about my mother's visit, or where she'd gone. My grandfather said that, for now, I'd be staying put, and that was that.

I began to wonder if I'd dreamed that encounter, or the one with the moose calf, or both.

After that, I had sporadic contact with my mother. She'd send me a pair of slippers every Christmas that were always too small. She came to my grandfather's funeral and my college graduation and two years after that died of ovarian cancer.

Years later when I went to live with the wolves, I would feel different about my mother. I would realize that what she did was no different from what any wolf mother does: put her child into the protective care of the elders, who can use their vast knowledge to teach the next generation everything it needs to know. But at that moment, sitting at the kitchen table eating breakfast in an uncomfortable silence, all I knew was that no animal in my life had ever lied to me; whereas the humans, I could no longer trust.

Edward

There are stages of shock.

The first one comes when you walk into the hospital room and you see your father, still as a corpse, hooked up to a bunch of machines and monitors. There's the total disconnect when you try to reconcile that picture with the one in your head: the same man playing tag with a bunch of wolf pups; the same man who stood eye to eye with you and dared you to challenge him.

Then there's hope. Every flicker of sunlight over the sheets, every hiccup in the ventilator's even sigh, every trick of your tired eyes has you jumping out of your seat, certain that you've just witnessed a twitch, a flutter, a rise to consciousness.

Except, you haven't.

This is followed by denial. Any moment now, you are going to wake up in your own bed cursing the crazy nightmares that always follow a tequila bender. It's laughable, really, theater of the absurd: the image of you playing nursemaid to a father you cut out of your life years ago. Then again, you know that you had no tequila last night. That you are not in your own bed but in a hospital.

That leads to catatonia, as you become just as unresponsive

as the patient. Nurses and doctors and technicians and social workers parade in and out, but you lose track of the number of visits. These nurses and doctors and technicians and social workers all know your name, which is how you realize that this has become a routine. You stop whispering – an instinct, since patients need their rest – because you realize your father can't hear you, and not just because ice water is being injected into his left ear.

It's part of a test, one of an endless series of tests, to measure eye movements. The way it's been explained to me, if you change the temperature of the inner ear, it should cause reflexive eye movements. In people who are conscious, it can be used to check for damage to the ear nerves that can cause balance problems. In people who are not conscious, it can be used to check for brain stem function.

'So?' I ask the neurology resident who's performing the test. 'Is it good news or bad news?'

She doesn't look at me. 'Dr. Saint-Clare will be able to tell you more,' she says, making notes on my father's chart.

She leaves a nurse to wipe my father's face and neck dry. The nurse is the fifteenth one I've met since I've been here. She's got intricately twisted braids swirled into a style on top of her head that makes me wonder how she sleeps at night, and her name is Hattie. Sometimes she hums spirituals when she's taking care of my father: 'Swing Low, Sweet Chariot' and 'I'll Take You There.' 'You know,' she says, 'it wouldn't hurt to talk to him.'

'Can he hear me?'

Hattie shrugs. 'Different doctors believe different things. Me, I think you've got nothing to lose.'

That is because she doesn't know my father. Our last

conversation had been far from a positive one; there's every chance that just the sound of my voice will trigger some angry response.

Then again, at this point, *any* response would do.

For twenty-four hours I have been living in this room, sleeping upright in a chair, maintaining a vigil. My neck hurts and my shoulders ache. My limbs seem jerky, unfamiliar; the skin of my face is slack as rubber. None of this feels real: not my own exhausted body, not being back here, not having my father comatose four feet away from me. Any minute now, I expect to wake up.

Or my father to.

I have subsisted on coffee and hope, making bets with myself: *If I'm still here, there must be a chance for recovery. If the doctors keep finding new tests, they must believe he's going to get better. If I stay awake just five more minutes watching him, he will surely open his eyes.*

When I was a kid, I used to get so scared of the monster that lived in my closet that sometimes I'd hyperventilate, or break out in hives. It was my father who told me to just get the hell out of bed and open the damn door. Not knowing, he said, is a thousand times more horrible than facing your fear.

Of course, when I was a kid and I bravely opened the closet door, there was nothing upsetting inside.

'Um,' I say, when Hattie leaves. 'It's me, Dad. Edward.'

My father doesn't move.

'Cara came to see you,' I tell him. 'She got banged up a little in the crash, but she's going to be fine.' I don't mention that she left in tears, or that I've been too much of a coward to go to her room and have more than a superficial discussion with her. She's like the only person in the village willing to point out that the emperor's not wearing any clothes – or in my case, that the role of dutiful son has been woefully miscast.

I try humor. 'If you missed me, you know, you didn't have to go to this extreme. You could have just invited me home for Thanksgiving.'

But neither of us finds this funny.

The door opens again, and Dr. Saint-Clare enters. 'How's he doing?'

'Aren't you supposed to be able to tell *me* that?' I ask.

'Well, we're still monitoring his condition, which appears to be unchanged.'

Unchanged, I remind myself, must be good. 'You know this from injecting water in his ear?'

'Actually, yes,' the doctor says. 'What we're looking for in the ice-water caloric test is a vestibulo-ocular reflex. If both eyes deviate toward the ear with the water in it, the brain stem is functioning normally and consciousness is mildly impaired. Likewise, nystagmus away from the water suggests consciousness. But your father's eyes didn't move at all, which suggests severe dysfunction of the pons and the midbrain.'

Suddenly I am tired of the medical jargon, of the parade of experts who come in to do tests on my father, who doesn't respond. *Get the hell out of bed and open the damn door.* 'Just say it,' I mutter.

'I'm sorry?'

I force myself to meet Dr. Saint-Clare's eyes. 'He isn't going to wake up, is he?'

'Well.' The neurologist sits down in a chair across from me. 'Consciousness has two components,' he explains. 'There's wakefulness, and there's awareness. You and I are both awake and aware. Someone in a coma is neither. After a few days in a coma, a patient might go one of several routes. He might lose all brain function, and become what we call brain-dead. It's quite rare, but he might develop locked-in syndrome, which would mean he has both wakefulness and awareness . . . but is unable to move or speak. Or he might evolve into a vegetative state – which would mean there's wakefulness . . . but no awareness of himself or where he is. In other words, his eyes may open and he will have sleep cycles, but he won't respond to stimuli. From there, a patient might either improve into a minimally conscious state, in which there's wakefulness and brief interludes of awareness, and eventually regain full consciousness. Alternately, he might remain in what we call a permanent vegetative state, never regaining awareness.'

'So you're saying my father *might* wake up . . .'

'. . . but the chances of him regaining awareness are extremely slim.'

A vegetative state. 'How do you know?'

'The odds are against him. In patients who've suffered traumatic brain stem injury, like your father, the outcome isn't good.'

I wait for these words to hit me with the force of a bullet: *he is talking about my father*. But it's been so long since I let myself feel anything for my dad that, actually, I'm numb. I listen to Dr. Saint-Clare speak, I acknowledge that I was expecting to hear this news from him, I accept it as fact. Ironically, I realize, this *does* make me the best person to keep the bedside vigil for him. 'So what happens?' I ask. 'Do we wait?'

'For a bit. We keep testing him to see if there's any change.'

'If he doesn't ever improve, does he stay here forever?'

'No. There are rehab centers and nursing homes that care for people in vegetative states. Some patients who've made their wishes known to discontinue life support will go into hospice and have their feeding tubes removed. Those who want to be organ donors might meet the protocol for DCD, donation after cardiac death.'

It feels like we are talking about a stranger. But then again, I guess we are. I don't really know my father any better than this neurosurgeon does.

Dr. Saint-Clare stands up. 'We'll keep monitoring him.'

'What should I do in the meantime?'

He puts his hands in the pockets of his white coat. 'Get some sleep,' he says. 'You look like hell.'

When he leaves the room, I pull my chair a little closer to my father's bed. If you had told me when I was eighteen that I would be back in Beresford, I would have laughed in your face. Back then, all I knew was that I had to get away from here as fast as possible. As a teenager, I never realized that the thing I was running from would still be here, waiting, no matter how far I ran.

Mistakes are like the memories you hide in an attic: old love letters from relationships that tanked, photos of dead relatives, toys from a childhood you miss. Out of sight is out of mind, but somewhere deep inside you know they still exist. And you also know that you're avoiding them.

If I were Hattie the nurse, I'd pray for my father. But I've never been religious. My father worshiped at the temple of nature, and my mother threw religion at me like a bucket of paint, but none of it ever stuck.

I find myself thinking of the first week I was in Thailand, when I noticed little decorative houses on pedestals in front of hotels, in the corners of restaurants, in front of local bars, in the middle of the woods, and in the yard of every house. Some were permanent, made of brick and wood. Some were temporary. Each house was filled with statues, furniture, figures of people or animals. On the balconies were incense holders, candlesticks, flower vases.

Most Thai are Buddhists, but bits of the old beliefs still creep through every now and then, like these spirit houses. Even now, the Thai feel that spirits need shelter when they aren't in the heavens, in caves, or trees, or waterfalls. The Guardian Spirits of the Land offer different types of protection: from helping in business affairs to safeguarding the home, from protecting animals, forests, water, and barns to watching over temples and forts. In the six years I've been in Thailand, I've seen spirit house offerings ranging from flowers and bananas and rice to cigarettes and live chickens.

Here's the interesting thing about spirit houses: when a family moves, there's a special ceremony to transfer the spirit from its original spirit house to its new place of residence. Only after that can you get rid of the place the spirit used to call its home.

Looking at the husk of my father in his hospital bed, I wonder if he's already moved on.

Luke

I hated college. There were too many buildings, too much concrete. It seemed counterintuitive to be studying zoology from textbooks instead of sitting quietly for hours in the woods, experiencing animals firsthand. I had my fair share of women and parties, but you'd be just as likely to find me hiking the Presidential Range, or camping in the White Mountains. It got to the point where I could pick out the distinctive voices of a great gray owl or a bohemian waxwing, a pine grosbeak or black-throated blue warbler. I tracked black bear and white-tailed deer and moose.

When I graduated with a degree in zoology, I got hired as a keeper at the only zoo in New Hampshire, down in the Manchester area. Wigglesworth Animal Park was a privately owned establishment that was half petting zoo with a handful of wild animals thrown into the mix. I worked my way up from the alpacas to the fisher cats to the red fox and finally to the wolves. The pack of five was kept in a small double-fenced enclosure with thick trees and a ridged rise that the wolves would sit on during the daytime hours. Every three days one of the keepers would bring in food – the carcass of a calf purchased from an abattoir. Anyone who entered would carry a ski pole – and it wasn't just the wolf keepers who did this but also those who worked with the cougars or the black bear or any other big animal. I don't know what damage any of us could really have inflicted with a ski pole, but it wasn't necessary, anyway. The wolves were far more scared of us than we were of them. The minute they heard the lock on the double gate being opened, they would rush through the thickest part of the wooded area to the den at the far northeast corner of the enclosure. We'd leave the carcass, and only long after we were out of the enclosure would they venture back to eat.

The day I first went in without a ski pole, I was checking the fence – part of the routine of a keeper. But instead of doing my duty and hightailing it out of the enclosure, I decided to sit and stay. Unarmed and uneasy, my blood racing with adrenaline, I sat down on the ridge where I'd seen the wolves settle daily, and I waited.

I was thinking that, like the deer and the moose I'd encountered as a child, these animals might eventually feel comfortable enough with me to go about their business as usual.

I was thinking wrong.

After five days of my sitting in the wolf enclosure, with the other keepers convinced I had a screw loose, not a single animal had approached me.

I have been asked so many times what made me choose this path in life. I think part of it was that animals have always been straight with me, but humans haven't. But the other part is that I don't take no for an answer very easily. So instead of giving up and going back to animal care with a ski pole, I thought about what I might be doing wrong.

And then I realized that I might not have a ski pole with me but I still had the advantage. When I'd been a boy, I'd *sneak out at dusk and dawn to see the animals – but they made themselves scarce midday. If I wanted to put the wolves at ease, I had to approach them when they had the upper hand. So I went to my boss and asked for permission to stay in the wolf enclosure overnight.*

Mind you, once the park closed its gates, at 6:00 p.m., the keepers all went home. There was a skeleton staff in place overnight, but only for emergencies. My boss told me I could do what I wanted, but I could see from the look on his face he thought he'd be hiring a new keeper after this one died of his injuries.

It's hard for me to describe what it was like, locking myself inside the enclosure that first time. At the beginning, all that existed was pure panic. The dark had a heartbeat, and I couldn't see well enough to know where the roots of the trees were sticking up. I could hear the movement of the wolves, but I also knew they had the ability to stalk silently if they were so inclined. I tripped my way to my usual spot – the ridge – and sat down. Unfamiliar sounds from all over the wildlife park pinned me in place. This is what you wanted, *I told myself.*

I tried to close my eyes and sleep, but I couldn't relax. Instead, I began counting stars, and before I knew it, the yolk of the sun was breaking on the horizon.

It was great to work with the wolves during the day, but I was really there to keep the people who came to the park from doing stupid things, like throwing them food or leaning too close to the fence. In the nighttime, though, I was alone with these magnificent animals, these kings and queens of the half-light. At the end of their day they weren't worrying about paying the bills, or what they were going to eat for breakfast, or what to do about the crack in the concrete, man-made pond. All that mattered was that they were together, and that they were safe.

For the next four nights, I locked myself into the wolf pen after the last zookeeper had gone home. And every night, the wolves stayed as far away from me as possible. On the fifth night, just after midnight, I got up and moved from the ridge to the rear of the fenced area. Two of the wolves bounded toward the spot where I'd been sitting. They sniffed the ground and one of them urinated. Then they moved away from the ridge, and spent the rest of their night staring at me with their yellow eyes.

On the sixth night, the wolf we called Arlo approached me. He moved in a slow circle, sniffing, before moving away.

He did the same thing on the seventh and eighth nights, too.

On the ninth night, he sniffed and circled and turned as if he were going to walk away but then whipped around and bit me on the knee.

It wasn't a painful bite. He could have easily gone for my throat if he'd wanted to. It was just a nip, and it scared me more than it hurt me.

The real power of a wolf isn't in its fearsome jaws, which can clench with fifteen hundred pounds of pressure per square inch. The real power of a wolf is having that strength, and knowing when not to use it.

I didn't move. I figured if I tried to get up and leave the enclosure, Arlo might take me down and deliver a lot worse than a nip. Paralyzed by fear, I waited for Arlo to trot away. I didn't move until the sunrise.

Much later I would learn that this terror probably is what

kept me alive that night. When a new member comes to a pack – a lone wolf, for example, filling a vacancy – he's tested to prove that he's capable of holding the position, and that he will not threaten the others in the family. This test takes the form of a bite. If the new wolf doesn't expose his throat to highlight his vulnerability and ask for trust, the wolves already in the pack will do what they must to teach him a lesson. If I'd flinched when Arlo nipped me, or gotten up and run out of the enclosure, I could have been killed.

The next night, Arlo bit me again. After two weeks, my knees, calves, and ankles were covered with bruises and cuts. Then one night, he brushed up against me. He was slightly damp from a light rain, and I thought at first he was trying to dry himself, but he rubbed his face, the top of his head, and his tail against me. When he pushed against me with all 120 pounds of his body and I fell backward, he nipped at me – another warning to stay in place. He continued to shimmy against me, until I smelled like a wet dog, too.

Which was exactly why he was doing it. A few weeks later he began to bring the other members of the pack to my spot on the ridge. They would hang back, wary, while Arlo bit me on the knee and shin. It was Arlo's way of showing them, I realized, that I could take direction.

That I could be trusted.

Georgie

'**D**rinking?' I say, stunned. 'You were *drinking*?'

The police are gone, chased away by a nurse after Cara dissolves into shoulder-wracking sobs that leave her gasping with pain. I don't know who I'm more angry at: the cops, for trying to accuse her of a DUI; or Cara, for lying to me in the first place.

'It was *one* drink—'

'Served in what? A bucket?' I ask. 'Blood tests are pretty damn accurate, Cara.'

'I went to a party with Mariah,' she says. 'I didn't even want to go, it was some guy from Bethlehem High she met at a track meet. And as soon as it started to get out of control, I called Dad and asked him to come get me. I'm telling you the truth. I swear I am.'

'Why didn't you say anything when the ER doctors asked if you had any drugs or alcohol in your system?'

'Because,' Cara says, 'I knew this was going to happen. I made a mistake, okay? Haven't you ever made a mistake?'

God, yes.

'If you couldn't admit it to the doctors,' I say, 'you might have at least told me. You made me feel like an idiot in front of those policemen.'

Cara's mouth twists. 'How do you think I feel? If it wasn't for me – if I hadn't been drinking – Dad wouldn't have gotten hurt. He would never even have been out on the road.'

That, finally, cuts through the red rage I've been seeing since hearing that my underage daughter was drinking while on Luke's watch. If I'd found out any other way, I would have called him on it. I would have yelled at him about not being a responsible parent, about changing the custodial agreement.

But I can't very well yell at him right now.

'Cara,' I say, sitting on the edge of the bed. 'It was a car accident. An *accident*. You can't blame yourself.'

She jerks away from me. 'You weren't there!' she snaps.

It's a criticism of me. I just don't know if she is upset with me for talking about the crash or for being with my other family when it happened.

I'd like to believe that if Cara had still been living under my roof, she wouldn't have been drinking. That if she had stayed with me, we wouldn't be in a hospital. Unlike Luke, who was always so wrapped up in his wolves, I would actually know what my own daughter was up to and I would never let her out late on a school night. But it is always easy to rewrite history after the fact. The truth is, even if Cara had not chosen to go live with her dad instead of me, I might have found myself the recipient of that phone call last Thursday from Cara, begging to be rescued.

There have been a handful of times in my life when I have suddenly had the perspective to be able to see myself from a distance, to trace how I got to that point. The first was the morning I read the note from Edward, telling me that he had left home. The second was at my wedding to Joe, when I was – maybe for the first time – unadulteratedly happy.

The third was when the twins were born. And the fourth, now, is at the crux of a nightmare – my first family, all drawn together again, and inextricably linked once more because of Luke's dynamic persona. *Be careful what you wish for.*

'You can tell Dad to ground me,' Cara says. 'When he wakes up.'

I don't have the heart to tell her that is an if, not a when.

Which means she's not the only person in this room who is a liar.

I met Luke when I was assigned to do a story on him for a local news show. I was convinced that I was going to be the next Katie Couric, even if I was currently slogging in the trenches of local New Hampshire television. Never mind that sometimes the anchors were so bad I watched the videotaped newscasts as a drinking game – every time a word was mispronounced I would have a sip of wine, and often downed an entire bottle in a thirty-minute newscast. My job was to spotlight the quirky, crusty, unique residents of the state in the last three minutes of the evening newscast.

I'd met my share of the weird – the farmer's wife who dressed up her barn cats in hand-sewn costumes and photographed them in the same positions as famous paintings; the bagel baker who had accidentally created a cheddar-dill concoction that bore an uncanny resemblance to the governor; the petite blonde elementary school teacher who had won a lumberjack contest in the north country. One day my crew (which meant me and a guy lugging a camera) was dispatched to the only zoo in New Hampshire, a sleepy little Manchester-area establishment with horseback trail rides, a dairy discovery barn, and a thin collection of wildlife.

We had been tipped off to the story by a viewer, who'd brought his toddler down to the zoo and who had been surprised to see a crowd gathered around the small enclosure where the wolves were kept. Apparently one of the zookeepers, Luke Warren, had begun to sleep overnight with the animals, and to spend part of the day inside the enclosure. His superiors – at first sure this was a suicide attempt – now realized the wolves had accepted him into their fold and encouraged Luke to interact with them during the park's open hours. His antics had single-handedly quadrupled the zoo's business.

When Alfred, my cameraman, and I arrived at the enclosure, we had to push our way through the crowd lined up along the fence. Inside were five wolves, and one human. Luke Warren was seated between two animals that were easily each over a hundred pounds. When he saw us, he walked toward the double gates leading out of the enclosure as people whispered and pointed. He greeted those who wanted to ask him questions about the wolves, and then he approached my cameraman. 'You must be George,' he said.

I stepped forward. 'No. That's me. It's *Georgie.*'

Luke laughed. 'You're definitely not what I expected.'

I could have said the same. I figured that this guy would be a nut job like most of the others I interviewed – peculiar to the point of dysfunctional. But Luke Warren was tall and muscular, with blond hair that reached down to his shoulders and eyes so pale and blue that, for a moment, I had trouble remembering what I was doing there. He wore a ratty old set of coveralls. 'Just let me get out of these,' he said, unzipping them to reveal the khaki uniform of a zookeeper. 'The wolves are used to this scent, but by now, my clothes could probably walk away by themselves.'

He disappeared into a keeper's hut and returned a moment later, his hair tied back neatly and his face and hands freshly washed. 'So,' I said. 'You don't mind if we film . . . ?'

'Go right ahead,' Luke replied. He led us to a bench that offered the best view of the wolves behind him, because – as he said – they were the real stars.

'I'm rolling,' Alfred said.

I folded my hands in my lap. 'You've been staying overnight in the enclosure for some time now . . .'

Luke nodded. 'Four months.'

'Continuously?' I asked.

'Yeah. It's gotten to the point where it's more comfortable for me than any bed.'

Already, I was wondering what this guy's angle was. You didn't go sleep with wild animals for four months unless you were trying to get attention drawn to you or you were mentally ill. I thought maybe he wanted his own talk show. In those days, everyone did. 'Don't you worry about the wolves attacking you while you sleep?'

He smiled. 'I'm not going to lie – the first night I went in, I didn't get any sleep. But on the whole, a wolf is far more afraid of a human than vice versa. At this point, because I allowed them to teach me instead of telling them what to do, they've accepted me as a low-ranking member of their pack.'

Definitely mental illness, I thought. 'Well, Luke, the obvious question is: why?'

He shrugged. 'I think if you want to know what a wolf is really like, you can't just observe. Most biologists would disagree, and say that you can watch the interaction of a wolf pack through your camera lens and draw your conclusions based on what you know of human behavior – but isn't that completely backward? If you want to understand a wolf's world, you have to be willing to live in it. You have to speak his language.'

'So you're telling me you speak wolf?'

Luke grinned. 'Fluently. I could even teach you a few phrases.' He stood up, setting one foot on the bench as he leaned in. 'There are three different types of howls a wolf makes,' he explained. 'There's a locating howl, which gives the whereabouts of any pack that's in the area. Not just my family, but rival packs, too. The defensive howl is a little deeper. It means *stay away*; it's a way to protect your territory and the pack inside it. The third type of howl is a rallying howl. That's the classic Hollywood howl – mournful, melancholy. It's used when a pack member is lost, and scientists used to think it was a measure of grief, but actually, it's a vocal beacon. A way for a missing family member to try to find his way back home.'

'Can you show me?'

'Only if you help,' Luke said. He pulled me up until I was standing. 'Take deep breaths, filling your lungs. Hold those breaths as long as you can, and then exhale. On the third breath, send the howl.' He inhaled three times, cupped his hand to his mouth, and a long, two-tone note swelled through the enclosure, rising over the tops of the trees. The wolves looked up, curious. 'Try it,' he said.

'I can't—'

'Of course you can.' He put his hands on my shoulders from behind. 'Breathe in,' he coached. 'Breathe out. In . . .

out. In . . . ready?' Leaning forward, he whispered into my ear. 'Let go.'

I closed my eyes, and all the air in my lungs poured forward on a vibration that started in my center and filled my body. Then I did it again. It was primal, guttural. Behind me, I could hear Luke howling a different pattern – longer, lower, more intense. When his voice tangled with mine, the result was a song. This time the wolves in the enclosure tipped their heads back and answered us.

'That's amazing!' I cried, breaking off to listen as their howls rolled in patterns, like waves. 'Do they know we're human?'

'Does it matter?' Luke asked. 'That was a locating howl. Pretty basic.'

'Do another one?'

He took a deep breath, rounding his mouth into an O. The sound that issued was completely different, like a distillation of grief. In that one note I heard the soul of a saxophone, a breaking heart.

'What does that one mean?'

He stared at me, so intense I couldn't look away. 'Is it you?' Luke whispered. 'Are you the one I'm looking for?'

Cara is trying – unsuccessfully – to eat the Jell-O on her dinner tray. She can chase the little bowl around with her left hand, but every time she tries to get a spoonful, it either tips over or scoots forward. 'Here,' I say, sitting down on the edge of the bed and feeding her myself.

She opens her mouth like a baby bird, swallows. 'Are you still mad at me?'

'Yes,' I sigh. 'But that doesn't mean I don't love you.' I

watch as she takes another bite, remembering how hard it was to get Cara to eat solid food. She was more likely to mash it into her hair, finger-paint on her high chair tray, or spit it in my face than eat it. At her well-child weigh-ins, she was always on the verge of undernourished, and I'd go out of my way to explain to the nurse practitioners that I wasn't starving her – she was starving herself.

When Cara was just a year old, we stopped at a McDonald's on the way home from one of Edward's Little League games. While I was busy opening up jars of baby food and digging in my purse for a bib, Cara reached from her high chair to Edward's Happy Meal place mat and started happily gumming a French fry. 'What about her baby food?' Edward asked.

'Well,' I replied. 'I guess she isn't a baby anymore.'

He considered this. 'Is she still Cara?'

Turn around, and the people you thought you knew might change. Your little boy might now live half a world away. Your beautiful daughter might be sneaking out at night. Your ex-husband might be dying by degrees. This is the reason that dancers learn, early on, how to spot while doing pirouettes: we all want to be able to find the place where we started.

Cara pushes away her dinner tray with her good hand and starts flipping through the television channels with the remote control. 'There's nothing on.'

It is five o'clock; all the networks are airing local evening broadcasts. 'The news isn't nothing,' I tell her. I look up at the screen, set on the station where I used to work. The anchor is a girl in her twenties who has too much eye makeup on. If I had stuck with broadcast journalism, I'd be a producer now. Someone who stayed behind the camera, who didn't have to worry about zits and gray roots and five extra pounds.

'In a stunning victory,' the anchor is saying, 'Daniel Boyle, the Grafton County attorney, has won a contentious trial that some say is a ringing victory for conservatives in the state. Judge Martin Crenstable ruled today that Merilee Swift, the pregnant woman who suffered an aneurysm in December, will be kept on life support for another six months, until her baby is delivered at full term. Boyle chose to prosecute the case himself when the woman's husband and parents asked the hospital to turn off Merilee Swift's respirator.'

'Pig,' I say under my breath. 'He wouldn't have blinked twice at the parents' request if it wasn't an election year.'

The screen cuts to a courthouse-steps interview with Danny Boy, as he likes to be called, himself. 'I'm proud to be the guardian of the smallest victims, the ones without voices,' he says. 'A life is a life. And I know if Ms. Swift could speak, she'd want to know her baby's being taken care of.'

'For the love of God,' I murmur, and I grab the remote away from Cara. I flip to the next channel, and my mouth drops open.

A picture of Luke, grinning as one of his wolves licks his face, fills the screen over the anchor's shoulder. 'WMUR has learned that Luke Warren, the naturalist and conservationist who made a name for himself by living in the wild with a pack of wolves, is in critical condition after a motor vehicle accident. Warren will be remembered for his cable television show, which detailed his experiences with wolves at New Hampshire's own Redmond's Trading Post—'

I push the button on the remote, and the screen goes

black. 'They'll say whatever they can to get viewers to watch,' I tell her. 'We don't have to listen.'

Cara turns her face against the pillow. 'They're talking about him like he's already dead,' she says.

It is ridiculous to think that after six years of my being continents away from Edward, he's now just a floor below where I'm sitting, and we're still separated.

I don't have to tell any mother what it's like to have a son leave. It happens a multitude of natural ways – summer camp, college, marriage, career. It feels as if the fabric you're made of has a hole in its center all of a sudden, yet whatever weave you use to fix it is sure to be a hatchet job. I don't believe any parent moves gracefully into the acceptance that a child doesn't need her anymore, but I was blindsided by the truth. Edward left when he was just eighteen, when he was still applying to colleges for the following year. I thought I'd have another six months to figure out how to surgically extract him from the pattern of my life, smiling all the while, so that he didn't think I was anything less than thrilled for his good fortune. But Edward never went to college. Instead, one awful morning, he left me a note and vanished, which is maybe why it felt as if I'd been shelled by a cannon.

I don't want to leave Cara alone, so I wait until she falls asleep again before I go to the ICU. Edward sits in a chair with his head bowed to his hands as if he's praying. I wait, not wanting to disturb him, and then realize he's dozed off.

It gives me a chance to look more carefully at Luke. The last time I'd been down here, with Cara and the social worker, I'd been more attuned to my daughter's reaction than I was to forming one of my own.

I've always thought of Luke as a verb. Something in motion, rather than at rest. Seeing him this still reminds me of times I used to will myself to wake up before he did, so that I could study him: the sculpted curve of his ear, the golden horizon of his jaw, the iridescent scars on his hands and neck that he'd accumulated over the years.

I must make some kind of noise in the back of my throat, because suddenly Edward is awake and staring at me. 'I'm sorry,' I say, but I'm not sure to whom I'm apologizing.

'It's weird, right?' Edward gets up and stands beside me. He smells like a man, I realize. Like Old Spice deodorant and shaving cream. 'I keep thinking he's just asleep.'

I slide my arm around my son's waist, hug him closer. 'I wanted to come down earlier, but . . .'

'Cara,' he says.

I face Edward. 'She didn't know you were here.'

He smiles crookedly. 'Hence the warm reception.'

'She's not thinking clearly right now.'

Edward smirks. 'Oh, she's clearly thinking I'm an asshole.' He shakes his head. 'And I'm kind of thinking she might be right.'

I look at Luke. He's not conscious, but it feels strange to be talking like this in front of him. 'I need a cup of coffee,' I say, and Edward follows me down the hall to a family lounge. It is a tired, sad little room with gray walls and no windows. There is a coffeemaker in the corner, and an honor box where you can pay a dollar per cup. There are two couches and a few extra chairs, some ancient magazines, a box of battered toys.

I brew one of the Keurig singles for Edward while he sinks down on a couch. 'Your sister may not realize it, but she needs you.'

'I'm not staying,' Edward says immediately. 'I'm out of here, as soon as . . .'

He doesn't finish his sentence. I don't finish it for him.

'I feel like a fraud. There's a part of me that knows I have to be in that room and talk to his doctors because I'm his son, right, and that's what sons do. But there's another part of me that knows I haven't been his son for a long time and that the last person he'd want to see if he opened his eyes was me.'

The coffee spits out of the machine in one final hiss. I realize I have no idea how Edward takes his coffee. Once, I could have told you any detail about this boy of mine – where the scar on the back of his neck came from, where he had birthmarks, which spots of him were ticklish, whether he slept on his back or his stomach. What else do I no longer know about my own child?

'You came home when I asked,' I say simply, handing him the coffee, black. 'That was the right thing to do.'

Edward runs his finger around the rim of the paper cup. 'Mom,' he says. 'What if?'

I sit down beside him. 'What if what?'

'You know.'

Hope and reality lie in inverse proportions, inside the walls of a hospital. Edward doesn't have to spell out what he's talking about; it's what I've worked so hard to keep from allowing myself to think. Doubt is like dye. Once it spreads into the fabric of excuses you've woven, you'll never get rid of the stain.

There is a lot I'd like to say to Edward. That this isn't fair; that this isn't right. After all Luke's done, all those times he could have died of hypothermia or an attack from a wild animal or a hundred other horrific natural disasters, it seems humiliating to think of him being felled by something as mundane as a car accident.

But instead I say, 'Let's not talk about that yet.'

'I'm out of my league here, Ma.'

'*Anyone* would be.' I rub my temples. 'Just keep gathering the information the doctors give you. So that when Cara's ready, you two can talk.'

'Can I ask you something?' Edward says. 'Why does she hate me so much?'

I think about hiding the truth from him, but that makes me think of Cara, and her drinking the night of the accident, and how I'm already being such a total hypocrite for being a cheerleader in front of her about Luke's condition, when clearly it doesn't warrant that kind of optimism. 'She blames you.'

'Me?' Edward's eyes grow wide. 'For what?'

'The fact that your father and I got divorced.'

Edward chokes on a laugh. 'She blames *me*. For *that*? I wasn't even here.'

'She was eleven. You vanished without saying good-bye. Luke and I started fighting, obviously, because of what had happened—'

'What had happened,' Edward repeats softly.

'Anyway, as far as Cara sees it, you were the first step in a chain of events that split her family apart.'

In the forty-eight hours since I got the phone call from the hospital about Cara and the accident, I have held myself together. I have been strong because my daughter needed me to be strong. When the news you don't want to hear is looming before you like Everest, two things can happen.

Tragedy can run you through like a sword, or it can become your backbone. Either you fall apart and sob, or you say, *Right. What's next?*

So maybe it is because I'm exhausted, but I finally let myself burst into tears. 'And I know you're feeling guilty, about being here, after everything that happened between you and your father. But you're not the only one who's feeling that way,' I say. 'Because as horrible as this has been, I keep thinking it's the first step in a chain of events that's put this family back together.'

Edward doesn't know what to do with a sobbing mother. He gets up and hands me the entire stack of napkins from the coffee amenities basket. He folds me into an awkward embrace. 'Don't get your hopes up,' he says, and as if by unspoken agreement we leave the family lounge side by side.

Neither one of us comments on the fact that I never did get the coffee I wanted.

Luke

*I*n the wolf world, it's in everyone's best interests to fill a pack vacancy. For the family that's lost one of its members – one that's been killed or has gone missing – the ranks are suddenly depleted. A rival pack trying to overtake their territory will become an even bigger threat, and the defensive howl sung by the family will change to an inquiry instead: a higher-pitched question, an invitation to lone wolves in the area to join the pack and battle the rival together.

So what would make a lone wolf answer?

Imagine being all alone in the wild. You are another animal's potential prey, a rival pack's enemy. You know that most packs will be prowling between dusk and dawn, so instead you move around during the daytime – but that makes you vulnerable and more easily seen. You walk a precarious tightrope, urinating in streams to disguise your scent, so that you cannot be tracked and challenged. Every turn you make, every animal you meet, is a danger. The best chance of survival you have is to belong to a group.

There is safety in numbers, and security. You put your trust in another member of your family. You say: *if you do what you can to keep me alive, I'll do the same for you.*

Edward

So my sister hates me because I ruined her childhood. If she understood the irony of that very statement, God, we'd have quite the laugh. Maybe one day, when we're old and gray, we actually *can* laugh about it.

As if.

It's always amazed me how, when you don't offer an explanation, other people manage to read something between the lines. The note I left my mother, pinned to my pillow so that she'd find it after I split in the middle of the night, told her I loved her, that this wasn't her fault. It said that I just couldn't look my father in the eye anymore.

All of this was the truth.

'Thirsty?' a woman says, and I jump back when I realize that the soda fountain I'm standing in front of in the hospital cafeteria is spilling Coke all over my sneakers.

'God,' I mutter, releasing the lever. I glance around to find something to sop up the mess. But the napkins are rationed by the cashiers, some sort of ecofriendly initiative. I look over at the cashier, who narrows her eyes at me and shakes her head. 'Luellen?' she yells out over her shoulder. 'Call the custodian.'

'Here.' The woman beside me removes a packet of Kleenex from her purse and starts patting my soaked shirt, my pants.

I try to take the ball of damp tissues from her, and we wind up bumping heads.

'Oh!'

'I'm sorry,' I say. 'I'm a little bit of a wreck.'

'I can see that.' She smiles; she's got dimples. She's probably about my age. She's wearing a hospital ID tag, but no medical coat or scrubs. 'Tell you what, the Coke's on me.' Refilling another cup, she moves my banana and yogurt from my tray onto hers. I follow her into the seating area after she swipes her ID card to pay.

'Thanks.' I rub my hand across my forehead. 'I haven't gotten a lot of sleep lately. This is really nice of you.'

'This is really nice of you, *Susan*,' she says.

'I'm Edward—'

'Nice to meet you, Edward. I was just correcting you, so you'd know my name for later.'

'Later?'

'When you call me . . . ?'

This conversation is moving in crazy circles I can't follow.

Immediately, Susan cringes. 'Shoot. I should have known better. I swear my gut instinct is permanently disabled. This is creepy, right? Trying to hit on someone in a hospital cafeteria? For all I know you're a patient or your wife's upstairs having a baby but you looked so helpless and my parents met at a funeral so I always figure it's worth taking the chance if you see someone you want to get to know better—'

'Wait – you were trying to *hit* on me?'

'Damn straight.'

For the first time during this conversation, I smile. 'The thing is, I'm not.' Now it is her turn to look confused. 'Straight, I mean. I bat for the other team,' I say.

Jodi Picoult

Susan bursts out laughing. 'Correction: my gut instinct isn't just disabled, it's irrevocably damaged. This might be a new single-girl career low for me.'

'I'm still flattered,' I say.

'And you got a free meal out of it. Might as well enjoy it while you're here.' She gestures to the seat across from her. 'So what brings you to Beresford Memorial?'

I hesitate, thinking about my father, still and silent, in the ICU. About my sister, who hates my guts, and who's swathed like a fallen soldier from neck to waist in bandages.

'Relax. I'm not going to violate HIPAA with you. I just thought it might be nice to have a conversation partner for a few minutes. Unless there's somewhere you need to be?'

I should be at my father's bedside. This is the first time I've left it in twelve hours, and I only came to the cafeteria to get enough food to keep me going for another twelve. But instead, I sit down across from Susan. Five minutes, I promise myself. 'No,' I tell her, the first in a series of lies. 'I'm good.'

When I walk back into my father's room, two policemen are waiting for me. I'm not even surprised. It's just one more item on a long list of things I never expected. 'Mr. Warren?' the first policeman asks.

It's strange to be called that. In Thailand I was called Ajarn Warren – *Head Teacher Warren* – and even that felt uncomfortable, like an oversize shirt that didn't fit. I've never actually known at what point a person becomes a grown-up and starts answering to titles like that, but I am pretty sure I'm not there yet.

'I'm Officer Whigby; this is Officer Dumont,' the cop says.

83

'We're sorry for your—' He catches himself, before he speaks the word *loss* out loud. 'For what's happened.'

Officer Dumont steps forward, holding a paper bag. 'We recovered your father's personal effects at the scene of the accident, and thought you might like them,' he says.

I reach out and take the bag. It's lighter than I think it's going to be.

They say their good-byes and head out of the room. At the threshold, Whigby turns around. 'I watched every single one of his Animal Planet episodes,' he says. 'You know the one with the wolf that almost gets poisoned to death? I cried like a baby, swear to God.'

He's talking about Wazoli, a young female who'd been brought to my father at Redmond's after being abused at a zoo. He built an enclosure for her and moved two brothers into it, forming a new pack. One day an animal-rights activist broke into Redmond's after hours and swapped meat that had been delivered from the abattoir for meat laced with strychnine. Since Wazoli was the alpha of the group, she ate first – and collapsed, unconscious, in the pond. The camera crews covered my father fishing her out of the water, carrying her to his trailer, wrapping her in his own blankets to warm her up until she began to respond again.

This policeman isn't just telling me he's a fan of wolves. He's saying, *I remember your dad back when.* He's saying, *That body in the hospital bed, that's not the real Luke Warren.*

When they're gone, I sit down beside my father and look through the bag. There's a pair of aviator sunglasses, a receipt from Jiffy Lube, spare change. A baseball cap whose bill has been chewed. A cell phone. A wallet.

I set the bag down, turning the wallet over in my hands.

It's hardly worn, but then, my father often forgot to carry one. He'd leave it in the console of the truck, because if he went into a wolf enclosure he was likely to have it snatched out of his back pocket by a curious animal. By the age of twelve I had learned to carry cash when I went out with my dad, to prevent the embarrassment of being stuck in a grocery line without the means to pay.

With clinical detachment, I open the wallet. Inside are forty-three dollars, a Visa card, and a business card from a large-animal vet in Lincoln. There's a feed-and-grain store customer-rewards punch card that says 'HAY?' on the back in my father's handwriting, and has a phone number scrawled beneath it. There's a wallet-size photo of Cara, with the cheesy blue background that school pictures always have. There's no indication that he even knew me, at all.

I will give all of this to Cara, I guess.

His driver's license is inside a laminated pocket. The photo on it doesn't even look like my father; he's got his hair pulled back and he's staring at the camera as if he's just been insulted.

In the bottom right-hand corner is a small red heart.

I remember filling out the paperwork for my own license when I was sixteen. 'Do I want to be an organ donor?' I had yelled to my mother in the kitchen.

'I don't know,' she'd said. '*Do* you?'

'How am I supposed to make that decision right now?'

She had shrugged. 'If you can't make it right now, then you shouldn't check the box.'

At that point my father had walked into the kitchen to grab a snack on his way back out to Redmond's. I remember thinking that I hadn't even known he was in the house that morning; my father would come and go with that sort of fluid frequency; we were not his home, we were a place to shower and change and eat a meal occasionally. 'Are you an organ donor?' I had asked him.

'What?'

'On your license. You know. I think it would freak me out.' I'd grimaced. 'My corneas in someone else's eyes. My liver in someone else's body.'

He had sat down at the table across from me, peeling his banana. 'Well, if it came to that,' he'd said, shrugging, 'I don't think you'd be physically capable of feeling freaked out.'

In the end, I hadn't checked off the box. Mostly because, if my father endorsed something, I was dead set on supporting its opposite.

But my father, apparently, had felt differently.

There is a soft knock on the open door, and Trina, the social worker, comes in. She's already introduced herself to me; she works with Dr. Saint-Clare. She was the one who'd been pushing Cara's wheelchair the first time my sister was brought in to see my father in his hospital bed. 'Hi, Edward,' she says. 'Mind if I come in?'

I shake my head, and she pulls up a chair beside mine. 'How are you doing?' Trina asks.

It seems like a strange question from someone who does this for a living. Is *anyone* she meets inclined to say 'Fantastic!' Would she even be skulking around near me if she thought I was handling this well?

At first I hadn't understood why my father, unconscious, had a social worker assigned to him. Then I'd realized Trina was there for me and for Cara. My previous definition of social worker involved foster care – so I wasn't quite sure what help she could offer me – but she's been an excellent resource. If I want to talk to Dr. Saint-Clare, she finds him. If I forget the name of the chief resident, she tells it to me.

'I hear you talked to Dr. Saint-Clare today,' Trina says.

I look at my father's profile. 'Can I ask you something?'

'Sure.'

'Have you ever seen someone get better? Someone who's . . . as bad off as him?'

I can't look at the hospital bed when I say this. I stare down at a spot on the floor instead. 'There's a wide range of recoveries from brain injury,' Trina says. 'But from what Dr. Saint-Clare has told me, your father's injury is catastrophic, and his chances of recovery are minimal at best.'

Heat floods my cheeks. I press my hands against them. 'So who decides?' I say softly.

She understands what I'm asking.

'If your father had been conscious when he was brought into the hospital,' Trina says gently, 'he would have been asked if he'd like to complete an advance directive – a statement explaining who is his health-care proxy. Who has the right to speak on his behalf for all medical decisions.'

'I think he wanted to donate his organs.'

Trina nods. 'According to the Anatomical Gift Act, there's a protocol for which family members are approached, and in what order, to give a directive for organ donation for someone who's medically incapacitated and unable to speak for himself.'

'But his license has an organ donor symbol.'

'Well, that makes it a little simpler. That symbol means that he's a registered donor, and that he's legally consented to donation.' She hesitates. 'But, Edward, there's another decision that needs to be made before you even start to consider organ donation. And in this state, there's no legal hierarchy to follow when it comes to turning off someone's life support. The next of kin of a patient with injuries like your dad's has to make the decision for withdrawal of treatment before anyone even starts talking about organ donation.'

'I haven't talked to my father in six years,' I admit. 'I don't know what he eats for breakfast, much less what he would want me to do in this situation.'

'Then,' Trina says, 'I think you need to talk to your sister.'

'She doesn't want to talk to me.'

'Are you sure about that?' the social worker says. 'Or is it that *you* don't want to talk to *her*?'

When she leaves a few minutes later, I tip back my head and let out a sigh. What Trina's said is a hundred percent true – the reason I'm hiding in this room with my father is because he's unconscious – he can't get mad at me for walking out six years ago. On the other hand, my sister can and will. First, for leaving without a word. And second, for coming back, and being thrust into a position that naturally belongs to her: the person who knows my father best. The person my father would probably want sitting next to him, now, if given the choice.

I realize that I am still holding my father's wallet. I take out the license, rub my finger over the little heart, the symbol for an organ donor. But when I go to slip it back into the laminated sleeve, I see there's something else in there.

It's a photo, cut down to fit the small pocket in the wallet. It's from 1992, Halloween. I had on a baseball cap, covered with fur, with two sharp ears sticking up. My face was painted to give me a muzzle. I was four years old, and I had wanted a wolf costume.

I wonder if I knew, even back then, that he loved those animals more than he loved me.

I wonder why he's kept this photo in his wallet, in spite of what happened.

Even though I was seven years older than Cara, I was jealous of her.

She had auburn ringlets and chubby cheeks, and people used to stop my mother as she was pushing the baby stroller down the street, just to comment on what a beautiful baby she had. Then they'd notice the second grader walking sullenly beside her – too thin, too shy.

But it wasn't Cara's looks that made me jealous – it was her mind. She was never the kind of kid who just played with dolls. Instead, she'd position them all around the house and make up some elaborate story about an orphan who travels across the ocean as a stowaway in a pirate ship to find the woman who sold her at birth in order to save her husband from a life in jail. When her report cards came home from elementary school, the teachers always commented on her daydreaming. Once, my mom had to go to the principal's office because Cara had convinced her classmates that her grandfather was an astrophysicist and that by 6:00 p.m., the sun was going to crash into the earth and kill us all.

Even though there was a significant age gap between us, sometimes when she asked me to play, I'd go along with it. One of her favorite games was to hide inside her bedroom closet and blast off. In the dark, she'd chatter away about the planets we were passing, and when she opened the door again, she gasped about the aliens with six eyes and the mountains that shivered like green jelly.

Believe me, even though I was old enough to know better, all I wanted was to see those aliens and mountains. I think even as a kid, when I realized I was different, my greatest hope was that change was possible, that I could be just like everyone else. Instead, I would open the closet door and glance around at the same old dresser and bureau, at my mother, putting away Cara's folded laundry.

It was no surprise that when my father went into the wild, Cara offered different explanations to anyone who asked: *He's on a dig with Egyptologists in Cairo. He's training for a space shuttle mission. He's filming a movie with Brad Pitt.*

I have no idea if she really believed the things she was saying, but I can tell you this much: I wished it were that easy for me to come up with excuses for my father.

The floor of the hospital where Cara and the other orthopedics patients are kept is considerably different from the ICU. There's more activity, for one, and the deathly quiet that makes you want to lower your voice to a whisper on my father's floor is replaced here by the sounds of nurses interacting with patients, the squeak of the book cart being pushed by a candy striper, the spill of voices from a dozen televisions bleeding past the thresholds of the rooms.

When I walk into Cara's room, she's watching *Wheel of Fortune.* 'Only the good die young,' she says, solving the puzzle.

My mother spots me first. 'Edward?' she says. 'Is everything all right?'

She means with my father. Of course she'd think that. The look on Cara's face makes my stomach hurt.

'He's fine. I mean, he's *not* fine. But he's not any different.'

I am already fucking this up. 'Mom, could I talk to Cara alone for a minute?'

My mother looks at Cara, but then she nods. 'I'll go give the twins a call.'

I sit down in the chair my mother vacated and drag it closer to the bed. 'So,' I begin, gesturing to Cara's bound shoulder. 'Are you in a lot of pain?'

My sister stares at me. 'I've been hurt worse,' she says evenly.

'I, uh, I'm sorry that this is the way we had to have a reunion.'

She shrugs, her mouth pressed into a tight line. 'Yeah. So why are you even here?' she asks after a minute. 'Why don't you just go back to whatever you were doing and leave us alone?'

'I will, if you want,' I say. 'But I'd really like to tell you what I've been doing. And I'd kind of like to know what you've been up to, too.'

'I've been living with Dad. You know, the guy you're downstairs pretending to know better than I do.'

I rub my hand over my face. 'Isn't this hard enough without you hating me?'

'Oh. Gosh. You're right. What am I thinking? I'm supposed to welcome you back with open arms. I'm supposed to ignore the fact that you tore our family to shreds because you're selfish and you left instead of trying to talk something out, so now you can ride in like some white knight and pretend you give a damn about Dad.'

There's no way to convince her that just because you put half a planet between you and someone else, you can't drive that person out of your thoughts. Believe me. I tried.

'I know why you left,' Cara says, jutting her chin up. 'You came out and Dad went ballistic. Mom told me so.'

Cara was too young to understand back then, but she's not now; she would have eventually asked questions. And of course my mother would have told her what she believed to be the answers.

'You know what? I don't even *care* why you left,' Cara says. 'I just want to know why you bothered to come back when no one wants you here.'

'Mom wants me here.' I take a deep breath. 'And *I* want to be here.'

'Did you find Jesus or Buddha or something in Thailand? Are you atoning for your past so you can move on to the next step in your karmic life? Well, guess what, Edward. I *don't* forgive you. So there.'

I almost expect her to stick her tongue out at me. *She's hurt*, I tell myself. *She's angry.* 'Look. If you want to hate me, fine. If you want me to spend the next six years saying I'm sorry, I'll do that, too. But right now, this isn't about you and me. We have all the time in the world to figure things out between us again. But Dad doesn't have all the time in the world. We need to focus on him.'

When she ducks her head, I take it as agreement.

'The doctors are saying . . . that his injuries aren't the kind that can heal—'

'They don't know him,' Cara says.

'They're *doctors*, Cara.'

'You don't know him, either—'

'What if he never wakes up?' I interrupt. 'Then what?'

I can tell, from the way her face pales, that she has not let herself go there, mentally. That she hasn't even let that hint of doubt creep into her head, for fear it will take root like the fireweed that grows along the road in summertime, rampant as cancer. 'What are you talking about?' she whispers.

'Cara, he can't stay hooked up to life support forever.'

Her jaw drops. 'Jesus. You hate him so much that you'd kill him?'

'I don't hate him. I know you don't believe it, but I love him enough that I'm willing to think about what *he'd* want, instead of what *we'd* want.'

'You have a truly fucked-up way of showing your love, then,' Cara says.

Hearing a curse word on my little sister's lips is like hearing nails on a blackboard. 'You can't tell me that Dad would want machines breathing for him. That he'd want to live with someone having to bathe him and change his diaper. That he wouldn't miss working with his wolves.'

'He's a fighter. He won't give up.' She shakes her head. 'I can't believe we're even talking about this. I can't believe *you* think you have the right to tell me what Dad would or wouldn't want.'

'I'm being realistic, that's all,' I reply. 'You have to be ready to make some hard choices.'

'Choices?' she says, choking on the word. 'I know all about hard choices. Should I have a total breakdown, or hold it together while my parents are splitting up? Even though the one person who'd understand what I'm feeling has totally abandoned me? Do I live with my mother or do I live with my father, because no matter what I decide, I know my answer's going to hurt the other person. I've made hard choices, and I picked Dad. So how dare you tell me I'm supposed to just give him up, now?'

'I know you love him. I know you don't want to lose him—'

'Before you left, you told Mom you wanted to kill him,' Cara snaps. 'So I guess now you have your chance.'

I can't blame my mother for telling her that. It's true.

'That was a long time ago. Things change.'

'Exactly. And in two weeks or two months or maybe longer, Dad just might walk out of this hospital.'

That is not what I've been led to believe by the neurologists. That is not what I'm seeing with my own eyes. I realize, though, that she is right. How can I make a family decision with my sister when I haven't been part of this family?

'For what it's worth,' I say, 'I'm sorry I left. But I'm here now. I know you're hurting, and this time, you don't have to go through it alone.'

'If you want to make it up to me,' Cara says, 'then tell the hospital *I* should be in charge of what happens to Dad.'

'You're not old enough. They won't listen to you.'

She stares at me. 'But you could,' she says.

The truth is, I want my father to wake up and get better, but not because he deserves it.

Because I want to leave as soon as possible.

In this, Cara is right. I haven't been part of this family for six years. I can't just walk in and pretend to fit seamlessly. I tell my mother this, when I walk out of Cara's room and find her pacing in the hall. 'I'm going back home,' I say.

'You *are* home.'

'Ma,' I say, 'who are we kidding? Cara doesn't want me here. I can't contribute anything valuable about what Dad would have wanted in this situation. I'm getting in the way, instead of helping.'

'You're tired. Overtired,' my mother says. 'You've been in the hospital for twenty-four hours. Get some rest in a real bed.' She reaches into her purse and pulls a key off a chain of many.

'I don't know where you live now,' I point out. As if that isn't proof enough that I don't belong.

'You know where you *used* to live,' she says. 'This is a spare key I keep in case Cara loses hers. There's no one in the house, obviously. It's probably good for you to go there anyway to make sure everything's all right.'

As if there would be a break-in in Beresford, New Hampshire.

My mother presses the key into my palm. 'Just sleep on it,' she says.

I know I should refuse, make a clean break. Start driving back to the airport and book the first flight to Bangkok. But my head feels like it's filled with flies, and regret tastes like almonds on the roof of my mouth. 'One night,' I say.

'Edward,' my mother says, as I am walking away from her. 'You've been gone for six years. But before that, you lived with him for eighteen years. You have more to contribute than you think you do.'

'That's what I'm afraid of,' I reply.

'That you can't make the right decision?'

I shake my head. 'That I *can*,' I tell her. 'But for all the wrong reasons.'

I'm having an Alice in Wonderland moment.

The house I step into is familiar, but completely different. There is the couch I used to lie on to watch TV after school, but it's not the same couch – this one has stripes instead of being a solid, deep red. There are photos of my dad with his wolves dotting the walls, but now they're mixed in with school pictures of Cara. I walk by them slowly, watching her grow up in increments.

I trip over a pair of shoes, but they aren't my little sister's light-up sneakers anymore. The dining room table is covered with open textbooks – calculus, world history, Voltaire. Sitting on the kitchen counter are an empty carton of orange juice, three dirty plates, and a roll of paper towels. It's the mess of someone who thought he was coming back to clean up later.

There's a nearly empty box of Life cereal on the counter, which feels more like a metaphor than a housekeeping oversight.

The house has a smell, too. Not a bad one – it's outdoorsy, like pine and smoke. You know how when you go to someone's house it smells a certain way . . . but when you go to your own house it doesn't smell at all? If I needed any other confirmation that I'm a stranger, this is it.

I push the blinking red button on the answering machine. There are two messages. The first is from a girl named Mariah, and it is for Cara.

Okay, I totally have to talk to you and your cell phone voice mailbox is full. Call me!

The second is from Walter, who lives at Redmond's Trading Post. Six years ago he was the caretaker for the wolves if my dad wasn't around – the one who sawed up the calves that came in from the abattoir for food, and who called my dad in the middle of the night if there was a medical problem and my dad happened to be home with us, instead of in the trailer on-site. I guess he's still the caretaker, because his message is asking a question about medication for one of the wolves.

It's been two days now that my father hasn't turned up at Redmond's. What if no one has told Walter what's happened?

I push all the buttons on the phone, but I can't figure out how to call the last incoming number. Well, there's got to be an address book somewhere around here, or maybe his contact information is on a computer.

My father's office.

It was what I called it back then, even though my father, as far as I knew, had never stepped foot in it. Technically it was the guest bedroom in our house, but it had a filing cabinet and a desk and the family computer, and we never had guests. It was where, twice a week, I sat down to pay family bills – my chore, just like Cara's was loading and unloading the dishwasher. We all had to pitch in when my father left for Canada to join the wild pack. I'm sure he expected my mother to be in charge of our finances, but she wasn't good with deadlines, and after having the heat turned off twice because of bills past due, we decided that I'd take over. So even at fifteen, I knew how much money it took to run a household. I learned about interest rates through credit card debt. I balanced the checkbook. And once my father came home, it was simply assumed that I'd continue. His mind was always a million different places, but none of them happened to be that office desk, paying bills.

You probably think it's strange that a teenager would be put in charge of the family finances, that this is bad parenting. I'd argue that taking your kids into wolf enclosures ranks right up there, too. But no one blinked when Cara, at age twelve, became my father's photogenic costar on his Animal

Planet series. My father excelled at making even the greatest naysayers believe that he was entirely in control.

The office chair is the same – one of those ergonomic jobs with pulleys and levers that adjust everything so your back won't hurt. My mom found it at a garage sale for ten bucks. But the computer is no longer a desktop – it's a sleek little MacBook Pro with a screen saver of a wolf staring out with so much wisdom in his yellow eyes that, for a moment, I can't look away. I pull open the file drawers and find one overflowing with envelopes – some marked PAST DUE. As if I'm being drawn by a magnet, I find myself sifting through them. I reach into the drawer on the right to find a checkbook, a pen, stamps. From the size of this stack of envelopes, you'd think no one had paid a bill since I left.

Which, frankly, wouldn't surprise me.

I have already forgotten what brought me to this office. Instead, I begin automatically sorting the mail, writing out checks, forging my father's signature. Every time I open an envelope, my heart skips a beat, and I know it's because I expect to see the same letterhead from six years ago, the bill that left me speechless. The one I wanted to wave in his face, and dare him to lie to me again.

But there is nothing like that. Just utilities, and credit cards that are maxed out, and warnings from collection agencies. I have to stop after the phone bill, the electric bill, and the oil delivery receipt, because the checkbook balance swings into the negative digits.

Where the hell has the money gone?

If I had to guess, I'd say to Redmond's. My father has five wolf enclosures now – five separate packs that he has to support. And a daughter, too. Shaking my head, I open the top drawer and begin to stuff the unpaid bills back in. This isn't my problem. I'm not his accountant. I'm not anything to him, anymore.

It's when I try to jam the envelopes into a drawer too small to contain them that I notice it – the yellowed, wrinkled piece of paper caught on the metal runner of the file drawer. I reach far into the back, trying to tug it free. The corner rips, but I manage to extract the page, and smooth it down beside the laptop.

And just like that, I'm fifteen again.

It was the night before my father was leaving, and Cara and I were hiding.

All day, there had been yelling. My mother would scream, and then my father would shout, and then my mother would burst into tears. *If you do this*, she said, *don't bother coming back.*

You don't mean that, he said.

Cara looked up at me. She was chewing on a pigtail, and it dropped out of her mouth, wet like a paintbrush. *Does she mean it?* Cara asked.

I shrugged. The only thing I knew about love was that it was always one-sided. Levon Jacobs, who sat in front of me in algebra, had skin the color of hot chocolate and knew the stats for every player on the Boston Bruins, but the only time he had ever spoken to me was when he needed to borrow a pencil, and besides, like every other guy in my class, he liked girls. My mother loved my father, but he could only think about his stupid wolves. My father loved the wolves, but even he would tell you that they didn't love him back, that thinking they might was attributing human emotion to a wild animal.

Lone Wolf

It's crazy, my mother yelled. *This is not how you act when you have a family, Luke. This is not how you act when you're an adult.*

You make it sound like I'm doing this to hurt you, my father replied. *This is science, Georgie. This is my life.*

Exactly, my mother said. *Your* life.

Cara pressed her back against mine. She was thin, and I could feel the ridges of her vertebrae. *I don't want him to die.*

My father was going to live in the forest without shelter, food, or any protection beyond a pair of heavy canvas coveralls. He planned to stake out one of the natural Canadian corridors for wolf migration and integrate himself into a pack, like he had before with captive groups. If he did, he'd certainly be the first person to really understand how a wild pack functioned.

That is, if he was still alive to talk about it when he was done.

My father's voice grew softer, like felt. *Georgie,* he said. *Don't be like this. Not on my last night here.*

There was a silence.

Daddy promised me he'd come back, Cara whispered. *He said, when I'm older, I can go there with him.*

Whatever you do, I said, *don't tell that to Mom.*

I couldn't hear them anymore. Maybe they had made up. There had been arguments like this for the past six months, ever since my father had announced his intention to go to Quebec. I wished he'd just leave, already, because at least that meant they'd stop fighting.

We heard a slam, and a few seconds later, there was a knock at my bedroom door. I motioned for my sister to stay put, and then opened it. My father stood on the other side of the threshold. *Edward*, he said, *we need to talk.*

When I opened the door, though, he shook his head and motioned for me to follow him. With a quick glance back at Cara to stay put, I trailed my father into the room we called the office, which was really just a collection of boxes, a desk, and a pile of mail no one bothered to sort through. My father cleared a stack of books off a folding chair so I could sit, and then he rummaged in one of the desk drawers and pulled out two shot glasses and a bottle of Scots whisky.

Full disclosure: I knew the bottle was there. I had even had a few swigs. My dad hardly ever drank because the wolves could smell it in his system, so it wasn't like he'd notice the level of the liquor inside slowly going down. I was fifteen, after all, and I could also tell you that buried in a stack of old *Life* magazines in the attic were two *Playboy*s – December 1983 and March 1987 – which I had read multiple times in the hope that I would finally feel a spark of arousal at the sight of a naked girl. But having my father offer me a drink was not something I'd anticipated, at least not till I turned twenty-one.

My father and I could not have been more different if we'd actively attempted to be. It wasn't that I was gay – I'd never seen or heard him act homophobic. It was because, while he was the modern version of a mountain man – all brawn and muscle and visceral instinct – I was more inclined to read Melville and Hawthorne. One Christmas, as a gift, I'd written him an epic poem (I was going through a Milton phase). He'd oohed and aahed and skimmed it, and then later, I overheard him asking my mother what the hell it meant. I know he respected the thirst I had for learning; maybe he even recognized it as the same itch he felt when he knew he had to get outside and hear the dry-throated leaves rasp beneath his footsteps. I used books to escape the same way my father used his work, but he would have been just as baffled by a copy of *Ulysses* as I would have been by a night spent in the wilderness.

You're going to be the man of the house, he said, in a way that let me know he had his doubts about my ability to pull off that role convincingly. He poured a centimeter of tawny liquid in the bottom of each glass and handed me one. He drank his in one smooth tip; me, I sipped twice, felt my intestines burst into flame, and set the glass down.

While I'm gone, you may have to make some difficult decisions, my father told me.

I didn't know what to say. I didn't have any idea what he was talking about. Just because he was off running with the wolves didn't mean my mother wasn't going to tell me I had to clean my room and finish my homework.

I don't think it's going to come to this, but still. He picked a piece of paper off the blotter on the desk and pushed it toward me.

It was handwritten, and simple.

If I cannot make a decision about my health, I give my permission to let my son, Edward, make any medical decisions that are necessary.

Then a line for his signature. And a line for mine.

My heart started booming like a cannon. *I don't get it.*

I asked your mother first, he said, *but she refuses to do anything that makes it seem like she was in favor of this trip. And it would be irresponsible to not think about . . . what could happen.*

I stared at him. *What* could *happen?*

I knew the answer, of course. I just needed to hear him say it out loud: he was risking everything for a bunch of animals. He was choosing them, over us.

My father didn't answer directly. *Look*, he said. *I need you to sign this.*

I picked up the piece of paper. I could feel the small ridges and hollows where the pen had dug deep, and it made me sick to my stomach to think that, just two minutes ago, my father had been contemplating his own death.

My father handed me a pen. I dropped it on the floor by accident. When we both went to reach for it, his fingers brushed over mine. I got a physical shock, as if he'd electrocuted me. And that's when I knew I'd sign the paper, even though I didn't want to. Because unlike my mother, I wasn't strong enough to let him leave – possibly forever – wishing that things had gone differently. He was offering me a chance to be something I'd never been before: the kind of son he'd always wanted, a boy he could depend on. I needed to be someone he'd *want* to come back to, or how could I be sure that he *would*?

He scrawled his signature on the bottom of the page, and then passed the pen again to me. This time I did not let it slip. I carefully formed the *E* of my name.

Then I stopped.

What if I don't know what to do? I asked. *What if I make the wrong choice?*

This is how I knew my father was treating me like an adult, not a kid: he dropped the pretense. He didn't say that nothing was going to go wrong; he didn't lie to me. *It's easy. If I can't answer for myself, and you're being asked . . . tell them to let me go.*

When people say growing up can happen overnight, they're wrong. It can happen even faster, in an instant. I picked up the pen, signed the rest of my name. Then I lifted the glass of whisky and drained it.

The next morning, when I woke up, my father was already gone.

For a long moment I stare at the spiky, spidered handwriting of my fifteen-year-old self, as if it is a mirror into my own mind. I had forgotten about this paper until now – and so had my father. A year and 347 days later, he emerged from the Canadian wilderness with hair down to his waist and dirt caked onto his bearded face, scaring the hell out of a bunch of schoolkids at a highway rest stop. He came home to find his household running without him in it, and slowly reaccustomed himself to things like showering and eating cooked food and speaking a human language. He never mentioned that piece of paper again, and neither did I.

More than once back then I'd hear footsteps in the middle of the night and I would slip downstairs to find my father out on the back lawn, sleeping underneath the night sky. I should have realized, even then, that once a person had made a home outdoors, any house would feel like a prison.

Still holding the yellowed paper, I leave the office. I head upstairs in the dark, passing the pink blur of Cara's room, hesitating at my old childhood bedroom. When I turn on the light, I see it hasn't changed. My twin bed is still covered with a blue blanket; my Green Day and U2 posters are still on the walls.

Continuing down the hallway, I walk into my parents' bedroom. My father's now, I suppose. The wedding ring quilt I remember is gone now, but there's a hunter-green blanket pulled tight with military precision, the top sheet crisply folded over. On the nightstand is a glass of water and an alarm clock. A phone.

It's not the house I remember; it's not my home. The thing is, neither is Thailand.

For a couple of days I've been thinking about what happens next – not just for my father but for me. I have a life abroad, but it's not much of one. I have a dead-end job, a few friends who, like me, are running away from something or someone. Although I came here dragging my feet, intending to fix whatever was broken and then retreat back to safety half a world away, things have changed. I can't fix what's broken – not my father, not myself, not my family. I can only try to patch it up and hope like hell it holds water.

It was a lot easier to tell myself that I belonged in Thailand when I could wallow in old hurts, and replay why I left over and over with every drink at a Bangkok bar. But that was before I saw the mistrust in my sister's eyes, or the walls of this house covered with no pictures of me. Now, I don't feel quite as self-righteous and expatriate. I just feel guilty.

Once, I made the radical, momentous decision to leave life as I knew it behind. Now, I make that decision again.

I pick up the phone and call my landlord in Chiang Mai, a very sweet widow who has me over to her apartment for dinner at least once a week, and tells me the same stories about her husband and how they met. In halting Thai I tell her about my father's condition, and ask her to box up my stuff and mail it to this address. Then I call my boss at the language school and leave a message on his voice mail, apologizing for leaving midterm, but explaining that this is a family emergency.

I take off my shoes and lie down. I fold the paper in half, and then in half again, and tuck it into the pocket of my shirt.

It was a long time ago, but once, my father trusted me enough to tell me what he wanted, should he wind up in the situation he's in now. It was a long time ago, but once, I promised him I would do what he asked.

I may never be able to tell him what I've been doing since I left, or make him understand me. I may never have a chance to offer an apology, to listen to his. He probably will never know I traveled back to be with him, to sit in his hospital room.

But I will.

In Thailand I always have trouble falling asleep. I blame it on the noise, the heat, the throb of a city. But tonight I fall asleep in minutes. When I dream, it's of pine needles under my bare feet as I run, of a winter that seeps through the skin.

Luke

O^n the day I walked into the woods north of the St. Lawrence River, I wore insulated waterproof coveralls, insulated boots, long underwear. In my pockets were extra pairs of socks and a hat and gloves; a roll of wire, some string, granola bars, jerky. My last eighteen dollars I gave to the trucker who let me hitchhike across the border with him. My driver's license I slipped into a zippered pocket of the coveralls. If things didn't work out, it might be the only way to identify what was left of me.

I didn't bring a backpack or a sleeping bag or a camp stove or matches. I wanted to be unencumbered, and I wanted to live as much like a lone wolf as I could. The idea, after all, was to find a pack with a vacancy that might allow me to join them. The last human I spoke to – for nearly two years – was the trucker who dropped me off. 'Bonne chance,' he said, in his Quebecois accent, and I thanked him and slipped into the fringe of pine trees that lined the edge of the highway. No fanfare. Nowadays, I'd probably have sponsorship endorsement patches all over my coveralls; I'd be swilling Gatorade from a CamelBak, and my progress would be simulcast on the Web and on a reality TV show. But then, fortunately, it was just me and the wolves.

I could tell you that I was a man on a mission, determined and brave and stalwart. The truth was, for twelve hours of the day, I was. I walked along old logging trails and would sometimes cover twenty miles of terrain a day, but I made sure I could get back to fresh water daily. I studied scat to see which animals were in the area, and rigged snares with the wire, string, and branches to catch squirrels, which I'd skin and eat raw. I urinated in streams, so that my scent couldn't be traced by predators. But the mountain man in me disappeared at around seven o'clock, when the sun set the tops of the pines on fire and slowly disappeared for the night.

Then, I was terrified.

Imagine your worst nightmare. Now imagine it's real. That's what it is like to feel the dark close around you like an angry fist. Every twitch and hoot and skittering leaf becomes a potential threat. When nature switches off her light, there's nothing you can do to turn it back on again. The first four nights I was in the wild, I slept in a tree, certain that I was going to be killed by a bear or a mountain lion. The fifth night, I fell out of the tree, and realized I was just as likely to die by breaking my neck. After that, I slept on the ground – but lightly, jumping alert at the slightest sound.

My learning curve was staggeringly steep. Within a week, I understood that in the wild, time moves much more slowly. A wind is never just a wind – it's the email system of the natural world, bringing in new information about weather patterns, animals coming into and leaving the area, potential predators. Rain isn't a nuisance – it's a respite from bugs and fresh water for drinking. A snowfall isn't an inconvenience – it's a new source for tracks and animals that might become a meal. The rustling of the trees or the song of a bird or the scrabble of a rodent is the key to your survival; being able to spot a flicker of movement through the dense block of foliage is essential. When it is a matter of life and death, the volume of nature gets turned up loud.

Everyone asks what I thought of, all by myself, alone for so long. The truth is, I didn't think about anything. I was too busy trying to keep myself alive and to read the signs that were presented to me, like some kind of hieroglyphic code without the Rosetta stone for guidance. If I thought about Cara and Edward and Georgie, I knew I'd be distracted enough to miss either an opportunity or a threat, and I could not risk that. So I didn't think. Instead, I survived. I spent the days amazed at the beauty of a spiderweb, laced between branches; at the jagged rise of a mountain ridge in the distance; at the dusk rolling over the woods like a purple carpet. I tracked herds of deer and watched two beavers engineer a phenomenal dam. I dozed off, because midday naps were safer than nighttime ones.

For a month, I didn't see or hear any wolves, and I began to wonder if I'd made a mistake.

The fourth week I was in the wild, a nor'easter hit. I moved away from the riverbank and huddled under evergreen trees, because they absorb moisture with their roots, and the ground beneath them would be that much drier. Unable to hunt and shivering and starving, I got sick. I drifted in and out of a feverish spell as the rain pelted me, wondering why the hell I'd ever thought of coming out here. I hallucinated that the forest had legs, that the roots of the trees were kicking me in the gut and the kidneys. I coughed until I vomited bile. There were points when I wished for a big cat or a bear, for anything that would swiftly put me out of my misery.

Lone Wolf

I think, looking back on it, that I had to get sick. I had to scrape away the very last bit of my humanity so that I would start behaving like a wolf, and not like a man. And in those dire straits, a wolf would not wallow in self-despair. Wolves do not give up. They assess the situation and ask, What can I eat? How can I protect myself? *Even wounded, they will run until they can no longer stand.*

Although it was only October, the elevation was high enough that it snowed. When my fever broke, I woke to find myself covered with a blanket of white, which I shook off as I sat upright. I glanced around to make sure I was safe, and that was when I saw it, pressed into the snow about three feet away from me: the paw print of a single, male wolf.

Scrambling to my feet, I searched the area for other prints – proof that a pack had been here – but found nothing. This animal either was scouting for his pack or was a lone wolf.

The wolf knew where I was. He could easily find his way back to me and, now that I wasn't feverish and unconscious, consider me a threat to be dispatched. The sane thing to do was to move on instead of putting myself in danger. But instead, I did something that jeopardized my safety, that made my position blatantly known, surely as if I was sending up a search flare.

I threw back my head, and I howled.

Cara

When my friend Mariah sees me in the hospital bed, she bursts into tears. It's almost ridiculous, the way I'm the patient but I have to hand her the box of Kleenex and tell her that it's going to be all right. She pushes a stuffed purple bear at me. It's holding a balloon that says congratulations. 'iParty ran out of the Get Well Soon bears,' she says, sniffling. 'God, Cara. I can't believe this happened. I'm so sorry.'

I shrug – or at least I would shrug, if my shoulder weren't immobilized. I realize she feels just as guilty about me being out at the party with her as I feel about my dad coming to get me there. If not for Mariah, I wouldn't have been in Bethlehem; if not for me, my father wouldn't have been on the roads that night. I hadn't even wanted to go out; we'd been planning pizza and a chick flick overnight at Mariah's house. But Mariah invoked the best friend code: *I would do it for you.* And so, like an idiot, I went.

'It's not your fault,' I tell her, although I don't really believe this when I say it to myself.

My mother, who has been living at the hospital, is in the family lounge down the hall with the twins and Joe. She hasn't brought them in to see me. She is afraid that all the bandages and bruises will give them nightmares, and she doesn't want Joe to have to deal with that while she's sleeping here with me. It makes me feel like the Frankenstein monster, like something that has to be hidden away.

Mariah stares into her lap. 'Is your dad . . . is he going to—'

'Tyler,' I interrupt.

She glances at me, her face red and puffy. 'What?'

'Tell me what happened.' Tyler is the reason we went to the party; he's the guy who invited Mariah. 'Did he drive you home? Did you hook up? Has he texted you?'

Even to my own ears, my voice sounds like a string that's been pulled too tight. Mariah's face crumples, and she starts crying again. 'You're stuck in a hospital and you had to have major surgery and your dad is, like, in some kind of coma and you want to talk about a guy? It's not important. *He's* not important.'

'No, he's not,' I say quietly. 'But he's what we'd be talking about if I wasn't in a hospital and if this never had happened. If you and I are talking about Tyler, then for five seconds I get to be normal.'

Mariah wipes her nose on her sleeve and nods. 'He's kind of a dick,' she says. 'He got wasted and started telling me how his ex had gotten a boob job over the summer and how he wanted to tap that.'

'*Tap that,*' I repeat. 'He actually used that phrase?'

'Gross, right?' She shakes her head. 'I don't know what I was thinking.'

'That he looked like Jake Gyllenhaal,' I remind her. 'That's what you said to me, anyway.'

Mariah leans back in her chair. 'Next time I decide to drag

you somewhere for the sake of my nonexistent love life will you just hit me with a two-by-four?'

I smile, and it's been so long that my face aches when I do. 'Next time,' I promise.

I let her tell me about how she's sure our French teacher has a brain tumor, because what else could be making her assign five poems to be memorized in a single week, and how the latest rumor in school is that Lucille DeMars, a goth kid who only talks to a sock puppet she wears on her right hand and who calls that performance art, was caught having sex with a substitute teacher in the music practice room.

I don't tell Mariah that when I first saw my father, I felt like all the air around me had gone solid, and that I couldn't for the life of me draw it into my lungs.

I don't tell her that I feel like I'm going to burst into tears all the time.

I don't tell her that this afternoon I went into the patient lounge and googled 'head injuries' and found more stories about people who never recovered than about people who did.

I don't tell her that after all those years of wishing my brother would come home, now that he's here, I wish he wasn't. Because then the doctors and the nurses and everyone who's taking care of my dad would come to me, instead of him.

I don't tell her that it's hard to fall asleep, and if I get lucky and *do* manage to drift off, I wake up screaming because I remember the crash.

I especially don't tell her what happened just before. Or after.

Instead, for the whole forty minutes Mariah is here, I let myself pretend that I'm the girl I used to be.

There are many moments I thought I'd get to experience with my brother that never happened because he quit the family. Like having him grill my first boyfriend before a date, or teach me how to drive in empty parking lots, or buy me a six-pack of beer to drink under the bleachers after prom. When he first left and my parents were separated, I used to write to him every night. Somewhere in my closet behind the stuffed animals I can't bear to throw away and the clothes that no longer fit is a shoe box filled with letters I never sent, because I didn't have an address for him.

I'll be honest, I used to imagine our reconciliation, too. I thought it might be seconds before I got married – Edward showing up just before I walked down the aisle, telling me he couldn't miss seeing his baby sister's wedding. I pictured everything fuzzy at the edges, like in a Lifetime movie, and him telling me I'd grown up even better than he'd ever imagined. Instead, I got a stilted hello over my father's respirator. My mom said Edward came down to check on me a couple of times after I had my surgery when I was still pretty out of it, but for all I know, she's just making that up to make me feel better.

Which is why it's still surreal to have him standing at the foot of my bed, holding a conversation with me. Behind him, muted, the television shows a contestant spinning the Wheel of Fortune.

'Are you in a lot of pain?' he asks.

No, I'm here for the gourmet food, I silently reply. Someone buys a vowel. There are two *A*'s.

'I've been hurt worse,' I tell him.

My dad used to tell me that a wounded wolf wasn't himself. He might know you as a brother but rip your throat out with his teeth. When pain factors into the equation, the outcome is unpredictable. I've told Edward that I'm not in pain, but that's a lie. My shoulder might not hurt, thanks to the drugs, but morphine's done nothing for my heart.

This is the only reason I can give for why I use every word like a weapon to shove him away, when all I really want is to be held right now.

'I know why you left,' I tell him. 'Mom told me.'

The fact that he's gay doesn't faze me. But I've always felt like the whole mystery surrounding my brother's exit was on a need-to-know basis. At first my mom said it was because Edward and my dad had a fight. Eventually I learned it was because Edward had come out to my dad, who said something that was apparently so god-awful Edward had to leave. Here's my take on it, though: millions of gay teens come out to their parents, and some have stupid reactions. Just because my father wasn't perfect, Edward bailed. And that led my mom to blame my dad, and eventually they broke up. The story of my life, as framed by my brother's impulsive decision to make a grand exit.

'You know what?' I say. 'I don't even care why you left.'

This isn't a lie, actually. I don't care why Edward left. All I really want to know is why I wasn't enough to make him stay.

I'm dangerously near tears right now, something I attribute to the fact that you can't get any goddamned sleep in a hospital, since someone's always waking you up to take your blood pressure or your temperature. I won't let myself believe it's because Edward has gotten underneath my skin. I've worked too hard building a brick wall around my feelings to admit that he might have chiseled his way inside so fast. 'Did you find Jesus or Buddha or something in Thailand?' I say. 'Guess what, Edward. I don't forgive you. So there.'

I sound like a spoiled brat. He's reduced me to that. I hate him even more for making me into someone I'm not than I do for the fact that he's been sitting downstairs with my dad, making *himself* into someone *he's* not.

But Edward doesn't even flinch; it's as if he's reading the text of me with some magic internal Rosetta stone that makes him understand what I say is not what I mean at all. 'Right now, this isn't about you and me,' he says patiently. Calmly. 'We have all the time in the world to figure things out between us again. But Dad doesn't.'

The fact that he's finally asking for my input about my father makes me dizzy. For a moment, I feel ridiculously happy – the way I used to when Edward picked me up from elementary school in his old beater, and all my friends had to go home instead with their moms in decidedly less cool vehicles. He let me name his car, actually. *Chase. Viper. Lucifer*, he had suggested. *Something badass.* Instead, I called it Henrietta.

'Cara, he can't stay hooked up to life support forever.'

Maybe it's the pain medication in my system; maybe it's just plain shock. But it takes me a few seconds to connect the dots. To realize that my brother, who'd left after a fight with my father, had grown that hatred like a spider plant until, years later, its offshoots threaten to fill every inch of him. 'You hate him so much that you'd kill him?'

Edward's eyes grow darker. Mine do that, too, when I'm

angry. It's strange to see it mirrored in someone else's face. 'You have to be ready to make some hard choices.'

That's when I lose it. Who is my brother to tell me about choices – my brother, who gave up on this family six years ago? He has no idea what it's like to hear your mother crying at night through the walls, to have a strange woman come up during your dad's daily wolf talk at Redmond's and slip you a piece of paper with her phone number on it. He has no idea what it is like to attend your own mother's second wedding, and then come home to find your father drinking himself under the table, asking what the ceremony was like. He has no idea how it feels to be responsible for buying groceries so the family doesn't starve, for forging signatures on report cards and making excuses when your father forgets a teacher conference. He has no idea what it's like to visit his mother and see her with the twins and feel obsolete. He has no idea.

The reason I've made the choices I have is because I wanted to save my family, just as much as Edward was hell-bent on destroying it. Because when you get down to it, the only person you can trust is the one you'd lay down your own life for. And I'm going to do that for my father now, no matter what Edward thinks.

I cannot look at him, so I stare over his shoulder. The contestant on *Wheel of Fortune* loses her turn.

'I know you're hurting,' Edward says after a moment. 'This time, you don't have to go through it alone.'

'It?'

He glances away. 'Losing someone you care about.'

He's wrong, though. Even with him standing three feet in front of me, I have never felt so isolated. So I do what any wolf would, if cornered. 'You're right. Because I'm going to do whatever it takes to make sure Dad gets better.'

Edward's mouth tightens. 'If you want to be taken seriously, then act like an adult,' he replies. 'You heard the doctors. He's not coming back, Cara.'

I stare at him. '*You* did.'

He tries to argue, but I pick up the remote control and turn on the sound on the television. There is a ringing as a contestant gets twelve hundred dollars for choosing a *W*. I push the buttons, so that the applause drowns out Edward's voice.

I am behaving like a two-year-old. But maybe that's okay, because, by definition, toddlers need their parents.

I stare at the Wheel of Fortune until Edward gives up and leaves the room. Under my breath, I solve the puzzle: *Blood is thicker than water.*

The next contestant guesses a *P;* the buzzer sounds.

People can be so stupid sometimes.

The first time I came face-to-face with a wolf, I was eleven years old. My father had just opened up the first enclosure at Redmond's. He waited until after hours and then took me past the first safety fence, and up to the second one. Inside were Wazoli, Sikwla, and Kladen, the first captive wolves he'd brought to the park. He made me crouch down, with the chain-link safely separating me from the wolves, and hold up my fists so that the knuckles just grazed the wire. This way, the wolves would get used to my scent.

Wazoli, the alpha female, immediately darted to the far end of the enclosure. 'She's more afraid of you than you are of her,' my father said quietly.

Sikwla was the tester, and Kladen the enforcer wolf. Big, with strong black markings down his back and tail, as if someone had taken a Sharpie marker to him, he came right up to the fence and stared at me with his wide eyes. Instinctively, I backed away into my father, who was standing behind me. 'They can smell your fear,' he told me. 'So don't give an inch.'

In a low, calm voice, he told me what was going to happen: he would open the outside gate that led into the enclosure, and then we would step into the little wire double gate and lock it behind us. Then he'd open the inside gate, and I would go in. I had to stay down low, and not move. The wolves might ignore me, or run away, but if I waited, they might also come closer.

'They can tell if your heart rate goes up,' my father whispered. 'So don't let them know you're afraid.'

My mother did not want me inside the wolf enclosure, and with good reason – who would willingly put a child right smack in the middle of danger? But I had watched my father insinuate himself into this pack now for months. I might never take my position at a carcass and rip away the meat with my teeth, like he did, while two wolves snapped on either side of him – but he was hoping Wazoli would have pups, and I wanted to help raise them.

I wasn't afraid of Wazoli. As the alpha, she would never come near me – she had all the knowledge of the pack and she would stay as far away from an unknown entity as possible. Kladen was big, 130 pounds of muscle, but he didn't scare me as much as Sikwla, who just a month ago had sent a park employee to the hospital after biting down on his finger all the way to the bone. The guy was a groundskeeper who had reached through the chain-link to pat Sikwla, thinking he was rubbing up against the fence for a scratch, and before he knew it the wolf had turned and bitten him. Screaming, he tried to pull away, which only made Sikwla bite down harder. Had he just stayed perfectly still, Sikwla would have probably let go.

Every time I saw the groundskeeper walking around Redmond's with his bandaged hand, I shuddered.

My father said that with himself in the enclosure, too, Sikwla would most likely leave me alone.

'Are you ready?' my father asked, and I nodded.

He opened the second gate, and we both went inside. I crouched down where my father had told me to crouch and waited as Kladen walked past me. I held my breath, but he just continued to lope toward the copse of trees in the back of the enclosure. Then Sikwla approached. 'Steady,' my father whispered, and all of a sudden Kladen came barreling at him, knocking him onto the ground in greeting.

Because of that, because my attention flickered, Sikwla seized his moment and went for my throat.

I could feel the pierce of his incisors, feel the wet heat of his breath. His fur was wiry and coarse and damp. 'Don't move,' my father grunted, unable to free himself fast enough to rescue me.

Sikwla was a tester wolf; this was his job in the family. I was a threat until proven otherwise; just because I'd come into the enclosure with my father, whom they accepted, didn't mean they wanted me around. Sikwla set the standards for this pack; this was his way of making sure I measured up.

At the time, though, I didn't think of any of this. I thought: *I am going to die.*

I didn't breathe. I didn't swallow. I tried not to let my pulse show what I felt. Sikwla's teeth pressed into the flesh of my neck. I wanted to shove at him with all my strength. Instead, I closed my eyes.

Sikwla let go.

By then my father had wrestled Kladen away and grabbed me into his arms. I didn't start to cry until I saw that he had tears in his eyes.

This is what I am thinking of when, just after three in the morning, I crawl out of bed. It is not easy, with a single hand, and I am certain I am going to wake up my mother, who is sleeping on a pullout chair beside me. But she only rolls over and starts snoring lightly, and I slip into the hallway.

The nurses' station is to the right, but the elevators are to the left, which means I don't have to pass by them and be interrogated about why I'm out of bed at this hour of the night. Keeping to the shadows, I shuffle down the corridor, careful to hold my bandaged arm tight against my stomach to keep my shoulder from being jostled.

I already know my brother won't be in my father's room. My mom told me she gave him the key to our house – something that makes me feel uneasy. Most likely Edward won't be poking around in my room – and it's not like I have anything to hide – but still. I don't like the thought of being here, while he is there.

The skeleton staff in the ICU doesn't notice the girl in the robe with the bandaged arm and shoulder who gets off the elevator. This is a blessing, since I really didn't know how to explain my migration from the orthopedic ward to this one.

My father is bathed in a blue light; the glow from the monitors surrounds him. He does not look any different to me than he did yesterday – surely this is a good thing? If he were, as Edward said, not coming back, wouldn't he be getting worse?

There is just enough space for me to sit on the bed, to lie down on my good side. It makes my bad shoulder ache like hell. I realize I can't hug him, because of the bandage, and he can't hug me, either. So instead I just lie next to him, my face pressed against the scratchy cotton of his hospital gown. I stare at the computer screen that shows that steady, solid beat of his heart.

The night after I went into the wolf enclosure for the first time I woke up to find my father sitting on the edge of my bed, watching me. His face was outlined with moonlight. 'When I was in the wild, I was chased by a bear. I was sure I was going to die. I didn't think there could be anything more terrifying,' he said. 'I was wrong.' He reached out one hand and tucked my hair behind my ear. 'The scariest thing in the world is thinking that someone you love is going to die.'

Now, I feel tears coming, a feather at the back of my throat. With a steady breath, I blink them away.

They can smell your fear, he taught me. *Don't give an inch.*

Luke

*T*wo weeks went by without any sign or sound of the wolf that had come so close to me when I was sick. And then one morning, when I was drinking from a stream, I suddenly saw an image rise in the reflection beside my own. The wolf was big and gray, with strong stripes of black on the top of his head and his ears. My heart started hammering, but I didn't turn around. Instead, I met his yellow eyes in the mirror of the water and waited to see what he would do next.

He left.

Any doubts I'd had about what I was doing vanished. This was what I had hoped for. If the big animal that had approached me at the stream was truly wild, he may have been just as curious about me as I was about him. And if that was the case, I might be able to get close enough to understand their behavior from within, instead of observing from outside.

I wanted nothing more than to see that wolf again, but I wasn't sure how to make that happen. Leaving food around the area would attract not just the wolf but also bears. If I called to the wolf, he might respond – even if he was a lone wolf, having a partner is safer than being alone – but that calling would also reveal my position to other predators. And *honestly, although I hadn't seen proof of any other wolves since I'd come into the wild, I couldn't be sure that this wolf was the only one in the area.*

I realized that if I was going to take the next step, it meant moving out of my comfort zone. Hell, it meant leaping blindfolded off the cliff of my comfort zone.

I adjusted my schedule so that I was sleeping during the day, and waking at dusk. I would have to travel in the darkness, even though my eyes and my body were not suited to it. This was much more threatening than any night I'd spent at the zoo in the captive pack's enclosure; for one thing, I was walking nearly ten miles in pitch darkness in a single night; for another, I didn't have to worry about other animals when I was in the wolf enclosure at the zoo. Here, if I tripped over an exposed tree root or splashed in a puddle or even stepped loudly on a branch, I was sending up a flare alerting every other creature in the wild to my location. Even when I was trying to be quiet, I was at a disadvantage; other animals were better at seeing and hearing in the dark and were watching every move I made. If I fell down, I was as good as dead.

What I remember about that first night was that I was sweating like mad, even though it was near freezing. I would take a step, and then hesitate to make sure I didn't hear anything coming toward me. Although there were only a scattered handful of stars that night, and the moon had a veil draped over its face, my vision adjusted enough to register shadows. I didn't need to see clearly. I needed to see movement, or a flash of eyes.

Because I was effectively blind, I used my other senses to their fullest. I breathed deeply, using the breeze to identify the scents of animals that were watching me pass. I listened for rustling, for footsteps. I stayed upwind. When the long fingers of dawn cupped the horizon, I felt as if I'd run a marathon, as if I'd conquered an army. I had survived a night in the Canadian forest, surrounded by predators. I was still alive. And really, that was all that mattered.

Georgie

By the fifth day after the accident, I can tell you what the soup of the day is going to be in the cafeteria and what times the nurses change shifts and where, at the orthopedics floor coffee station, they keep the packets of sugar. I've memorized the extension of Dietary, so that I can get Cara extra cups of pudding. I know the names of the physical therapist's children. I keep my toothbrush in my purse.

Last night, the one night I'd tried to go home, Cara had spiked a fever – an infection at the incision site. Although the nurses told me it was common, and although my absence wasn't correlative, I still felt responsible. I've told Joe I'm going to stay at the hospital as long as Cara does. A heavy dose of antibiotics has brought down her fever some, but she's out of sorts, uncomfortable. Had she not faced this setback, we might have been wheeling her out of the hospital today. And although I know this isn't possible – that you can't will yourself to have an infection – there is a part of me that thinks Cara's body did this in order to make sure she could stay close to Luke.

I am pouring myself my fifth cup of coffee of the day in the small supply room that has the coffee machine in it, a godsend provided by a nurse with a kind heart. It's amazing, really, how quickly the extraordinary can start to feel like the commonplace. A week ago I would have started my morning with a shower and a shampoo and would have packed lunch for the twins and walked them to the bus stop. Now, it feels perfectly normal to wear the same clothes for days in a row, to wait not for a bus but for a doctor doing rounds.

A few days ago the thought of Luke's brain injury felt like a punch in my gut. Now, I am just numb. A few days ago I had to fight to keep Cara in her bed, instead of at her father's bedside. Now, even when the social worker asks her if she'd like to visit him, she shakes her head.

I think Cara is afraid. Not of what she'll see but of what she won't.

I reach into the little dorm-size fridge for the container of milk, but it slips through my hands and falls onto the floor. The white puddle spreads beneath my shoes, under the lip of the refrigerator. 'Goddammit,' I mutter.

'Here.'

A man tosses me a wad of industrial brown napkins. I do my best to mop up the mess, but I'm near tears. Just once – once – I'd like something to be easy.

'You know what they say,' the man adds, crouching down to help. 'It's not worth crying over.'

I see his black shoes first, and his blue uniform pants. Officer Whigby takes the sopping napkins from my hands and tosses them into the trash. 'There must be something else you need to do,' I say stiffly. 'Surely someone's speeding, somewhere? Or an old lady needs help crossing the street?'

He smiles. 'You'd be surprised at how many old ladies are self-sufficient these days. Ms. Ng, honestly, the last thing I want to do is bother you at a time when you're already under a lot of stress, but—'

'Then don't,' I beg. 'Let us get through this. Let me get my daughter out of the hospital and let my ex-husband . . .' I find I can't finish the sentence. 'Just give us a little space.'

'I'm afraid I can't, ma'am. If your daughter was driving drunk, then she could be looking at a negligent homicide charge.'

If Joe were here, he'd know what to say. But Joe is back in my old life, making lunches for the twins and walking them to the bus stop. I straighten my spine and, with a confidence I didn't know I still had, turn my full gaze on the policeman. 'First of all, Luke isn't dead. Which means your charge is irrelevant. Second, my ex may be many things, Officer, but he's not a fool, and he wouldn't have let Cara drive home if she was drunk. So unless you have hard facts and evidence that can prove to me my daughter was responsible for that accident, then she's just a minor who made a bad choice and got drunk and needed to be picked up by her dad. If you're going to arrest her for underage drinking, I will assume you've already arrested every other teenager who was at that party. And if you haven't, then it turns out I was right the first time around: you've got something else you need to do.'

I push past him, sailing back to Cara's room with my chin held high. Joe would be proud of me, but then again, he's a defense attorney, and anything that sticks it to The Man is a mark of honor in his book. What I find myself thinking about is Luke, instead. *There's a fire in you*, he used to say. It was why he wanted to marry me. Underneath my reporter's silk blouse and my graduate degree in journalism, he said, was someone who always came up swinging. I think he believed that someone with a spark like that could understand a man who lived on the edge of death every day. It truly took him by surprise to find out that I wanted the house, the garden, the kids, the dog. I may have had a spark inside me, but I needed sturdy, solid walls to keep it from being snuffed out.

When I get back to Cara's room, I realize that I've left my coffee with Officer Whigby, and that my daughter is wide awake and sitting up. Her cheeks are flushed, and her hairline is damp, which suggests that the fever's broken. 'Mom,' she says, her words tumbling, 'I know how to save Dad.'

Luke

*T*hree weeks later, I was walking northeast when a wolf suddenly stepped out from behind a tree in front of me. To be honest, I couldn't tell you if it was the same gray wolf that had come to the stream before, or a new one. His golden eyes locked on mine for nearly half a minute, which feels like forever when you are facing a wild animal. He didn't bare his teeth or growl or show any fear, which led me to believe that he'd known of my presence much longer than I'd known of his.

The wolf turned away and walked into the woods.

After that, I saw the wolf every few days when I least expected it. I'd be springing fresh kill from a trap and would feel myself being watched – only to turn and find him there. I would open my eyes from a catnap and catch him staring, a distance away. I didn't speak to him. I didn't want the wolf to see me as a human. Instead, every time he appeared, I lay on the ground or rolled onto my back, offering up my throat and my belly, the universal sign of trust. By exposing my weakest areas, I was acknowledging that he could kill me – quickly or slowly, whatever he wished – and asking, How balanced an individual are you? *What would happen then – what* should *happen then – was that the dominant wolf* would change his energy level, squeezing my throat with his muzzle and then letting go as if to say, I could hurt you . . . but I choose not to. *And just like that, our hierarchy of roles would be established.*

One evening, when I was sitting under a tree and wondering if I smelled snow in the air, the wolf stepped into the clearing before me. But then a second wolf stepped out. A third. Three more. They began to dart in and out of the trees, sewing up the space around me. There were four males and two females, and from the looks of it, the wolf that had been visiting me was one of the younger ones. He had probably been sent by the alpha female to learn more about me.

The next day, I tried to find the pack. But although I looked for weeks, they had made themselves all but invisible. Crushed – was this the extent of the wolf interaction I'd have in the wild? Had I gotten this close only to be disappointed? – I fell into my former habits. During the nights I'd wander, but in the daytime I went back to the spot where I had first met up with the entire pack.

Several weeks went by, and then they returned. They were down to five members – one of the males was absent – and seemed more skittish than they had been the last time. They settled in about forty yards away. The young male I'd seen first played with his sister, rolling in the snow and chasing each other like puppies. Occasionally one of the older wolves would warn them off with a throaty growl, and eventually they collapsed in a tired heap.

I wish I could explain to you what it felt like to be near them. To know that, of all the places in the woods where they might have relaxed, they chose to be near me. I had to believe it was intentional; there were plenty of places they would not have had to keep a wary eye on the stranger in the distance. The combination of euphoria and hope, of feeling like I'd been chosen in some way, was enough to sustain me during the weeks when they would vanish – weeks of ice storms and snow when it sometimes felt like I was the only living thing left in the universe.

I would sleep during the day, when it was warmest, but even then, sometimes, the temperatures were brutal. Then, I'd find shelter from the cold: a rock cave, a fallen tree with a hollow inside it, even a little burrow in a pile of snow – a personal igloo. I'd line the space with pine boughs for warmth. I'd pile green branches to keep out falling snow or a wild wind. I'd eat whatever I could trap, and when that failed, I'd split open a rotten log with my hands and pick off the ants.

One night, the pack howled. It was low, painful, mournful – the type of cry meant to search for someone who was missing. In this case I figured it was for the big gray male that had not returned. They howled every night that week, and on the fourth night, I replied. I called the way a lone wolf would call, if he thought there might be a position in a pack for him.

At first, there was only silence.

And then, like a miracle, the whole pack howled back.

Edward

The wolf has chewed through the seat belt of the rental car.

'Goddammit,' I say, tugging the belt away from the latticed grate of the cage. 'Didn't he teach you any manners?'

I wonder if the optional insurance I took on the rental car covers damage by wild animal.

I wonder how much trouble I'm going to get into.

Mostly I wonder why I let Cara talk me into doing this.

I had headed to the hospital this morning with the best intentions – and clutching the piece of paper I'd found with my signature on it. I'd tried to show it to Cara before, but my timing was off: a surgical resident was examining her sutures in the morning and then she was being sponge bathed by a nurse and then my father had been taken down for another CT scan, and then she was running a fever. Today, I had been determined to show it to her. Cara might not believe I had any right to speak for my father, but I had proof otherwise.

After checking on my father (no change, as if I needed any more reason to talk to my sister), I had gone upstairs to the orthopedics floor. Cara was sitting up in bed, sweaty and disheveled. My mother stood beside her. They both turned when I walked in. 'I have something to show you,' I'd said, but Cara interrupted me before I could show her the paper.

'The wolves,' she announced. 'That's what he needs.'

'What?'

'Dad's always saying that the wolves communicate on a different level than humans do. And he can't hear *us* telling him to wake up. So what we have to do is bring him to Redmond's.'

I had blinked at her. 'Are you crazy? You can't transport a guy on a ventilator to some crappy theme park—'

'Oh, right, I forgot I was talking to *you*,' she snapped. 'Instead we should just *kill* him.'

I'd felt the paper burning where it rested against my chest. 'Cara,' I'd said evenly, 'no doctor is going to sign off on a field trip for Dad.'

'Then you have to bring a wolf here instead.'

'Because nothing says "sterile environment" like "wolf."' I turned to my mother. 'Don't tell me you agree with her.'

Before she could answer, Cara had interrupted. 'You know Dad would move heaven and earth to save one of the animals in his packs. Don't you think they'd do the same for him?' She swung her legs over the bed.

'Where do you think you're going?' my mother asked.

'To call Walter,' Cara said. 'If you two won't help me, I'm sure *he* will.'

I had looked at my mother. 'Can you explain to her why this is impossible?'

My mother touched Cara's good arm. 'Honey,' she said. 'Edward's right.'

Hearing those words on her lips – well, on *anyone's* lips – I can't tell you how it made me feel. When you are the family fuckup, receiving credit is almost overwhelming.

This is really the only explanation I can offer as to why I did what I did. 'If I do this,' I had said to Cara. 'If I do this for you, and it doesn't work . . . then will you listen to what I have to say?'

Her eyes met mine, and she'd nodded, a nonverbal contract. 'Tell Walter to give you Zazigoda,' she said. 'He's the one we take to schools. Once, when he got spooked, Dad kept him from jumping through a window.'

My mother shook her head. 'Edward. How are you going to—'

'And he has to ride in the front seat,' Cara interrupted. 'He gets carsick.'

I had zipped up my coat. 'In case you were even wondering,' I told her, 'Dad's condition is the same as it was last night.'

Cara smiled at me then. It was the first real smile she'd offered me since I came home. 'But not for long,' she had said.

Redmond's Trading Post is a sorry anachronism from a time before 3D and Sony PlayStations – a poor man's Disney World. In the winter, it's even more depressing than it is during its high season. Closed to everyone but a few animal caretakers, it feels like the land that time forgot. This was only reinforced by the sight that greeted me the minute I hopped over the turnstiles and let myself into the park: a faded animatronic dinosaur with icicles dripping off its chin that roared at me and tried to swing a massive tail mired in snowdrifts.

It felt strange to walk up the hill to the wolf enclosures, as if I were peeling back years with each footstep, until I was a kid again. As I passed by one of the pens, a pair of timber wolves trotted along the fence line with me, watching to see if I might lob a rabbit over the chain-links as a treat. My father's old trailer stood at the crest of the hill, above the enclosures. A curl of smoke pumped from the woodstove vent in the trailer, although when I knocked no one answered.

'Walter?' I called out. 'It's Edward. Luke's son.' The door swung open at my touch, and I found myself knocked backward by a memory. Nothing had changed in this trailer. There was the sofa with foam cushions that had been ripped by the teeth of countless wolf pups, where I had read dozens of books while my father gave the daily wolf talk to the trading post visitors. There was the bathroom with a toilet flushed by a foot pump.

There was the narrow bed, where everything had gone to hell.

This was a bad idea; I never should have listened to Cara; I should just go back to the hospital . . . I slammed my way out of the trailer, and heard a whistle of bluegrass coming from the wooden shack where the fresh meat brought in for the wolves was refrigerated. I poked my head inside and found Walter in a butcher's apron, quartering a deer with a gigantic knife. Half Abenaki, Walter is six foot four and bald, with spirals of tattoos up both arms. As a kid, I'd been alternately mesmerized and terrified by him.

Walter looked up at me as if he was seeing a ghost.

'It's me,' I said. 'Edward.'

At that, he dropped the knife and folded me into a bear hug. 'Edward,' he said. 'If you're not the spitting image . . .' He stepped back, frowning. 'Did he—?'

'No,' I said quickly. 'Nothing's changed.'

I glanced outside the abattoir, where a trio of wolves were staring at me from behind a fence. My father used to talk about the wisdom in a wolf's eyes; even a layperson who comes in contact with the species will often feel unnerved the first time he is face-to-face with a wolf. They don't just look *at* you; they look *into* you. Maybe, I thought, Cara had a point.

I'd called Walter last night from my father's house and had explained his condition, but now I told Walter why I'd come here today – namely, what Cara felt a wolf encounter would do for my father. He listened quietly, his mouth twisting, as if he could chew on the plan and spit out the bits he didn't like. When I finished speaking, he folded his arms. 'So you want to bring a wolf into the hospital.'

'Yeah,' I said, ducking my head. 'I know it sounds ridiculous.'

'The thing is, you don't know how to handle a wolf. Just cause it looks like a dog don't mean it *is* one. You want me to come along?'

For a moment I gave this serious consideration. 'It's better if I'm alone,' I said finally. That way only one of us would get in trouble.

I followed Walter out of the abattoir, down the hill to the enclosures. As we approached one fence, a pair of gray wolves bounded toward him. The smaller one only had three legs. 'Morning, boys,' he said and pointed to the one that was racing back and forth in front of the fence, completely unimpeded by his lack of a limb. His gaze slipped like a splinter under my skin. 'That's Zazigoda,' Walter told me. 'His name means *lazy*. Your dad, he's got a sense of humor.'

Walter reached into the game pouch of his jacket and

tossed a frozen squirrel into the woods at the rear of the enclosure. The other wolf trotted off to claim it as Zazigoda waited for his own reward. But instead of taking another squirrel from his jacket, Walter extracted a brick of Philadelphia cream cheese. He tore off a corner, and Zazi began to lick it. 'Milk products calm 'em down,' he explained.

I vaguely remembered my father telling me how an alpha female who knows she's going to give birth soon might direct her pack to kill the lactating doe in a herd of deer, simply because she knows the hormones running through the prey animal's system will take the edge off the emotions of those that eat it. Then, by the time the pups are born, the rest of the pack will be more mellow and likely to accept them.

'We rescued Zazi,' Walter said, moving into the enclosure without any hesitation. 'A hunter found him when he was about a year old. His leg had gotten caught in a bear trap, and he chewed it off. Your dad played nursemaid. The vet said he was a goner; he was too weak; his wound was infected; he'd be gone before the end of the week. But Zazi, he blew those odds away. You know how in life, there are people, and then there are *people*? Well, there are wolves, and then there are *wolves*. Zazi's one of those. You tell him he ain't going to make it, and he'll prove you wrong.'

I wondered if this was why Cara wanted me to bring Zazi, in particular. Because his story so closely mirrored what she wanted to happen to my father.

Walter looked up at me. 'Since your dad nursed him, he's always been more comfortable around humans than a wolf ought to be. Great with kids, great with film crews. That's why we've always used him for community outreach.' He dragged a crate into the pen and easily loaded the wolf inside.

'One day we were at a school with Zazi. Your dad, he likes to pick a couple of kids from a class to come up and touch the fur of a wolf, hands on, if you get what I mean. To make them curious but not terrified about wolves. But he eyeballs the kids to make sure he's not picking the class clowns, and before he does this, he lays down the rules – mostly to keep the wolf safe from the kids. If a kid moves a certain way, or comes up too fast, or just doesn't pay attention, all hell can break loose.'

Walter leaned down to the mesh wire at the front of the crate and let Zazigoda lick his knuckles. 'One day an aide brought a kid with special needs up to the front of the room. Kid was maybe ten years old and had never spoken a word; he was in a wheelchair and had profound disabilities. The aide asked if the boy could touch the wolf. Now, your dad, he didn't know what to say. On the one hand, he didn't want to turn the kid away; on the other hand, he knew that Zazi could easily read anxiety and could turn on the boy quickly, thinking he had to defend himself. Zazi's not a hybrid; he's a wild animal. So your dad asked the aide if the boy could communicate any signs of fear or distress, and the aide said no, he couldn't communicate at all. Against his better judgment, your father lifted Zazi up to the table, where he could be eye level with the boy's wheelchair. Zazi looked at the boy, then leaned forward and started licking around his lips. Your dad leaned forward to intervene, figuring Zazi had smelled food, and that the boy was going to freak out and push Zazi away. But before your dad could pull Zazi back, the boy's mouth started working. It was garbled, and it was hard to hear, but that boy said his first word right in front of us: *wolf.*'

I leaned down and grabbed the handle of the crate with Walter, beginning the long climb uphill. 'If you're telling me this to make me feel any better about taking a wild animal to a hospital, it's not helping.'

Walter glanced at me. 'I'm telling you this,' he said, 'because Zazi's no stranger to miracles.'

It's actually something Walter has said that gives me the idea: *Just cause it looks like a dog don't mean it is one*. Since no one would ever be stupid enough to bring a wild animal into a hospital, folks who see me with Zazi will assume he is a domestic animal instead. That means all I have to do is come up with a valid reason to have a dog there in the first place.

The way I see it, I have two options. The first is a therapy dog. I have no idea if they use them at this particular hospital, but I know there are trained volunteers who bring Labs and springers and poodles into pediatric wards to boost the spirits of the sick kids. From what I understand, these dogs are usually older, calmer, unruffled – which pretty much leaves Zazi out of the running.

The only other kind of dog I've ever seen in a hospital is a Seeing Eye dog.

At a gas station, I buy a pair of hideous, oversize black sunglasses for $2.99. I call my mother's cell, to tell her that I am on my way and that she should meet me in my dad's room, with Cara. Then I park in the hospital lot, as far away from other cars as I can get.

The front seat has been moved back on its runners to accommodate Zazi's crate, which takes up every inch of available space. I get out of the car and open the passenger door, eyeballing the wolf through the metal door of the crate. 'Look,' I say out loud, 'I don't like this any more than you do.'

Zazi stares at me.

I try to convince myself that when I open this crate the wolf isn't going to sink his teeth into my hand. Walter's already put a harness on him; all I have to do is attach the leash.

Well. If he does bite me, at least I'm already at the hospital.

With brisk efficiency I open the crate and snap the heavy carabiner onto the metal hook of the wolf's harness. He jumps out of the crate in one smooth, graceful motion and starts tugging me forward. I barely have time to close the car door, to whip my sunglasses out of my pocket.

The wolf takes a piss on every lamppost lining the walkway into the hospital. When I yank on his leash once to get him moving, he turns around and snarls at me.

If the volunteers sitting at the welcome desk of the hospital think it's strange to see a blind man who's dragging his dog, instead of the other way around, they don't say anything. I am blissfully thankful that we are the only ones in the elevator that takes us up to the third-floor ICU. 'Good boy,' I say when Zazi lies down, paws crossed.

But when the bell dings just prior to the door opening, he leaps to his feet, turns around, and nips my knee.

'Shit!' I yelp. 'What was *that* for?'

I lean down to see if he's drawn blood, but by then the doors have opened and a candy striper is waiting with a stack of files. 'Hi,' I say, hoping to distract her from the fact that I have a wolf on a leash.

'Oh!' she says, surprised. 'Hello.'

That's when I realize that if I'm blind, I shouldn't have known she was there.

Suddenly Zazi starts loping down the hall. I struggle to keep up, forgetting about the candy striper. An Amazon of a nurse follows. She is taller than me, with biceps that suggest she could probably beat me in arm wrestling. I saw her the first day I came to the hospital, but she hasn't been at work again until today – so she doesn't recognize me, or question my sudden new disability. 'Excuse me, sir? Sir?'

This time I remember not to turn around until she calls me.

'Are you talking to me?' I ask.

'Yes. Can you tell me which patient you're here to see?'

'Warren. Lucas Warren. I'm his son, and this is my guide dog.'

She folds her arms. 'With three legs.'

'Are you kidding me?' I say, grinning with my dimples. 'I paid for four.'

The nurse doesn't crack a smile. 'We'll have to get clearance from Mr. Warren's doctors before the dog can go inside—'

'A guide dog can go in all places where members of the public are allowed and where it doesn't pose a direct threat,' I recite, information gleaned from Google on my phone after my sunglasses purchase at the gas station. 'I find it hard to believe a hospital would violate the Americans with Disabilities Act.'

'Service dogs are allowed into the ICU on a case-by-case basis. If you'll just wait here for a second I can—'

'You can take it up with the Department of Justice,' I say as Zazi starts pulling hard on the leash.

I figure I have five minutes max before security gets here to remove me. The nurse is still shouting as Zazi drags me down the hall. Without any direction from me, he leads me through the doorway of my father's room.

Cara is cradled against the canvas sling of a wheelchair; my mother stands behind her. My father is still immobile on the bed, tubes down his throat and snaking out from beneath the waffle-weave blanket. 'Zazi!' Cara cries, and the wolf bounds over to her. He puts his front paws on her lap and licks her face.

'He bit me,' I say.

My mother has backed into a corner, not too thrilled to be in the same room as a wolf. 'Is he safe?' she asks.

I look at her. 'Isn't it a little late to be asking that?'

But Zazi has turned away from Cara and is whimpering beside my father's bed. In a single, light leap, he jumps onto the narrow mattress, his legs bracketing my father's body. He delicately steps over the tubes and noses around beneath the covers.

'We don't have a lot of time,' I say.

'Just watch,' Cara replies.

Zazigoda sniffs at my father's hair, his neck. His tongue swipes my father's cheek.

My father doesn't move.

The wolf whines, and licks my father's face again. He drags his teeth across the blanket and paws at it.

Something beeps, and we all look at the machines behind the bed. It's the IV drip, needing to be changed.

'Now do you believe me?' I say to Cara.

Her jaw is set, her face determined. 'You just have to give it a minute,' she begs. 'Zazi knows he's in there.'

I take off the sunglasses and step in front of her, so that she has to meet my gaze. 'But Dad doesn't know Zazi's here.'

Before she can respond, the door bursts open and the desk nurse enters with a security guard. I shove the sunglasses onto my face again. 'It was my sister's idea,' I say immediately.

'Way to throw me under the bus,' Cara mutters.

The nurse is practically having a seizure. 'There. Is. A dog. On the bed,' she gasps. 'Get. The dog. Off. The. Bed!'

The security guard holds me by the arm. 'Sir, remove the dog immediately.'

'I don't see a dog in here,' I say.

The nurse narrows her eyes. 'You can drop the blind act, buster.'

I take off my sunglasses. 'Oh, you mean *this*?' I say, pointing to Zazi, who jumps down and presses himself against my leg. 'This isn't a dog. *This* is a wolf.'

Then I grab the leash and we run like hell.

The hospital decides not to press charges when Trina the social worker intervenes. She is the only member of the staff who understands why I had to bring the wolf to the hospital. Without it, Cara wouldn't broach a conversation about my father's condition and his lack of improvement. Now that my sister has seen with her own eyes how even his wolves can't elicit a reaction, Cara can't help but understand that we're running out of options, out of hope.

I think Zazi knows what's up, too. He goes into his crate without any fight and curls up and sleeps for the entire ride back to Redmond's Trading Post. This time when I drive up to the trailer, Walter comes out to greet me. His face is as open as a landscape; he's waiting for the good news, for the story of how my father suddenly returned to the world of the living. But I can't speak around the truth that's jammed like a cork in my throat, so instead I help him haul the crate out of my car, and carry it down to the enclosure where Zazi's companion is keeping watch along the perimeter of the fence. When Walter releases Zazi, the two wolves slip between the army of trees standing at attention at the back of the pen. I watch Walter lock the first gate to the enclosure, and then walk to the second gate. He's holding the leash and harness in his hands. 'So,' he prompts.

'Walter,' I say finally, testing the size and shape of these words in my mouth, 'whatever happens, you'll still have a job. I'll make sure of it. My dad would want to know someone he trusts will still take care of the animals.'

'He'll be back here in no time, telling me what I'm doing wrong,' Walter says.

'Yeah,' I say. 'No doubt.'

We both know we're lying.

I tell him I have to get back to the hospital, but instead of leaving Redmond's right away, I stop to watch the animatronic dinosaurs. I dust snow off a cast-iron bench and wait the twelve minutes to the hour, so that I can hear the *T. rex* come to life. Just like earlier, he cannot thrash his tail the way he should, because of the snowdrifts.

In my sneakers and my jeans, I jump the fence so that I am knee-deep in the snow. I start clearing it out with my bare hands. It only takes a few seconds before my fingers are red and numb, before the snow melts into my socks. I smack the green plastic tail of the *T. rex*, trying to dislodge the ice, but it stays stuck. 'Come on,' I yell, striking it a second time. 'Move!'

My voice echoes, bouncing off the empty buildings. But I manage to do something, because the tail begins to sweep back and forth as the fake *T. rex* goes after the same fake raptor once again. I stand for a second, watching, with my hands tucked under my armpits to warm them up. I let myself pretend that the *T. rex* might actually reach the fraction of an inch that's necessary to finally get his prey, that instead of his going through the motions there will be progress. I let myself pretend that I have, successfully, turned back time.

A lot can happen in six days. As the Israelis will tell you, you can fight a war. You can drive across the United States. Some people believe six days is all it took for God to create a universe.

I'm here to tell you that a lot might *not* happen in six days, too.

For example, a man who's suffered a severe head trauma might not get any worse, or any better.

For four nights now, I've left behind the hospital room to go to my father's home, where I pour a bowl of stale cereal and watch Nick at Nite. I don't sleep in his bed; I don't really sleep at all. I sit on the couch and listen to endless episodes of *That '70s Show*.

It's weird, walking out of the hospital every night during a vigil. The whole day has somehow passed me by, and the stars reflect on the snow that's fallen while I was unaware. My life is moving forward in a weird empty narrative, missing one key character, whose current life is a continuous loop. I bring back things I think my father would want to find at the hospital if he were to awaken: a hairbrush, a book, a piece of mail – but this only makes the house feel even emptier when I'm in it, as if I'm slowly liquidating its contents.

After the wolf debacle, when I got back to the hospital, I went to Cara's room. I wanted to show her the letter I'd found in Dad's file drawer. But this time there was a team of physical therapists in there talking about shoulder rehab and testing her range of motion, which had her in tears. Whatever I had to say to her, I decided, could still wait.

Now, the next morning, as I am headed to her room, I am ambushed by Trina the social worker. 'Oh good,' she says. 'You heard?'

'Heard what?' There are a hundred red flags waving in my mind.

'I was just headed downstairs to get you. We're having a family meeting in your sister's room.'

'Family meeting?' I say. 'Did she put you up to this?'

'She didn't put me up to anything, Edward,' Trina says. 'It's a meeting to share medical information about your father with both of you at the same time. I suggested we do it in Cara's room because it would be more comfortable for her than being transported to a conference room.'

I follow Trina into the room and find a handful of nurses I've seen going in and out of my father's room and some I haven't; Dr. Saint-Clare; a neurology resident; and Dr. Zhao from the ICU. There's also a chaplain, or that's who I am assuming he is, since he's wearing a white collar. For a moment I think this is a setup, that my father has already died and this is the way they thought best to tell us.

'Mrs. Ng,' Trina says, 'I'm afraid I'm going to have to ask you to step outside.'

My mother just blinks. 'What about Cara?'

'Unfortunately, this meeting is for Mr. Warren's next of kin,' the social worker explains.

Before my mother can go, Cara grabs her sleeve. 'Don't leave,' she whispers. 'I don't want to be alone for this.'

'Oh, baby,' my mother says. She smoothes Cara's hair back from her face.

I step into the room and maneuver around everyone until I am standing beside my mother. 'You won't be,' I tell Cara, and I reach for her hand.

I have a sudden jolt of memory: I am crossing the street so that I can walk my little sister into school. I don't let go of her hand until I know both her feet are firmly planted on the opposite sidewalk. *You have your lunch?* I ask, and she nods. I can tell she wants me to hang around because it's cool to be the only fifth grader talking to a senior, but I hurry back to my car. She never knows it, but I don't drive off until I see her walk through the double doors of the school, just to be safe.

'Well,' Dr. Saint-Clare says. 'Let's get started. We're here today to update you on your father's medical condition.' He nods to the resident, who sets a laptop on Cara's bed so we can all see the scanned images. 'As you know, he was brought into the hospital six days ago with a diffuse traumatic brain injury. These are the CT scans we took when he was first brought into the ICU.' He points to one side of the image, which looks muddy, swirled, an abstract painting. 'Imagine that the nose would be here, and the ear here. We're looking up from the bottom. All this white area? That's blood, around the brain and in the ventricles of the brain. This large mass is the temporal lobe hematoma.'

He clicks the mouse pad so that a second scan appears beside the first. 'This is a normal brain,' he says, and he really doesn't have to say anything else. There are clear, wide black expanses in this brain. There are strong lines and edges. It looks tidy, organized, recognizable.

It looks completely different from the scan of my father's brain.

It's hard for me to understand that this fuzzy snapshot is the sum total of my father's personality and thoughts and movements. I squint at it, wondering which compartment houses the animal instincts he developed in the wild. I wonder where language is stored – the nonverbal movements he used to communicate with his wolves, and the words he forgot to say to us when we were younger: that he loved us, that he missed us.

Dr. Saint-Clare clicks again so a third scan appears on the screen. There is less white around the edges of the brain, but a new gray patch has appeared. The surgeon points to it. 'This is the spot where the anterior temporal lobe used to be. Removing it and the hematoma, we were able to reduce some of the swelling in the brain.'

Dr. Saint-Clare had said that taking out this piece of my father's brain would not affect personality but would probably mean the loss of some memories.

Which ones?

His year with the wolves in the wild?

The first time he saw my mother?

The moment he knew I hated him?

The neurosurgeon was wrong. Because losing any one of those memories would have changed who my father was, and who he'd become.

Cara tugs my arm. 'That's good, right?' she whispers.

Dr. Saint-Clare pushes another button, and the image on the laptop refreshes. This is a different angle, and I tilt my head, trying to make sense of what I'm seeing. 'This is the brain stem,' he explains. 'The hemorrhages reach into the medulla and extend into the pons.' He points to one spot. 'This is the area of the brain that controls breathing. And this is the area that affects consciousness.' He faces us. 'There's been no distinguishable change since your father's arrival.'

'Can't you do another operation?' Cara asks.

'The first one was done to alleviate high pressure in the skull – but that's not what we're seeing anymore. A hemi-craniectomy or a pentobarb coma isn't going to help. I'm afraid your father's brain injury . . . is unrecoverable.'

'Unrecoverable?' Cara repeats. 'What does that mean?'

'I'm sorry.' Dr. Saint-Clare clears his throat. 'Since the prognosis for a decent recovery is so poor, a decision needs to be made whether to continue life-sustaining treatment.'

'*Poor* isn't the same as *impossible*,' Cara says tightly. 'He's still alive.'

'Technically, yes,' Dr. Zhao replies. 'But you have to ask yourself what constitutes a meaningful existence. Even if he were to recover – which I've never seen happen to a patient with injuries this severe – he wouldn't have the same quality of life that he had before.'

'You don't know what will happen a month from now. A year from now. Maybe there will be some breakthrough procedure that could fix him,' Cara argues.

I hate myself for doing this, but I want her to hear it. 'When you say the quality of life would be different, what do you mean exactly?'

The neurosurgeon looks at me. 'He won't be able to breathe by himself, feed himself, go to the bathroom by himself. At best, he'd be a nursing home patient.'

Trina steps forward. 'I know how difficult this is for you, Cara. But if he were here, listening to everything Dr. Saint-Clare just said, what would *he* want?'

'He'd want to get better!' By now Cara is crying hard, working to catch her breath. 'It hasn't even been a full week!'

'That's true,' Dr. Saint-Clare says. 'But the injuries your father has sustained aren't the kind that will improve with time. There's less than a one percent chance that he'll recover from this.'

'See?' she accuses. 'You just admitted it. There's a *chance.*'

'Just because there's a chance doesn't mean there's a good probability. Do you think Dad would want to be kept alive for a year, or two, or ten based on a one percent probability of *maybe* waking up and being paralyzed for the rest of his life?' I ask.

She faces me, desperate. 'Doctors aren't always right. Zazi, that wolf you brought here yesterday? He chewed off his own leg when it got caught in a trap. All the vets said he wouldn't make it.'

'The difference is that Dad can't compensate for his injuries, the way Zazi did,' I point out.

'The difference is that *you're trying to kill him,*' Cara says.

Trina puts her hand on Cara's good shoulder, but she jerks her body away in a twist that makes her cry out in pain. 'Just leave!' Cara cries. 'All of you!'

Several machines behind her start to beep. The nurse attending her frowns at the digital display. 'All right, that's enough,' she announces. 'Out.'

The doctors file through the door, talking quietly to each other. Another nurse comes in to fiddle with Cara's morphine pump as the first nurse physically restrains her.

My mother bursts through the doorway. 'What the hell just happened?' she asks, looking at me, and the nurses, and then at Cara. She makes a beeline for the bed and gathers Cara into her arms, letting her cry. Over my mother's shoulder, Cara fixes her eyes on me. 'I said *leave*,' she mutters, and I realize that when she told this to the doctors, she was including me.

Within seconds, the morphine kicks in and Cara goes limp. My mother settles her against the pillows and starts whispering to the duty nurse about what happened to get Cara into this state. My sister is glassy-eyed, slack-jawed, almost asleep, but she fixes her gaze directly on mine. 'I can't do this,' Cara murmurs. 'I just want it to be over.'

It feels like a plea. It feels as if, for the first time in six years, I might be in a position to help her. I look down at my sister. 'I'll take care of it,' I promise, knowing how much those words have cost her. 'I'll take care of everything.'

When I leave Cara's room, I find Dr. Saint-Clare on a phone at the nurses' station. He hangs up the receiver just as I come to stand in front of him.

'Can I ask you something?' I say. 'What would actually . . . you know . . . happen?'

'Happen?'

'If we decided to . . .' I can't say the words. I shrug instead, and rub the toe of my sneaker on the linoleum.

But he knows what I'm asking. 'Well,' he says. 'He won't be in any pain. The family is welcome to be there as the ventilator gets dialed down. Your father may take a few breaths on his own, but they won't be regular and they won't continue. Eventually, his heart will stop beating. The family is usually asked to leave the room while the breathing tube is removed, and then they're invited back in to say good-bye for as long as they need.' He hesitates. 'The procedure can vary, though, under certain circumstances.'

'Like what?'

'If your father ever expressed interest in organ donation, for example.'

I think back four days ago – was it really only that long? – when I sifted through the contents of my father's wallet. Of the little holographic heart printed on his license. 'What if he did?' I ask.

'The people from the New England Organ Bank get contacted with every case of severe brain trauma, whether or not the patient has previously expressed a desire to donate. They'll come talk with you and answer any questions you have. If your father is a registered donor, and if the family chooses to withdraw treatment, the timing can be coordinated with the organ bank so that the organs can be recovered as per your father's wishes.' Dr. Saint-Clare looks at me. 'But before any of that happens,' he says, 'you and your sister need to be on the same page about removing your father from life support.'

I watch him walk down the hallway, and then I slip along the wall closer to Cara's room again. I hang back so that I will not be seen but can still peer inside. Cara's sleeping. My mother sits beside the bed, her head pressed to her folded hands, as if she's praying.

Maybe she still does.

When I used to walk Cara to school, and then sat in my car making sure she went all the way into the double doors, it wasn't just because I wanted to make sure that she wasn't snatched by some perv. It was because I couldn't be who she was – a little kid with pigtails flying behind her; her backpack like a pink turtle shell; her mind full of what-ifs and maybes. She could convince herself of anything – that fairies lived on the undersides of wild mushrooms, that the reason Mom cried at night was because she was reading a depressing novel, that it wasn't a big deal when Dad forgot it was my birthday or missed her performance in a holiday concert because he was too busy teaching Polish farmers how to keep wolves off their land by playing audiotapes of howls. Me, I was already jaded and tarnished, skeptical that a fantasy world could keep reality at bay. I watched her every morning because, in my own little Holden Caulfield moment, I wanted to make sure someone was keeping her childhood from getting just as ruined as mine.

I know she thinks I abandoned her, but maybe I got back at just the right time. I'm the only one who has the power to let her be a kid a little while longer. To make sure she doesn't have herself to blame for a decision she might second-guess for the rest of her life.

I can't do this, my sister had said.

I just want it to be over.

Cara needs me. She doesn't want to talk to the doctors and the nurses and the social workers anymore. She doesn't want to have to make this choice.

So I will.

The best day I ever spent with my father was nearly a disaster.

It was just after Cara was born. My mother had been

reading parenting books, trying to make sure that a little boy who'd been the sole focus of her attention for seven years wouldn't freak out when a baby was brought home. (I did try to feed Cara a quarter, once, as if she was an arcade pinball machine, but that is a different story.) The books said, *Have the new baby bring the sibling a gift!* So when I was brought to the hospital to meet the tiny pink blob that was my new sister, my mother patted the bed beside her. 'Look at what Cara brought,' she told me, and she handed me a long, thin, gift-wrapped package. I stared at her belly, wondering how the baby had fit inside, much less a present this big, and then I got distracted by the fact that it was mine. I unwrapped it to find a fishing pole of my own.

At seven, I was not like other boys, who ripped the knees of their jeans and who caught slugs to crucify in the sunlight. I was much more likely to be found in my room, reading or drawing a picture. For a man like my father, who barely knew how to fit into the structure of a traditional family, having a nontraditional son was an impossible puzzle. He didn't know, literally, what to do with me. The few times he'd tried to introduce me to his passions had been a disaster. I'd fallen into a patch of poison ivy. I'd gotten such a bad sunburn my eyes swelled shut. It reached the point where, if I had to go to Redmond's with my dad, I stayed in his trailer and read until he was finished doing whatever he needed to do.

I would have much rather had a new art kit, all the little pots of watercolor paint and markers lined up like a rainbow. 'I don't know how to fish,' I pointed out.

'Well,' my mother exclaimed. 'Then Daddy needs to teach you.'

I'd heard that line before. *Daddy'll show you how to ride a bike. Daddy can take you swimming this afternoon.* But something always came up, and that something wasn't me.

'Luke, why don't you and Edward go test it out right now? That way Cara and I can take a little nap.'

My father looked at my mother. 'Now?' But he wasn't about to argue with a woman who'd just given birth. He looked at me and nodded. 'It's a great day to catch a fish,' he said, and just those words made me think that this could be the start of something different between us. Something wonderful. On television, dads and sons fished all the time. They had deep conversations. Fishing might be the one thing that my father and I could share, and I just didn't know it yet.

We drove to Redmond's. 'Here's the deal,' he said. 'While I'm feeding the wolves, you're going to dig up worms.'

I nodded. I would have dug to China for worms if that were a prerequisite. I was with my father, alone, and I was going to fall in love with fishing if it killed me. I pictured a whole string of days in my future that involved us, bonding over walleye and stripers.

My father took me to a toolshed behind the cage where the gibbons were kept and found a rusted metal shovel. Then we walked to the manure pile behind the aviary, where all the keepers carted their wheelbarrows daily after cleaning the animal cages. He overturned a patch of earth as rich as black coffee and put his hands on his hips. 'Ten worms,' he said. 'Your hands are going to get dirty.'

'I don't care,' I said.

While he checked on his pack, I carefully plucked a dozen worms out of the soil and confined them in the Ziploc bag my dad had given me. He returned with a fishing rod of his own. Then we ducked out the back gate behind the lions and I followed my father into the woods, parting the green fingers of ferns to walk down a muddy path. I was getting bitten by mosquitoes and I wondered how long it would be until we were there (wherever we were headed), but I didn't complain. Instead, I listened to my father whistle, and I imagined how awesome it would be to show my fishing pole to my best friend, Logan, who lived next door, and who couldn't stop bragging about the Sonic the Hedgehog 3 game he'd gotten for his birthday.

After about ten minutes the woods opened up to the edge of a highway. My father held tight to my hand, looked both ways, and then jogged across the road. Water sparkled, like the way my mother's ring sometimes made light dance on the ceiling. There was a fence, and a white sign with black letters.

'What's NO TRESPASSING?' I asked, sounding it out.

'It means nothing,' my father said. 'No one owns the land. We're all just borrowing it.'

He lifted me over the fence and then hopped it himself, and we sat side by side at the edge of the reservoir. My father's fishing rod was rusty where mine was gleaming. And mine had a red and white bobber on the line, like a tiny buoy. I sat on my knees, then on my bottom, and then got up on my knees again. 'The first rule of fishing,' he told me, 'is to be still.'

He showed me how to release the hook from the eye where it was safely tucked, and then he reached into the plastic bag to pull out a worm. 'Thank you,' he said under his breath.

'For what?'

He looked at me. 'My Native American friends say an animal that gives its life to feed another animal should be honored for the sacrifice,' my father said, and he speared the worm onto the hook.

It kept wriggling. I thought I might throw up.

My father knelt behind me, and put his arms around me. 'You push the button here,' he said, pressing my thumb against the Zebco reel, 'and you hold it. Swing from right to left.' With his body flush against mine, he swayed us in tandem, and at the last minute he let go of the button so that the line arched over the water, a silver parabola. 'Want to try?'

I could have done it myself. But I wanted to feel my dad's heartbeat again, like a drum between my shoulder blades. 'Can you show me one more time?' I asked.

He did, twice. And then he picked up his own fishing rod. 'Now, when the bobber starts going up and down, don't pull. There's a difference between a nibble and taking the bait. When it goes down and stays down, that's when you pull back and start reeling in.'

I watched him thank another worm and thread his hook. I held my rod so tightly my knuckles were white. There was a wind coming out of the east, and that made the bobber bounce around on the water a little bit. I worried that I might miss a fish because I thought it was the breeze. But I also worried that I'd reel in my line too early; that my worm would have given its life for nothing.

'How long does it take?' I asked.

'Rule number two of fishing,' my father said. 'Be patient.'

Suddenly there was a yank on my line, as if I had woken up from a dream in the middle of a game of tug-of-war. I nearly dropped the pole. 'Itsafishitsafish,' I cried, getting to my feet, and my father grinned.

'Then you'd better bring it in, buddy,' he said. 'Nice and slow . . .'

Before he could help me, though, he got a fish on his line, too. He stood up as the fish zipped further into the middle of the reservoir, bending the tip of his pole like a divining rod. Meanwhile, my fish broke through the surface of the water with a splash. I had reeled as far as I could; the fish was thrashing and flailing inches away from my chest.

'What do I do now?' I shouted.

'Hold on,' my father instructed. 'I'll help you as soon as I get mine in.'

The fish was a perch, tiger-striped, with tiny jagged edges along its fins. Its eyes were glassy and wild, like those of the porcelain doll that used to belong to my mom's grandma and that she said was too old and special to do anything but sit on a shelf. I tried twice to grab the perch, but it slithered and flapped out of my grasp.

But my father had told me to hold on, and so, even though I was afraid those spikes on its fins would poke into me, even though the fish smelled like the inside of a rubber boot and slapped me with its tail, I did.

My fist closed around the fish, which was no bigger than six inches long, but which seemed huge. My fingers didn't fit all the way around its belly, and it was still struggling against me and trying to dislodge the hook in its mouth, which broke through the silvery skin of its throat and made me feel sick to my stomach. I squeezed a little harder, to make sure it wouldn't get away.

But I guess I squeezed a little too hard.

The eyes of the perch bulged, and its entrails squirted from its bottom. Horrified, I dropped my fishing rod and stared at my hand, covered with fish guts, and at the dead perch still hooked to the line.

I couldn't help it; I burst into tears.

I was crying for the fish and the worm, which had both died for no good reason. I was crying because I had screwed up. I was crying because I thought this meant my father wouldn't want to fish with me again.

My father looked at me, and at the remains of the perch. 'What did you *do*?' he said, and in that single moment of distraction, his own line snapped. Whatever huge fish he'd been reeling in was gone.

'I killed it,' I sobbed.

'Well,' he pointed out. 'You were going to kill it anyway.'

This did not make me feel any better. I cried harder, and my father looked around, uncomfortable.

He was not the parent who held me when I was sick, or who calmed me down when I had a nightmare – that was my mother. My father was as out of his element with a terrified kid as I was with a fishing pole.

'Don't cry,' he said, but I had crossed the line of panic that small children sometimes do, where my skin was hot and my breath came in gasps, a punctuation of hysteria. My nose was running, and that made me think of the slime of the fish between my fingers, and that made me cry even harder.

He should have hugged me. He should have said that it didn't matter and that we could try again.

Instead, he blurted out, 'Did you hear the joke about the roof? No? Well, it's probably over your head anyway.'

I don't know what made him tell a joke. A bad joke. But

it was so awkward, so different from what I needed at that moment, that it shocked me into silence. I hiccuped, and stared up at him through spiked lashes.

'Why do doctors use red pens?' he said, the words fast and desperate. 'In case they need to draw blood.'

I wiped my nose on my sleeve, and he took off his shirt and used it to gently wipe my face and settle me on his lap. 'Guy walks into a bar with a salamander on his shoulder,' my father said. 'The bartender says, "What's his name?" And the guy says, "Tiny. Because he's my newt."'

I didn't understand any of the jokes; I was too young. And I'd never really thought of my father as a closet comedian. But his arms were around me, and this time there was no casting lesson involved.

'It was an accident,' I told him, and my eyes filled up again.

My father reached for the knife he carried in his pocket and snipped the line, kicked the remains of the fish into the water, where I wouldn't have to see it anymore. 'You know what the dad buffalo said to his kid when he went to work in the morning? "Bye, son."' He wiped his hands on his jeans. 'Rule number three of fishing: what happens at the pond stays at the pond.'

'I don't know any jokes,' I said.

'My grandfather used to tell them to me when I got scared.'

I could not imagine my father, who thought nothing of wrestling with a wolf, being scared.

He helped me to my feet and picked up my rod and his. The wisps of loose fishing line flew through the air like the silk from a spider.

'Did your dad tell you jokes, too?' I asked.

My father took a step away from me then, but it felt like

a mile. 'I never knew my dad,' he said, turning away from me.

It was, I realized, the one thing we had in common.

I'm sitting in the dark in my father's room, the green glow from the monitors behind him casting shadows on the bed. My elbows rest on my knees, my chin is cupped in my hands. 'How do you know Jesus likes Japanese food?' I murmur.

No reply.

'Because he loves miso.'

I rub my eyes, which are burning. Dry. Tearless.

'Did you hear about the paranoid dyslexic?' I say. 'He's always afraid he's following someone.'

Once, bad jokes had distracted my father enough to stop being scared. It isn't working for me, though.

There is a soft knock on the open door. A woman steps inside. 'Edward?' she says. 'I'm Corinne D'Agostino. I'm a donation coordinator with the New England Organ Bank.'

She's wearing a green sweater with leaves embroidered on it, and her brown hair is in a pixie cut. She reminds me of Peter Pan, which is ironic. There's no Neverland here, no everlasting youth.

'I'm so sorry about your father.'

I nod. I know that's what she's expecting.

'Tell me a little bit about him. What did he like to do?'

Now *that* I'm not expecting. I'm hardly the most qualified person to answer that question. 'He was outside all the time,' I say finally. 'He studied wolf behavior by living with packs.'

'That's pretty amazing,' Corinne says. 'How did he get involved in that?'

Did I ever ask him? Probably not. 'He thought wolves got

a bad rap,' I reply, remembering some of the talks my father used to give to the tourists who swarmed Redmond's in the summertime. 'He wanted to set the record straight.'

Corinne pulls up a chair. 'It sounds like he cared a lot about animals. Often, folks like that want to help other people, too.'

I rub my hands over my face, suddenly exhausted. I don't want to beat around the bush anymore. I just want this to be over. 'Look, his license said he wanted to be an organ donor. That's why I asked to speak to you.'

She nods, taking my lead and dropping the small talk. 'I've talked to Dr. Saint-Clare and we've reviewed your father's chart. I understand that his injuries were so severe that he's never going to enjoy the quality of life he used to have. But none of those injuries have damaged his internal organs. A donation after cardiac death is a real gift to others who are suffering.'

'Is it going to hurt him?'

'No,' Corinne promises. 'He's still a patient, and his comfort is the most important concern for us. You can be with him when the life-sustaining treatment is stopped.'

'How does it work?'

'Well, donation after cardiac death is different from organ donation after brain death. We'd begin by reviewing both the decision you made with the medical team to withdraw treatment and your father's status as a registered donor. Then, we'd work with the transplant surgeons to arrange a time when the termination of life support and the organ donation could be done.' She leans forward, her hands clasped between her legs, never breaking my gaze. 'The family can be present. You'd be right here, along with your father's neurosurgeon and the ICU doctors and nurses. He'd be given intravenous morphine. There would be an arterial line monitoring arterial pressure, and one of the nurses or doctors will stop the ventilator that's helping him breathe. Without oxygen, his heart will stop beating. As soon as he is asystolic, which means his heart has stopped, you'll have a chance to say good-bye, and then we take him to the operating room. Five minutes after his heart stops, he'll be pronounced dead, and the organ recovery will begin with a new team of doctors, the transplant team. Typically in donations after cardiac death, the kidneys and liver are recovered, but every now and then hearts and lungs are donated, too.'

It seems almost cruel to be discussing this, literally, over my father's unconscious body. I look at his face, at the stitches still raw on his temple. 'What happens after that?'

'After the organ recovery, he's brought to the holding area of the hospital. They'll contact whatever funeral home you've made arrangements with,' Corinne explains. 'You'll also receive an outcome letter from us, telling you about the people who received your father's organs. We don't share their names, but it often helps the family left behind to see whose lives have been changed by the donor's gift.'

If I looked into the eyes of a man who had received my father's corneas, would I still feel like I didn't measure up?

'There's one thing you need to know, Edward,' she adds. 'DCD isn't a sure thing, like donation after brain death. Twenty-five percent of the time, patients wind up not being candidates.'

'Why not?'

'Because there's a chance that your father will not become asystolic in the window of opportunity necessary to recover the organs. Sometimes after the ventilator is turned off, a patient continues to breathe erratically. It's called agonal breathing, and during that time, his heart will continue beating. If that goes on for more than an hour, the DCD would be canceled because the organs wouldn't be viable.'

'What would happen to my father?'

'He would die,' she says simply, honestly. 'It might take two to three more hours. During that time he'd be kept comfortable, right here in his own bed.' Corinne hesitates. 'Even if the DCD isn't successful, it's still a wonderful gift. You'd be honoring your father's wishes, and nothing can take away from that.'

I touch my father's hand where it lies on top of the covers. It's like a mannequin's hand, waxy and cool.

If I fulfill my father's last wish, does that wipe clean the karmic slate? Am I forgiven for hating him every time he missed a meal with us, for breaking up my parents' marriage, for ruining Cara's life, for running away?

Corinne stands. 'I'm sure you need some time to think about this,' she says. 'To discuss it with your sister.'

My sister has trusted me with this decision, because she's too close to make it.

'My sister and I have talked,' I say. 'She's a minor. It's ultimately my decision.'

She nods. 'If you don't have any more questions, then—'

'I do,' I say. 'I have one more question.' I look up at her, a silhouette in the dark. 'How soon can you do it?'

That night, I tell my mother that Cara and I have talked, that she doesn't want to deal with this nightmare anymore, and I don't want her to *have* to. I tell my mother that I've made the decision to let Dad die.

Lone Wolf

I just don't tell her when. I am sure she's thinking that the termination of life support will be a few days from now, that she will have time to help Cara process all those emotions, but really, that's completely pointless. If I'm doing this to protect Cara, then it should happen fast, before it hurts more than it has to. It's not enough that I'm making the decision; it has to be carried out as well, so that there's no more second-guessing and she can't tear herself up inside.

My mother holds me close and I rest my head on her shoulder as she cries a little. She may have split with my father, but that doesn't mean she didn't love him once. I know she's lost in her thoughts about her life with him, which is probably what keeps her from asking too many questions I cannot answer truthfully. By the time she remembers to ask them, everything will already be done.

After she goes to keep vigil in Cara's room again, I sign the paperwork and call a funeral home on the list Corinne has given me, and then I leave the hospital. Instead of going to my father's house, though, I drive to the highway that runs past Redmond's and park along the shoulder near the reservoir where we once went fishing.

It takes some bushwhacking to find the overgrown trail that my father led me down years ago, the one that heads back toward the wolf enclosures. In the dark, I curse myself for not bringing a flashlight, for having to navigate by the glow of the moon. The snow in these woods is up to my knees; it's not long before I am soaked and shivering.

I see a light on in the trailer at the top of the hill. Walter's still awake. I could knock on his door, tell him about this decision I've made on my father's behalf. Maybe he'd break out a bottle and we'd toast the life of the man who was the link between us.

Then again, Walter probably doesn't have a bottle there. My father always said a wolf's sense of smell is so advanced it doesn't just notice shampoos and soaps – it can scent what you've digested and when and how, days after you indulged. It can smell fear, excitement, contentment. A wolf pup is born deaf and blind, with only its sense of smell to recognize its mother, and the other members of its pack.

I wonder if the wolves know I am here, just because I am my father's son.

Suddenly I hear one mournful note, which breaks and falls a few steps into another. There is a beat of silence. The same note sounds again, as clear as a bow drawn across a violin. It makes something inside me sing like a tuning fork.

At first I think the wolves are calling an alarm, because they can smell an intruder, even from this distance.

Then I realize it is an elegy.

A requiem.

A song for a pack member who isn't coming back.

For the first time since I received that phone call in Thailand, for the first time since I've been home, for the first time in a long time, I start to cry.

It is a funeral. We just don't have the body, yet.

I stand awkwardly next to my father's bed. It is 9:00 a.m. on the dot. The transplant team is ready in the OR. Corinne is here, and two ICU nurses, and Trina. There's a woman in a suit – I've been told she's from the legal department. I guess the hospital needs to have all its *i*'s dotted and *t*'s crossed before they turn off life support.

Trina steps beside me. 'Are you all right?' she asks softly. 'Can I get you a chair?'

'I'd rather stand,' I say.

In five minutes, my father will be pronounced dead. And somebody else will get a new lease on life.

Dr. Saint-Clare slips into the room, followed by Dr. Zhao, the ICU physician. 'Where's Mr. Warren's daughter?' Dr. Zhao asks.

All eyes turn to me. 'Cara told me to take care of everything,' I reply.

Dr. Zhao frowns. 'As of yesterday she wasn't too keen on the idea to discontinue her father's life support.'

'Edward assured me that she'd given her consent before he signed the paperwork,' Dr. Saint-Clare says.

Don't they understand that this is what my father would have wanted? Not just for him to be released from this vegetative hell but for me to protect Cara. I'm saving her from having to make a decision that will break her heart. And I'm saving her from wasting her life as the caretaker of an invalid.

'That's all very well and good,' the lawyer says, stepping forward, 'but I need to hear it from Cara herself.'

Luke

*T*wo days after the pack howled in reply to me, I was sitting beneath a tree untangling a trap when the big male wolf stepped out of nowhere and ran toward me at full tilt. The other four wolves appeared like ghosts between the trees, coming to stand like sentries in a line. I was defenseless, sitting down like this. I was certain this was the moment I'd die. I could roll onto my back and offer my throat, but I didn't know if I had the time to ask the animal for trust before his jaws sank into my flesh.

At the last moment he stopped dead in front of me. He craned his neck, as if he wanted to smell me but didn't want to get any closer. Then, without warning, he nipped at my knee in exactly the same spot I'd been nipped years ago by Arlo at the zoo. Abruptly he turned and walked back to the rest of his pack, which started licking him like mad around the mouth.

The next day, the big male returned, this time with two pups, a male and a female. They flanked him, watching carefully. The big wolf sniffed my boots, and then circled me, as if he was trying to suss out if there was anything new about me that might be a threat. The youngsters came closer to investigate, and the big wolf snapped at their muzzles.

Three times he nipped at me, pinching the flesh under my knees, leaning into my shoulder. After each bite he looked at me, inscrutable. He rubbed his body against me, like a cat on a scratching pole.

Then he moved behind me, leaving the pups in front. I started to sweat – it just didn't feel comfortable having a wild animal somewhere I couldn't see him – and in that instant the wolf's jaws closed around my neck from behind. I could feel his long teeth scraping against my jugular.

The female pup darted forward and took a sizable nip at my knee at that moment, just as the big male let go of my neck. When he sauntered back to the two remaining wolves that were waiting at the edge of the clearing, the pups in tow, I did something I still cannot believe I had the nerve to do.

I followed.

I was on my hands and knees, stumbling, awkward. Twice, the big male looked over his shoulder and clearly saw me behind him. I figured he could very easily teach me a lesson if he thought that was a bad idea, but instead, he just kept going. I had never been this close to the wild pack before; I could smell the mud caked into their paws and the wet musk of their coats.

Of the two wolves that had stayed back from me, one was the alpha female. She was smaller, with black lines marking her back and tail and the top of her head, thick as if she'd been striped with paint. Staring at me, she bared her teeth, curled her tongue.

I was about twenty-five yards away when she started growling.

Immediately, the pups ran to her side and glowered at me. The big male stepped between us, but she snapped at him and he fell into line, too. The alpha female flattened her ears and barked, low and threatening. Then she turned and took the others back through the tree line.

The big male hesitated, capturing my gaze.

A lot has been said about the stare of a gray wolf. It's level, measured, eerily human. A wolf is born with blue eyes, but after six or eight weeks, they turn golden. And if you've ever been lucky enough to look into a wolf's eyes, you know that they penetrate. They look at you, and you realize they are taking a snapshot of every fiber of your being. That they know you better even than you know yourself.

The wolf and I sized each other up. Then he dipped his head, turned, and loped into the woods.

I didn't see the pack for another six weeks. From time to time I heard them calling, but it wasn't a rallying call to replace a missing member anymore – just a locating call to make sure they kept other packs and animals at bay. My invitation had been revoked. I had replayed in my mind what had happened between us, whether that last look from the big male had been his way of communicating to me that I had been given a chance, and clearly had not measured up. But the fact that he hadn't chosen to rip out my throat made me believe this couldn't be the case. That even if the alpha female wasn't very fond of me, more than half her pack was.

They appeared on the first day that felt like spring – when it was warm enough for me to break through the ice of the stream to drink without having to use a rock or stick, when I had unzipped my coveralls so that the breeze could cool me. Just like before, they came silently, a wall of gray mist. I immediately dropped so that my body was lower than theirs. Even the alpha female inched closer.

Lone Wolf

They were energetic and rowdy, more active than the last time they'd come. I felt an overwhelming relief that they were back, that I wasn't alone in this wilderness. The big male came running at me again, as he had weeks before, and pinned me on my back with his full weight. In this vulnerable pose, I was offering my life to him, and frankly I was so happy to see him again that I wasn't even as terrified as I probably should have been.

Maybe it was because my guard was down, maybe it was because the world felt like it was thawing and I was cocky after surviving the winter – there are a dozen reasons why I did not anticipate what happened next. The big wolf was suddenly gone, and the alpha female had taken his spot. Her front paws held my shoulders down on the ground, her weight was on my lower body. She was an inch from my face, and she was snarling and snapping at me. When the male moved closer, she lunged and bit him, and he slunk away.

Her breath came in hot gusts; her saliva streaked my forehead, but every time I thought she was going to tear into my flesh, she pulled the punch. I stayed perfectly still for the five minutes it was going on, and then she released me. She loped away, but instead of vanishing into the woods, she lay down on a rock in the sun. The big male settled beside her.

I was amazed that they had chosen to keep company with me, instead of disappearing like usual. And then, to my shock, the other three wolves left the protection of the trees and came into the clearing. They stretched out on either side of me. The younger female yawned and crossed her front paws.

We weren't touching, but I could feel the heat of their bodies, and I was warmer than I'd been in months. I did not move for over an hour. Lying between them in the pool of sunlight, I listened to the sound of their breathing.

Unlike the wolves, I couldn't sleep. Part of me was too excited; part of me kept glancing at the alpha female.

I realized she hadn't been trying to kill me.

She'd been teaching me a lesson.

In those five minutes, I could have died. Instead, I was getting a new lease on life.

Cara

I'm being discharged. Now that my fever's down and it seems I will survive this shoulder surgery, they want the bed for someone more needy. The bad news is that I cannot go back to school yet because I still can't do things like hold a fork or a pencil or unzip my own jeans to pee. The good news is that I will be staying at my mom's, and will have plenty of time to research traumatic brain injury and other cases like my father's. Other cases where the patients, against all odds, have gotten better.

My mother promises that as soon as she gets the final papers from the nurse, we can go downstairs so I can see my father before I leave the hospital.

For the past hour I have been ready to go. I'm sitting on the bed, showered and dressed, champing at the bit. My IV line has already been removed. From what the nurses' station has told my mother, the paperwork is ready; it's just a matter of my orthopedic surgeon coming by to give me discharge instructions, and to officially sign us out.

My mom is on her iPhone with Joe, telling him that we'll be coming home. Her eyes are dancing in a way that they haven't the whole time we've been cooped up here. She wants

Jodi Picoult

to get back to her old life, too. It's just a little easier for her than it is for me.

When the door opens, she stands up. 'Gotta go, honey,' she says, hanging up. We both turn, expecting my doctor, but instead Trina the social worker walks in with a woman I've never seen before in a pencil skirt and a kelly-green silk blouse.

'Cara,' Trina says, 'this is Abby Lorenzo. She's a lawyer for the hospital.' Immediately I panic – thinking of the two cops, and the blood test that showed I'd been drinking that night. My mouth goes dry, my tongue feels as thick as a mattress.

Does this mean they've figured out what happened?

'I wanted to ask you about your father,' the lawyer says, and in that instant I am sure that I've turned to stone, that I can no longer escape.

'You seem upset,' Trina says, frowning. 'Edward said you two had talked.'

'I haven't talked to him since yesterday,' I answer.

My mother puts her hand on mine, squeezes. 'My son told me that he and Cara decided that Edward would make the medical decisions for their father from here on.'

'What?' I blink at her. 'Are you *kidding* me?'

The lawyer looks at Trina. 'So you *haven't* given consent to terminate your father's life support today?'

I don't even think. I just stumble off the bed, barefoot, and use my good shoulder to shove my way between the two women. And I run. To the stairwell, down to the ICU floor, clutching my bad arm to my chest and fighting off the pain I feel with each jostle and turn.

Because this time, when I save my father, I'm not going to screw it up.

Luke

*M*y *Native American friends call it the dance of death: the moment that two predators size each other up. For a wolf in the natural world, the brain doesn't have a choice. It doesn't get to say,* There's a bear coming and I'm going to die. *Instead, it thinks,* What do I know about this bear? What do I know about my environment? What members of my family do I need to protect myself? *Suddenly the bear is no longer a threat. He knows that you're a predator, and you know that he's a predator. You respect each other's ground, turning very slowly, eyeball to eyeball. The space between you is the difference between life and death. Does he see you as a prey animal? Or does he see you as something that can injure him as he comes after you? If you can put that doubt in his mind, chances are, he will leave you be.*

Edward

She is a five-foot, three-inch storm: red-faced, tear-streaked, hair flying out wild. And she's coming right for me.

'Stop!' Cara says. 'He's a liar!'

The doctors have gone, ready to be paged once we get the attorney's permission. Corinne has been anxiously pacing; there is a narrow window of opportunity for organ donation that is slipping away moment by moment. I was just doing what Cara had asked. She wanted this to be over, but she was too close to my father; I understood that. It was like the little kid who holds out his arm for a vaccination and shuts his eyes tight, because he doesn't want to look until it's all over.

But apparently Cara's changed her mind. Before she can scratch my eyes out, a nurse grabs her around the waist. Corinne steps forward. 'Are you saying that you didn't give consent to the organ donation?'

'It's not enough to kill him?' Cara yells at me. 'You have to cut him into pieces, too?'

Maybe I should have asked my sister if she wanted to be here. Based on what she'd said yesterday, I figured she wouldn't have been emotionally capable of it. This outburst only reinforces that.

'It's not what Dad wanted. He told me so.'

By now, the hospital lawyer and Trina and my mother have reached the room. 'Well, that's not what Dad told *me*,' I say.

'When?' she scoffs. 'You haven't lived with us for six years!'

'All right, you two,' the lawyer says. 'Nothing's going to happen today, I'll tell you that much. I'll ask for a temporary guardian to be appointed to review your father's case.'

Cara visibly relaxes. She falls back against my mother, who is staring at me as if she's never seen me before.

What I do next, I do because I have a letter burning in my breast pocket that's validation.

Or because I know better than Cara how you have to live with the choices you make.

Or because, for once, I want to be the son my father wanted.

I lean over, bracing my hands on my knees, as if I'm disappointed. Then I dive down to the linoleum, pushing aside the nurse who is sitting beside the machine that's breathing for my father, waiting for a cue that isn't going to come.

'I'm sorry,' I say out loud – to my father, my sister, myself – and I yank the plug of the ventilator from its socket.

Part Two

If you call one wolf,
you invite the pack.

– Bulgarian proverb

Cara

A t first, when the alarm goes off, I don't even realize what's happened.

Then I look up from my mother's shoulder and see Edward on his knees, still gripping the electrical cord that trails from the ventilator. He is holding the plug in his hand as if he cannot believe it is actually there.

I start to scream, and all hell breaks loose.

The nurse near Edward stumbles upright as another nurse calls for security. A burly orderly rushes into the room, shoving my mother out of the way as he tackles Edward. He slams Edward's hand against the floor, and the electrical cord flies free; immediately, the nurse plugs the machine in again and hits the Reset button.

Maybe all of this takes twenty seconds. It's the longest twenty seconds of my life.

I hold my breath until my father's chest starts to rise and fall again, and then I give myself permission to burst into tears.

'Edward,' my mother gasps. 'What were you thinking?'

Before he can answer, security arrives. Two guards stuffed like sausages into their uniforms grab Edward's arms and haul him upright. Dr. Saint-Clare runs into the room, short of breath. He bends over my father, immediately assessing the damage Edward's done, as a nurse brings him up to speed.

I can feel my mother tensing behind me. 'Where are you taking him?' she demands, trailing the officers as they start to drag Edward off. Abby Lorenzo, the hospital lawyer, follows them.

'Stop! Please. He's been here round the clock, hardly sleeping,' my mother begs. 'He wasn't thinking clearly.'

'I can't believe you're defending him!' I say.

I can see the storm in her eyes, the one that's tearing her in two. I take a step back, putting distance between us. After all, she did it first.

My mother looks at me, apologetic. 'He's still my son,' she murmurs, and she leaves the room.

Immediately, Trina approaches. 'Cara, why don't we sit down somewhere quiet while your mother sorts all this out?'

I ignore her. 'Is my dad okay?' I ask Dr. Saint-Clare.

The neurosurgeon looks at me. I know what he's thinking: *Your father wasn't okay to start with.* 'It depends on how long he spent without oxygen,' Dr. Saint-Clare says. 'If it was longer than a minute, it might be clinically significant.'

'Cara,' Trina says again. 'Please.'

She touches my good arm, and I let myself be led away. But the whole time, my mind is racing. What kind of person pulls the plug, literally, on his own father? How much hate did Edward have to be nursing to deliberately go behind my back, to tell all these doctors and nurses that I had agreed to terminate life support, and then, when it didn't go according to plan, to take matters into his own hands?

Trina leads me down the hall to a lounge. There are a few

on the ICU floor, for families who are in for a long wait. This one is empty, with uncomfortable orange couches and magazines from 2003 on the coffee tables. I curl into a ball in the corner of one of the couches. I feel impossibly small, overlooked.

'I know you're upset,' she says.

'Upset? My brother lied to everyone so that he could kill my father. Yeah, I'm a little upset.' I swipe a hand across my eyes. 'My dad stopped breathing. What's *that* going to do to his recovery?'

She hesitates. 'Dr. Saint-Clare will let us know as soon as he can if there was any damage. I know that you have to be without oxygen for about ten minutes for it to lead to brain death, if that's any comfort.'

'What if my brother tries this again?'

'First of all, he won't have the opportunity,' Trina says. 'The hospital will press charges for assault; Abby's having him brought down to the police station right now. And second of all, even though Edward's the one legally capable of making a decision about your father, we never would have scheduled a DCD if we didn't believe you'd given your consent. I'm sorry, Cara. The donor coordinator told me that Edward had your permission, but someone should have asked you directly. I can assure you that won't happen again.'

I don't believe a word she's saying. If Edward found a way to snow them once, he can find a way to snow them again.

'I want to see my father,' I insist.

'I'm sure you do,' Trina says. 'But let's give the doctors some time to make sure he's all right.'

My father taught me that wolves can read emotion and illness the way humans read headlines. They know when a woman is pregnant before she does and will treat her more gently; they single out the visitor who suffers from depression and try to engage him. Already the medical community has learned that canines can actually sniff out an invisible illness, like heart disease or cancer. In other words, you cannot fool a wolf.

But you sure as hell can fool a human.

I stare down at my lap, widening my eyes until they tear up, and then I look up at Trina. 'I want my mom,' I say, making my voice small and wounded.

'She's probably downstairs talking to the hospital attorneys,' Trina says. 'I'll get her. Why don't you just wait here?'

So I do, counting to three hundred, until I'm sure Trina is gone from the ICU hallway. Then I peek my head out the lounge door and start walking calmly to the staircase. I know, from my father's prior visit to the hospital for stitches in his arm, that the ER doors are on a completely different side of the hospital, and that's where I'm headed. To an exit where I won't run into my mother, my brother, or anyone else who might stop me.

I'm not thinking about what I'm going to do, once I'm outside in my street clothes without a winter coat or a phone or transportation.

I'm not thinking about the fact that I haven't technically been discharged yet, either.

I'm just thinking that desperate times call for desperate measures, and that *someone's* got to keep my brother from doing this again.

Really, I ought to become a professional liar. Apparently, I have a gift: I have now managed to fool the cops, my mother, a social worker, and a woman at the Starbucks right down the street from the hospital. I told her that my boyfriend and I had a fight and he drove off in his car, leaving me without my coat and my purse and my phone – and did she have a phone I could borrow so I could call my mom to come get me? Having my arm wrapped like the broken wing of a bird helps with the sympathy votes. Not only did the lady give me her cell but she also bought me a hot chocolate and a poppy-seed muffin.

I don't call my mother. Instead, I call Mariah. The way I see it, she owes me big-time. If she hadn't been stalking some loser, I never would have been at that party in Bethlehem. If I hadn't been at the party in Bethlehem, I wouldn't have been drinking. And my father wouldn't have had to come get me. And, well, you know the rest.

Mariah is in French class when I call her. I hear her whisper, 'Hang on,' and then, over the drone of Madame Gallenaut conjugating the verb *essayer*, Mariah says, 'May I go to the bathroom?'

J'essaie.

Tu essaies.

I try. You try.

'*En français*,' Madame says.

'*Puis-je aller aux toilettes?*'

There is a flurry of static, and then Mariah's voice. 'Cara?' she says. 'Is everything okay?'

'No,' I tell her. 'Things are totally messed up. I need you to come pick me up at the Starbucks that's on the corner before the turnoff to the hospital.'

'What are you doing there?'

'Long story. I need you to come *now*.'

'But I'm in the middle of French. I have a free period fifth—'

I hesitate, deploying the big guns: 'I would do it for you,' I say, the same words Mariah used to convince me to go to that party in Bethlehem in the first place.

There is a beat of silence. 'I'll be there in ten minutes,' she answers.

'Mariah,' I say. 'Fill up the gas tank.'

The county attorney's office looks nothing like the way law offices look on TV. It's got crappy furniture and a secretary punching away at a computer so old it probably still runs BASIC. There's a framed poster of Machu Picchu on the wall, and also two photographs – one of a serene Obama, and one with Danny Boyle shaking Governor Lynch's hand. A rubbery plant is dying in the corner.

Mariah's waiting in the parking lot in her car. She wasn't thrilled about a road trip to North Haverhill, but she drove me all the same, and she even helped me figure out a ruse to get me into the county attorney's office. 'Danny Boyle,' she'd said. 'Sounds like he ought to be dancing on a Lucky Charms box.'

That had gotten me thinking – someone whose name sounded like he had relatives in Killarney, and who built his political platform on saving unborn babies was most likely a devout Catholic. I couldn't be sure, but it was a decent guess. And every Catholic kid I knew in my school seemed to have a thousand cousins.

So I approach the secretary's desk and wait for her to finish her phone call. 'Thanks, Margot,' she says. 'Yes, it's the Fox News segment about his recent conviction. DVD format would be great.'

When she hangs up, I try to give my most pathetic smile. After all, I'm standing there in a freaking arm sling. 'Can I help you?' the secretary asks.

'Is Uncle Danny in?' I say. 'It's kind of an emergency.'

'Dear, did he know you were coming? Because he's quite busy right now—'

I tighten my voice to the knife edge of hysteria. 'Didn't my uncle tell you I had a really bad car accident? And I just got into this huge fight with my mom and she told me I can't drive again until I'm forty and I have to pay off the insurance premium and I might as well find someone else to fund my college education and oh, *God*, can't I just please talk to Uncle Danny right now?' I start crying.

Seriously, I am becoming an Oscar contender.

The secretary blinks at the onslaught of words, then recovers and gets up to comfort me, gently patting me on my good shoulder. 'You just go right on back to his office, honey,' she says. 'I'll buzz him and tell him his niece is here.'

When I knock on the door that says DANIEL BOYLE, COUNTY ATTORNEY in gold lettering on glass, he tells me to come in. He's sitting behind a big desk stacked with files. His hair gleams, black like the wing of a crow, and his eyes look like he hasn't gotten a lot of sleep lately. He stands up, assessing me as I walk through the door.

'You're not as tall as you look on TV,' I blurt out.

'And you don't look like any of my nieces,' he replies. 'Look, kid, I don't have time to help you do your extra-credit project in Civitas. Paula can give you a packet about local government on your way out—'

'My brother just tried to kill my father and I need your help,' I say.

Danny Boyle frowns. 'What?'

'My father and I, we were in a car accident,' I explain. 'He hasn't regained consciousness. My brother left six years ago after a fight with my dad. He's been living in Thailand but he came home after the accident. It's only been seven days since the crash – my dad just needs time to get better – but my brother doesn't see it that way. He wants to turn off the ventilator and donate my father's organs and then go back to living his life. He managed to convince the hospital to do it, and when I freaked out and tried to stop them, Edward shoved a nurse out of the way and pulled the plug out himself.'

'What happened?'

'The nurse reset the ventilator. But the doctors still don't know if being without oxygen hurt my dad even more.' I take a breath. 'I've seen you on the news. You're good at what you do. Can't you prosecute Edward?'

He sits down on the edge of his desk. 'Listen, honey—'

'Cara,' I say. 'Cara Warren.'

'Cara. I'm really sorry – about your father, and about your brother's behavior. But this is a family issue. I prosecute criminal cases.'

'It's attempted murder!' I say. 'I may just be a high school student, but I know that when you shove a nurse out of the way, and unplug someone who's unconscious from a ventilator, you intend to kill him! What's more murderous than that?'

'Intent to kill isn't the only piece in the puzzle,' Boyle says. 'You have to prove malice, too.'

'My brother hates my father. It's why he walked out six years ago.'

'That may be,' Boyle says, 'but pulling out a plug is

significantly different than coming after someone with a knife or a gun. I'll pray for your father, but I'm afraid I can't help you.'

I stiffen my spine. 'If you don't, then my brother's going to try again. He'll go to court and say that my opinion doesn't matter, because I'm younger than him. He'll get the procedure rescheduled. But with a criminal charge against him, he can't be named a legal guardian for my father.' When Boyle looks at me, surprised, I shrug. 'Google,' I explain. I'd used Mariah's iPhone on the drive over.

Boyle sighs. 'All right. I'll look into it,' he says. He reaches onto his desk and hands me a legal pad and a pen. 'Give me your name and phone number.'

So I write these down for him. I hand back the pad. 'My dad may not be doing so well right now,' I tell him. 'But that doesn't give my brother the right to play God. A life,' I say, parroting Boyle's own words, 'is still a life.'

As I walk down the hallway to the reception area again, I can feel Danny Boyle's stare, like an arrow in my back.

Luke

I have been asked repeatedly why a pack of wild wolves would accept a human into their ranks. Why bother with a creature that follows too slowly, stumbles in the dark, can't speak their language fluently, and inadvertently disrespects their leaders? It was not as if the pack didn't know I wasn't a wolf, or didn't realize that I couldn't help bring down a kill for food, or protect them with teeth and claws. The only answer I can come up with is that they realized they needed to study a human as much as I needed to study them. The human world is encroaching closer and closer to the wolf world. Instead of just denying that fact, they wanted to find out as much as they could about people. From time to time you will find a feral dog adopted by a wolf pack for the same reason; accepting me into their ranks just brought them one step closer.

My goal, once they seemed to relax with me in their company, was to be allowed to follow them when they slipped between the trees and vanished. Now, this wasn't the brightest idea I'd ever had – I could easily get lost; and if they'd started hunting, I wouldn't have been able to keep up. But I couldn't let myself get this close and give up now, so when the wolves got up and left, I went with them.

At first I was able to follow. But it was night, pitch-black, and as soon as we reached a thickly wooded area I lost them; my eyes were no match for theirs. On the way back to the clearing, I smacked my head on a low-lying branch and was knocked out cold.

When I woke up, the sun was already high in the sky and the young female wolf was licking the cut on my head. (Of all the injuries I had in those years, not a single one became infected. If I'd been able to bottle the medicinal properties of wolf saliva, I'd be a rich man.) I sat up gingerly, temples throbbing, and watched the wolf pick up a haunch from a deer, hoof still attached. She rolled it around in the dirt a bit, batting it with her paws, and then dropped it on my leg.

I would come to learn that an alpha female can read every single bit of food you put into your body. Make a choice that's going to keep you strong and fit for the pack and you will pass muster; make a choice that's the equivalent of chocolate cake in the human world and you'll wind up urinating in streams to disguise your scent, or else suffer the consequences. There are nutritional foods, eaten daily to foster strength and health. Social foods help reinforce pack roles – when six wolves are feeding on a single carcass, the alpha will go to the internal organs, and the beta will get the muscle-packed rump and thigh meat, and the omega gets the intestinal contents and nonmovement meat, like the neck, spine, and rib cage. The tester wolf will get about 75 percent nonmovement meat and 25 percent vegetable matter; the numbers wolf will get 50 percent nonmovement meat and 50 percent stomach contents; the lookout will have 75 percent stomach contents and 25 percent nonmovement meat. If you go for a portion that's not yours, even by accident, you'll find yourself flat on your back.

Lone Wolf

Emotional foods like milk or stomach contents take a wolf back to a time in its life when it was placid and accepting of anything given by its mother; feed the same foods to older wolves and they'll mellow out. At first I didn't know if the young female wolf was testing me, if she wanted to see whether I'd try to take her food away. But she picked it up and dropped it again. So I lifted the deer leg to my mouth and started to eat.

How did the raw meat taste?

Like the finest filet.

It had been months since I'd eaten anything more substantial than rabbit and squirrel. I had been brought this food by a wild wolf, which may not have wanted me to go hunting but still wanted me well-fed, like any other member of the pack.

As I tore at the meat with my teeth, the wolf watched me calmly.

From then on, every time the pack went hunting, they brought me back food. Sometimes it was rolled in droppings or urinated upon. After a hunt, they'd stay in my company or let me follow them; then suddenly they would leave me. Sometimes I would howl, and if they were within hearing range, they'd answer. On their way back, they would howl to me. Without fail, that sound would bring me to my knees. It felt like the phone call you receive when someone you love has been out driving on a sheet of ice: I'm back, I'm safe, I'm yours again.

It made me realize that I had a new family.

Georgie

I knew that my son was gay before he did. There was a gentleness to him, an ability to see the world for its pieces instead of its whole, that made him different from the other boys in his nursery school class. When they picked up a stick, it was a gun or a whip. When Edward picked up a stick, it was a spoon to bake mud cookies, a magic wand. At playdates when he and a friend dressed up, Edward was never the knight but rather the princess. When I wanted to know if an outfit made me look fat, I never turned to Cara for frank advice but instead, to Edward.

You'd think that someone like Luke – someone virile enough to literally tear a carcass to shreds with his teeth when wolves were on either side of him – might have a problem with a gay son, but that's not something I ever anticipated. He was a firm believer that nothing trumped family. Just like wolves could maintain individuality within the pack and not have to prove themselves on a daily basis, to Luke, if you were family, you were respected for your differences, and your role was secure. He'd even told me once of same-sex wolves mounting each other during mating season, something that had more to do with domi-nance and subordinance than with sexuality. Which is why

I was so shocked when Edward came out to Luke, and Luke said . . .

Well. The truth is, I have no idea what Luke said.

All I know is that Edward went up to Redmond's to talk to his father, and when he came home, he wouldn't speak to me or Cara or anyone else. When I asked Luke what had happened, his face turned red. 'A mistake,' he said.

Two days later, Edward was gone.

No matter how often I asked him over the next six years, he would never tell me what his father had said that was so offensive. And in the way that imagination sometimes works, what I didn't know turned out to be more devastating than what I did. I would lie in bed imagining the foulest remarks Luke might have made, the demeaning expressions, the reactionary response. There was Edward offering his heart on a silver platter. But what was the reply? Did Luke tell Edward he could change, if he really wanted to? Did he say that he'd always known there was something *wrong* with his son? Because I didn't know the truth, and neither party would tell me what had happened, I pictured the worst.

You do not know what failure feels like until your eighteen-year-old son quits your family. That's the way I've always thought of it, because Edward was too smart to hop on a bus to Boston or even California. Instead, he took his passport from the filing cabinet in Luke's office, and with the money he'd reaped from tutoring over the summers (money he was going to put toward college), he bought a plane ticket to a place he knew we couldn't easily follow. Edward had always been impulsive – right back to when he was in nursery school and threw a jar of paint at a boy who'd been making fun of his artwork; or later, yelling at an unfair teacher without thinking through the consequences. But this was behavior I just couldn't understand. The farthest Edward had ever traveled alone was to a mock trial conference in Washington, DC; what could he possibly know about foreign countries and finding housing and making his own way in the world? I tried involving the police, but at eighteen, he was legally an adult. I tried calling Edward's cell phone, but the number had been disconnected. At home, I would wake up in the middle of the night and for two glorious seconds forget that my son was gone. And then, when the truth crept under the covers, clinging to me like a jealous lover, I would start sobbing.

One night I drove to Redmond's, leaving Cara alone and asleep in an empty house – more evidence of my bad parenting. Luke wasn't in the trailer, but his research assistant was. A college girl named Wren who had a giant wolf tattoo on her right shoulder blade, she split the time with Walter to make sure someone could be present overnight with the animals when Luke wasn't living with one of his packs – which was most of the time, these days. Wren was wrapped in a blanket and half asleep when I knocked. She looked terrified to see me – not surprising, since I was wild and furious – and pointed me toward the enclosures. This being nighttime, Luke was wide awake in the company of his wolf family, wrestling with a big gray wolf when I came to stand like an apparition against the fence. It was enough to make him do something he never did: break character, and be human. 'Georgie?' he said, guarded. 'What's wrong?'

I almost laughed at that; what *wasn't* wrong? Luke's way of dealing with his son's absence had been to gather his family closer – not Cara and me but his brotherhood of wolves. He hadn't been home long enough to see me set a place at the table for Edward and burst into tears; he didn't sit on his son's bed and hold the pillow, which still smelled like Edward. 'I need to know what you said to him, Luke,' I replied. 'I need to know why he left.'

Luke came through the double gates of the pen until he was standing, like me, on the outside.

'I didn't say *anything*.'

I just stared at him in disbelief. 'Do you actually think less of your son because he's gay? Because he doesn't care about wild animals or like being outside all the time? Because he didn't turn out like *you*?'

Anger flashed across Luke's face, quickly held in check. 'You really think that's what I'm like?'

'I think Luke Warren is all about Luke Warren. I don't know, maybe you're afraid that Edward doesn't fit your TV persona.' By now I was screaming at him.

'How dare you. I *love* my son. I love him.'

'Then why is he gone?'

Luke hesitated. I can't even remember what he said after that brief caesura, but it didn't matter nearly as much as the hiccup of space, that infinitesimal delay. Because that one faltering moment was a canvas, and I could paint upon it all of my greatest fears.

Three weeks after Edward left he sent me a postcard from Thailand. He included a new mobile phone number. He said that he had gotten a job teaching English, and an apartment, and that he loved me and Cara. He did not mention his father.

I told Luke I wanted to see him. Even though there was no return address on the postcard, even though Thailand was a big country – how hard could it be to find an eighteen-year-old Caucasian teacher? I called the travel agent to book a flight, planning to use money we kept in an emergency fund.

Then one of Luke's precious wolves got sick and needed surgery. And suddenly that money no longer existed.

The next week, I filed for divorce.

These were my irreconcilable differences: My son was gone. My husband was to blame. And I couldn't forgive him for that, ever.

But here's the dirty little secret I still hide: I was the one who told Edward to go to Redmond's that day, who urged him to come out to his own father the way he had to me. If I hadn't made that suggestion – if I'd *been* with Edward when he told his father – would Luke have still reacted as badly? Would Edward never have left?

If you look at it from this angle, it's my fault I lost my son for six years.

Which is why, now, I won't make the same mistake twice.

I would be the first to tell you I'm not perfect. I only floss before dentist appointments. I sometimes eat food that I've dropped on the floor. Once, I even spanked one of the twins when she ran into the middle of the road.

And I know how it must look when I do not stay with my daughter, who is wrapped and bandaged and wounded more than bone-deep, but instead choose to follow the son who has tried to pull the plug from his father's ventilator. I know that people are talking as I walk behind the security guards and the hospital lawyer, calling out to Edward, so he understands he isn't alone.

I look like a bad mother.

But if I *didn't* run after Edward – if I didn't try to explain to the hospital and the police that he didn't mean it – well, wouldn't that make me a *worse* mother?

I don't deal well with stress. I never have – it's why you never saw me on any of Luke's TV episodes; it's why, when he went to Quebec to live in the wild, I started taking Prozac. Over the past week I have done my best to hold myself together for Cara, even though being in this hospital at night feels like wandering through a ghost town, even though walking into Luke's room and seeing him with his head shaved and the stitches bisecting his scalp makes me want to turn tail and run. I stayed calm when the police came asking questions to which I did not want to know the answers. But now, I willingly throw myself into the fray. 'I'm sure that Edward can explain,' I tell the hospital lawyer.

'He'll have a chance to do that,' she says. 'Down at the police station.'

On cue, the sliding doors of the hospital entrance open and two officers walk in. 'We'll need the nurse's statement, too,' one of the cops says, while the other one handcuffs my son. 'Edward Warren, you're being arrested for simple assault. You have the right to remain silent—'

'Assault?' I gasp. 'He didn't hurt anyone!'

The hospital lawyer looks at me. 'He shoved a nurse. And you and I both know that's not all he did.'

'Mom,' Edward says, 'it's okay.'

Sometimes I think I have spent my entire life being torn in two directions: I wanted a career, but I also wanted a family. I loved the way Luke's wildness could barely be contained inside his skin, but that didn't necessarily make him the best husband, the best father. I want to be a good parent to Cara, but I have two little children now who demand my complete attention.

I love my daughter. But I also love my son.

I stand rooted to the floor as the security guards and the hospital lawyer leave, as the police lead Edward into a day so bright I have to squint, and even then I lose sight of him too fast.

The automatic doors whisper like gossip as they close. I rummage in my purse and find my phone, so that I can call my husband. 'Joe,' I say when he answers. 'I need your help.'

Luke

An alpha female can choose a specific prey animal from a herd of hundreds by the smell it leaves behind. A moose with a scratch on its foreleg will leave behind the scent of pus with every footstep. The alpha reads this as vulnerability, and she can track it as if each footfall were a visible bread crumb. She can sniff at the tufts of grass the moose has fed upon and know, from the scent of its teeth, how old the animal is. Long before she ever comes into contact with this moose, she already knows volumes about it.

Eventually she stops focusing on the ground and instead breathes deeply into the air. The dust coming off the moose's coat leaves particles in the wind, so even from miles away, she will know this is still the same animal. She will start to run, her hunters keeping stride, and when she reaches the herd, she will hold herself back – she's far too valuable to put herself in danger – and signal a plan of attack to the others. There is a gland on a wolf's spinal area near the tail. To get a hunter to move right, the alpha will lift her tail up to the left, letting out a directional scent that her hunter can read. If she wants the hunter to speed up, she'll circle her tail. If she wants her hunter to slow down, she'll drop her tail. Through these tail postures, and her scent, she communicates with her team, directing them. Even if another moose is closer, the hunters will not strike until their leader gives them the signal, and even then, they will only take the animal she's pointed out.

An alpha will put two wolves in front of the moose's shoulders, and then listen for its heart rate. The moose may stamp or snort or throw its rack around to show how mighty a foe it is, but it can't affect its own adrenal system. When the alpha cues a third hunter to the back of the moose, and its heart skips a beat, she may instruct her team to terrorize it. This may take hours; it may take weeks.

It's not that wolves are cruel. It's that the alpha also knows, for example, that to the east is a rival pack that's bigger and stronger than her own. If this moose gets frightened, adrenaline will saturate its system – it's the emotional price of death. If her pack can then feed off that moose, those rivals to the east will smell the adrenaline in the urine and scat her pack leaves to mark the boundaries of the territory. And suddenly, her pack is less vulnerable. The wolves to the east would never come steal the food or kill the offspring of a pack whose scent is redolent with emotion, power, dominance.

In other words, what looks cruel and heartless from one angle might, from another, actually be the only way to protect your family.

Edward

Suffice it to say I was not the most popular kid in middle school. I was the quiet one, the brainiac who always got A's, the boy you only struck up a conversation with if you needed the answer to number 4 on your homework. At recess, I was more likely to be found in the shade reading than dunking on the basketball court. That was long before I discovered the benefits of circuit training, so my biceps back then were about as thick as rigatoni noodles. And obviously, I didn't stare after girls with skirts so short that their panties peeked out from behind – but every now and then, when no one was looking, I stared after the guys who were staring.

I had friends, but they were like me – kids who would far rather spend their days blending into the scenery than being noticed, because being noticed usually meant being the punch line to some popular kid's joke. Which is why, on my thirteenth birthday, I know I did the right thing, even though it wound up netting me a week of detention and a month of being grounded.

We were lining up to head to the cafeteria for lunch, and had to wait for other classes to march out first. I had this part of the day down to an art; I was never at the front of the line (popular kid territory) or the back of the line (troublemaker territory), because either spot would make me an easy target. Instead I sandwiched myself in the middle, between a girl who wore a full-body brace for her scoliosis and another girl who'd recently transferred from Guatemala and hardly spoke English. In other words, I was very busy making myself invisible when something awful happened: my teacher, who was old and sweet and fairly deaf, decided to pass the time by drawing attention to the fact that it was my birthday.

'Did you all know that today is Edward's thirteenth birthday?' Mrs. Stansbury said. 'Let's sing to him while we're waiting. Happy birthday to you . . .'

I turned crimson. We weren't five, after all. We were eighth graders. Having the class sing to you went out of vogue about the same time we stopped believing in the tooth fairy.

'Please stop,' I whispered.

'You going to do something special to celebrate?' my teacher continued.

'Yeah,' said one kid, loud enough for me to hear but not for the teacher to notice. 'He's going to have a gay old time, right, Eddie?'

Everyone laughed, except for the girl from Guatemala, who probably didn't understand.

Mrs. Stansbury peered into the hallway to see if it was our turn yet. Unfortunately, it wasn't. 'How old are you now,' she started singing. 'How old are you now! How old are you, Ed-waaaaard . . .'

I balled my hands into fists, and shouted, 'Shut *up!*'

That Mrs. Stansbury heard.

So did the principal, moments later. And my parents. I

was punished for being rude to a teacher, who was only trying to be nice to me by making me feel special on my birthday.

A month after my dad grounded me (as he put it in wolf terms, a subordinate would never act that way to a pack leader), he asked me if I'd learned anything. I made sure not to answer. Because I'd have done exactly the same thing all over again.

This is just my way of pointing out that we people who leap without looking are not stupid. We know damn well we might be headed for a fall. But we also know that, sometimes, it's the only way out.

The interrogation room is freezing cold. I'd cynically assume it's a secret police tactic to get people talking, if not for the fact that the officers have been really kind – bringing me coffee and a slice of sponge cake from the staff room. Many of them are fans of my dad's, from the TV show; I happily trade on his fame for food. I honestly can't remember the last time I ate; this tastes like manna.

'So, Edward,' the detective says, sitting down across from me. 'Why don't you tell me what happened today.'

I open up my mouth to respond, and then snap it shut. Years of *Law & Order* reruns on Thai TV have taught me something after all. 'I want my lawyer,' I announce.

The detective nods, and walks out of the room.

Never mind that I don't actually *have* a lawyer.

But a moment later the door opens again and a man walks in. He's small and wiry, with black hair that keeps falling into his eyes; he's wearing a suit and tie and carrying a briefcase. It takes me a moment to place him, because I only met him once – two days ago when he brought my mother's twins to see her at the hospital.

'Joe,' I breathe. I don't think I've ever been so happy to see someone. I had forgotten that my mom's new husband practiced law. I've done stupid, impulsive things before, but this is the first time I've been handcuffed for it.

'Your mother called me,' he says. 'What the hell happened?'

'I didn't shove the nurse, no matter what they say. She fell back when I . . .' I trail off.

'When you what?'

'When I pulled my father's ventilator plug out of the wall,' I finish.

Joe sinks into a chair. 'Do I even have to ask *why* . . . ?'

I shake my head. 'I was going to donate my dad's organs, which is what he wanted – he was a donor, according to his license. I just wanted to carry out his last wishes, you know? The doctors had barely started when Cara came in and made a huge scene. As if this was all about her, and not my dad.'

'From what Georgie's told me, Cara wasn't in favor of terminating life support. You had to know that.'

'She told me yesterday that she didn't want to have to deal with all this stuff anymore; that she couldn't talk to the doctors about my dad, much less make a decision about what to do. I wasn't trying to hurt anyone. I was trying to *help*—'

He holds up a hand, silencing me. 'What happened, exactly?'

'I bent down and grabbed the cord of the ventilator. I didn't push the nurse, she was just standing between me and the machine. All I did was pull the plug out of the wall to turn it off. Because that's what was *supposed* to happen.'

Joe doesn't ask me to explain myself. He just looks at the

facts and accepts them at face value. 'This is a bailable offense, a misdemeanor,' he says. 'In this state, if you've got no criminal record and you've got family around, you can be released on your own recognizance. Granted, you haven't been a resident for some time, but I think we can work around that.'

'So what happens?'

'I'll get a bail commissioner down here, and we'll take it one step at a time.'

I nod. 'Joe?' I say. 'I, um, don't really have any money to post bail.'

'You can pay off your debt by babysitting the twins so I can get reacquainted with my beautiful wife,' he replies. 'Seriously, Edward. Your job from here on in is to sit down, be quiet, and let me handle everything. No outbursts. No grand heroic efforts. Understand?'

I nod, but the truth is, I don't like to be beholden to anyone. I've been forging my own way for so long that it makes me feel totally vulnerable, as if I've suddenly found myself stark naked in the middle of a crowded street.

As he stands up to find an officer, I realize what it is that I like so much about Joe Ng. 'You're the first person who hasn't said how sorry you are that this happened to my father,' I muse aloud.

He pauses at the threshold of the door. 'The world knows your father as a brilliant conservationist and wildlife researcher. Well, I know him as the man who made Georgie's life hell and who threw away his marriage for a bunch of glorified dogs,' Joe says bluntly. 'I'm happy to be your lawyer. But I'm not doing it because of any great affection I have toward Luke Warren.'

For the first time in what feels like days, I smile. 'I can live with that,' I say.

The holding cell in the police station is very small and dark, and faces a wall with a few yellowing posters and an Agway calendar from 2005. I'm stuck here, waiting for a bail commissioner to arrive.

My father used to say that an animal will only feel like it is in captivity if its home feels not like a territorial boundary but instead like a cage. What's at stake is the lack of the natural world – not the fact that the space has been limited. After all, animals have their families with them – so the only thing you're changing, by putting wolves into captivity, is their ability to defend themselves. You're making them vulnerable the minute you put up the fence.

If you enrich their enclosures, though, a pack can be happy in captivity. If you play tapes of rival wolf packs howling, you force the males in the pack to bond together against this supposed threat. If you change their environment from time to time, or play multiple pack howls at once, the females have to think on their feet and make new decisions to keep the pack safe – should they divide the pack? Should they switch howls? Investigate around that new boulder? If you provide hunting enrichment, and avoid just sticking prey inside a fence (where it will be killed every time), you teach the wolves how to behave in the wild against a predator. If a wolf makes a kill once in every ten hunts in the wild, then in captivity you need to keep him guessing whether or not today's the day food's coming. Basically, a cage stops feeling like a cage when you can convince the wolf inside that he needs his family to survive.

When I hear footsteps, I stand up and grab the bars, expecting to be told the bail commissioner has finally arrived. Instead, I am assaulted by fumes of alcohol long before I see their source – a drunk man being held upright by an officer. He is weaving back and forth, red-faced and sweaty, and I am pretty sure that's a streak of vomit on his checkered flannel shirt. 'Brought you a roommate,' the officer says, and he opens the metal door so that the man staggers inside.

'Happy New Year,' the guy says, although it is February. Then he collapses facedown on the cement floor.

I gingerly step over him.

Once when I was around ten, I was sitting underneath the empty bleachers near the wolf enclosure at Redmond's. Each day at 1:00 p.m. my father gave a wolf talk there to the summer visitors, but the rest of the time, it was a cool spot to hide with a book in the otherwise overcrowded, overheated park. I was not really paying attention to my father, who was in an adjoining pen digging out a pond while the wolves were relegated to another section of the enclosure. Suddenly a guy named Lark, who worked with my dad as a caretaker before he hired Walter, came back from his lunch break. He was stumbling, weaving. As he walked past the wolves, they started to go berserk – hurling themselves against the fencing, snapping and whining, running back and forth the way they did when they could smell food coming.

My dad dropped his tools and ran for the gates, until he reached Lark and slammed him down on the floor. With his forearm against the man's throat, he growled, 'Have you been drinking?'

My father had firm rules for the people who worked with his animals – no perfumed shampoos or soaps, no deodorant.

And absolutely no alcohol. A wolf could smell it in your system days after you'd drunk it.

'Some guys took me out to celebrate,' Lark sputtered. He'd just had his first baby.

Gradually, the wolves calmed down. I'd never seen them act so crazy around a person, especially one of their keepers. If a human was being upsetting, like the annoying toddlers who waved and screamed from the security fence, the wolves would just lope into the rear of the enclosure, disappearing between the trees.

My father released his hold on Lark, who rolled away, coughing. 'You're fired,' he said.

Lark tried to argue, but my father just ignored him and walked back into the enclosure where he'd been working on the pond. I waited until Lark cursed a blue streak and stalked up the hill to the trailer to collect his belongings. Then I let myself through the safety gate and sat on the grass outside the enclosure where my father was working.

'I don't care that he had a few drinks,' he said bitterly, as if we had been in the middle of a conversation and he needed to defend himself. 'But he should know better than to do it on the job.' He dug his shovel into the ground and upended a heavy chunk of earth. 'Think about it. A drunk guy staggering around. What's that look like to you?'

'Uh . . . a drunk guy staggering around?' I said.

'Well, to a wolf, it looks a hell of a lot like a calf that's been wounded. And that triggers the prey drive. Didn't matter that the wolves know Lark, or work with him every day. The way he was moving was enough to make him lose his identity to the pack. They would have killed him, if they could have.'

He jabbed his shovel into the ground so that it stood upright like a soldier. 'It's a good life lesson, whether or not you ever work with wolves, Edward,' my father said. 'No matter what you do for someone – no matter if you feed him a bottle as a baby or curl up with him at night to keep him warm or give him food so he's not hungry – make one wrong move at the wrong moment, and you become someone unrecognizable.'

That comment, of course, would become personal years later. My father had made one wrong move at the wrong moment. I realize, with a start, that after this morning he might accuse me of the same.

The drunk at my feet begins to snore. A moment later, a police officer walks in. 'Showtime,' he says. I look up at the clock and realize I've spent three hours in here, most of it in the quicksand of memories about my father.

It just goes to show you: you can put nine thousand miles between you and another person. You can make a vow to never speak his name. You can surgically remove someone from your life.

And still, he'll haunt you.

We are back in the same interrogation room I was in before, except now, in addition to the detective and Joe, there's a guy with a very bad comb-over and eyes so red I would assume he was stoned if I didn't think that was particularly risky behavior for someone who routinely works in a police station. 'All right,' the bail commissioner says. 'I've got a doctor's appointment to get my conjunctivitis diagnosed, so let's make this snappy. What've you got, Leo?'

The detective hands him a piece of paper. 'This is a pretty

serious case, Ralph. It's not just second-degree assault; the accused also interfered with the duties of hospital personnel and adversely affected the health of a patient.'

What does that mean? I think. *Is my father worse off than he was before?*

'We're asking that bail be set at the amount of five thousand dollars with surety,' the detective finishes.

The bail commissioner reads the paper the detective has handed him. 'Pulled the *plug*?' he says, looking at Joe. 'Mr. Ng? What do you have to say?'

'This is my stepson we're talking about,' Joe begins. 'This is the town where he grew up, and he's surrounded by family and friends. He's got ties to the community, and no funds with which to flee. And I give you my word I will personally not let him out of my sight.'

The commissioner rubs his eyes. 'The purpose of bail is to secure the accused's attendance in court. We don't practice preventative detention in Beresford, Mr. Warren, so I'm going to set bail in the amount of five thousand dollars personal recognizance. You'll be released on your own promise to appear in court tomorrow morning, to keep the peace, and to be of good behavior. You won't be able to leave the state of New Hampshire while this matter is pending. I'm going to make it a condition of your release that you have a psychiatric evaluation, and I'm going to issue a no trespass order in and around the hospital.'

'Wait a second,' I say, already breaking my promise to Joe to be silent. 'That's not going to work. My father's in there, and he's dying—'

'Not quick enough for you, from the sound of it,' the detective says.

'I will not let my client be harassed,' Joe argues.

The bail commissioner holds up his hands. 'Shut up. Both of you. I've already got pinkeye; I don't need a migraine. You'll be arraigned tomorrow in district court.'

'What about my father?' I press.

That's when Joe stomps hard on my foot.

'What did you say, Mr. Warren?' the commissioner asks.

I look at him. 'Nothing,' I murmur. 'Nothing at all.'

Luke

A *kill is a scary place to be, six inches away from the snarling, snapping jaws of a wolf on the other side of you. It's feast or famine for wolves, and most of the time during a kill they haven't eaten for several days, so this is a battle for survival. If you move too far to the left or turn the wrong way, they'll let you know, growling and biting at you, and yet even in all that tremendous energy and frenzied excitement and hot anger, they pull their punch, so that the discipline you suffer isn't nearly what the prey animal has coming.*

Most of the time, the wolves knew I couldn't keep pace with them and would be more of a hassle during a hunt than an attribute. In a straight chase, I couldn't move fast enough; I didn't have the same weaponry to bring down prey, I couldn't even defend myself with my thin skin. But after the snows came, the hunting technique changed to an ambush. For the few months that two feet of snow covered the ground, I was not only invited to participate in the hunt, I was expected to be there.

In an ambush, the pack needs the weight of the big males. Sometimes they need a prey animal to turn and run into some brush, where other wolves jump out and surround it while the hunters make the kill. I was settled in a little bowl dug out of the snow with the youngsters in the pack and the alpha, waiting for the big black wolf and the other adult female to run the quarry toward us.

We had been waiting for days – not moving because we'd disturb the snow and tip off the prey. Even with wolves on either side of me, I was cold, and I started to occupy myself by letting my mind run wild. These wolves were masters of camouflage. They knew the wind direction, and how to disguise their scent. But was the deer working on instinct, too? Would it know, from years of ancestral experience, that if a wolf chases you like this at this speed in this formation, it's going to lead to an ambush rather than a straight chase? Would it know from some rogue change in the wind that there is trouble up ahead?

My thoughts abruptly scattered as the alpha started eating snow. The young male immediately followed her lead, burying his muzzle into the snow and chowing down. The young female reached up to a branch where an icicle was hanging like the ornament on a Christmas tree, and snapped it off between her teeth. She sucked on it like a lollipop.

Why on earth are they doing that? *I wondered. It wasn't anything I'd seen in the three days we'd been camped in this copse. Maybe the wolves just needed to move around a bit because we'd been in one place for so long. Maybe they were thirsty.*

But the wolves never had been skittish before, and since I wasn't thirsty, they probably weren't, either.

I was wondering if the deep snow was dehydrating them in some way when the alpha snapped silently at me and wrinkled her muzzle, then buried it in the snow again. I got the hint. I began scooping up handfuls of snow and eating it like there was no tomorrow.

Then it hit me: the only thing the prey animal could see as it ran toward us in our hiding spot was our frozen breath on the air. Holding snow and ice on our tongues meant that even our breath was invisible.

A moment later, a deer came crashing into the copse.

Somehow, the alpha had known that the ambush was imminent. But then again, what's the job of the alpha if not to hold the family together, so that, at the most crucial moment, its members all do as they're told?

Cara

I am expecting World War III when I get back home, and I'm not disappointed. My mother runs up to Mariah's car and starts to yank me out of the passenger seat, remembering too late that I've got an injured shoulder. I wince as she grabs my arm and see Mariah's silently mouthed *Good luck* as she zips away. 'You are grounded until you're . . . until you're *ninety*! For God's sake, Cara, where have you been?'

I can't tell my mom that. So instead, I look down at the ground. 'I'm sorry,' I say. 'After Edward did . . . you know . . . I had to get out of there. I couldn't stand it anymore, so I just ran. Mariah came to pick me up.'

My mother flips an internal switch, and suddenly she's hugging me so tightly I can't breathe. 'Oh, baby. I was so worried . . . By the time I got back upstairs, you were gone. Security looked everywhere. I didn't know if I should stay at the hospital or come back here . . .'

The front door opens, and the twins poke their heads out into the cold, reminding me (1) why my mother wound up here instead of the hospital and (2) why I should never believe I might actually come first in her list of priorities.

'Elizabeth, Jackson, get back inside before you catch pneumonia,' she orders. Then she turns to me again. 'Do you have any idea how frantic I've been? I even had the police out looking for you—'

'I bet you did. It would mean fewer cops focusing on Edward.'

My mother slaps me so fast I don't have time to see it coming. She's never done that to me in my life, and I think she's just as shocked as I am. I wrench away from her, holding my hand to my cheek. 'Go to your room, Cara,' she says, her voice trembling.

With tears in my eyes, I run away from her, into the house. Elizabeth and Jackson are sitting on the steps. 'You got a time-out,' Jackson says.

I stare at him and say, 'Remember when I told you there wasn't a monster in your closet? I was totally lying.' Then I step over their little bodies and head to my room, where I slam the door and throw myself facedown on the bed.

When I start to cry, I know it's not because my cheek stings – the humiliation hurt more than the slap. It's because I feel like the only person left in the world. I'm not part of this nuclear family; my own mother has taken sides with my brother; my father is floating somewhere I can't reach. I am truly, horribly on my own now which means I can't just sit around and wait for someone to fix things.

It is not that I think the hospital will try to turn off my father's life support again, even if Edward asks. It's that if I can't figure out a way to derail him, he's going to take the next step and get himself legally appointed as my dad's guardian – something I can't be, because I'm only seventeen.

But that doesn't mean I can't try.

Pulling myself together, I wipe my face on the gauze from my sling and sit up, cross-legged. I reach for my laptop and turn it on for the first time in a week, bypassing the sixteen million emails from Mariah asking me if I'm all right that she must have sent before she knew I was in the hospital.

I type some words into the search engine and click on the first name that pops up on my screen.

Kate Adamson, completely paralyzed in 1995 by a double brain stem stroke, was unable to even blink her eyes. Her medical staff removed Kate's feeding tube for eight days, before it was reinserted due to the intervention of her husband. Today, she is nearly completely recovered – still partially paralyzed on her left side, she has full control of her mental faculties, and is a motivational speaker.

I click on another link.

A victim of a car crash believed to be in a persistent vegetative state for 23 years, Rom Houben was actually conscious the entire time and unable to communicate. Doctors had originally used the Glasgow coma test to assess his eye, verbal, and motor responses and to describe his condition as unrecoverable, but in 2006, new scans were developed that suggested his brain was functioning fully. He now communicates via computer. 'Medical advances caught up with him,' says his physician, Dr. Laureys, who believes that many patients are misdiagnosed in vegetative states.

And another:

Carrie Coons, an 86-year-old from New York, was in a vegetative state for over a year. A judge granted her family's wish to remove her feeding tube. However, she regained consciousness unexpectedly, ate food by mouth, and conversed with others. Her case raises the question of how reliable a diagnosis of irreversible consciousness is – and legally, raises questions about when life-sustaining treatment should be discontinued.

I start to bookmark the documents. I'll make a PowerPoint presentation, and I'll go back to Danny Boyle's office and prove to him why what Edward did is no different than holding a gun to my father's head.

When my cell phone rings – it's plugged in and happily recharging – I reach for it, assuming it's Mariah asking me if I've been flayed alive by my mom. The caller ID, though, is a number I don't recognize. 'Please hold for the county attorney,' Paula's voice says, and a moment later, Danny Boyle is on the line.

'You really want to do this?' he says.

I think of poor Kate Adamson and Rom Houben and Carrie Coons. 'Yes,' I tell him.

'Tomorrow the grand jury's convening in Plymouth. I want you to come to the courthouse so I can put you on the witness stand.'

I have no idea how I'm supposed to get all the way back to Plymouth. I can't ask Mariah to miss school again. I don't have a car, I'm virtually crippled, and oh, right, I'm also grounded.

'Is there any chance you'd be passing by Beresford on your way to Plymouth?' I ask as politely as possible.

'For the love of God,' Danny Boyle says. 'Can't your parents drive you?'

'My mother's tied up doing everything in her power to make sure my brother's not going to be sent to jail. And I wish my father could drive me. But he's too busy fighting for his life in Beresford Memorial Hospital right now.'

There is a beat of silence. 'What's the address?' he asks.

Joe doesn't come home that night. It turns out that the only way to keep Edward out of jail is to make sure he's supervised, and wisely, Joe didn't think it was a particularly good idea to bring my brother back here in close proximity with me. It's weird that Joe and my mom wouldn't just switch places, so that my mom would be living in her old home with Edward, if only for one night. But then again, Joe thinks my mom is the reason the sun comes up in the morning, and he would do anything to make sure she doesn't have to set foot in that house again, and face all those memories of my father.

It also means that the next morning, when Danny Boyle comes to get me, my mom is down at the end of the block with the twins waiting for their school bus, and completely unaware that the snazzy silver BMW that zips by her and around the corner is about to pull into her very own driveway.

I get into Danny Boyle's car, and he looks at me. 'What the hell are you wearing?'

Immediately, I realize I've made a mistake. I wanted to look nice for court – I mean, aren't you supposed to? – but the fanciest dresses I have are the strapless one I wore to my spring formal and a hot pink, shoulder-padded number

I was forced to wear at Joe's sister's Bring Back the '80s theme wedding. My mother had insisted on hemming it to the knee, so that I could wear it again, although the only place I could ever imagine wearing something like that again is at a *Saved by the Bell* reunion costume party.

'You look like a Pat Benatar fan club refugee,' Danny says.

'Very good guess,' I reply, impressed. I buckle my seat belt and shade my face with my hand as we drive by my mother at the bus stop.

'I take it your mother has no idea you're doing this today,' Danny says.

My guess is that my mother will be too busy championing my brother, wherever he is, to even notice I've left the confines of my room.

'Here's what you need to understand,' he continues. 'You're the one who wants this to be a murder charge, and that means it has to meet all three criteria. Malice, premeditation, and intent to kill. We don't have to prove those to a grand jury, but we have to be able to point to the dots so that they can connect them. If you don't have all three dots, it's not murder. Do you understand what I'm telling you?'

I look at him. It's not what he's *saying*, it's what he's *not* saying that's important. 'I'll do whatever you need me to do as long as it keeps my father alive.'

He glances at me and nods, satisfied.

'Can I ask you something?' I say. 'What made you change your mind?'

'I got a call from my sister yesterday. She was all upset because of something that happened at work.' He flexes his hand on the steering wheel. 'Turns out a man went nuts in his dad's hospital room – the same hospital room where she was stationed at the ventilator.' He glances at me. 'She's the nurse your brother shoved out of the way.'

I guess I'm expecting a richly paneled courtroom, with a high bench that has a white-haired judge presiding. I'm pretty surprised to find out that, instead, a grand jury is a small clot of ordinary people in jeans and sweaters sitting around a table in a room with no windows.

Immediately I try to pull my sweater over my too-fancy pink dress.

There's a tape recorder on the table, which makes me even more nervous, but I focus on Danny Boyle's face, just like he told me to do. 'This is Cara Warren,' he announces to the little group. 'Does anyone know the witness?'

The people clustered around the table shake their heads. One, a woman with a blond pageboy that angles toward her chin, reminds me of one of my teachers. She stands up and holds out a Bible. 'Can you raise your right hand . . . ,' she says, before she realizes my right arm is in a sling. There is a bit of uneasy laughter around the table. 'Can you raise your *left* hand and repeat after me . . .'

This part is just like on television: I swear to tell the truth, the whole truth, and nothing but the truth, so help me God.

'Cara,' Danny says, 'state your name and address, please.'

'Cara Warren. Forty-six Statler Hill, Beresford, New Hampshire,' I answer.

'Who do you live with?'

'My dad. Until a week ago.'

The county attorney gestures at me. 'We can see that you've got your arm in a sling – what happened?'

'My father and I were in a serious car accident a week

ago,' I explain. 'I broke my scapula. My dad's been unconscious since then.'

'In a coma?'

'A vegetative state, that's what the doctors call it.'

'Do you have any other family?'

'My mom – she's remarried now. And my brother, who I
haven't seen in six years. He lives in Thailand, but when my
dad got hurt, my mom called him up and he came back
home.'

'What's your relationship with your brother?' Danny asks.

'What relationship,' I say flatly. 'He left and he didn't want
to talk to any of us after that.'

'How long has your father been in the hospital?'

'Eight days.'

'What is the doctors' prognosis for your father?'

'It's too early to tell anything,' I say. Because really, isn't
it?

'Have you and your brother discussed your father's situation?'

All of a sudden my stomach feels as empty as a pocket.
'Yes,' I say, and even though I don't want to, I can feel my
eyes welling with tears. 'My brother just wants this to be
over. He thinks the outcome isn't going to change. But me,
I want to keep my dad alive long enough to prove him wrong.'

'Has your father contacted your brother during the six
years he's been in Thailand?'

'No,' I say.

'Does he ever talk about your brother?'

'No. They had a big fight, which is why my brother left.'

'Have you been in touch with your brother, Cara?' Danny
asks.

'No.' I look at one of the members of the jury. She is shaking her head. I wonder if she's reacting to Edward leaving, or to me not contacting him.

'Now,' the county attorney says, 'yesterday you told me about something very upsetting.'

'Yes.'

'Can you tell the ladies and gentlemen of the grand jury what happened?'

Danny and I had practiced this in the car. Sixteen times, actually. 'My brother made a decision to terminate my father's life support – without asking for my opinion. I found out by accident, and ran downstairs to my father's hospital room.' I can hear, as clearly as if it's happening now, the alarm that sounded as my brother pulled that plug. 'There were doctors and nurses and a lawyer from the hospital and other people I didn't recognize, all gathered around my father's bed. My brother was there, too. I yelled at them to stop, to not kill my father – and everyone backed away. Everyone except my brother, anyway. He bent down, pretending like he was catching his breath, and he yanked the plug of the ventilator out of the wall.'

I hesitate, looking around the table. The faces of the jurors might as well be balloons, they are that smooth and unemotional. I suddenly remember what Danny said in the car, about the three criteria of murder. Premeditation, intent to kill, and malice. It's clear that my brother had planned this, or all those doctors and nurses wouldn't have been convened. It's equally clear that he wanted to kill my father. It's malice that's the sticking point.

I think about being sworn to tell the truth, the whole truth, nothing but the truth. But then again, it wasn't like I raised my right hand. I *couldn't*, logistically. So maybe the way I was sworn in is the equivalent of crossing your fingers behind your back when you tell your mom a white lie – that you've brushed your teeth, that you walked the dog, that you didn't put the empty milk carton back in the fridge.

It's not really a lie, is it, if the ends justify the means? If, because of it, my father has a chance to get better? By the time everyone finds out I embellished the truth, I will have bought my father a few more hours, a few more days.

'He yanked the plug out of the wall,' I repeat, 'and he yelled, "Die, you bastard!"'

At that, one of the jurors covers her mouth with her hand, as if *she* was the one who said it.

'Someone tackled him,' I continue. 'And the nurse plugged in the ventilator again. The doctors are still figuring out how much damage was done while my father was without oxygen.'

'Is it fair to say that your brother and father had a very contentious relationship?'

'Totally,' I say.

'Do you know why, Cara?'

I shake my head. 'I know they had a huge fight when I was eleven. It was bad enough to make Edward pack up and leave and never talk to him again.'

'When your brother called your father a bastard, he was angry, wasn't he?'

I nod. 'Yes.'

'There's no question in your mind that he intended to kill your father, is there?' Danny asks.

I glance directly at him. 'No. And there's no question in my mind that if he has the chance, he'll do it all over again.'

Luke

In captivity, a wolf might live for eleven or twelve years, although I've heard of some living even longer than that. In the wild, though, a wolf would be lucky to make it to age six. The level of experience and knowledge in a wolf is irreplaceable, which is why the alpha will stay in the den near the young most of the time, sending other pack members out to do patrols, to hunt, to safeguard. This is also why, when an alpha gets taken down, so many packs fall apart. It is as if the central nervous system has suddenly lost its brain.

So what happens when an alpha is killed?

You might think that there is promoting from within – that maybe the beta, the number two man, will fill his former boss's shoes. But in the wolf world, that's not how it happens. In the wild, recruiting would start. A call would go out to lone wolves, letting them know there is a vacancy in the pack. The candidates would be challenged to make sure that the one chosen is the smartest, surest, and most capable of protecting the family.

In captivity, of course, recruiting like that can't happen. Instead, a mid- or low-ranking animal that is by nature suspicious and shy finds itself in the decision-making role. Which is a disaster.

From time to time you'll see documentaries about low-ranked wolves who somehow rise to the top of the pack – an omega that earns a position as an alpha. Frankly, I don't buy it. I think that, in actuality, those documentary makers have misidentified the wolf in the first place. For example, an alpha personality, to the man on the street, is usually considered bold and take-charge and forceful. In the wolf world, though, that describes the beta rank. Likewise, an omega wolf – a bottom-ranking, timid, nervous animal – can often be confused with a wolf who hangs behind the others, wary, protecting himself, trying to figure out the Big Picture.

Or in other words: There are no fairy tales in the wild, no Cinderella stories. The lowly wolf that seems to rise to the top of the pack was really an alpha all along.

Edward

When I come into the kitchen, where Joe is standing at the counter eating a bowl of cereal and flipping through the high school sports section of the newspaper, he glances up at me. 'Is *that* what you were planning on wearing?' he says, in the tone of someone who had something completely different in mind.

I've never really paid much attention to clothes; I'm not the stereotypical gay man in that respect. I'm perfectly happy wearing the jeans I've had since high school and a sweatshirt so old that it's threadbare in the elbows. Of course, I had starched shirts and ties for my teaching assignments, but they are somewhere between here and Chiang Mai in a box, I imagine. Given that I flew to New Hampshire on a moment's notice, with only a small carry-on bag, my sartorial choices are pretty limited. 'Sorry,' I say. 'When I was packing, I didn't realize I'd need a good courtroom look.'

'Do you at least have a collared shirt?'

I nod. 'But it's denim.'

Joe sighs. 'Come with me.'

He puts down his bowl and walks out of the kitchen, heading upstairs to my father's bedroom. I realize too late what his intention is. 'Don't bother,' I say, as Joe begins to rustle through my father's closet. 'He didn't even own a tie when I was growing up.'

But Joe reaches into the bowels of the closet and pulls out a white dress shirt, pressed and still hanging in its plastic dry cleaning bag. 'Put this on,' he orders. 'You can borrow one of my ties. I keep an extra in the trunk of my car.'

'It's going to be huge on me. My dad's built like the Hulk.'

Joe flinches almost imperceptibly. 'Yeah, I'd noticed.'

He leaves me so that he can go get the tie. I sit down on the bed, trying to keep myself from giving this moment more symbolism than it is due. As a boy I never felt like I measured up to my father – who was larger than life, literally and figuratively. Putting on his shirt will be like a little kid playing dress-up, pretending to fill shoes that arc too big for me.

I rip open the plastic and begin to unbutton the shirt. When did my father start wearing stuff like this, anyway? I cannot remember a moment in my life when he wasn't wearing flannel, thermals, coveralls, battered boots. You don't dress for success when you're spending 24/7 in a wolf pen; you wear whatever will give you protection against nips and scratches and mud and rain. Had he changed in the time I'd been away, enough to be able to acclimate himself to the world of people as seamlessly as he blended into the company of wolves? Did he go to wine bars, to poetry slams, to theater?

Is the father I kept imagining in my mind, on an endless home-video loop, now someone different?

And if he is, can I really be sure that what he said to me over a shot of whisky when I was fifteen was still what he believed?

Yes, I tell myself. It has to be, because I can't let myself face the alternative.

I pull my sweatshirt over my head and shrug into my father's shirt. The cotton is cool on my skin, wings settling over my back. I button the placket and then slip my hand into the starched breast pocket, peeling open the starched skin of the fabric.

When I was really tiny, my father had a red and black buffalo check wool jacket that he used to wear to work. It had two breast pockets, and whenever he came home, he'd tell me to choose a pocket. If I picked the right one and reached inside, I'd find a piece of penny candy. It took me years to realize there were no right and wrong pockets. They both had candy; I couldn't help but be a winner.

I turn around on impulse and look in my father's closet to find that jacket. At first I think it's not there, and then I find it hanging behind a pair of ripped Carhartt coveralls.

I notice my reflection in the mirror that is glued to the back of the closet door. To my surprise, the shirt isn't big on me at all. I fill out the shoulders, and the arms are exactly the length I'd choose if I were buying this for myself. With a start I realize that, now, I could easily pass for my father, with my features and my height.

I reach for the buffalo plaid jacket and put it on, too.

'It's a statement,' Joe argues, the same argument he's made since I walked downstairs wearing my father's coat. 'And in court, you don't want to do anything to get a judge riled up.'

'It's a coat, not a statement,' I say. 'It's freaking fifteen degrees out. And this is New Hampshire. You can't tell me every defendant wears Armani.'

Before we can bicker any further, the sheriff walks into the courtroom. 'Hear ye, hear ye, hear ye, all rise!' He faces the gallery. 'All those having business before the district court shall now join near, give their attendance, and they shall be heard. The Honorable Nettie McGrue presiding!'

The judge is a tiny bird of a woman with a cap of frighteningly yellow hair and a sharp, pointed nose. Her judicial robe has a profusion of lace at the collar that makes me think of a rabid, frothing dog. 'Counsel,' she says, 'I will take any formal matters that are scheduled for arraignment.'

Beside me, Joe stands. 'Your Honor, I'm ready in the matter of Edward Warren.'

'Mr. Warren, come forward,' the judge says, as Joe hauls me upright. 'Clerk, arraign the defendant.'

We walk to the front of the courtroom, and I give my name and address – well, I give my father's address, anyway. 'Mr. Warren,' the judge says, 'I see you're represented by counsel . . . Would Counsel identify himself for the record?'

'Joe Ng, Your Honor.'

'Mr. Warren, you're before the court having been charged by complaint with second-degree assault against Maureen Cullen, a nurse at Beresford Memorial Hospital. What say you to this charge?'

My fingers curl around the cuff of my father's jacket. 'I'm not guilty, Your Honor.'

'I see bail was set at five thousand dollars personal recognizance. The defendant, having appeared here voluntarily, is released on the same recognizance. Mr. Warren, I'm going to set the same bail conditions that were set by the bail commissioner: you are ordered to have a psychiatric evaluation, and there's a no contact order with your father, and a no trespass order with Beresford Memorial Hospital.' She fixes her bright, black eyes on me. 'You realize that if you fail to have the evaluation performed within the next ten days, or if you go to the hospital to see your father, you could be brought back and held without bail at the county jail pending a hearing? Do you understand the terms and conditions of your release?'

She asks me to raise my right hand and swear that I'll be back here in ten days for a probable cause hearing, whatever that is.

'Next matter,' the judge says, and then it's over.

The whole procedure takes about two minutes, tops.

'That's it?' I say to Joe.

'Would you prefer it to drag on longer?' He pulls me out of the courtroom.

I follow him through the parking lot to his car.

'Now what?' I ask, my words shifting shape in the cold. I stamp my feet while he unlocks the door.

'Now you do what the judge said. You get your psychiatric evaluation and you sit tight while I try to figure out how to get this case thrown out.' He turns on the ignition and backs out of his spot. 'I'll drive you back to your father's—'

He is interrupted by a blast of Queen's 'Bohemian Rhapsody.' Startled, I fiddle with the radio to turn it down, but it isn't even switched on. 'Joe Ng,' he announces out loud, to nobody.

Then I hear another voice, broadcast through the hands-free phone system. 'Joe? This is Danny Boyle, the county attorney.'

'Danny,' Joe says, wary. 'What can I do for you?'

'Actually, it's the other way around. Your stepson was indicted today for the attempted murder of his father—'

'What the *hell*?' I burst out.

Joe punches me in the arm. 'Sorry. Let me turn down the radio here,' he says, and he shoots me a deathly look and puts his finger to his lips: *silence.* 'I think you might have that charge wrong,' Joe continues. 'He was arraigned for second-degree assault.'

'Well, Joe' – the other voice is smooth, oily – 'I have the indictment sitting right here in my hand. This was a professional courtesy call, to be frank. Instead of having him picked up, I thought you might prefer to surrender him to the police department.'

'Yes,' Joe replies. 'I'll bring him in. Thanks for the call.' He pushes a button on his steering wheel, disconnecting the call, and looks at me. 'You,' he says, 'are in deep shit.'

'I wasn't trying to kill my father,' I insist, as Joe drains his cup of coffee in a single gulp, then holds it out to the diner waitress to refill. 'Well, I mean, I *was,* but not because I wanted him dead. Because it's what *he* wanted.'

'And you know this how?'

I fumble in my coat pocket for the letter I signed for my father – but then realize it's in my sweatshirt back home. 'I have a note he signed, giving me the power to make medical decisions for him if he wasn't capable of making them,' I say. 'He told me if he was ever in a condition like this, he wouldn't want to be kept alive.'

At this, Joe raises his brows. 'When did he sign this note?'

'When I was fifteen,' I admit, and Joe buries his face in his hands.

'I'm going to work this out,' he promises, 'but you have to tell me exactly what happened yesterday.'

'I already have—'

'Tell me again.'

I draw in my breath. I tell him about the meeting at Cara's bedside, how the neurosurgeon and the ICU doctor both said my father wasn't going to recover, and that we would have to make some choices about his health care. I tell him how Cara went ballistic, how the nurse shooed everyone out. 'Cara said she couldn't do this,' I explain. 'She couldn't keep listening to all these doctors telling her there wasn't any hope. So I told her I'd take care of everything. And I did.'

'So she never actually *said* that she wanted you to terminate your father's life support . . .'

'Of course not. Neither of us *wanted* it. Who *would*, when it means someone in your family is going to die? But Cara couldn't face the fact that my father isn't ever going to *live* again, either.' I shake my head. 'There is no miracle around the corner, if we give it a week or a month or a year. It is what it is. And that sucks, but it means our options are sticking him in a nursing home forever or terminating life support, and either one of those choices is something Cara doesn't want to make. I may not have been around much when she was growing up, but I'm still her big brother, and I'm supposed to be the one who protects her – from bullies, and from crappy boyfriends, and from horrible situations like this. That's why I decided I'd make the call. That way, she didn't have to carry around that little bit of guilt for the rest of her life.'

'But *you* would,' Joe says.

I look up at him. 'Yeah.'

'So what did you do?'

'I talked to my father's surgeon. I wanted to make sure that what he was really saying was that my dad wasn't coming back. Ever. I told him I wanted to talk to the organ donation people.'

'Why?'

'My dad's license says he wanted to be a donor,' I say. 'So I met with them, and signed all the forms, and they scheduled everything to happen the next morning.'

'Why didn't you go back and talk to Cara about this?'

'She was sedated. That's how upset she got after the doctors told her there wasn't a chance in hell for my father.' I shrug. 'You can ask my mother if you don't believe me.'

'Then what happened?'

'At nine, I was in my father's hospital room with a couple of nurses and the hospital lawyer and the neurosurgeon, and the ICU doctor asked where Cara was. Next thing I know, she bursts into the room screaming that I'm trying to kill my father.' I pick up my fork, toying with it. 'The hospital lawyer told everyone to step back, that this couldn't continue as planned. But all I could think was, *I can't let this drag on anymore.* It wasn't going to get any easier, no matter how long we waited, whether or not Cara wanted to admit it. So I bent down and pulled the plug of the ventilator out of the wall.' I glance at Joe. 'I bumped into the nurse when I reached for the plug, but I didn't shove her.'

'The nurse is the least of your worries now,' Joe says. 'Did you say anything when you pulled out the plug?'

I shake my head. 'I don't think so.'

'Did you ever do anything that might have made people think you were angry at your father?'

I hesitate. 'Not *yesterday.*'

He leans back in the booth. 'Here's the deal. The state has to prove beyond a reasonable doubt that you intended to kill your father, that you thought about it in advance, and that you wanted to do it with malice. You clearly wanted to hasten your father's death. Premeditation counts, even if you thought about it only seconds before you acted. So the sticking point here – the one we can use to hang our hat on – is malice.'

'You know what's malicious? Keeping someone alive with machines,' I argue. 'How come it's okay to prolong life artificially, but not to let someone die by getting rid of all those special measures?'

'I don't know, Edward, but I don't really have time to argue the philosophy of euthanasia right now,' Joe says. 'What happened after you pulled the plug?'

'I got tackled by an orderly, and then security came and brought me to the lobby. The cops picked me up.'

I watch Joe take a pen from his pocket and scribble something on a napkin. 'So here's our spin: this isn't murder, it's mercy.'

'Exactly.'

'I'll need you to get me that letter your father signed,' he says.

'It's at the house.'

'I'll pick it up later.'

'Why not now?' I ask.

'Because I'm going to talk to everyone else who was in that hospital room.' Joe slaps a twenty-dollar bill down on the table. 'And you,' he says, 'are going to the police station.'

The bail commissioner is the same one I met yesterday. 'You know, Mr. Warren,' he says, 'you don't get frequent flyer miles for coming back.'

It is like a massive déjà vu, with another criminal complaint being handed to the commissioner, another detective with his arms crossed, and Joe by my side. The commissioner reads over the charge, but this time, I can tell, he's surprised.

'Attempted murder is a very serious offense,' he says. 'And it's your second arrest in as many days. This one's out of my comfort zone, Mr. Warren. I'm setting bail at five hundred thousand dollars.'

'*What?*' Joe explodes out of his seat. 'That's astronomical!'

'Take it up tomorrow with the judge,' the commissioner says.

Joe turns to the cop in the room. 'Can I have a moment with my client?'

The bail commissioner and the detective finish up and leave us alone in the interrogation room. Joe shakes his head. I'm sure he's wishing he wasn't married to someone whose baggage includes a son like me, who can't seem to stay out of trouble.

'Don't worry,' he says. 'When you go to superior court for your arraignment, the judge will never hold you to those bail guidelines.'

'But what do we do in the meantime?'

'We need fifty thousand dollars to post bail,' Joe explains, looking down at the floor. 'And, Edward, I just don't have that kind of money available.'

'I don't understand.'

'It means,' he says, 'that you have to spend the weekend in jail.'

If you had told me a week ago that I'd be in a New Hampshire county correctional facility, I would have told you that you were insane. In fact, I had believed that by now, my father would be on the mend, and I'd be on a plane back to my students in Chiang Mai.

Life has a way of kicking you in the teeth, though.

The correctional officer who's processing my information types with one finger. You'd think that since this is his job, he'd be better at it by now. Or he would have taken a keyboarding course. He is so slow that I wonder if I will spend any time in a cell, or if I will still be sitting here when they come to get me for the arraignment.

'Empty your pockets,' he tells me.

I take out my wallet, which has thirty-three U.S. dollars in it and a smattering of *baht*, the key to my father's house, and the rental car keys.

'Will I get this stuff back?' I ask.

'If you get released,' the officer says. 'Otherwise, the money will be set up in an account for your pending trial.'

I cannot even let myself think about that. This is a misunderstanding, that's all, and tomorrow Joe will make the judge see that.

But there are doubts that keep running across my mind like shadows in an alley. If this weren't serious, why would the bail have been set so high? If this weren't serious, why would the county attorney himself have been the one who called Joe to tell him I'd been indicted? If this weren't serious, why would I have been driven to the county jail in the back of a sheriff's car?

I am no expert on law, that's for sure. But I know enough of the basics to understand that while the hospital might have filed the complaint that got me charged with assault, the state would have to be the one to file criminal charges for murder.

How could the county attorney even have *heard* so quickly about what happened?

Someone told him.

It would not have been the doctors, who – let's face it – were crystal clear in explaining my father's bleak prognosis. It would not have been the hospital lawyer, who (if all had gone according to plan) would welcome the turnover of the bed for a patient they could actually help. It wouldn't have been the organ donation coordinator, because that would be counterproductive for her organization.

Which leaves one of the nurses, possibly. I'd met all sorts coming in and out of my father's room. Some were funny, some were kind, some brought me snacks, and others brought me prayer cards. I guess it's possible that someone conservative who believed in the sanctity of life at all costs might become a nurse to preserve that gift – and that terminating life support would morally upset her, even if it were part of her job description. Add to that Cara's outburst and—

Suddenly, I trip over my own thoughts. *Cara.*

For all I know, she sold me out. After all, who'd pick an alleged murderer to be someone's legal guardian?

I find myself shivering, even though the heat has been cranked up to approximately the eighth circle of Hell in here. I fold my arms, hoping I can hide it.

'You got a hearing problem?' the officer yells, standing over me. I realize I have not been listening to a thing he's been saying.

'No. I'm sorry.'

'This way.'

He leads me into a tiny, airless room. 'Get undressed,' he demands.

I don't have to tell you the stereotypes about gay men and jail. But when he says that, I cannot pretend this isn't real and happening anymore. I, who have never even returned a library book late, now have a criminal record. I am about to be strip-searched. I will be locked in a cage with someone who actually *deserves* to be here. 'You mean, like, in front of you?'

'Oh!' the officer says, widening his eyes in mock horror. 'I'm so sorry! You must have booked the private cabana with the beach view. Unfortunately, that package isn't available right now.' He folds his arms. 'I can, however, offer you this choice: *You* can take your clothes off, or I can take them off for you.'

Immediately my hands go to the belt of my pants. I fumble with the zipper and turn my back to the officer. I unzip my father's jacket, unbutton my father's shirt. Then my socks and finally my boxer briefs. He picks up each item of clothing and inspects it. 'Face me and raise your arms,' the officer says, and I do, closing my eyes. I can feel his eyes on me, like a minesweep. He snaps on a pair of latex gloves and lifts up my testicles. 'Turn around and bend over,' he instructs, and when I do I can feel him moving my legs apart, probing.

Once at a bar in Bangkok I met a man who was a prison guard. He'd kept us all in stitches with stories of inmates rubbing themselves with their own feces – which the guards called self-tanning – of one guy who dove from the top bunk into his toilet as if it were a swimming pool, of the booty they found during body cavity searches: shanks, soda cans, screwdrivers, pencils, keys, baggies of heroin, once even a live sparrow. 'But the female inmates,' he had said. 'They're the ones you gotta watch. They could smuggle in a *toaster.*' At the time I'd thought it was hilarious.

I don't, now.

The officer snaps off the gloves and tosses them in a trash can. Then he hands me a laundry sack. Inside are blue scrubs, some T-shirts, underwear, shower shoes, a towel. 'This is a complimentary gift from the manager on duty,' he says. 'If you have any questions, you can call the front desk.' He starts laughing, as if this is actually funny.

I am taken to a nurse, who checks my blood pressure and my eyes and ears and sticks a thermometer in my mouth. When she leans down to listen to my lungs with a stethoscope, I whisper in her ear. 'There's been a mistake,' I murmur.

'Beg pardon?'

I look around to make sure that the door is closed and that we are alone. 'I don't belong here.'

She pats my arm. 'You and me both, sweetheart,' she says.

She turns me over to a different officer, who marches me into the belly of this jail. There are double gates at several steps, manned on both sides by people in control towers, who slide the doors open and closed in sequence. When we step through one of the portals, the officer reaches into a bin and hands me another laundry sack. 'Sheets, blankets, and a pillowcase,' he says. 'Laundry's every two weeks.'

'I'm only here for the weekend,' I explain.

He doesn't even look at me. 'Whatever you say.'

We are on a catwalk, with metal that clangs every time I put down my foot. The cells are on one side. Each has a bunk bed, a sink, a toilet, a television with a plastic casing so that you can see its guts. The inmates we pass are mostly asleep. The ones who are awake whistle or call out as I walk by.

Fresh meat, I hear.

Lone Wolf

Ooh, we got us a baby.

I find myself thinking of my father, instructing me as I approached the wolf enclosure for the first time: *They can tell if your heart rate goes up, so don't let them know you're afraid.* I keep my eyes straight ahead. My watch has been confiscated, but surely it's already late afternoon; it is only a matter of hours before I can leave.

And again, I hear my father's voice. *It's hard for me to describe what it was like, locking myself inside the enclosure that first time. At the beginning, all that existed was pure panic.*

'Vern,' the officer says, and he stops in front of a cell that has one inmate inside. 'Got a roommate for you. This is Edward.' He unlocks the door and waits for me to move peacefully inside.

I wonder if anyone has ever just absolutely refused. Hung back, clawed at the iron bars, hurled himself over the catwalk's railing.

When the door is locked behind me again, I look at the man sitting on the bottom bunk. He has a buzz of red hair and a beard with food caught in it. One of his eyes bounces and veers to the left, as if it's not tethered inside his head. He has tattoos on every inch of skin I can see – including his face – and his fists look like Christmas hams. 'Fuck,' he says. 'They brought me a faggot.'

I freeze, holding the bag with my sheets and towels. Which is all the confirmation he needs.

'You try to suck my cock in the middle of the night and I swear I'll cut your balls off with a butter knife,' he says.

'That won't be a problem.' I move as far away from him as possible (not easy, in a space that is six feet by eight feet)

242

and climb into the upper bunk. I don't bother to make the bed. Instead I lie down and look at the ceiling.

'What are you in for?' Vern asks after a minute.

I consider telling him I'm waiting to be arraigned for murder. Maybe it will make me seem tougher, like someone who should be left alone. But instead I say, 'The free food.'

Vern snorts. 'It's cool. I get it. You don't want anyone knowing your business.'

'I'm not trying to be an enigma—'

'Yeah, damn straight you're not sticking some hose up my ass—'

It takes me a minute to figure that one out. 'Not an *enema*,' I say. 'And I'm not hiding anything. It's that I don't belong here.'

'Shit, Eddie,' Vern says, laughing. 'None of us do.'

I turn to my side and put the pillow over my head so I don't have to hear him anymore. *It's just a few nights*, I tell myself again. *Anyone can survive a few nights.*

But what if it isn't? What if Joe isn't able to make all this go away, and I have to wait here for six months or a year until we go to trial? What if, God forbid, I wind up convicted of attempted murder? I couldn't live like this, in a cage.

I'm afraid to close my eyes, even after the lights go out hours later. But eventually I fall asleep, and when I do, I dream of my father. I dream he's in a jail cell, and I am the only one with the key.

I reach into my pocket to get it, but there's a hole in the lining of my pants, and no matter how hard I search, I can't find it.

Luke

I once saw a wolf commit murder.

   There was a lone wolf that kept crossing the boundaries of the other packs and poaching off the livestock from farms in the area. No matter how many times my pack warned him off through howling, he wouldn't stay away. It wasn't my decision to act upon, however, but rather the alpha female's. Every time this wolf was near our territory, tension rose. The wolves in my pack would fight with each other. At night, other packs would call, telling him to get lost.

   One day, the big black wolf – the beta rank – disappeared on a patrol with the other female. That in and of itself was not unusual; it was his job within the pack. However, this time, he didn't return. Four days passed . . . five . . . six. I started to worry – to believe he was gone for good – and then the female came back alone, confirming my fears. That night, our pack howled, but it wasn't a location call. It was pain, wrapped in the skin of a single note. It was what we did, when we wanted to sing someone home to us.

I have been on the receiving end of that call. In the forest you have no direction, so when this constant vocal tone comes out of nowhere like the beacon of a lighthouse, it gives you a direction to follow, to tell you where your pack is waiting. But the beta didn't turn up. Three nights of calling, and he never answered.

I was sure he had been killed.

Then one night, when we howled, there was an answer. Not from the black wolf but from the lone wolf who'd been such a hassle to our pack.

The alpha continued to call to him. Far be it from me to question her motives, but I imagined this would be a disaster. Here she was advertising the vacancy in the pack, inviting him to join, and he would be nothing but a nuisance.

Eventually the calls of this lone wolf came closer, and he approached the pack. Everyone was on guard; after all, this was an unknown quantity for the family, and the first meeting would feel like an awkward dance, the beginning of an arranged marriage. No sooner had he loped into the clearing where we were waiting for him, however, than the big black beta wolf barreled out of the cover of the forest and ambushed him. Immediately the other female and the young male leaped forward to help fight.

The lone wolf was dead within seconds. Lying still on the ground, he had the look of a cross between a feral dog and a wild animal, which would explain his bad behavior. The beta was surrounded by the rest of our pack, which licked at his

muzzle and rubbed against him in solidarity, in welcome.

I don't think I'm reading human emotion into what happened that day when I say it was a coordinated attack. For the pack to intentionally create a ruse, where the beta was sent off to lie in wait – in silence – in order to lure the lone wolf closer; for the beta to wait for the lone wolf to be drawn out from his cover, so that he could be taken down with the help of the rest of the waiting pack – well, it was premeditated, and malicious, and very, very necessary at the moment to keep the family safe.

You call it murder.

A wolf might call it opportunity.

Cara

I used to wonder about prisoners who had been given a life sentence. What if one has a heart attack and is pronounced dead and resuscitated by doctors? Does that mean he's served his time? Or is that why, sometimes, sentences are written for two or three life terms?

The reason I'm asking is because I'm currently grounded until I'm 198.

My mother, of course, had returned home from the bus stop to find me missing. I couldn't very well let her know I was en route to the grand jury in Plymouth, so I had left her a very passionate note about how it was killing me to know my dad was alone in the hospital, so Mariah was going to drive me there for a visit, but that I promised not to overtax myself and she shouldn't feel that she had to come down and sit with me since she hadn't seen the twins for a week, thanks to my shoulder surgery, yadda yadda yadda. I figured compassion would trump fury, and I was right: how can you be mad at a kid who sneaks off to visit her hospitalized father?

If Danny Boyle thinks it's weird that I ask him to drop me off at the end of my block so I can walk the rest of the way without my mother asking about the strange Beemer that dropped me off, he doesn't say anything. My mother, actually, gives me a careful hug when I come in and apologizes for yelling at me the night before and asks, 'How's he doing?'

For a second I think she's talking about the county attorney.

Then I remember my fake alibi. 'No change,' I say.

She follows me into the kitchen, where I start to open and close cabinet doors in search of a glass. 'Cara,' my mother says, 'I want you to know that this is your home, forever, if you want it to be.'

I know she means well, but my home is across town – complete with a ratty couch that has indentations on it in the spots where my father and I tend to sit. My home has natural shampoos and shaving cream so that the wolves aren't assaulted by perfume when my father is working with them. My home has a single bathroom with two toothbrushes: pink for me, blue for my dad. Here, I have to rifle through six different drawers before I find what I'm looking for. Home is the place where you know where the silverware lives, where the cups hide, where the clean plates go.

I run the water in the faucet so that I can get myself a drink. 'Um,' I say, embarrassed. 'Thanks.'

I try to imagine a life where I have to constantly expect a little pest hiding under my bed to scare the hell out of me, where I have a curfew, where I am given a list of chores instead of made an equal partner in the household. I try to imagine a life without my dad. He may be an unorthodox parent, but he's still the one that fits me best. You remember the controversy when Michael Jackson dangled his kid over a railing? I bet no one asked the kid how he felt about it.

Probably he was delighted, because to him the safest place in the world was his dad's arms.

I hear a door slam, and a moment later Joe comes into the kitchen. He looks rumpled and pretty distracted, but my mother acts like it's Colin Farrell. 'You're home early!' she says. 'I hope that means you got that ridiculous charge against Edward thrown out—'

'Georgie,' he interrupts, 'I think you'd better sit down.'

My mother's features freeze. I turn my back to the sink again, dumping out my water and refilling it, wishing I wasn't caught in the web of this conversation.

'I got a call from the county attorney,' Joe explains. 'They've amended the charge against Edward from assault to attempted murder.'

'What?' my mother says, stunned.

'I'm not sure where the push is coming from. It could be political – he's built a platform on being pro-life and this is an election year and could net him the vote of every conservative in the state. He may be grandstanding, and Edward's just the fall guy.' Joe looks up at my mother. 'You were in the hospital room when it all happened. Did Edward say or do anything that could have been publicly interpreted as malice?'

Yes, I think. *He tried to* kill *my father.*

'I . . . I can't remember. It was very fast. One minute the hospital attorney was saying the procedure would be canceled, and the next, there was an alarm and an orderly grabbing Edward . . .' She faces me. 'Cara, did he say anything?'

He said *nothing*. And that's the whole point they're missing. He didn't ask me first if it was okay to kill off our father; he didn't care at all that I objected completely. 'I think

I need to go lie down,' I reply, dumping my water into the sink for a second time.

My mother sits down at the kitchen table. 'Where is Edward now?'

Joe hesitates. 'He has to spend the weekend in jail. His arraignment's on Monday morning.'

I guess I didn't think about the fact that actions have consequences, that what I did might mean my brother is stuck in a cell. That he might wind up there for years. I'd wanted him somewhere out of the way, so that I could get the doctors to listen exclusively to me, but I hadn't considered where that somewhere would actually be.

When I said I needed to lie down, I was just making up an excuse, so that I could get out of the kitchen before Joe realized I was the one to blame for my brother's situation. But now, I think I actually may *have* to lie down.

Because I'm the one responsible for breaking up this family.

For making my mother cry.

For not listening to anyone else's reason but my own.

Which means that everything I've accused my brother of doing in the past, I've just done myself.

Luke

*Y*ou can be evicted from a pack.

     I've seen both sides. There are wolves that are highly respected for their knowledge and their experience, who may fall sick or lame and will be nursed back to health by the entire pack. They will have food brought to them, they will be kept warm, the pace will be adapted to accommodate them until they are well again.

    I've also seen wolves who know they are no longer any use to the pack get that sidelong look from the alpha. This may be because of illness; it may be because of age. And maybe on the next patrol, or the next hunt, they will choose to intentionally slip away. Lie down beneath a copse of trees. Let go.

Joe

The thirty-second television ad for my law practice shows me stern and focused in front of my desk, my arms folded. *Joe Ng*, a voice-over announces, the guttural stop of my last name ringing through the speakers. 'The name stands for Not Guilty,' I say, and there's the sound of a gavel being struck.

Yeah, it's cheesy. And Ng of course doesn't really stand for Not Guilty, but I don't mind it when law clerks high-five me and call me that. I am the first kid in my family to go to college, much less law school. My father was a Cambodian fisherman and my mother a seamstress, and they moved to Lowell, Massachusetts, just before I was born. Me, I was the golden boy, the American dream swaddled in disposable diapers.

I have been lucky my whole life. I was born at 9:09, on 9/9, and everyone knows that nine is a lucky number in Cambodia. My mother tells a story about how, when I was a toddler, she found me holding a snake in the backyard, and never mind that it was a common garter snake, the fact that I could kill such a creature with my chubby bare hands surely meant that I was special. My father is convinced that the reason I made law review was not because I had straight

A's but because he had prayed to Ganesha to remove all obstacles from my rise to greatness.

Like everyone else in America, I remember when Luke Warren stumbled out of the forest looking like some sort of missing link, and terrified a group of Catholic schoolgirls whose bus stopped for a lunch break at a highway rest stop along the St. Lawrence River. I watched the interviews he did with Katie Couric and Anderson Cooper and Oprah. I probably even skimmed the profile of him in *People* magazine, which had a picture of Georgie in it, sitting with Luke on the front steps of a house he hardly ever slept in, their kids flanking them like bookends.

Still, when Georgie came into my office in Beresford asking if I could represent her in the divorce, I didn't recognize her by name or by face. I just thought that, even after I'd paid an interior designer named Swag fifty thousand dollars to give my office feng shui, it wasn't until Georgie walked through the door that anything really looked like it belonged there.

The divorce was a nonevent; all Luke wanted was shared custody and some crappy trailer on the grounds of Redmond's Trading Post. I managed to get Georgie a portion of the proceeds he'd earned doing the Animal Planet specials on wolf behavior, too. I called her Ms. Warren, and was a hundred percent professional, until the day the divorce decree was handed down. And then I called her cell phone and asked if she wanted to go out sometime.

I didn't really believe that someone who had fallen in love with Luke Warren would ever even look twice at a guy like me. It's not that I'm a hideous beast or anything, but I am certainly not the kind of fellow who'd be a dead ringer for the bare-chested heroes sculpted onto romance novel covers. I have a little bald spot that I try to ignore, and at five six, I'm a half inch shorter than Georgie. But she didn't seem to care.

I have to admit, every night before I go to bed I wing a little prayer to Luke Warren. Because if he hadn't been such an asshole, I might never have looked so good to Georgie by comparison.

Something is bugging the crap out of me.

Even though Georgie manages to hold it together through dinner, I know she's thinking about Edward. She begs off reading the twins *One Fish Two Fish* and instead says she has a headache. She goes up to our bedroom, but even with the door closed, I can hear her crying.

After the kids are tucked in, I knock on Cara's door. The lights are out, but I can hear music playing. When I come in I find her sitting on the bed with her laptop open. She immediately clams it shut. 'What?' she asks, challenging.

I shake my head. There's a very fine ethical line I'm skating here, as Edward's attorney, even if he happens to be related to my stepdaughter. Technically I shouldn't be here, much less asking her about the circumstances that led to Edward's arrest.

'Just wanted to make sure you're feeling okay,' I say. 'The shoulder doesn't hurt?'

She shrugs. 'I'm tough.'

This I know. I had to work hard to break through her defenses when Georgie and I were first a couple. She was convinced that I was after the money I had won in the divorce settlement for Georgie. It was because of Cara that I actually drew up a prenuptial agreement – not to protect her mother from me but to reassure the daughter that I was in this for the right reasons.

'You know I can't talk to you about what happened at the hospital, Cara. But if you volunteer the information, that's a different story.' I hesitate. 'You might actually be able to save your brother.'

Her eyes shutter, suddenly dark and unreadable. 'I have no idea why Danny Boyle decided to pick Edward for a witch hunt,' Cara says.

I hesitate, my hand on the doorknob. 'Maybe I'll go over his head to Lynch,' I muse out loud.

'Who?'

I look at her and shake my head. 'Nobody.'

But as I pull the door shut again, I think how incredibly normal it would be for a modern teenage girl to have no idea that John Lynch is the governor of New Hampshire.

Which makes it even more odd that, without me mentioning it first, she referred to the county attorney by his given name.

That night I place a phone call to Danny Boyle and arrange to meet with him first thing in the morning.

It's only 7:30, and since it is Saturday, Boyle's secretary isn't in the office. He meets me with his hair still wet and a faint odor of chlorine clinging to his skin. 'Whatever you have to say, Joe,' he tells me, leading me back to his office, 'you can say in front of the judge.'

He gestures to a seat, but I stand. I pick up one of the framed photos on his desk. A girl about Cara's age smiles back at me, her cheeks flushed with sun. 'You got kids?' I ask.

'No,' he says, rolling his eyes. 'I keep pictures of random young girls on my desk just for the hell of it. Come on, Joe. I don't really have time to shoot the breeze right now, and neither should you.'

'I have twins. And two stepkids, too,' I say, as if he hasn't spoken. 'And the thing is, this whole nightmare is just eating away at my family. My wife's practically torn in two, and I don't know what to say to her. I don't know how to make this right, without hurting someone else.' I look up at him. 'I'm appealing to you not as a lawyer, but as a father and a husband. I need my discovery before this arraignment happens.'

'The grand jury was sitting *yesterday*,' Boyle says. 'I'll get you the transcript as soon as I can.'

'You could give me the recording of the proceedings *now*,' I reply.

The county attorney looks at me for a long moment, and then reaches into his desk drawer and passes over a CD. 'Family's everything,' he says. 'That's why I'm giving this to you.' I grab the disc and head out of his office. 'And Joe?' he calls after me. 'That's also why this charge is gonna stick.'

I hurry out to my car and listen to the CD on the stereo system. There's some discussion with the grand jury; and Danny's voice, asking the witness his first question.

And then, clear as a bell, I hear Cara answer.

It goes without saying that the security guards running the metal detector at the entrance to the jail do a double take when they see me, a forty-six-year-old lawyer, carrying a briefcase in one hand and a toy Sing-A-Long Karaoke player in the other. I can't exactly carry a car stereo into the building, and the CD drive on my computer is broken, and I need Edward to hear this. I was weighing the location of the nearest Best Buy and the cost of a crappy boom box when I spied the toy we got Elizabeth for Christmas, sitting in the backseat. You pop in the karaoke CD, and the kid grabs the attached microphone and starts to sing along to Yo Gabba Gabba! or the Wiggles.

I feel like a moron, but it works. I put the brightly colored, chunky plastic toy on the conveyor belt and empty my pockets of change and electronics. The security guard who waves me through snickers. 'Now, Luther,' I say genially. 'I know for a fact that I'm not the only closet Hannah Montana fan.'

Edward has already been brought to a client-attorney meeting room. When I walk inside, I do a quick assessment: I know Georgie will ask me how he's fared overnight.

His eyes are bloodshot, which isn't extraordinary – I wouldn't imagine he'd sleep well in jail. But he's clearly jittery, on edge. 'Joe,' he says, the minute we are alone, 'you have to get me out. I can't stay in there. My cellmate is the poster child for the Aryan Brotherhood.'

'I'm going to do my best,' I promise. 'There's something you need to hear.'

I set the CD player on the table between us and hit the Play button. Edward cocks his head closer to the speaker. 'What is this?'

'The grand jury proceedings.' I hesitate. 'The witness is Cara.'

Edward pushes the Pause button. 'My sister sold me out?'

'I don't know how she got to the county attorney. Or why he decided to listen to her. But yes, it seems that she's the connection.'

'When I get out of here, I'm going to kill her,' Edward mutters.

Immediately I grab his arm. 'If you say anything like that again, I can pretty much promise you that you'll be shacking up with Hitler Junior for a long time. This isn't a joke, Edward. The cops say so during the arrest: *Everything you say can and will be used against you.* And something you said in that hospital room, even if you didn't mean it, must have been enough for the county attorney to think he could convict you.'

I hit the Pause button again, and the CD starts. Edward's mouth twitches; he's angry, but he's managing to control himself. Which is a damn good lesson to learn before he steps into the courtroom.

Cara's voice sounds younger than it does in person. *I yelled at them to stop*, she says. *To not kill my father – and everyone backed away. Everyone except my brother, anyway. He bent down, pretending like he was catching his breath, and he yanked the plug of the ventilator out of the wall.* She hesitates. *He yelled,* Die, you bastard!

Edward jumps up from his seat. 'That's a lie! I never said that! I told you what happened, and that wasn't it. Ask anyone else who was in the room!'

I intend to. But even if Cara lied under oath, the real question is whether Boyle knew she was lying.

To say it is a tense weekend at the Ng household would be an understatement. Georgie is on edge, thinking of her son rotting in a jail cell – even though I have assured her he'll survive. Cara has locked herself in her room, unwilling to face her mother's wrath. Even the twins are cranky and out of sorts, picking up on the tension in the air. Me, I've made the decision to *not* tell Georgie – or Cara – that I know Cara was the one to testify against her brother. Part of this is because my allegiance is to my client, Edward. And part of this is because I have a strong self-preservation instinct and don't want the shit to hit the fan until Edward's arraignment is done.

For all these reasons, I've never been so happy for Monday to roll around. I'm parked in the superior courthouse lot before they even open the building for business. The first tip I have that this is no ordinary criminal arraignment is that the courtroom is crowded. Usually, the only people who show up for arraignments are the defendants and their lawyers, and occasionally, a stringer for a local paper who has to cover the courtroom beat and list the names of those who were accused of beating their wives or stealing televisions or breaking into cars. Today, however, there are cameras rolling in the back, and I have a sinking feeling they're here for Edward. And that it was Danny Boyle, who needs media attention the way plants need sunlight, who has tipped them off.

Our case is the third arraignment of the day. 'State of New Hampshire versus Edward Warren,' the clerk calls, and Edward is brought up from the underground maze of the courthouse. He looks like he hasn't slept in a week. He sits next to me, his foot jiggling nervously. At the table beside us is Danny Boyle, who has changed into a suit with a shirt so starched the collar and cuffs could probably cut through steak. He sits almost sideways, so that the cameras will catch his profile and not the back of his head.

He smiles at me. 'Always good to see you, Joe,' he says,

although prior to our Saturday morning discussion, I had only met him once at a bar association dinner.

'Same,' I reply. 'And let me commend you on your choice of tie. I hear red looks great on camera.'

I don't do many criminal arraignments. Let's face it, New Hampshire isn't a bastion of depravity; my cases tend toward civil suits or custody battles, not attempted murder. So I have to admit that even if I'm not showing it visibly like Edward is, I'm just as nervous.

The judge is a small man with a runner's build and a handlebar mustache. 'Mr. Warren, please rise,' he says. 'I have before me indictment 558 from the grand jury that charges you with one count of attempted murder on Luke Warren. What say you to this indictment?'

Edward clears his throat. 'I'm not guilty.'

'I see your attorney has already entered an appearance on your behalf. I'd like to hear the parties. Mr. Boyle, what's your position on bail?'

The county attorney stands up and frowns gravely. 'Your Honor, this is a very serious case,' he says. 'There are strong elements of premeditation, of expressed intent, of malice. This was a plan devised by someone with intense animosity toward Luke Warren, who is fighting for his life in a hospital and unable to defend himself right now. We fear that Mr. Warren's estranged son will attempt this again, and further-more, we feel that his presence in the community presents a danger. He's been gone for the past six years and has had no contact with his family, Judge. There's nothing to keep him from leaving the country before trial.'

The judge scratches his cheek. 'Mr. Ng, what do you have to say?'

'Your Honor,' I begin, 'my client came home immediately when he found out about his father's tragic accident. If he really harbored any ill will toward his father, would he have jumped on a plane? Would he have spent the past week at his father's bedside?'

I am pretty sure I hear Danny Boyle comment under his breath, 'Waiting to make his move . . .'

'Edward Warren came here because of the love and concern he has for his father's well-being. He has no animosity toward his father; he only wishes to carry out his father's wishes – as he was asked by Luke Warren to do. There's no motive, there's no financial gain for Edward if his father dies. If Mr. Boyle is concerned about Edward being a flight risk, we are happy to surrender his passport, and we have no objection to him reporting weekly for probation, or to any other conditions the court might set.'

'Your Honor,' Boyle says, 'we'd ask that the court take into consideration that there are those who need to be protected against Edward Warren's rages – most notably Luke Warren and his daughter, Cara.'

The judge looks at me, and then at Boyle. 'I'm releasing the defendant on fifty thousand dollars surety, with the conditions that he surrender his passport, have a psychiatric evaluation and no contact with his father or sister. He'll report to the probation department every Thursday. Next?'

As the clerk calls the next set of attorneys in front of the judge, I stand up. 'Sorry you didn't get what you want, Danny,' I say. 'Especially considering you brought your audience with you.'

He snaps shut his briefcase and shrugs. 'See you in court, Joe,' he replies.

Fifteen minutes later, I've signed all the paperwork necessary to have Edward released. He has buried himself in his father's buffalo plaid jacket and keeps zipping and unzipping it like it's some kind of relaxation technique. 'So where do we go now?'

'*We* don't go anywhere. *I* go,' I say, as we turn the corner.

Danny Boyle is standing in the lobby, holding court with six or seven television reporters. 'It's not up to us to decide what kind of life is worth living,' he says, grandstanding. 'You think Helen Keller's parents felt her existence wasn't worth the trouble? Or how about Stephen Hawking's family? Life is precious, period. And you can go all the way back to the Bible to know that taking the life of another before his time is an injustice and an abomination. *Thou shalt not kill,*' Boyle quotes. 'Can't get any clearer than that.'

Edward stares for a moment. 'So it's okay to let doctors help people who shouldn't live, live,' he calls out, 'but not to help people who should be dead die?'

The reporters pivot, the heavy heads of the cameras swiveling to catch Edward. 'Shut *up,*' I say, grabbing his arm.

But he's bigger and stronger, and shakes me off. 'How many of you have taken an old, sick pet to the vet to be put down, because you don't want them to suffer? You think that's murder, too?'

'Edward, *stop talking,*' I yell. I pull him with all my might in the other direction, away from Danny Boyle, who is grinning from ear to ear.

And why shouldn't he be; Edward's just compared his father to a dog.

Although I am tempted to lock Edward in a closet so that he cannot dig himself a deeper hole, I settle for a blistering lecture the whole way back to his father's house, and a promise that I will duct-tape his mouth the next time we're in public if I have to. Then I drive to the hospital, calling Georgie to let her know that Edward's out on bail and safe, for the time being.

Dr. Saint-Clare is in surgery, I'm told when I go to his office. So I get a cup of coffee and park myself in front of the ICU nurses' desk. 'Hi there,' I say, grinning at a woman with curves as broad as the Great Wall of China. 'You look like a woman who's in charge.'

She glances up over her computer screen. 'And you look like a pharmaceutical rep. You can leave samples in the closet.'

'Actually, I'm a lawyer,' I say.

'My condolences.'

'I'm trying to find the nurse who was involved in Thursday's . . . incident? There's a chance she could wind up with some monetary compensation in a settlement—'

'Figures. Maureen gets all the luck. I'm stuck with the chronic vomiter in 22B while she gets bumped into and cries whiplash.' The nurse points down the hall to another woman wearing scrubs, and stuffing soiled linens into a hamper. 'That's her.'

I walk down the hall until I reach her. 'Maureen?' I say. 'My name's Joe Ng. I'm an attorney.'

'Oh, for the love of Pete,' she sighs. 'I suppose my brother sent you?'

Her brother probably heard what happened and saw dollar signs. It's guys like that who make my living possible.

'Yes,' I lie.

'I really shouldn't be talking to you. The hospital's sure it's going to be slammed with a lawsuit,' Maureen says, shaking her head. 'But that poor man. He's only here for six days, and the son makes the decision to terminate life support?'

'From what I understand, Mr. Warren's prognosis isn't very good . . .'

'Miracles happen,' Maureen says. 'I see it every day.'

'What exactly went on in there?'

'The son signed the papers for organ donation, and the harvest was scheduled. We all thought he'd gotten consent from his sister. She's a minor, so technically, she doesn't get a legal vote, but the policy is to get the whole family on board before terminating life-sustaining measures. When the hospital lawyer realized that wasn't the case, they went to talk to her.'

'Where were you during all this?'

'Sitting in front of the ventilator,' she says, lifting her chin. 'I don't necessarily agree with the decisions some families make, but it's still my job to do what I'm told.'

'What was Mr. Warren's son doing?'

'Waiting,' she says. 'With the rest of us. He wasn't talking. It was a difficult moment for him, as you can imagine.'

'And then?'

'The girl came in like a bat out of you-know-where. And before I knew what was going on, the son pushed past me and yanked the plug out of the wall.'

'What did he say?'

'Nothing.' Maureen shrugs. 'It happened very fast.'

'You never heard him say "Die, you bastard"?'

She snorts. 'I think I'd remember something like that.'

'Are you sure you didn't miss what he said because he pushed you out of the way?'

'He bruised my hip, not my ears,' she says. 'Look, I have to get back to work. And anyway, I told my brother all of this last week.'

'Your brother?'

'Yes.' She rolls her eyes. 'Danny Boyle? The one who sent you here?'

Danny Boyle, I am told, is taking a deposition and cannot meet me without an appointment. 'Oh, he wants to see me,' I insist, and I walk past the secretary, opening doors until I find the one that is a conference room. Boyle is sitting across from an attorney and a client, and when he notices me, he looks like he's going to burst into flame.

'I'm a little busy right now,' he says, his voice serrated.

By now the secretary has caught up to me. 'I tried to tell him, but—'

I smile beatifically. 'I think it's really in Attorney Boyle's best interests to hear what I have to say,' I announce. 'Considering my next stop is the press.'

Boyle flattens his mouth into a two-dimensional smile. 'Excuse me a moment?' he says to his client, and he leads the way toward his office. Dismissing his secretary, he closes the door behind us. 'This better be fucking important, Ng, because I swear I will have the bar slap you with misconduct if you—'

'You are in serious trouble, Danny,' I interrupt. '*Die, you bastard*? Really?'

He shrugs. 'That's what she told me. She testified under oath.'

'Here's what I know: You spoke to your sister and you knew damn well Edward had never said anything even remotely like that. So you intentionally allowed perjured testimony into the grand jury proceeding. You may think a high-profile case like this will get you the conservative vote and settle you back into office before your chair even gets cold, but most people in this county prefer knowing that their attorney is honest and upright, not a weasel who's willing to twist the law in order to gain a political advantage.'

'The girl came to *me*,' Boyle says. 'Not the other way around. I'm not the one to blame here if she's an outright liar.'

I take a step toward him and poke him in the chest, even though I'm a full head shorter than he is. 'Did you ever hear of due diligence, Danny? Did you speak to any of Luke Warren's doctors to find out whether Cara really understood her father's prognosis? Did you ask anyone else who was in the hospital room – anyone who isn't a blood relative of yours, that is – if there was intent or malice? Or did you just choose to believe a seventeen-year-old kid who's distraught and desperate to keep her father alive?'

Taking my phone out of my pocket, I hold it up between us. 'I've got the *Union Leader* on speed dial, and you're going to be above the fold tomorrow morning unless you do something right now.' Then I sit down in his office chair. 'In fact, I'm going to wait right here until I know you've done it.'

He gives me a dirty look and then crosses to his desk, pressing the speakerphone button before dialing one of his contacts. To my surprise, though, the voice on the other end of the line is not that of the editor of the biggest newspaper in New Hampshire but one I recognize. 'Cara,' Boyle says when she answers her cell phone, 'it's Daniel Boyle.'

'Is something wrong?' she replies.

'No . . . I just have a really important question to ask you.'

There's a beat of silence. 'Um. Okay.'

'Did you lie to the grand jury?'

Her voice comes back in a flood of words. 'You told me I needed to make them believe it was premeditated and that Edward intended to kill my father and that there was malice, too, so I did what I needed to do. I didn't lie, I just said what you told me to say.'

Boyle's face goes white. It's a beautiful thing, really.

'I didn't tell you to say anything. You swore under oath—'

'Well, technically I didn't. My right arm's in a sling.'

'Are you admitting, Cara, that your brother never actually said, *Die, you bastard*, in your father's hospital room?'

She is quiet for a heartbeat. 'If he didn't say it,' she finally mutters, 'I know he was thinking it.'

I lean back in Boyle's chair and put my feet up on his desk.

'You fight all the time for people you don't even know; this is my father's life we're talking about,' Cara adds. 'Imagine how I felt? I didn't have any choice.'

Boyle briefly closes his eyes. 'This is a real problem, Cara. This indictment came about under false circumstances. I never have participated and never will participate in any fraud . . . and I would never support perjury,' he grandstands. 'You misunderstood me. I realize you're upset right now, and you probably weren't thinking straight, but I'm going to make this indictment go away before either one of us suffers any greater embarrassment.'

'Wait!' Cara cries. 'What am I supposed to do about my father?'

'That's a civil matter,' Boyle says, and he hangs up the phone.

I swing my legs down. 'Since you're in the middle of a deposition, I'll let you send me a cell phone photo of the dismissal form you're going to file in court before the end of the day. Oh, and Danny?' I walk past him, smiling broadly. 'That assault charge against my client is going to disappear, too.'

When I first met Cara, she was twelve and angry at the world. Her parents had split up, her brother was gone, and her mom was infatuated with some guy who was missing vowels in his unpronounceable last name. So I did what any other man in that situation would do: I came armed with gifts. I bought her things that I thought a twelve-year-old would love: a poster of Taylor Lautner, a Miley Cyrus CD, nail polish that glowed in the dark. 'I can't wait for the next Twilight movie,' I babbled, when I presented her with the gifts in front of Georgie. 'My favorite song on the CD is "If We Were a Movie." And I almost went with glitter nail polish, but the salesperson said this is much cooler, especially with Halloween coming up.'

Cara looked at her mother and said, without any judgment, 'I think your boyfriend is gay.'

After that, she made herself scarce whenever I visited Georgie or came to take her mother out on a date. When Georgie and I decided to get married, though, I knew that I had to connect with Cara somehow. So one morning, I presented Georgie with a surprise trip to a day spa, and then I straightened up her kitchen and started cooking the Cambodian food my mother used to make for me.

Let's just say if you haven't experienced *prahok* in your lifetime, you might want to keep it that way. It's a staple in the Cambodian diet, one of those you-wouldn't-understand-unless-you-grew-up-with-it foods, like Marmite or gefilte fish. My mother used it at every meal as a dipping sauce, but that morning, I was frying it in banana leaves as a main dish.

It didn't take long before Cara stumbled into the kitchen in her pajamas, her hair a mess and her eyes still swollen with sleep. 'Did something *die* in here?' she asked.

'This,' I announced, 'is a good home-cooked Cambodian meal, for your information.'

She raised a brow. 'Well, it smells like butt.'

'Actually, what you're smelling is fermented fish paste. On the other hand, durian smells like butt,' I said. 'It's a fruit Cambodians eat. I wonder if they sell them at Whole Foods . . .'

Cara shuddered. 'Yeah. Next to the rotten whale meat, probably.'

'Some things,' I told her, 'are an acquired taste.'

I had been talking about the *prahok* but also about me. As a stepfather, as a partner for her mother – maybe I was an addition to the family that would grow on her.

'Just try it,' I urged.

'I'd rather die,' Cara told me.

'I was afraid you might say that,' I replied. 'Which is why I made this, too.' I opened up a wok and used tongs to serve her some *mee kola*, a noodle dish that I'd never seen a kid turn away from.

She picked at the crushed peanuts on top, and stuck her finger into the sauce. 'This,' she conceded, 'is decent.' And she proceeded to eat three full bowls, while I sat down across from her with the dreaded *prahok*. While we ate, I asked her questions – gently, the way I approached traumatized witnesses. Cara told me that some kids in her class only wanted to be her friend because her father was famous on television, and that it was easier to be alone than to try to guess someone's motivations for sharing their Thin Mint cookies with you at lunch. She talked about a teacher who had made a mistake on an answer grid for a test, and how unfair it was that she still marked students wrong. She said she desperately wanted a cell phone but her mom thought she was still too young. She said she secretly thought the Jonas Brothers had been sent by aliens to judge the reactions of humankind. She told me that she could take or leave ice cream, but that if she were told she would never be able to eat another Twizzler in her life, she would probably kill herself.

Cara left the kitchen thinking she'd had breakfast. But as I rinsed the dishes and pots and pans, I knew that what she'd really had was a conversation.

After Georgie and I got married and moved into our house, I'd get up on Sunday morning and I'd start cooking. *Amok trei, ka tieu.* I'd make desserts like *sankya lapov* and *ansom chek.* Georgie would sleep in, but Cara would get up and pad into the kitchen. We'd talk while she worked beside me, cutting up papaya or ginger-root or cucumbers. Then we'd sit at the kitchen table and devour our creations. As she grew older, our discussions changed. Sometimes she complained to me about a punishment Georgie had lobbed at her, hoping I would intercede. Sometimes she turned the topic to me – asking what it was like to grow up first-generation American, or how I knew I wanted to be a lawyer, or if I was nervous about having twins. After Georgie had the kids, and even after Cara moved out to live with her father, if she was visiting us over the weekend as part of the custodial arrangement, I always knew to set out a second plate for her on Sunday mornings.

Which is why, when I get back to the house and am filling Georgie in on the turn of events, I start cooking. I haven't gone to the Asian grocery in a while, so I have to make do with the ingredients we have in the fridge. 'So he's free?' Georgie says to me. 'Like, really truly free?'

'Yup,' I reply, and squint into the bowels of the refrigerator. 'Didn't we have some stew meat?'

Suddenly I am pulled backward by my wife, who's grabbed me around the neck to kiss me. 'I love you,' she says against my lips. 'You are my superhero.'

I hold her tight, kiss her like I'm never going to get to kiss her again. I'd like to say I'm an optimist, but I keep waiting for the other shoe to drop, for Georgie to tell me she's made a mistake and is leaving me. When things are this good, I have to believe that they can't last.

Case in point: I need to tell her the reason Edward wound up indicted for attempted murder in the first place. 'Georgie,' I confess. 'Cara is the one who testified against Edward.'

She shakes her head a little, as if she has to clear it. 'That's ridiculous. She's been here or at the hospital, not at the grand jury.'

'Were you the one to take her to the hospital?'

'No, but—'

'Then how do you know it's where she actually went?'

Georgie's mouth tightens. 'She would never do that to her brother.'

'She would if she thought it would save her father,' I argue.

I know Georgie will not fight me on this one. If Luke Warren is larger than life for most people who know of him, he's absolutely mythic to Cara.

'I'm going to kill her,' Georgie says calmly. 'And then I'm going to ask her what the hell she was thinking.'

'You might want to reverse the order,' I suggest. I pour oil into the wok and turn up the flame beneath it; then with a sizzle and a flash of steam, I toss the beef cubes and vegetables in. The room fills with the smells of onions and pepper.

She sits down on a kitchen stool, rubbing her temples. 'Does Edward know?'

'Does Edward know what?' Cara says, suddenly standing in the doorway, her face stricken. 'Did something happen to Dad?'

Georgie stares at her, her features rigid. 'I don't even know what to say to you right now. You know how you feel about losing your father? Like a piece of you would be missing? That's how I've felt, every day, since your brother left home. Now he's back, and you try to get rid of him by getting him charged with attempted murder?'

Cara's face flushes. 'He started it,' she says.

'You are not seven years old! This isn't about who broke a lamp!' Georgie cries.

'He would have killed Dad if I hadn't found out what he was doing in time to stop it,' Cara answers. 'I'm seventeen and three-quarters, and no one gives a crap,' she says. 'My vote still doesn't count. So you tell me how else I was supposed to get everyone's attention.'

'Maybe by acting like a grown-up, instead of a spoiled brat with a grudge,' Georgie argues. 'If that's what people see, they'll treat you like one.'

'You're criticizing *my* behavior?' Cara laughs, incredulous. 'You know what I see? I see Edward, who's been pissed off at Dad for six years. I see the doctors, who would rather have a new patient who can pay the hospital bills. I see that you wish deep down I was the kid who disappeared, and not Edward.' She swipes at her eyes with the back of her free hand. 'But you know what I don't see? Anyone who gives a shit about me or my father.'

'Do you really think I don't love you? Or Luke, for that matter?'

I can't help it. Chopping lettuce and tomatoes, I flinch.

'You've got your perfect little family now,' Cara says bitterly. 'I'm just here till you pull the plug, right?'

Georgie reels back. 'That's not fair,' she replies. 'I've never chosen between you and the twins.'

'But you *did* choose between me and Edward, didn't you,' Cara says flatly. 'You followed him downstairs at the hospital. You made excuses for him. You got him a lawyer.'

'I love him, Cara. I'm doing what I *have* to do for him.'

Cara folds her arms. 'I'm doing what I have to do for Dad.'

There is a long silence. Then Georgie comes forward and pushes Cara's hair out of her eyes. 'I'm not making excuses for your brother, and I don't love him more than I love you. But Edward doesn't want to kill your father. He just wants to let him die. There's a difference, Cara, even though you won't let yourself see it.'

She slips out of the kitchen, and Cara throws herself onto a stool, burying her face in her hands. 'I don't mean to get her all worked up, you know.'

I slide a plate of *loc lac* in front of her. 'Guess it's a gift you have.'

'Will you take me to the hospital?'

'Nope. I still have to go talk to my client. If you want to visit your dad, you're going to have to reinstate diplomacy with your mother.'

'Great,' she mutters. Then she looks up at me. 'Does Edward know what I did?'

'Oh yeah.' I rest my elbows on the counter, across from her. 'He heard the whole testimony.'

'I bet he wants to kill me.'

'If I were you, I'd be a little more careful about throwing that phrase around,' I say. 'You could have wound up in jail yourself, you know. For perjury.'

'I wouldn't have let him go to jail, for real. If it got that far, I would have said something—'

'Unfortunately, the law doesn't bend to the whims of a seventeen-year-old. Once the state pressed charges, it would have been out of your hands.'

She grimaces. 'I really didn't mean to lie. It just sort of slipped out.'

'Just like it slipped out when you lied to the police about drinking the night of the accident?' I ask.

Cara lifts her face to mine. Her eyes are wide, and I can see secrets swimming in them, like koi in the dark shallows of a pond. 'Yes,' she admits.

'That's not the only thing you lied about, is it?' I press.

She shakes her head, silent.

I am hoping that, this time, our shared Cambodian cooking moment might bleed into a conversation. I am hoping that, because I'm not part of the universe of this family, but only a satellite, she will be more willing to talk to me. But then there is the sound of a door slamming, and the helium bubbles of the twins' voices spill into the hallway. 'Daddy! Daddy!' Elizabeth cries. 'I made a mermaid picture for you!'

'Jackson, let me unlace your boot,' Georgie says. Her voice is still shaky, and I know her well enough to realize she is grateful for the distraction, for the pudgy hands that grip her shoulders as she works off our son's shoe and for the smell of him, pure child, when she buries her face in the right angle of his neck. A moment later, the twins bounce into the kitchen and cling to my legs like mollusks. Elizabeth thrusts the damp finger painting upward; it droops over her hands.

'That is some mermaid,' I say. 'Don't you think so, Cara?'

But the stool where she's been sitting is empty. Her plate of *loc lac* is full and steaming – the first Cambodian meal I've cooked for her that she hasn't devoured.

I wonder how someone can leave in the blink of an eye without you even noticing.

And just like that, my mind drifts to Luke Warren.

Later that day, I receive a text from Danny Boyle. There's no message, just a snapshot of the dismissal form he's filed in court.

I drive over to Georgie's old place. Edward opens the door wearing a Beresford High School T-shirt and a pair of thread-bare sweatpants. 'He kept my clothes,' Edward says. 'They were in a box in the attic. What do you think that means?'

'That you're overthinking,' I tell him. I hand him his passport. 'Congratulations. You've got your life back.'

'I don't understand.'

'The indictment's been voided. The whole charge has been

revoked. You can go to the hospital and see your dad; you can go back to Thailand if you want; you can do anything and go anywhere you like. It's like none of this ever happened.'

Edward envelops me in a bear hug. 'I don't know what to say, Joe. Honestly. What you've done for me . . .'

'I did it for your mom,' I tell him. 'So do me a favor and consider how she's going to feel before you jump off the deep end again.'

Edward ducks his head, nods.

'You want to come over to the house? See your mother? I know she'd like that.'

'I'm going to head to the hospital,' Edward says. 'See if anything's changed.'

I am about to wish him well when the doorbell rings. I follow him into the mudroom as he opens the door to a man wearing a leather jacket and a wool fisherman's cap. 'Sorry to bother you,' the man says. 'I'm looking for Edward Warren?'

'That's me,' Edward answers.

The man holds out a small blue folder. 'You've been served,' he says, and he smiles and walks away.

Edward takes the folded legal documents out of the folder. *In Re Luke Warren*, I read across the top. 'What *is* this?' he asks.

I take it from him and quickly scan the pages. 'It's a lawsuit that's been filed by the hospital in probate court,' I explain. 'A temporary guardian has already been appointed by the court for your father; an expedited hearing is going to be held on Thursday to appoint a permanent guardian for him.'

'But I'm his son,' Edward says. 'Cara's not even legal yet.'

'It's possible that the judge will decide, given the . . . recent turn of events . . . to make the temporary guardian appointment a permanent one.' I look up at him. 'In other words, neither you nor Cara would be calling the shots.'

Edward stares at me, his chest rising and falling. 'A total stranger? That's crazy. That's what you do when no one steps up to the plate for the job. For God's sake, I have a signed letter from my father *telling* me to make this decision for him.'

'Then you'd better play nice with this woman when she comes to interview you,' I suggest. 'Because I'm ninety-nine percent sure that Cara got a little blue folder just like this, and that she's going to work very hard to get the temporary guardian to believe she's the best candidate to take care of your father.'

There is a standard in probate court unlike any other civil suit. In order to get a guardian appointed for someone, the plaintiff has to prove beyond a reasonable doubt that this person is irrevocably incapacitated. In other words, to take away someone's civil rights and liberties, you have to prove a criminal burden.

'Edward,' I say, 'I think it's time I saw that letter.'

Luke

Years after I came out of the wild, when I was working with Ukrainian farmers to divert wolf packs from their land and their cattle, I observed the most remarkable thing. There was a pack whose pups had been separated by biologists. One was sent off in one direction, the other was sent off in the opposite direction. Years later, they had formed rival packs, and one day, I saw them meet on a breach line of territory. They stood with their brethren, bristling, teeth bared, on two facing ridges.

As soon as the litter mates saw each other, they ran to the no-man's-land between the territories and greeted each other, brother and sister rolling in the grass and having a grand old reunion.

It wasn't until some of the other adult wolves went down and reminded each of them that the sibling was part of a rival pack that they stopped.

And then the two wolves fought each other as if they'd never met before in their lives.

Georgie

It's not politically correct to say that you love one child more than you love your others. I love *all* of my kids, period, and they're all my favorites in different ways. But ask any parent who's been through some kind of a crisis surrounding a child – a health scare, an academic snarl, an emotional problem – and we will tell you the truth. When something upends the equilibrium – when one child needs you more than the others – that imbalance becomes a black hole. You may never admit it out loud, but the one you love the most is the one who needs you more desperately than his siblings. What we really hope is that each child gets a turn. That we have deep enough reserves to be there for each of them, at different times.

All this goes to hell when two of your children are pitted against each other, and both of them want you on their side.

For years after Edward left us, I used to wake up in the middle of the night and imagine all the worst that could happen to him in a foreign country. I pictured drug busts, deportation, rapes in alleys. I pictured him mugged and beaten, bleeding, unable to find someone to help. Like a missing tooth, sometimes an absence is more noticeable than a presence, and I found myself worrying about him even more than I had when he was here. I loved him most because I thought that might be the spell that would bring him back to me.

Meanwhile, Cara blamed me for the divorce when Luke moved out for good; and she blamed me for replacing our old, broken family with a shiny new one. I admit, sometimes I agree with her. When I am with the twins, I think that this is my second chance, that maybe I can bind these two little people to me more closely than I managed to do with my first pair of children.

I am out front watching the kids as they play in the snow fort we built two weeks ago – before the car accident, before Edward came home, before I had to take sides. After my confrontation with Cara, it's liberating to sit on the porch steps and listen to Elizabeth and Jackson pretending that they live in a frost palace and that the icicles are magic talismans. I'd give anything, right now, to dream away reality.

When I hear a car coming down the driveway, I stand up and walk between the road and the twins, as if that would be enough to protect them. They poke their heads out from the window of their little igloo as a stranger rolls down the window. 'Hi,' he says. 'I'm looking for Georgiana Ng?'

'That would be me,' I reply. I wonder if Joe's had flowers sent to me again; sometimes he does that – not to apologize for missing my birthday or anniversary, like Luke, but just because.

'Great.' The man hands me a blue folded packet, legal papers, and reverses out of the driveway.

I don't need Joe to translate; it's a petition to appoint a permanent guardian for Luke. The reason I've been served is because Cara, as a party of interest, is still a minor. Which is exactly why she has all the odds stacked against her.

'Hey, guys,' I say, 'time for hot chocolate!' The twins won't want to come inside yet, but I have to tell Cara about this. So I negotiate a deal that includes an extra half hour of television time this afternoon, install the kids on the couch in front of Nickelodeon, and then walk upstairs to her room.

She is sitting at her desk, watching a YouTube video of her father bent over a carcass, feeding between two wolves. It was probably uploaded by a visitor to Redmond's; you find hundreds if you Google Luke's name. The novelty of watching a grown man defend himself between the snapping jaws of two wild beasts never gets old, I guess. I wonder how those amateur videographers would react if they knew that eating the raw innards of the calf gave Luke such bad diarrhea that he started having the organs removed and flash-fried by Walter, then tucked back into the carcasses in small plastic bags. The animals were never the wiser – they thought he was just eating his allotted portion of the calf – but Luke's digestive system stopped rebelling.

No matter how much he liked to think of himself as a wolf, his body betrayed him.

Cara swivels in her chair when she sees me. She looks nervous. 'I'm sorry for sneaking out,' she begins. 'But if I'd told you where I wanted to go, you never would have taken me.'

I sit down on her bed. 'An apology with a defense built in isn't much of an apology,' I point out. 'And I actually can forgive you for that, because I know you were thinking of your father. What's harder to forgive is the other stuff you said downstairs. This isn't a contest between you and your brother. Or you and the twins.'

Cara looks away from me. 'It's just hard to compete with a tortured runaway or supercute toddlers.'

'There's no competition, Cara,' I say. 'Because I wouldn't have traded you for anything. And no one's better at being you than you.'

She bites the cuticle on her thumb. 'When Edward first left? You used to come into my room when I was asleep and curl up behind me. You thought I was asleep and didn't know, but I did,' Cara says. 'I used to wish on every star and every stray eyelash that he would stay where he was, so you'd keep doing it. It was just the two of us, and then one day, it wasn't anymore.' She swallows. 'First Edward was gone, and the next minute you were gone. So for the longest time, it's just been Dad and me.'

Cara may think I don't love her as much as I do her brother, but parents aren't the only ones who play favorites. Both Cara and Edward, they loved Luke best. How could they not, when he was the one who took them orienteering in the woods and showed them what kind of clover is edible and who put wolf puppies into their laps to chew on their sleeves. Me, I was the one who told them to clean up their rooms and eat their broccoli.

I want to reach out to Cara, but the wall she's put between us is invisible and thick and strong. 'Do you know when I found out I was pregnant with you I burst into tears?'

Cara's jaw drops, as if she expected an admission like this but never thought I'd have the guts to say it out loud.

'I didn't think I could possibly love another baby as much as I loved the one I'd already had,' I continue. 'But the strangest thing happened when I held you for the first time. It was like my heart suddenly unfolded. Like there was this secret space I didn't even know existed, and there was room for both of you.' I stare at her. 'Once my feelings were stretched like that, there was no going back. Without you, it just would have felt empty.'

Cara leans forward, her hair obscuring her face. 'It doesn't always feel that way on the receiving end.'

'I didn't choose Edward over you,' I say. 'I choose you both. Which is why I'm giving this to you.' I hand her the legal papers. 'On Thursday a court's going to appoint a permanent guardian for your father.'

Cara's eyes widen. 'And whoever they pick is the one the hospital has to listen to?'

'Yes,' I say.

'And your name is on the papers because you're *my* legal guardian.'

'I assume so. And I assume that Edward's gotten the same set of papers.'

She gets up so fast the chair spins backward. 'They have to pick you,' she says. 'You need to get a lawyer . . .'

Immediately I hold up my hand. 'Cara, there's no way I'm getting involved in your father's life again.' *Or his death*, I think.

'It's just for three months, until I turn eighteen,' she begs. 'All you have to do is say what I say, and the doctors will listen. And who knows, by then, Dad could even be recuperating.'

'I know how much you love him, honey, but this is outside my comfort zone. Your father is a roller coaster, and I can't handle that ride again.'

'You don't understand,' Cara says. 'I can't lose him.'

'Actually, I *do* understand,' I tell her softly. 'There was a time when I felt the same way. There's no one else in this world like your father. But I had to remind myself that he wasn't the same man I'd fallen for, anymore. That he'd made some bad choices.'

Cara glances up, dry-eyed, determined. 'He didn't choose this,' she answers. 'Maybe he left you, Mom, but he would never, ever leave me.'

Her words take me back. I am pregnant with Cara, and Luke sleeps with his arms around me. *An alpha female can have a phantom pregnancy*, he tells me.

I'm pretty sure this one's real, I tell him, turning slightly in the hope I can find a comfortable position for my bulk. *I can't imagine wanting to fake this.*

It puts every other wolf on his best behavior. They're busy advertising themselves as potential nannies, or proving to the alpha that they're still good at protecting the pack or diffusing the pack or whatever their jobs are that will make those pups safe and sound. And then, at the very end of it, when the alpha's got everyone acting just the way she wants, she turns off the hormones that have been in her urine and her scent and says, Gotcha.

That's pretty impressive, I say.

He cups his hands over my belly. *You don't know the half of it. Four or five months before she even comes into season, an alpha female knows the number of pups she is going to have, their gender, and if they'll stay in her pack or be dispersed to form a new one*, he says.

I laugh. *I'd settle for knowing whether to buy blue or pink clothes.*

It's amazing, he whispers. *These babies are part of the family before they even are conceived.*

Now, I realize Cara is right. Luke may have been a singularly selfish, lousy husband, but he loved his children. He showed it the only way he knew how: by bringing them into the world he couldn't live without. For Edward, that turned out to be a clash. For Cara, it was a delight.

I had defended Edward when he needed an advocate; I would do no less for Cara. I can't be the guardian she wants me to be for her father, but that doesn't mean I can't help her. Resolved, I stand up. 'Meet me in the car. We'll have to take the twins with us, but they might fall asleep on the way . . .'

'Where are we going?' Cara asks.

'To track down Danny Boyle,' I tell her. 'He's going to find you a lawycr.'

The county attorney is not in his office, but as it turns out, old reporters don't die – they just arrange playdates instead of secret meetings with sources, and wear homemade Play-Doh instead of pencil skirts. It only takes one call to a former colleague to find out that Boyle's holding a press conference in the Beresford Grange Hall. An attempted murder charge in a small New England town – even a revoked one – is enough to merit a top story, and the county attorney isn't one to let a golden opportunity pass him by.

By the time Cara and I arrive, the press conference is in full swing. The twins have fallen asleep in the car, and we're each holding one, a damp, warm weight. Among the reporters and television crews we stick out, so even though we hover at the lacy edge of the crowd, I'm not surprised when I see Boyle's eyes light on Cara, and he pauses just the slightest bit during his speech.

'I consider myself a champion of justice,' he says. 'Which is why I will do whatever it takes to always make sure justice doesn't get out of hand. We will not become a litigious society with trumped-up charges based on false evidence, if I have any say.'

It's curious that he doesn't mention that he is the one who let the charges get out of hand in the first place.

'What about the wolf guy in the hospital?' some reporter calls out, and beside me, I feel Cara flinch.

'Our thoughts and prayers continue to be with him and his family,' Boyle says soberly, and then he holds up a hand. 'Sorry, folks, no more questions today.'

He pushes his way through the crowd until he reaches Cara, and grasps her upper arm. 'What are you doing here?' he hisses.

'You owe me,' she says, lifting her chin.

Boyle looks around to see if anyone's listening and then drags Cara into the Grange's community kitchen. I follow them, clutching Jackson as he sleeps against my shoulder. 'I *owe* you?' Boyle says, incredulous. 'I ought to be putting you in jail.' He frowns, noticing me. 'Who's this?'

'My mom,' Cara says.

This makes Boyle tone down his attitude a little. After all, I'm a voter. 'If I didn't firmly believe that your whole scheme was a result of you being overwrought by your father's condition, I would have indicted you myself. I don't owe you anything; I'm cutting you a colossal break.'

'Well,' Cara replies, undaunted, 'I need a lawyer.'

'I already told you I don't try civil suits—'

'A temporary public guardian was appointed for my father. I don't even know what that is, really. But there's a court

date on Thursday to pick a permanent guardian, and I have
to let the judge know that I'm the only person who wants to
keep my father alive.'

Watching Cara in action, I am impressed. She is a terrier
with her teeth sunk into the mailman's pants cuff. She may
be the underdog in size and in scope, but she isn't giving up
without a fight.

Boyle looks from Cara to me. 'Your kid,' he says, 'is quite
a piece of work.'

When he says that, I realize who Cara reminds me of at
this moment.

Me, back when I was a reporter, and wouldn't stop until
I got the answer I wanted.

'Yes,' I say. 'I couldn't be more proud.'

Maybe Cara chose to live with Luke instead of Joe and
me. Maybe she is willing to give up everything, now, to care
for her father. Yet in spite of her infallible allegiance to Luke,
it turns out she is very much her mother's daughter.

Danny Boyle scribbles something on the back of one of
his business cards. 'This woman used to work for me. She
practices law part-time now. I'll call and tell her you'll be in
touch.' He hands the card to Cara. 'And after that,' he says,
'I never want to hear from you again.'

Luke

There is a very real pecking order in a wolf pack, a fluid and constant test of dominance and respect. If a higher-ranking wolf comes toward me, I am supposed to move my weaponry – my teeth – from right to left, horizontally. If, on the other hand, I am passing by that wolf, I should not approach too quickly or I'll find him stiffening and leaning forward, holding the position until I lower myself. Once he looks at me, making the eye contact to beckon me forward, I can inch closer – and even then, I have to pass on the side, avert my head and my teeth to greet him, proving that I am not a threat.

Needless to say, I didn't know any of this at first. Instead, I was just my stupid human self with a true gift for getting in the way of wolves who ranked higher than me. The first time I tried to get too close to the beta without a formal invitation, he schooled me. We were in the clearing, and it had started to rain – a nasty, cold sleet. The beta had the good fortune to be positioned under the thickest cover of trees, and I thought there was plenty of room beside him. So the other young male wolf and I decided to share the space.

The beta's eyes slitted and he growled, a low rumble, but I didn't get the message. When I was about twenty feet away, he showed his teeth. The young male immediately ducked sideways, but when I didn't, the beta growled again, deeper in this throat.

I still didn't see this as a warning. After all, he'd been the one to engage me first, to invite me to travel with the pack. So you can imagine how my heart rate skyrocketed when, in an instant, he closed the distance between us and snapped at me, his teeth clamping centimeters away from my face.

I was rooted to the spot with fear. I couldn't move, couldn't breathe. The beta gripped me with his jaws, his teeth and breath sealing over my face. He roughly turned my head to the left and down, teaching me the correct response. Then he snapped at me, growled deeply, showed his teeth, and growled lightly, reversing the lesson.

Later that day I was sitting with my knees drawn up when the beta loped closer and suddenly lunged, grabbing my throat on the underside. I could feel his teeth sinking into my skin, and instinctively I rolled to my back, a position of utter subordination. He wanted to make sure I'd learned what he'd been trying to teach me earlier, I realized. He squeezed my neck harder, stealing my breath. You know what I am capable of, *he was saying.* And yet this is all I'm going to do to you. This is why you can trust me.

The highest-ranking wolf in the pack isn't the one that uses brute force. It's the one who can, and chooses not to.

Helen

It is telling, I suppose, that all of my work outfits are different shades of gray. Not just for the metaphorical value, but because it means that in the morning, I don't have to agonize over whether I should wear the green blouse or the blue and if one is too showy for my job as a public guardian. The sad truth is that when it comes to making personal decisions, I find it difficult to commit, whereas when it comes to organizing the affairs of others, I am a natural.

The Office of Public Guardian in New Hampshire is a nonprofit that serves nearly a thousand people who are mentally ill or developmentally disabled, who have Alzheimer's or who have suffered a traumatic brain injury. We are assigned to cases by judges who receive requests for temporary and permanent guardianship. Yesterday, my boss tossed another file onto my desk. It was not the first time I'd been appointed a temporary advocate for someone with a brain injury, but this case was different. Usually, our office is pressed into service when a hospital can't find someone willing or able to make medical decisions for a ward. From what I've read, however, the problem here is that both of the man's children are jockeying for that position, and things have spiraled out of control.

Apparently I am the only person in my office who has never heard of the ward, Luke Warren. He is famous, or at least as famous as a naturalist can be. He had a television show on a cable network that showcased his work with wolf packs, but I only listen to the news and to PBS. It is La-a (pronounced La*dash*a, which leads me to wonder if she's as frustrated by her moniker as I am by my own) who drops the book off on my desk this morning. 'Helen,' she says, 'thought you might like this. Hank left it behind when he moved out, the pig.'

Who knew that Luke Warren was not only a television personality and wildlife conservationist but also an author? I run my hand over the raised foil lettering of the title of this autobiography. LONE WOLF, it reads. ONE MAN'S JOURNEY INTO THE WILD. 'I'll give it back when I'm done,' I promise.

La-a shrugs. 'It's Hank's. Which means you can burn it as far as I'm concerned.' She touches the cover of the book, with its photo of Luke Warren being smothered in kisses by a presumably wild animal. 'Sad though. That someone could go so fast from *this*' – she moves her hand to the dark case folder – 'to *this*.'

Most of the wards I've worked with have not published autobiographies and do not have YouTube footage of themselves in their prime at work. In this, it is easier to get a sense of who Luke Warren was before his accident. I pick up the book and read the first paragraph:

What I get asked all the time is: How could you do it? How could you possibly walk away from civilization, from a family, and go live in the forests of Canada with a pack of wild wolves? How could you give up hot showers, coffee, human contact, conversation, two years of your children's lives?

When I become someone's guardian, even in a temporary position, I try to slip under that person's skin, to find something within myself that's similar to him. You would think that a forty-eight-year-old single woman with a monochromatic wardrobe and a manner so quiet that librarians ask her to speak up might not be able to relate to a man like Luke Warren, but the connection I feel is immediate, and intense.

Luke Warren would have been deliriously happy to shed his human skin and become a bona fide wolf.

And like him, I've spent my whole life wishing I were someone I'm not.

My mother's name on her birth certificate is Crystal Chandra Leer. She worked at the Cat's Meow Gentlemen's Club as their star attraction until, amid a night of tequila and moonlight, the bartender seduced her in the stockroom on top of boxes of Absolut and Jose Cuervo. He was long gone by the time I was born, and my mother raised me by herself, supporting us by hosting home parties to sell sex toys instead of Tupperware. Unlike other mothers, mine had hair bleached so white that it looked like moonlight. She wore high heels, even on Sundays. She didn't own a piece of clothing that did not incorporate lace.

I stopped having friends over after my mother told them during a sleepover party that when I was a baby, I was so colicky the only thing that could calm me down was tucking a vibrator along the side of my baby car seat. From that day on I made it my mission to be the antithesis of my mother.

I refused to wear makeup and dressed in shapeless, washed-out clothing. I studied incessantly, so that I had the highest GPA in my graduating class. I never dated. Teachers who met my mother at open school night would say, with amazement, that we didn't seem related at all, which was exactly how I liked it.

Now, my mother lives in Scottsdale with her husband, a retired gynecologist who, for Christmas, bought her a powder-pink convertible with the vanity license plate 38dd. For my last birthday she sent me a Sephora gift card, which I regifted on Secretary's Day.

I am sure that my mother didn't mean to hurt me by putting my birth father's last name on my birth certificate. I'm equally sure that she thought my name was a cute play on words and not a moniker fit for a drag queen.

Let's just say this: whatever your response is when I introduce myself to you . . . I've heard it all before.

'I'm here to see Luke Warren,' I say to the ICU nurse manning the main desk.

'And you are?'

'Helen Bedd,' I reply, primly.

She smirks. 'Well, good for you, sister.'

'I spoke to one of your colleagues yesterday? I'm from the Office of Public Guardian.' I wait while she finds me on a list.

'He's 12B, on the left,' the nurse says. 'I think his son might be in with him.'

That, of course, is what I'm counting on.

I am struck, when I first walk into the room, by the resemblance between father and son. You'd have to know Luke Warren from before his accident, of course, but this young man curled like a question mark in the corner looks exactly like the man on the cover of the book in my bag, albeit with a much more metrosexual haircut. 'You must be Edward,' I say.

He looks me up and down with bloodshot, wary eyes. 'If you're with the hospital counsel, you can't make me leave,' he says, immediately on the offensive.

'I'm not with the hospital,' I tell him. 'My name's Helen Bedd, and I'm the temporary guardian for your father.'

It is as if an entire opera plays across his features: the opening salvo of surprise, a crescendo of mistrust, then an aria of realization – I am the one who will be presenting my findings to the judge on Thursday. He cautiously stands up. 'Hi,' he says.

'I'm sorry to intrude on your private time with your father,' I tell him, and for the first time I really look at the man in the hospital bed. He is like every other ward I've worked with: a husk, an object at rest. My job isn't to see him the way he is now, though. It's to figure out who he used to be, and think the way he would have thought. 'When you have a moment, though, I'd like to speak with you.'

Edward frowns. 'Maybe I should call my lawyer.'

'I'm not going to talk to you about any of the criminal matters of the past few days,' I promise. 'That's not my concern, if that's what's worrying you. All I care about is what's going to happen to your father.'

He looks over at the hospital bed. 'It's already happened,' he says quietly. Behind Luke Warren, something beeps, and a nurse comes through the door. She lifts a full bag of urine that's been collecting on the side of the bed. Edward averts his eyes.

'You know,' I say, 'I could use a cup of coffee.'

*　　*　　*

We sit at a table near the window in the hospital cafeteria. 'I imagine this is incredibly hard for you. Not just because of what happened to your father, but because you've been away from home, too.'

Edward folds his hands around his coffee cup. 'Well,' he admits, 'it wasn't the way I thought I'd come back here.'

'When did you leave?'

'When I was eighteen,' Edward says.

'So as soon as you could fly the coop, you did.'

'No. I mean, no one ever would have suspected that of me. I was a straight-A kid, I'd applied to half a dozen colleges, and I pretty much just got up one morning and walked away from home.'

'That sounds like a radical decision,' I reply.

'I couldn't live there anymore.' He hesitates. 'My father and I . . . didn't see eye to eye.'

'So you left because you didn't get along?'

Edward laughs mirthlessly. 'You could say that.'

'It must have been quite an argument, if it made you angry enough to leave your home.'

'I was angry long before that,' Edward admits. 'He ruined my childhood. He left for two years to go live with a pack of wolves, for God's sake. He used to say all the time that if he could have, he would have chosen to never interact with humans again.' Edward glances up at me. 'When you're a teenager and you hear your dad saying that to a television crew, believe me, it doesn't exactly make you feel warm and fuzzy inside.'

'Where have you been all this time?'

'Thailand. I teach ESL there.' Edward shakes his head. '*Taught* ESL.'

'So you've moved back here permanently?'

'I honestly don't know where I'll wind up,' he says. 'But I've made my way before. I'll do it again.'

'You must want to get back to your own life,' I suggest.

He narrows his eyes. 'Not enough to kill my father, if that's what you're thinking.'

'Is that what you think I was thinking?'

'Look, it's true that I didn't want to come back here. But when my mother called me and told me about the car accident, I got on the first flight I could. I've listened to everything that the neurosurgeon has said. I'm just trying to do what my father would want me to do.'

'With all due respect, after six years without contact, what makes you think you're a decent judge of that?'

Edward glances up. 'When I was fifteen, before my dad left to go into the wild, he signed a letter giving me the right to make medical decisions about him if he couldn't do it himself.'

This is news to me. I raise my brows. 'You have this letter?'

'My lawyer has it now,' Edward says.

'That's quite a lot of responsibility for a fifteen-year-old,' I point out. I'm not just learning whether Luke Warren wanted to terminate life support. I'm learning about his parenting skills. Or lack thereof.

'I know. At first, I really didn't want to do it, but my mother couldn't even face the fact that my father was leaving for two years – she was a mess about it – and Cara was a little kid. There were times, when he was gone, that I used to lie in bed and hope he'd die out there with the wolves, just so I wouldn't be forced to make that kind of decision.'

'But you're willing to do it now?'

'I'm his son,' Edward says simply. 'It's not a decision anyone wants to make. But it's not like this hasn't happened before. I mean, that's what my father always asked of his family – to give him the freedom to go places we didn't want him to go.'

'You know your sister feels differently.'

He toys with a sugar packet. 'I wish I could believe that my dad is going to open his eyes and wake up and recover, too . . . but my imagination just isn't that good.' He stares down at the table. 'When I first got here, and people would come into the room to talk to me about my dad's condition, I always lowered my voice. As if we were going to wake him up because he was asleep. But you know what? I could have yelled at the top of my lungs and he wouldn't have budged. And now . . . after eleven days . . . well. I don't lower my voice.' The sugar packet slips out of his hands and lands on the floor beside my tote bag. Edward bends to retrieve it, and spies a copy of his father's book inside. 'Homework?' he asks.

I take *Lone Wolf* out of my bag. 'I just started it this morning. Your father is a very interesting man.'

Edward reverently touches the gold lettering on the cover. 'May I?' He picks up the book and riffles through the pages. 'I was gone when it was published,' he says. 'And then one day I was in an English language bookshop, and there it was. I sat down right in the aisle and read the whole thing, six hours straight.' He flips through the middle section, a sheaf of black-and-white photos of Luke Warren with his wolves – as pups, as adults. Feeding, playing, resting.

'See this?' Edward points to a picture that shows Luke in one of the enclosures while a small child sits on the hillside, watching. The child is viewed from the back, head covered with a sweatshirt hood. *Cara Warren watches her father teach Kladen and Sikwla how to hunt.* 'That's not Cara,' Edward says. 'That's me. My sweatshirt, my skinny ankles, even my book on the grass. It was *A Wrinkle in Time*, by Madeleine L'Engle – if you go look it up online, you'll see the same cover.' He traces the caption again with one fingertip. 'Years ago, when I first saw that, I wondered if some publishing minion got the citation wrong, or if my dad just gradually edited me out of his life after I left.'

He looks up at me, his eyes suddenly sharp and intense. 'In other words,' he tells me, 'don't believe everything you read.'

The inside of the house looks like a snow globe that's been upended. There are tiny white feathers coating the floor, the couch, and the hair of the woman who opens the door. 'Oh,' she says weakly. 'Is it already two?'

I had called to speak with Georgie Ng while still at the hospital, asking if now might be a good time to chat with Cara. But from the looks of the tiny twin demons shrieking and sliding through the feathers in their stocking feet, I'm wondering if there's ever a good time to do anything in this household.

As I step through the entryway, feathers coat my gray skirt like metal filings drawn to a magnet. I wonder how long it will take me to get them off with a lint brush. Georgie is holding the neck of a vacuum cleaner. 'I'm so sorry about . . . this. Kids will be kids, right?'

'I don't know,' I tell her. 'I don't have any.'

'Wise choice,' Georgie murmurs, grabbing the exploded pillow out of the hand of one of the kids. 'What part of *stop* do you not understand?' she asks. She turns to me again, apologetic. 'It might be easier if you go upstairs to talk to Cara,' she suggests. 'She's in the room to the right at the top of the stairs. She knows you're coming.' Then she disappears around a corner, still holding the vacuum in a death grip, in hot pursuit of her children. 'Jackson! Do *not* put your sister in the clothes dryer!'

Gingerly picking my way through the fluff, I walk upstairs. It is odd to reconcile Georgie Ng with the woman that Luke Warren mentions briefly in his book – a former reporter who fell for him on the job because of his passion for wolves, and realized too late that left no room for a passion for her. I imagine she is happier now, with a more attentive husband and another family. Cara would not be the first child of divorce to shuttle between parents, but the difference in lifestyle between the two must have been drastic.

I knock softly on the door. 'Come in,' Cara says.

I admit, I'm curious to meet a girl who has the wherewithal to get the county attorney to listen to her. But Cara looks young, slight, a little nervous. Her right arm is wrapped tight against her body like a broken wing, and between that and her shoulder-length, wavy dark hair and fine features, she calls to mind a bird that's been pushed from a nest. 'Hi,' I say. 'I'm Helen, your father's temporary guardian.' Something flashes over her face when I say that, but it is gone too quickly for me to interpret. 'Your mother thought if we talked up here, we might be less . . .'

'Allergic?' she suggests.

She offers me the seat at the desk, while she sits on the bed. The room is painted a serviceable blue, with a wedding ring quilt on the bed and a single white dresser. It looks like a guest room, but not for a frequent guest. 'I'm sure this is very hard for you,' I begin, taking out my notebook. 'I'm sorry to have to ask you all these questions right now, but I really need to talk to you about your dad.'

'I know,' she says.

'You two were living together before the accident, is that correct?'

She nods. 'For the past four years. At first I was living with my mom, but when she had the twins, it was sometimes hard to feel like I wasn't a fifth wheel. I mean, I love her and I love Joe and I love having a little brother and sister, but . . .' Her voice trails off. 'My dad says, with the wolves, every day begins and ends with a miracle. Here, every day begins and ends with a cup of coffee, a newspaper, a bath, and a bedtime story. It's not that I don't like being here or that I'm not grateful for being here. It's just . . . different.'

'So you're a bit of an adrenaline junkie, like your father?'

'Not really,' Cara admits. 'I mean, there were times my dad and I would just rent a movie and have popcorn for dinner, and that was just as good as the times that I got to go to work with him.' She feeds the edge of her quilt through her fingers. 'It's like a telescope. My dad, no matter what he's doing, zooms right in so he can't see anything except what's right there with him at that minute. My mom, she's always on wide angle.'

'It must have been hard, then, when his focus was on the wolves and not you.'

She is quiet for a moment. 'Have you ever been swimming in the summer,' she asks, 'when a cloud comes in front of the sun? You know how, for a few seconds, you're absolutely freezing in the water and you think you'd better get out and dry off? But then all of a sudden the sun's back out and you're warm again and when you tell people how much fun you had swimming you wouldn't even think to mention those clouds.' Cara shrugs. 'That's what it's like, with my father.'

'How would you describe your relationship with him?'

'He knows me better than anyone else on the planet,' she says immediately.

'When was the last time you saw him?'

'Yesterday morning,' Cara replies. 'And my mom promised she'll take me to the hospital as soon you leave.' She looks up at me. 'No offense.'

'None taken.' I tap my pen on the pad. 'Could we talk a little bit about the accident?'

She folds in on herself, pulling her bandaged arm tighter against her body with her free arm. 'What do you want to know?'

'There's some question about whether or not you'd been drinking that night.'

'It was hardly anything. I had a beer before I left—'

'Left where?' I ask.

'This stupid party. I went with a friend, and I freaked out when I saw how drunk everyone was getting, so I called my dad. He came all the way to Bethlehem to pick me up.' She looks at me, earnest. 'I wasn't driving the car, even if that's what the police think. He never would have let me do that.'

'Was he angry at you?'

'He was disappointed,' she says quietly. 'That was worse.'

'Do you remember the accident?'

She shakes her head.

'The paramedics said that you dragged your father from the car before it caught fire,' I say. 'That was incredibly brave of you.'

Cara slips her free hand beneath her thigh. Her fingers are shaking. 'Can we . . . can we just not talk about the accident anymore?'

Immediately I back off into safer ground. 'What do you love most about your dad?'

'That he doesn't give up,' she says. 'When people told him he was crazy for wanting to go live with a wild wolf pack, he said he could do it, and that when he was done, he'd know more about them than anyone else on this planet. And he was right. When someone brought him a wolf that was injured or starving to death or once even kept as a pet in some idiot lady's apartment in New York City, he didn't ever say the wolf was a goner. Even if they died during the process, he still tried to save them.'

'Did you and your father ever have a conversation about what he'd want if he was in this kind of situation?'

Cara shakes her head. 'He was too busy living to talk about dying.'

'What do you think should happen, now?'

'Well, obviously I want him to get better. I know it's going to be hard and everything, but I'm practically done with school and I could go to community college instead of some-where out of state so I could help him through rehab—'

'Cara,' I interrupt, 'your brother feels differently. Why do you think that is?'

'He thinks he'll be putting my father out of his misery. That living with a traumatic brain injury isn't really living. The thing is, that's what Edward thinks. My father would never look at a chance at life as miserable – no matter how small that chance is,' she says tightly. 'Edward's been gone for six years. My father wouldn't recognize him if they bumped into each other on the street. So I have a really hard time believing that Edward knows what's best for my dad.'

She is fierce in her convictions, evangelical. I wonder what it would feel like to be on the receiving end of that unconditional love. 'You've talked to your dad's doctors, haven't you?' I ask.

Cara shrugs. 'They don't know anything.'

'Well, they know a lot about medicine,' I counter. 'And they have a lot of experience with people who have brain injuries like your father.'

She looks at me for a long moment, and then gets off the bed and walks toward me. For an awkward moment, I think she's going to hug me, but she reaches past my shoulder to push a button on her laptop. 'You ever hear of a guy named Zack Dunlap?' she asks.

'No.'

I turn the chair around so that I can see the computer screen. It is a clip from the *Today* show, of a young man in a cowboy hat. 'He got into an ATV accident in 2007,' Cara explains. 'Doctors declared him brain-dead. His parents decided to donate his organs, because he said he wanted to on his license. But when they went to turn off the life support machines, one of his cousins – who was a nurse – had a hunch and ran a pocketknife blade along his foot, and the foot jumped. Even though another nurse said it was just a reflex, the cousin dug his fingernail underneath one of Zack's, and Zack swatted his arm away. Five days later, he opened his eyes, and four months after the accident he left rehab.'

I watch the montage of Zack in his hospital bed, of his parents recounting their miracle. Of Zack receiving his hero's welcome in his hometown. I listen to Zack talk about the memories he's lost, and the ones he remembers. Including one where he heard the doctors pronouncing him dead, although he couldn't get up and tell them he wasn't.

'Doctors said Zack Dunlap was brain-dead,' Cara repeats. 'That's even worse off than my dad is now. And today Zack can walk and talk and do just about everything he used to do. So don't tell me my dad isn't going to recover, because it happens.'

The video clip ends, and the next Favorite in Cara's YouTube queue rolls into play. Transfixed, we both watch Luke Warren rubbing the tiniest, squinting squeal of a wolf pup with a towel. He tucks it underneath his shirt, warming it with his own body heat.

'She was one of Pguasek's babies,' Cara says quietly. 'But Pguasek got sick and died, so my dad had to raise the two pups in her litter. My dad fed them with eyedroppers. When they were old enough, he taught them how to function in the pack. This one, he named Saba, *Tomorrow*, so that she'd always have one. It was the one thing he never got used to in the wild – how a litter would die, in order to teach the mom wolf how to do a better job next time. He said he had to interfere, because how can you throw out a life just like that?'

On the tiny rectangular screen, Luke Warren's hair falls forward, obscuring the pinched face of the wrinkled pup. *Come on, baby girl*, he murmurs. *Don't you quit on me.*

Luke

*W*ho tells the new generation what they need to know? In a household, it's a parent. In a wolf pack, it's the nanny. The position is a coveted one, and when an alpha is pregnant, several wolves in the pack will advertise themselves for the role, like beauty pageant contestants, trying to convince this mother-to-be to pick one over the rest. You are awarded the job because of the experience you have – often an older alpha or beta who can no longer perform the tasks necessary to keep the pack safe will take care of the new pups. In this, wolf culture is a lot like Native American culture, where age is revered – and nothing like most Americans, who stick their aging parents in rest homes and visit twice a year.

I didn't audition for the nanny role in the wild; I would have been a disaster, since I could barely keep myself safe and my own learning curve was so steep. But I watched the wolf who became the caretaker, and committed her actions to memory. And it was a good thing, too, because I became a nanny by default. When I was back at Redmond's years later and Mestawe refused her pups, Cara and I saved three out of the four – and someone was going to have to teach them how to function as a pack. That meant guiding them into positions of leadership – by the time I was done, I would

305

rank higher only than Kina, who was destined to be a tester wolf.

You teach wolves by example; you discipline by taking away the warmth the pups crave. When the pups were behaving well, I would be in the tumble of their play. When they got out of hand, I'd nip them, roll them over, and bare my teeth over their throats so that they knew they could trust me. I started their differentiation in hierarchy through their food source, because wolves truly are what they eat. It's a cycle: what the wolves feed on determines their rank in the pack; their rank in the pack determines what they feed on. So as soon as Cara and I weaned the pups off Esbilac and onto rabbit, I gave them the three different parts of the animal. Kina, the lowest-ranking pack member, could have the stomach contents. Nodah, the tough beta, got the 'movement meat' – the rump and leg muscle. Kita was given the precious organs. As we moved on to single calf carcasses, I directed the wolves to the appropriate parts, the way my wolf brothers had done for me in Canada.

Nodah, who was a bully, sometimes shoved Kita out of the way to get to the good stuff – the heart, the liver. When that happened, I'd go off and have a fake fight with Kina for a few minutes, and then I'd come back with my blood racing and my adrenaline levels raised. Just like that, Nodah would back down and do what I told him to do.

I taught them their own language: that a high-pitched whimper is encouraging, that a low whimper is calming. That a growl is a warning, and an uff, uff *sound means danger.*

But the hardest lesson I had to teach them was the order of importance. If a pack is in danger, they protect the alpha at all costs. Anyone else can be replaced, but if you lose the alpha, the pack will likely break apart. So after digging rendezvous holes – deep holes they could run to and hide in if danger came in the form of a bear or a human or any other threat – I would play tag, biting at their legs and hindquarters as if a predator was in pursuit. I directed them toward the RV holes, so they'd learn that the only way to get away from me was to burrow. But I had to make sure they always let Kita in first. Compared to this future alpha, Nodah and Kina were nonessential.

It killed me, every time. Because as much as I wanted to be a wolf, I was only human. And what parent chooses one child at the expense of another?

Cara

Zirconia Notch lives on a sustainable farm so high up in the state of New Hampshire it's practically Canada. There are goats and llamas milling free-range in her yard when my mother drives in, which delights her, because it means that she can let the twins pat the animals to kill time while I'm meeting with my brand-new lawyer.

She told me on the phone that she doesn't do much with her law degree these days; instead, she's got a new profession: a medium to pets that have passed. It wasn't until five years ago that she realized she had this gift, when the spirit of her neighbors' dead Labrador came to her in the middle of the night and started barking. Sure enough, the neighbors' house was on fire. Had Zirconia not roused them, it could have been a disaster.

When I walk into the house, I smell incense. A window with twenty-five tiny panes has a jelly jar in each cubicle, filled with what looks like water with food coloring mixed in. The result is a cross between a rainbow and what I always imagined *Romeo and Juliet*'s apothecary shop to look like, when I read the play in tenth grade. There is a curtain of crystal beads hanging in the doorway, but if I stand at a certain angle, I can see Zirconia sitting with a client at a table draped with purple lace and strewn with heather. Zirconia has long white hair and a tattoo of a sweet pea vine that wraps around her neck and disappears into her collar. She's wearing a furry, sleeveless vest that looks like it started its life on the back of one of the llamas in the yard, and she's holding a pet's rope chew toy. 'Nibbles wants you to know that she didn't mean to soil the Oriental rug,' Zirconia says, her eyes shut, her body swaying just the tiniest bit. 'And that she is with your grandma Jane—'

'June?' the client says.

'Yes. Sometimes it's hard to understand the dialect in a bark . . .'

'Can you tell her we miss her? Every day?'

Zirconia purses her lips. 'She doesn't believe you. Hang on . . . I'm getting a name.' Zirconia opens her eyes. 'She's talking about a bitch named Juanita.'

'Juanita's our Chihuahua puppy,' the client gasps. 'I guess technically she's a bitch, but she hasn't replaced Nibbles. No other dog could do that.'

Zirconia holds a hand to her temple and squints. 'Nibbles is gone now,' she says. She sets down the chew toy.

The woman sitting across from her is frantic. 'But you have to get a message back to her! Tell her we love her!'

'Trust me.' Zirconia touches the client's hand. 'She knows.' Briskly she gets to her feet, spying me in the mudroom through the crystal curtain. 'That's three hundred dollars,' she says. 'I take personal checks.'

As Zirconia leads the client into the mudroom to get her coat, I see that she's wearing hot pink tights under her black skirt. 'You must be Cara,' she says. 'Come right in.' She gives a parting hug to the other woman. 'If Nibbles comes through during any other readings, I have your phone number.'

The crystal beads sing as I walk through them. 'So,' Zirconia says. 'You found your way here.'

I take a seat. 'My mom did. She's outside with my half brother and half sister.'

'Does she want to come in? I can make her some tea. Read the leaves for her.'

'I'm pretty sure she's okay out there,' I say.

Zirconia disappears through another crystal curtain and returns with two steaming cups of what seems to be dishwater with tobacco at the bottom. 'Thanks for agreeing to represent me, Ms. Notch.'

'Zirconia. Or better yet, Z.' She shrugs. 'I was born in a yurt at the base of Franconia Notch. My parents thought about naming me Diamond – for its strength and beauty – but they were afraid it sounded too much like a madam in the Wild West, so they went for the next best thing.'

A cat, which I'd thought was a statue on the mantel, suddenly yowls and jumps onto the middle of the table, getting its claws tangled in the lace. Zirconia absently extracts it as she continues talking. 'I know you're probably wondering why Danny Boyle recommended me, given that I cherry-pick my cases. I'll tell you, I never thought I'd become a lawyer. I wanted to fight The Man. But then I realized I'd get farther if I fought The Man from the inside. You hear me?'

She talks like someone who smoked way too much dope in the sixties. I nod. 'Loud and clear,' I say, and I wonder what the heck Danny Boyle was thinking.

'Turns out that I was really gifted at prosecution. I like to think it's because my chakras are aligned, and let me tell you, there wasn't a single person in the county attorney's office who could make the same claim. I had a higher conviction rate than Danny Boyle.'

'So why aren't you still a prosecutor?'

She strokes the cat twice and releases him onto the floor, where he races through the crystal curtain. 'Because one day I woke up and questioned being in a profession that, by definition, suggests you'd never be proficient. I mean, how long did I have to *practice* law before I got it right?'

I laugh, and take a sip of the tea. To my surprise, it tastes decent.

'A lot of people would tell you that a pet medium is a colossal hack. I would have told you that myself, before my first experience with contact from the other side.' She shrugs. 'Who am I to question a talent that brings closure to so many grieving families? I'll be honest with you – it's a blessing, and a curse.'

I admit I was pretty skeptical of Zirconia when she told me what she did for a living now. And sure, maybe every dead dog wants to apologize to its owner for taking a whiz on the nice rug in the house . . . but then again, how would she have known that this family's new dog was named Juanita? I'm not saying I'm a believer, but I will admit it gave me pause.

'Now, Cara,' Zirconia says, 'I'm your advocate. That's what lawyers used to be called, you know, and I hold true to the definition. I want to know what you want the outcome to be, and then I want to figure out how I can advocate for you to get there.' She leans forward, her hair falling down her back like a glacial avalanche.

'I just want my dad to get better,' I tell her. It's what I told that guardian yesterday, too, but this time I have a lump in my throat. I think it's because I feel like I've been an army of one, and all of a sudden, there's someone fighting next to me.

Zirconia nods, visibly moved. 'You know what we're going to do? We're going to light a special candle for your dad right now, so that it's like he's here with us.'

She rummages through a cabinet and comes out with a Yankee Candle. She sets it down between us on the table and lights it. The room smells like a pine forest, all of a sudden, and it takes me by surprise, because that's what my dad always smells like, coming in from the outdoors.

'Now that we have the goal in sight, we have to begin to chip away at the obstacles,' Zirconia says. 'And the biggest problem is that you're seventeen.'

'My mom says she'll sign anything,' I tell her.

'Unfortunately, to the state of New Hampshire, you're still a minor, and minors aren't allowed to make medical decisions for someone incapacitated.'

'It's just a number. First of all, in three months, I'll be eighteen. And besides, I've been taking care of myself and my dad for years.'

'Unfortunately, that's not how the law sees it. So what could I say to the court that would help them decide to override the legal technicalities?'

'I've lived with my dad for four years,' I say. 'We've made every decision together. I drive. I go to school. I babysit to make money. I do the grocery shopping, and I'm listed on my dad's bank account. I pay all the bills, and I take care of the business questions that come in about his TV series and answer his fan mail. The only thing I can't do is vote.'

'To be honest,' Zirconia says, 'there haven't been a wealth of wonderful candidates anyway in the past twelve years.' She looks up at me. 'What was this about drinking?'

'I don't. Drink, I mean. But I did, the night of the crash.'

Zirconia steeples her hands in front of her face. 'How much?'

'One beer.'

'One?'

I pick at the cuticle on my thumb. 'Three.'

Zirconia raises her brows. 'So you've basically lied to everyone about that.' She waves her arms in a circular motion. 'This is a circle of truth. Whatever you say to me from now on better be exactly what happened. If it didn't happen that way, I don't want to hear it.'

'Okay,' I say, ducking my head.

'Those are the two sticking points that your brother's lawyer is going to use against you,' Zirconia says.

'There's plenty that makes him an unfit guardian,' I point out. 'Starting with a murder charge.'

'Which has been vacated,' Zirconia replies, 'so it's like it never happened.'

We speak for another three hours, talking about my dad, and how he lived his life, and all the names on the Internet I've found of people who recovered when given a second chance. Zirconia writes notes on a recycled paper napkin and then on the back of an old Southwest Airlines e-ticket that is tucked into her skirt pocket. She stops only once, to make banana-soy shakes for the twins, who are watching a movie in my mother's van.

Finally, she puts down her pen. 'I'm going to give you some homework,' she says. 'I want you to go to your dad's hospital room and lay your head on his chest. Then tell me what thoughts come to you.'

I promise her I will, even though it is way too New Age for me. We talk about the logistics of court on Thursday; where I have to go, where I will meet her. It isn't until she's walking me through the questions she's going to ask me on the stand that it suddenly hits me: This is happening. I'm standing up against my brother in court, in the hope that I will win guardianship for my father.

Zirconia is watching me carefully. 'It just got real,' she hypothesizes.

'Yeah.' My heart is racing. 'Can I ask you something?'

I am afraid to phrase the question out loud, but I have to, because there's no one else I can pose it to. And she did say she was my advocate, my helper, and God knows I need help. So I whisper the words that have been cycling around my heart, squeezing when I least expect it. 'Do you think I'm doing the right thing?'

'The right thing,' Zirconia repeats, turning the words over in her mouth as if they are hard candy. 'I once talked with a mastiff that had passed. The vet said it was remarkable he lived as long as he did; given the medical tests, he should have died three years earlier. The mastiff's owner was a little old woman, lived by herself. When he started to talk to me from the other side, he said he was so tired. It had been exhausting work, staying alive for the lady all that time. But he couldn't let himself go because he knew he'd be leaving her alone.'

Zirconia looks at me. 'I think that you're asking the wrong question. It's not whether your dad would want to die. It's whether your dad would want to leave this world without knowing that someone was going to be here to take care of you.'

Until she hands me a clean napkin, I'm not even aware that I'm crying.

When I get to my father's hospital room, Edward is there.

For a moment, we both stare at each other. Part of me understands that now that he's not in jail, he would of course be back here; the other part of me wonders how he could possibly have the nerve to walk through the ICU after the stunt he pulled. His eyes darken, and for a second I think he's going to cross the tiny space and throttle me for getting him into all that trouble, but my mother steps between us. 'Edward,' she says, 'why don't you and I grab dinner while your sister has some private time with your dad?'

Edward nods tightly and walks past me without saying a word.

I'd like to tell you that my father opened his eyes just then and rasped my name and that I got my happy ending, but that's not true. He is still lying the way he had been lying a day ago, when I last saw him; if anything, he looks even more sunken and transparent, as if he were already an illusion.

Maybe I am kidding myself. Maybe I am the only person who can look at my father and see a miracle. But I *have* to. Because otherwise, what he said to me that night would be true.

Thinking of Zirconia, I crawl onto the bed and lie down. I curl up against my dad, who is still warm and solid and familiar. This makes my throat prickle like a cactus. Underneath my ear his heart is beating.

How am I supposed to believe he's not coming back, when I can feel that?

When my father rescued the pups that Mestawe rejected – the brothers of little Miguen, who died on the way to the vet – he had to somehow teach them to act like a family without the help of their biological mother. There was Kina, the shy one; and Kita, the smart one; and then Nodah, the burly tough guy. But for all of Nodah's bravery, he was terrified of lightning. Anytime a storm came, he would start freaking out, and the only way to calm him was for my dad to pick him up and cradle him against his chest. It was easy, of course, when he was a four-week-old. It was a little more challenging when he was fully grown. I used to laugh, watching this brute of a wolf clamber up my father to hear his heartbeat.

It turns out that it's not so funny anymore; not now, when I'm in the middle of the storm.

I close my eyes and picture my father, back when he was the nanny for these pups, when I used to stand at the fence and watch him. *You have to teach them to play?* I said. *Don't they already know how to do that?*

My dad would stick his bum in the air, front half crouched in a prey bow – from that position a wolf could spring six feet in all directions. Every time the tussles and tumbling got too rough for the wolves, he'd collapse into this prey bow and everyone would stop and mimic him. *A family can have a mock fight*, my father said, *but they need to know when it's time to stop.*

I'm teaching them balance, my father used to explain.

I'm teaching them how not to kill each other.

Luke

I know I was a curiosity for my wolf family. Sometimes when I was asleep, I'd wake to a hundred pounds of wolf pouncing on me, to see what my reaction would be. When we went out on a hunt and they chose to bring me along, they'd zigzag in front of me, trying to see if they could trip me up, as if they wanted to catalog all my flaws before an enemy did. In retrospect I realize that my role for them was akin to an alien abduction of a human: they wanted to know what they were up against, now that our worlds and our territories were bleeding into each other.

One summer evening at dusk, the alpha had taken the hunters out on a journey somewhere to the south. I was left behind with the young male wolf and his sister, who was on patrol around the perimeter of our territory. It was blisteringly hot; I kept making trips to the stream to douse my head with water; then I'd come back to our clearing and doze, drifting off to the gossip of mosquitoes and the belly laughs of bullfrogs. Even though I knew I should have been keeping a wary eye like the young male, the heat and the humidity had softened my edges and instincts.

I woke with a start and saw the young male sitting beside me. The female was still gone. In other words, nothing had changed. So I hitched myself upright, intent on cooling down once again at the stream. No sooner had I reached the water, however, than the young male tackled me, knocking all the wind from me. He growled and snapped at my face, eyes blazing and teeth bared, in full attack mode. I immediately rolled over, asking this wolf for trust, stunned by this behavior. It was the first time since I'd been accepted by the pack that I truly believed my life was in danger – and, worse, at the hands of one of my wolf brothers.

He continued to snarl at me, his ears flattened, as he backed me away from the stream and into the twisted skeleton formed by several enormous trees that had been felled during a thunderstorm. I lay with my face pressed into the earth, breathing in twigs and soil, sweating and shaking. Every time I tried to move, the wolf leaned closer and snapped his powerful jaws centimeters from my face.

You can imagine what went through my mind during that hour. That the biologists were right: that I could never infiltrate a wild pack; that the wolves were wild animals and would never consider me one of their own; that this young male was only waiting for the rest of his pack to get back to kill me because the alpha had told him I wasn't necessary anymore. I thought of all the lost knowledge I'd accumulated about these remarkable creatures, how no one would ever learn what I had. I wondered if anyone would ever find my body, given that I wasn't even sure how far away from civilization I was at this point. And for the first time in a long time, I thought about Georgie, and my kids. I wondered whether they would grow up hating me for leaving them. I wondered if they even thought of me anymore, after all this time.

As night fell, the sounds in the forest changed. The symphony of crickets gave way to the violin-cry of an owl; the wind picked up, and the earth began to cool beneath my cheek. After four hours of aggressively trapping me in this makeshift cave, the young wolf suddenly sat down, leaving room for me to crawl out. He glanced back at me, his yellow eyes calm.

I thought for sure it was a trick.

The minute I came out of that hole, he was going to go for my throat.

When I didn't emerge, he leaned in again. Instinctively I reared back, but instead of snapping at me, he began to lick my mouth and cheeks, the way he might welcome back the wolves in the pack when they returned.

Still terrified, I crawled into the open, making sure I kept my body lower than his to show submission. He turned and trotted toward the stream, stopping to look over his shoulder at me. It was an invitation to follow him, so I did, still keeping my distance.

When he reached the stream, he lifted his leg and scented the matted grass where I'd been kneeling earlier. Glancing down, I saw a pile of scat that did not resemble that of any animal I'd ever encountered. Beside it, in the soft mud, was a perfectly preserved paw print from a mountain lion.

Cougars are rare here in eastern Canada, but there have been sightings in New Hampshire and Maine and New Brunswick. They are solitary hunters, and the summertime is when the juveniles leave their mothers to search out their own territories. They compete with wolves directly for prey. A solitary mountain lion is more powerful than a single wolf, but a pack can bring down a mountain lion.

The only other fact I knew about cougars is that they kill by ambush, by jumping onto the back of the prey animal and breaking its neck with a bite.

I did not have the safety of the pack surrounding me, the strength in numbers. I had been kneeling at the stream by myself, ripe picking for a cougar in the vicinity to leap onto me and deliver a death blow.

The young wolf had not been trying to kill me. He'd been trying to save my life.

There isn't love among wolves. It's an unconditional commitment. If you do your job, a lifetime tour of duty, then you are part of the family. You need the others in your pack to complete you. The young wolf had protected me not because of any emotional bond, but because I was a valuable member of the pack – a makeshift numbers wolf who bolstered the ranks at ambush hunts, or against rival packs; but also an individual from whom they could learn more about the humans with which they were increasingly forced to share territory.

Yet deep down, in the part of me that was still human, I wished he'd protected me because he loved me as much as I loved him.

The day after I was nearly killed by a mountain lion, I knew it was time to leave my pack. I put some meat from the previous night's kill in my coverall pocket and started to walk east. The wolves let me go; they probably assumed I was headed to the stream or out on patrol; there was no reason for them to believe I wouldn't return.

The last I saw of my family, the young male and female were play-wrestling under the watchful eye of the big beta wolf. I wondered if I would hear them howling for me that night.

People assume that the reason I walked away from the pack that day was because the harsh conditions had finally become overwhelming – the weather, the cold, the near starvation, the constant threat of predators. But the real reason I came back is much simpler.

If I hadn't left at that moment, I knew I would have stayed forever.

Joe

There are natural alliances formed in a courtroom. When I walk into the probate court, the hospital's lawyer is already sitting at the counsel table on the left. With her is the neurosurgeon.

At the table on the right is Cara, and her lawyer.

Immediately I steer Edward toward the hospital lawyer's table.

The last person to walk in is Helen Bedd, the temporary guardian. She looks at the seating arrangement and plants herself, wisely, between the tables, in the space that separates Edward and Cara.

Georgie is in the row behind me. 'Hey, baby,' I say, leaning over the bar to give her a quick peck. 'How are you holding up?'

She looks over at her daughter. 'Pretty well, given the circumstances.'

I know what she means. This morning while she fed Cara oatmeal and juice and got ready to drive her to the hospital and then to court to meet her attorney, I grabbed a granola bar and drove to Luke Warren's house to pick up my client. We can't really talk about the case, because we have aligned ourselves with different camps. I feel like my marriage is a

Venn diagram, and the only shared space between us right now is an awkward silence.

Don't think I haven't wondered about my own motivations in this case. I am representing Edward, of course, and might never have been pressed into service if not for Georgie desperately asking me to get him out of the police station. Professionally, I want a win for my client. But is that because I really believe in Edward's right to make a medical decision for his father . . . or because I know what that medical decision will be? If Luke Warren dies, he is out of the picture. He'll never come between me and Georgie again. If, on the other hand, he is moved to a long-term care facility, and Cara winds up as his guardian, Georgie will continue to play a significant role – until Cara is eighteen, and perhaps even after that.

Edward is wearing his father's buffalo check jacket again; I think it's morphed in status from outerwear to a talisman. When Cara sees him in it, her eyes widen and she comes halfway out of her seat, only to have her attorney pull her down and start whispering furiously.

'You remember everything I told you?' I murmur to Edward.

He jerks his chin, a nod. 'Stay calm,' he says. 'No matter what.'

I fully expect him to be painted as a hothead, as someone who makes rash decisions. Who else walks away from home after an argument and moves to Thailand? Or, frustrated by a turn of events, yanks the plug of a ventilator out of the wall? It doesn't help, too, that even if the criminal charge can't be admissible in court since it's been vacated, this is a small town. Everyone knows what Edward did.

It's up to me to spin it so he looks like an angel of mercy instead of a disgruntled prodigal son.

The clerk looks around at everyone who's clustered at the tables. 'We all ready, folks?' he asks. 'All rise, the Honorable Armand LaPierre presiding.'

Although I haven't argued before this judge before, I am well aware of his reputation. He's allegedly an empathetic man. So empathetic, in fact, that he has trouble making any decisions. He often leaves court during his lunch hour to go down the street to Sacred Heart, the closest Catholic church, where he says novenas for the parties involved and prays for guidance.

The judge enters in a cloud of black – black robe, black shoes, jet-black hair. 'Before we begin,' he says, 'this is a deeply disturbing case for everyone here. We are convened to determine the permanent guardianship of Luke Warren. I understand that his medical condition hasn't changed since I appointed a temporary guardian last Friday. Today I see that the hospital is represented, as well as the ward's two children as parties of interest.' He frowns. 'This is a very unconventional hearing, but these are unconventional circumstances. And what the court hopes to keep in mind is that ultimately we're trying to make a decision that would be in line with what Luke Warren would want, if he were here to speak for himself. Are there any preliminary matters that need to be discussed?'

That's my cue. I rise from my chair. 'Your Honor, I'd like to bring to the court's attention that one of the parties of interest here today is a minor. Cara Warren is not the age of majority, which suggests that she is legally incapable of being vested with the authority to make decisions about her father's end-of-life care.' I look directly at the judge, unable to face the heat of Cara's eyes. 'I ask the court to strike her appearance here today and have her leave the courtroom, and to have her representative, Ms. Notch, dismissed from the proceedings, as her client doesn't have the legal standing to make this sort of choice on her father's behalf.'

'What are you talking about?' Cara cuts in. 'I'm his daughter. I have every right to be here—'

'Cara,' her attorney warns. 'Judge, what my client *meant* to say—'

'I'm quite sure what your client meant to say had a few choice expletives in it,' the judge replies. 'But people, seriously. We're thirty seconds into the proceeding and we're already at each other's throats? I know emotions are running high, but let's be calm and just look at the legal precedent.'

Zirconia Notch stands. She is dressed like a lawyer from neck to knees, but her tights are a shocking lime green with red stripes, and her pumps are sunshine yellow. It's as if the top half of her body fell on the bottom half of the Wicked Witch of the West. 'Your Honor,' she says, 'my client is seventeen, true, but she is also the only person in this courtroom who has been intimately involved in the day-to-day life of Mr. Warren. Under RSA 454-A, a guardian must merely be competent. The fact that Cara's birthday isn't for three months doesn't have any impact on whether the court can vest her with the authority to make decisions regarding her father's life. Indeed, if she'd been charged with a felony, like her brother, she would have been tried as an adult in court—'

'Objection,' I say. 'That charge was dismissed. Ms. Notch is trying to bring up this irrelevant claim to prejudice my client.'

'People,' the judge sighs, 'let's confine ourselves to the matter before the court this morning, all right? And Ms. Notch, could you remove those wrist bells? They're distracting.'

Undaunted, Zirconia strips off her bracelets and continues. 'Once the court begins hearing her testimony, I'm certain Your Honor will determine that this young woman is of sufficient age, maturation, and intelligence to have an opinion and to be considered competent, as the criteria of the statute state.'

The judge looks like he's having an ulcer attack. His mouth twists, his eyes water. 'I'm not inclined to dismiss Cara from the proceedings at this time,' he says. 'I have yet to hear the evidence, and I need to hear her perspective just as much as I need to hear from her brother, Edward. I'm going to ask you two to present brief opening arguments. Ladies first, Ms. Notch.'

She stands up and walks toward the bench. 'Terry Wallis,' she says. 'Jan Grzebski. Zack Dunlap. Donald Herbert. Sarah Scantlin. You've probably never heard of these people before, so let me introduce you. Terry Wallis spent nineteen years in a minimally conscious state. Then one day, he spontaneously began to speak and regained awareness of his surroundings. Jan Grzebski, a Polish railroad worker, woke up from a nineteen-year coma in 2007. Zack Dunlap was declared brain-dead after an ATV accident and was on the verge of having life support terminated so his organs could be donated, when he showed signs of purposeful movement. After five days, his eyes were open; two days later, he was off a ventilator, and today he can walk and talk and continues to improve.'

She walks toward Edward. 'Donald Herbert,' she continues,

'suffered a severe brain injury while fighting a fire in 1995. After ten years in a vegetative state, he uttered his first words. Sarah Scantlin was a pedestrian hit by a drunk driver in 1984. After a six-week coma she entered a minimally conscious state, and then, in January of 2005, she started talking again.' Zirconia spreads her hands, a plea. 'Each of these men and women had injuries from which they were never expected to recover,' she says. 'Each of these men and women had lives ahead of them that their families had given up hope of them living. And each of these men and women are here today because someone loved them enough to believe in their recovery. To give them time to heal. To *hope*.'

She walks back to her table, her hand resting on Cara's good shoulder. 'Terry Wallis, Jan Grzebski, Zack Dunlap, Donald Herbert, Sarah Scantlin. And just maybe, Your Honor, Luke Warren.'

The judge looks up at me as Zirconia sits down. 'Mr. Ng?'

'Different people believe life starts at different places,' I say, standing up. 'Tibetan Buddhists say it begins at orgasm. Catholics trace life to the moment the sperm meets an egg. Those who use stem cells say an embryo isn't alive until it is fourteen days old, when it develops a primitive streak – the thickened bit that becomes a backbone. *Roe v. Wade* says life begins at twenty-four weeks. And the Navajo, they believe that life begins the first time a baby laughs.'

I shrug. 'We've gotten used to there being a multitude of beliefs about the start of life. But what about the end of life? Is its definition as muddy? In the 1900s, Duncan McDougal believed that you could put a dying patient on a scale and know the exact moment death occurred, because he'd lose three-quarters of an ounce – the weight of the human soul.

Nowadays, the Uniform Determination of Death Act defines death as the irreversible cessation of circulatory and respiratory functions or the irreversible cessation of all brain functions. That's why brain death qualifies as death, and why cardiac death qualifies as death.'

I look at the judge. 'We're here today, Your Honor, because Luke Warren did not leave us a directive that would show us how he defines death. But we do know how he'd define life. Life, to Mr. Warren, meant being able to run with his wolves . . .'

Leaving your wife and kids at home, I think.

'It meant becoming an expert on pack behavior . . .'

Even though you knew nothing about how to keep your own family close.

'It meant seamlessly integrating himself with nature . . .'

While his wife waited up for him.

'It didn't mean lying in a hospital bed, unconscious, unable to breathe on his own, with no presumptive hope for recovery. Your Honor, you're the one who said that we should be making a decision in line with what Luke Warren would want.' As I pause, I meet Edward's gaze. 'Luke Warren,' I say, 'would ask us to let him go.'

During the first fifteen-minute recess, Edward and I head to the restroom. 'Do you believe it?' he asks, while we are both standing at the urinal. 'What that lawyer said?'

'You mean about all those people who recovered from brain injury?'

He nods, flushing and then heading to the sink to wash his hands. 'Yeah.'

'I don't know. But I'm sure as hell going to ask the

neurosurgeon about them,' I say. I finish up and find Edward staring into the bathroom mirror, as if he cannot place his own face. 'Look,' I tell him. 'Today you don't have to make any decisions about your father. You just have to win the right to make that decision.'

We leave to grab a soda before we have to go back to the courtroom. In the vending machine area, Zirconia and Georgie are seated at the small industrial table across from Cara.

'Ladies,' I say. I wink at Cara.

She looks down at the table, nursing a Coke.

'How's your dad doing?' I ask. I know that Cara had asked to visit Luke before coming to court today.

She narrows her eyes. 'As if you care.'

'Cara!' Georgie draws in her breath. 'Apologize to Joe.'

'In the grand scheme of things, I think he owes me one first.' She picks up her Coke and stands. 'I'll wait upstairs.'

But before she can leave, Edward blocks her exit. He pushes a pack of Twizzlers toward her, candy from the vending machine. 'Here,' he says.

'What makes you think I want these?'

'Because you used to,' Edward tells her. 'You used to beg me to buy them for you when we were on the way home from school, and I stopped off at a gas station to fill up. You'd bite off the ends and stick one in the milk carton you saved from school, like a straw. Said it was a strawberry shake that way.' He looks at Georgie. 'We kept it a secret from Mom, because she said you were a sugar addict and you'd lose all your teeth before you hit puberty.'

Holding her soda, she can't grab the package; she only has one hand free. 'I forgot about that,' she murmurs.

Edward tucks the candy into a fold of her sling. 'I didn't,' he says.

The hospital attorney, Abby Lorenzo, begins by calling Dr. Saint-Clare to the stand. He's sworn in and rattles off his neurosurgeon credentials, looking the whole time like he could be doing something so much more important, such as saving lives. 'Do you know Luke Warren?' she asks.

'Yes. He's one of my patients.'

'When did you meet him?'

'Twelve days ago,' the doctor says.

'Can you tell us about Mr. Warren's condition, when he arrived at the hospital?'

'He was brought in after a motor vehicle accident,' Saint-Clare says, 'where he was found outside the vehicle. The EMTs on the scene assumed that he had a diffuse traumatic brain injury, based on the circumstances. He was given a five on the Glasgow Coma Scale, and came into the hospital presenting with an enlarged right pupil, left-side weakness, and a laceration on his forehead. When a CT scan revealed severe swelling around his brain and a periorbital edema around his eyes, I was called in.'

'Then what happened?' the lawyer asks.

'Mr. Warren was again tested on the coma scale and still scored a five—'

'What does that mean exactly?'

'It's a neurological scale to measure responsiveness, or lack thereof, after head injury. The scale ranges from three to fifteen, with three being a person in the deepest coma and fifteen being a normal, healthy individual. For patients who test between five and seven after twenty-four hours, fifty-three percent will die or remain in a vegetative state.'

Lorenzo nods. 'How did you treat Mr. Warren?'

'The emergency CT scan suggested that he had a temporal lobe hematoma and subarachnoid hemorrhage, an intraventricular hemorrhage, and hemorrhages in the brain stem in the medulla, extending into the pons.'

'In layman's terms?'

'Mr. Warren came in with blood around his brain, blood in the ventricles of his brain, and hemorrhages in the parts of his brain that affect breathing and consciousness. We put him on a drug called Mannitol to reduce pressure in the brain, and performed a temporal lobectomy – a surgery that would give room inside the cranium for his brain to expand, so that the swelling could go down. We removed the hematoma, as well as part of the anterior temporal lobe. After his surgery, he was still not breathing on his own and did not wake up; however, his right pupil became reactive again, which suggests the swelling did indeed go down in the brain. The temporal lobectomy means that Mr. Warren would probably lose some memories, but not all; however, since consciousness has been so severely compromised by the injuries to his brain stem, it's unlikely that he's ever going to be able to access any of those memories.'

'So he's not brain-dead, Dr. Saint-Clare?'

'No,' the surgeon replies. 'His EEG shows cerebral cortex activity. But none of it's accessible, because he can't regain consciousness.'

'How is Mr. Warren being kept alive?'

'A ventilator is breathing for him, and he's being nourished via feeding tube.'

'What's your professional opinion regarding Mr. Warren's chances of recovery?'

I look at Cara while the surgeon answers. Her eyes are narrowed, her jaw set firmly, as if his words are a bracing wind. 'We've done a repeat CT scan every two days. Although we know the pressure in his brain has gone down, the hemorrhages in the brain stem have become a bit larger. He's still unconscious, he's in a vegetative state. In my opinion this is a serious brain injury from which we do not expect recovery.'

Cara flinches.

'Even if there was a chance, which would be extremely unlikely, the best-case scenario for Mr. Warren would be life in a long-term care facility with limited function, never regaining consciousness.'

'How certain are you of your professional opinion, Dr. Saint-Clare?' Lorenzo asks.

'I've been a neurosurgeon for twenty-nine years, and I've never seen a patient recover from a brain injury as traumatic as this one.'

'What's the hospital's position with respect to Mr. Warren's care and recovery?'

'He's a patient, and will receive the best care we can possibly give him to ensure his comfort. However, because we don't expect improvement in the quality of his life functioning, a decision needs to be made. Either Mr. Warren will have to be moved to another facility to provide round-the-clock care, or if the choice is made to terminate life support, he is a candidate for organ donation.'

'If Mr. Warren isn't brain-dead, how can he be a candidate for organ donation?'

The neurosurgeon leans back in his seat. 'You're correct,

he doesn't meet the medical criteria for brain death. However, he does meet the criteria for donation after cardiac death. Patients who have a severe brain injury and who aren't breathing on their own can still be organ donors, if they've made their wishes known. The hospital connects their families with the New England Organ Bank. After the decision is made to terminate life support, the ventilator is effectively turned off and the patient stops breathing. A countdown is started, and after five minutes the patient is declared dead, brought into an OR, and the organs are harvested. In Mr. Warren's case, the viable organs would be liver and kidneys, possibly even his heart.' The doctor pauses. 'For many families who are faced with this kind of no-win situation, knowing that their loved one can help save someone else's life through organ donation is a great comfort.'

'Thank you, Dr. Saint-Clare,' Abby Lorenzo says. 'Nothing further.'

I get up, ready to cross-examine the neurosurgeon. 'Doctor,' I begin, 'are you familiar with the case of Zack Dunlap?'

'I am.'

'You're aware that Mr. Dunlap was in an ATV accident, declared to be brain-dead, and then spontaneously recovered, correct?'

'That's what people think.'

'What do you mean by that?'

'The medical community believes that Mr. Dunlap was never actually brain-dead but misdiagnosed,' the doctor replies. 'If he *had* been brain-dead, he wouldn't have recovered. In fact, I was part of a national group that was going to look into Mr. Dunlap's case – review the records and give an official public statement about what really happened – but the family didn't want us to.' He shrugs. 'They preferred to call it a miracle.'

'What about Terry Wallis?'

'Again, Mr. Wallis was diagnosed to be in a vegetative state for nearly two decades, but he wasn't. He was in a minimally conscious state, which is quite different. Patients who are minimally conscious have some degree of awareness of self and environment but can't communicate their thoughts and feelings. They may respond to painful stimuli, or follow a command, or cry at the sound of a loved one's voice. Minimal consciousness can be a chronic condition, but there is a better chance of recovery than there is for someone in a vegetative state.'

'Is it possible that Mr. Wallis moved from a vegetative state to a minimally conscious state?'

'Yes. There's a range of consciousness, from coma to vegetative state to minimally conscious state. Some patients move from one state to another.'

'So isn't it possible that the same might happen to Mr. Warren?'

'Terry Wallis's recovery was a remarkable and unexpected one, but his initial trauma was markedly different from Mr. Warren's. He had a diffuse axonal injury, which occurs without intracranial pressure, and which doesn't damage the neurons – just the axons. Your neurons are in your brain's cortex. Then there's gray matter. The axons go from there into the white matter. A head injury that leads to a DAI means that the cells in the gray matter are intact but aren't connected to anything, because those connections – the axons – have been sheared away. It's a very bad form of head trauma,

334

but it's one that spares the cells, the neurons. Mr. Wallis's recovery came about through regrowth of the axons. Mr. Warren's injury is caused not by severed axons but rather by damaged neurons. And unlike axons, once a neuron is destroyed, it can't regenerate.'

For all of the other lucky individuals mentioned by Zirconia in her opening argument, Dr. Saint-Clare has a medical reason why recovery was possible. 'So let me get this clear,' I recap. 'Each of the people Ms. Notch mentioned recovered either because they were initially misdiagnosed or because their injuries were substantially different from what Mr. Warren suffered?'

'Exactly,' the neurosurgeon says. 'No one is debating the fact that Mr. Warren's EEG shows signs of activity. It's possible he's retained the same verbal and motor ability he used to have, in the frontal lobes of his brain. But with injuries to his brain stem, it doesn't matter what happens in the frontal lobes. He can't plug into it, so to speak.' Dr. Saint-Clare looks at the judge. 'It's a little like going on vacation and seeing your destination from a plane, when all of a sudden a tornado blocks your landing. You might still be able to see the most beautiful resort – with a gorgeous beach and five-star service – but there's no way you're going to get from where you are to where you want to visit.'

'Will Mr. Warren always be dependent on a ventilator for breathing and tubes for feeding?' I ask.

'In my opinion, yes.'

'Can you predict how long he'll live if that treatment is continued?'

'Most patients with this sort of injury die within weeks or months of pneumonia or some other complication.' The doctor shakes his head. 'All these machines, they really just prolong the dying process. We're sustaining a life, but it's not much of one.'

'Thank you,' I say. 'Your witness.'

Zirconia Notch frowns at the neurosurgeon as she approaches. 'Who's paying for Mr. Warren's care?'

'From what I understand, he does not have health insurance. He's a guest of the state.'

'A guest who's costing you approximately five thousand dollars per day, excluding doctor fees.'

'We don't consider that when we're providing health care—'

'Isn't it true that your hospital lost two million dollars last year?'

'Yes . . .'

'So isn't it possible that part of the hospital's motivation to force a decision about Mr. Warren's welfare is so that you can free up a bed for a *paying* patient?'

'That's not my concern as a physician.'

'Doctor, you said that Mr. Warren is a candidate for donation after cardiac death?'

'That's correct. A man in his physical condition would be an excellent donor.'

'Isn't it true that a quarter of DCD cases don't go according to plan?'

He nods. 'Sometimes when the ventilator is turned off, the patient breathes sporadically on his own. If it doesn't stop within an hour or so, the donation is called off and the patient is left to die.'

'Why is the donation called off?'

'Because the patient won't have enough oxygen in his bloodstream to keep the organs viable, but he'll have too much oxygen to lead to cardiac cessation – which is the criterion for death.'

'So,' Zirconia says, pursing her lips. 'You basically wait for the heart to stop, and then count off five minutes, and then you harvest the organs?'

'That's correct.'

'Have you ever heard of Dr. Robert Veatch?' she asks.

Dr. Saint-Clare clears his throat. 'I have.'

'Isn't Dr. Veatch a renowned medical ethics professor who questioned DCD?'

'Yes.'

'Can you summarize for the court what Dr. Veatch's position is?'

Dr. Saint-Clare nods. 'Dr. Veatch points out that a heart that stops can be started again – in fact, that's exactly how a heart transplant is done. In his opinion the cessation of cardiac function and circulation is not irreversible in DCD patients – which means it doesn't meet the accepted standard of determination of death.'

'So basically, you're telling me that Mr. Warren can be declared dead once his heart stops. But it can then be donated to someone else . . . and start beating again.'

'That's right.'

'Then isn't it a little hasty to consider Mr. Warren dead in the first place, given that his heart technically could be defibrillated into action again while still inside his own body?'

'The circulatory determination of death is a standard medical practice in the developed world, Ms. Notch,' the doctor says. 'The five-minute waiting time is meant to ensure that the heart doesn't start beating again by itself, without medical intervention.'

Zirconia nods, but you can tell she's not buying it. 'Is Mr. Warren in any pain in his current condition?'

'No,' the doctor says. 'He's unconscious; he can't feel anything. We're doing our best to keep him comfortable.'

'So he's not currently suffering?'

'No.'

'He's not in distress?'

Dr. Saint-Clare shifts in his seat. 'No.'

'And he could continue in this state, not suffering, for how long?'

'If he didn't contract an illness that further compromised his bodily systems, and was sent to a long-term care facility, it could be several years.'

Zirconia folds her arms. 'Now, you've told Mr. Ng that the five people I listed initially who had severe brain injuries were misdiagnosed, which is why they eventually recovered?'

'Yes. Disorders of consciousness are notoriously hard to diagnose accurately.'

'Then how can you be sure Mr. Warren won't be the next case study of so-called miraculous recovery?'

'It's possible, but highly improbable.'

'Are you aware of total locked-in syndrome, Doctor?'

'Of course,' he says. 'LIS is a condition in which the patient is aware and awake but can't move or communicate.'

'Isn't it true that evidence of a brain stem lesion and a normal EEG are both symptomatic of LIS?'

'Yes.'

'And doesn't Mr. Warren's brain injury reflect brain stem lesions and a normal EEG?'

'Yes, but patients in classic locked-in syndrome have pinpoint pupils and other signs that lead to its recognition. Most neurologists consider it as a diagnosis when a patient appears to be in a coma, and test for it by asking the patient to look up and down.'

'But not in total locked-in syndrome, correct? Total LIS patients can't look up and down voluntarily, by definition.'

'That's right.'

'So wouldn't it be extremely difficult, without that voluntary eye movement, to know if a patient has total locked-in syndrome or is in a vegetative state?'

'Yes. It could be hard,' Dr. Saint-Clare says.

'Are you aware, Doctor, that LIS patients often communicate with assistive devices, and some of them may go on to lead long lives?'

'So I hear.'

'Can you tell this court with a hundred percent degree of certainty that Mr. Warren *doesn't* have locked-in syndrome?'

'Nothing in medicine is a hundred percent,' he argues.

'Then I guess you can't say with one hundred percent certainty, either, that Mr. Warren won't progress from a vegetative state into a minimally conscious one, and maybe even into consciousness?'

'No. But what I *can* tell you is that the treatments and interventions we've tried have not been successful in altering his state of consciousness, and I have no medical reason to believe that would change in the future.'

'You must be aware, Doctor, that people who suffered spinal cord injuries and were told they would never walk again have, in some cases, been able to walk due to advances in medicine.'

'Of course.'

'And the soldiers coming home from Iraq and Afghanistan

with missing limbs today have the use of amazing prosthetic devices that would have only been science fiction for a soldier from Vietnam. Isn't it fair to say that medical research advances every day?'

'Yes.'

'And haven't many people who were given dire – even terminal – diagnoses gone on to live rich, full lives? You can't say that five years from now, someone might not develop a technique that helps someone with lesions in the brain stem to recover, can you?'

Dr. Saint-Clare sighs. 'That's true. However, we have no way of knowing how long it will be before we start seeing these hypothetical cures you're talking about.'

Zirconia levels her gaze at him. 'I'm guessing it's more than twelve days,' she says. 'Nothing further.'

Dr. Saint-Clare stands up, but before he can leave the witness stand, the judge interrupts. 'Doctor,' he says. 'I have one more question for you. I don't understand a lot of the medical jargon you've used today, so I want to cut to the heart of the matter. If this man were your brother, what would you do?'

The neurosurgeon sinks slowly back into his chair. He turns away from the judge, and he looks at Cara, his gaze bruised and almost tender. 'I'd say good-bye,' Dr. Saint-Clare answers, 'and I'd let him go.'

Luke

I must have walked for six or seven days, trying to find my
   way back to humanity. Much of the time I cried, already
feeling the loss of my wolf family. I knew they'd survive
without me. I just wasn't sure if the same could be true in
reverse.

Understand I hadn't seen myself in two years, except for
the occasional muddy reflection in a pool of water. My hair
reached halfway down my back and was matted into unintentional dreadlocks. My beard was full and thick. My face
was full of healing scratches incurred during play with the
wolves. I hadn't fully bathed in months. I had lost nearly
sixty pounds, and my wrists stuck out like twigs from the
cuffs of my coveralls. I looked, I am sure, like anyone's biggest
nightmare.

I heard the highway long before I saw it, and I realized
how keen my senses had become – I could smell the hot tar
of the summer pavement miles before the trees thinned and
the embankment of the road rose in front of me. As I stepped
into the full sunlight, I squinted; a passing tractor-trailer
was so loud I nearly staggered backward at its roar. The hot
gust of wind it left behind blew my hair away from my filthy
face.

Lone Wolf

When I came to the chain-link fence, I touched it, the cool steel pressing like a lattice into my palm and so unlike anything I'd touched for so long that I stood for a moment, just feeling the strength and the clean lines of the metal. I started to climb up it, deftly leaping over the top edge and dropping to the ground silently: these were the skills I'd been honing. When I heard the voices, every hair on the back of my neck rose and I dropped into a natural crouch. I crossed so that I was upwind, so that they wouldn't know I was coming.

They were a group of Girl Scouts, or whatever Girl Scouts are called in Canada. They were having a picnic at this highway rest stop, while their motor coach slept like a hulking beast in the shade of the parking lot.

I felt edgy, wild, too exposed. There wasn't any tree cover; there wasn't anyone flanking me willing to fight beside me if I needed it. I could hear the high, ripping sound of cars whizzing by on the road, and each noise seemed to me a bullet skating too close for comfort. The laughter of the girls was deafening; it had me covering my ears with my palms.

In retrospect, I can imagine what it was like for them: to be joking around one minute and the next to have a beast at their picnic table, hulking and ragged and reeking. Some of the girls started screaming, one ran for the bus. I tried to calm them down, but my immediate instinct was to lower myself, duck my head. Then I remembered I had a voice.

One I hadn't used in two years, except to howl and growl. It was rusty, thin, a yelp. A sound I didn't remember.

It hurt, to make this sound. To try to shape it on the bowl of my tongue into a word. As I stuttered and choked on the syllables, the bus driver came running over. 'I've already called the police,' he threatened, holding me at bay with a gigantic flashlight, a makeshift weapon.

That's when speech returned to me. 'Help,' I said.

It actually was a blessing in disguise when the police showed up. It was at first hard to convince them of my ID, even though in the breast pocket of my tattered coveralls was the driver's license I'd walked into the woods with two years ago. I'm sure, given the looks of me, they thought that I was a homeless bum who stole some guy's wallet. It was when they called Georgie and she broke down sobbing on the phone that they finally believed me and let me shower in the precinct locker room. They gave me a police-issue T-shirt and a pair of sweats. They bought me a hamburger from McDonald's.

I ate it in about five seconds. Then I spent the next hour in the bathroom, throwing up.

The police chief brought me water and saltines. He wanted to know what the hell would make a guy go live with a pack of wolves. He especially wanted to know how I didn't wind up as their dinner. The more I talked to him, the more my voice lost its rasp, and the words that had been hovering like ghosts on the roof of my palate landed softly, solid and real.

He apologized for making me sleep in the holding cell, on the thin cot. It was the first bed I had been in in two years, though, and I could not get comfortable. The walls felt like they were closing in on me, even though the officers left the cell door unlocked. Everything smelled like ink and toner and dust.

When Georgie was brought into the holding area in the morning, having driven through the night to reach me, I was fast asleep on the floor of the cell. But like any wild animal,

I became one hundred percent alert before her footstep crossed the threshold. I knew she was coming because the scent of her shampoo and perfume rolled in like a tsunami before I could even see her.

'Oh, God,' she murmured. 'Luke?'

She rushed toward me.

I think that's what did it – made the instinct take over, and the reason in my mind shut down. But at any rate, when Georgie came running at me, I did what any wolf would have done in that situation.

I ducked away from her, wary.

No matter how long I live, I will always remember the way the light went out of her eyes, like a candle flame caught in an unexpected wind.

Edward

While I'm on the witness stand being sworn in, I stick my hand into the pocket of my father's jacket, and feel a tiny piece of paper there. I don't want to be obvious and pull it out and see what it is, especially while I'm in the hot seat, but I'm dying to know. Is it a note? A grocery list, in my dad's handwriting? A receipt from the post office? A laundry ticket? I have a fleeting vision of a dry cleaner's employee, wondering why the trousers Luke Warren dropped off weren't picked up last Monday, like they were supposed to be. I wonder how long they'd keep the clothes, if they'd call my father and ask him to come pick up his belongings, if they'd donate the pants to charity.

But when I manage to slide the paper secretly out of the pocket and hold it beneath the bar of the witness stand so that it would look, to anyone else, like I am just staring down into my lap, I see that it's a fortune from a cookie at a Chinese restaurant.

Anger begins with folly, and ends with regret.

I wonder why he kept it. If he felt like it was speaking personally to him. If he would read it from time to time and consider it a warning.

If he just shoved it in his pocket and forgot it was there.

If it reminded him of me.

'Edward,' Joe says, 'what was it like growing up with your father?'

'I thought I had the coolest dad on the planet,' I admit. 'You have to understand, I was kind of quiet, a brainiac. Most of the time I could be found with my head buried in a book. I was allergic to, well, practically all of nature. I was the bull's-eye for bullies.' I can feel Cara's eyes on me, curious. This is not the big brother she remembers. From the point of view of a little kid, even a geek can be cool if he's in high school and drives an old beater and buys her licorice. 'When my dad came back from the wild, he was an instant celebrity. I was suddenly more popular just because I was related by blood.'

'What about the relationship you and your dad had? Were you close?'

'My father spent a lot of time away from home,' I say diplomatically, and a phrase pops into my head: *Don't speak ill of the dead*. 'There was his trip to Quebec, to live with the wild wolves, but even after he got back home and started building the packs at Redmond's, he'd stay overnight there in a trailer, or sometimes in the enclosures. The truth is that Cara liked tagging along with him more than I did, so she'd spend more time at the theme park, and I stayed with my mom.'

'Did you resent your father for not being with you?'

'Yes,' I say bluntly. 'I remember being jealous of the wolves he raised, because they knew him better than I did. And I remember being jealous of my sister, too, because she seemed to speak his language.'

Cara looks down, her hair falling into her face.

'Did you hate your father, Edward?'

'No. I didn't understand him, but I didn't hate him.'

'Do you think he hated you?'

'No.' I shake my head. 'I think he was baffled. I think he expected that his kids would naturally be interested in the same things he was – and to be totally honest, if you *weren't* into the same things he was, he couldn't really hold up his end of a conversation.'

'What happened when you were eighteen?'

'My father and I had . . . an argument,' I say. 'I'm gay. I'd just come out to my mother, and at her suggestion, I went to my father's trailer at the theme park to tell him, too.'

'Things didn't go very well?'

I hesitate, picking my way through a minefield of memory. 'You could say that.'

'So what happened?'

'I left home.'

'Where did you go?'

'Thailand,' I say. 'I started teaching ESL, and traveled around the country.'

'And you've been there for how long?'

'Six years,' I reply. My voice cracks in between the two words.

'During the time you were away, did you have any contact with your family?' Joe asks.

'Not at first. I really wanted – needed – to make a clean break. But eventually I got in touch with my mother.' I meet her gaze, and try to communicate that I'm sorry – for putting her through hell, for those months of silence. 'I didn't speak to my father.'

'What were the circumstances under which you came back from Thailand?'

'My mother called me and said that my father had been in a very bad accident. Cara had been in it, too.'

'How did you feel when you heard that?'

'Pretty freaked out. I mean, it doesn't really matter if you haven't seen someone for a long time. They never stop being your family.' I look up. 'I got on the next plane out to the States.'

'Tell the court, please, about the first time you saw your father in the hospital.'

Joe's question takes me back. I am standing at the foot of my father's bed, looking at the tangle of tubes and wires snaking out from beneath his hospital johnny. There's a bandage on his head, but what gets me like a fist in the gut is the tiniest fleck of blood. It's on his neck, just above his Adam's apple. I could easily see how it might have been mistaken for a bit of stubble, a scratch. But when the evidence of trauma has been so carefully cleaned from him already by the attentive nurses, this one tiny reminder nearly brings me to my knees.

'My father was a big man,' I say softly, 'but when you met him, he looked even bigger than he was. His energy alone probably added two inches. He was the guy who didn't just walk somewhere; he ran. He didn't eat, he devoured a meal. You know how you meet people who live at the very edge of the bell curve? That was him.' I pull his jacket closed around me. 'But the man in the hospital bed? I'd never seen him before in my life.'

'Did you speak to his treating neurosurgeon?' Joe asks.

'Yes. Dr. Saint-Clare came in and talked to me about the tests they'd done, and the emergency surgery they had performed to relieve pressure on his brain. He explained how even though the swelling had gone down, my father still had suffered a severe trauma to the brain stem and that no further surgery could fix that.'

'How often have you seen your father in the hospital?'

I hesitate, figuring out how to say that I've been there constantly – except for the moments I was legally barred from his room. 'I've tried to make some time to visit every day.'

Joe faces me. 'Did you and your father ever have a conversation about what he'd want to do if he became incapacitated, Edward?'

'Yes,' I say. 'Once.'

'Can you tell us about it?'

'When I was fifteen, my father decided to go into the forests of Quebec and try to live with wild wolves. No one had ever done anything like it before. Biologists had tracked wolf corridors along the St. Lawrence River, so he figured he would try to intercept them, and then infiltrate a pack. He'd gotten a few captive packs earlier in his career to accept him, and this was a natural extension, he thought. But it also meant living on his own during a Canadian winter without any shelter or food.'

'Was your father concerned about his welfare?'

'No. He was just doing what he felt like he had to do – for him, it really was a *calling*. My mom didn't see it quite the same way. She felt like he was running out on her and leaving her with two kids. She was certain he was going to die. She thought it was irresponsible and insane, and that he'd come to his senses and decide to stay home, where he belonged . . . except he didn't.'

My mother is stone-still in her seat in the front row, her

eyes cast down onto her lap. Her hands are clenched together. 'The night before he left, my father called me into his office. He had two glasses and a bottle of whisky on his desk, and he told me I should have a drink, because I was going to be the man of the house now.'

The alcohol feels like fire; I cough and my eyes water and I think I might die right there, but he pats my back and tells me to breathe. I wipe my face with the bottom of my shirt and swear that I will never, in a million years, drink that crap again. When my vision clears, I notice something on the desk that wasn't there before. It's a piece of paper.

'Do you recognize this document?' Joe asks.

And there it is again, wrinkled and torn at one edge, the letter I found wedged in the file cabinet. He enters it into evidence and then asks me to read it out loud. I do, but it's my father's voice I hear in my head.

And then, my own reply: *What if I make the wrong choice?*

'Is that your signature at the bottom of the page?' Joe asks.

'Yes.'

'And is that your father's signature?'

'Yes.'

'In the past nine years did your father ever advise you that he was revoking this medical power of attorney?'

'Objection!' Cara's lawyer stands up. 'This note isn't a valid legal medical power of attorney.'

'Overruled,' the judge mutters. He tears at his hair again. It's a wonder he's not bald by now, actually.

In some parallel universe, Cara and I would laugh over that.

'We never talked about it again. And one day, he came home from Quebec, and that was that.'

'When did you remember this contract?'

'When I was going through his papers at his home a few days ago, trying to find the number of the caretaker who stays with the wolves up at Redmond's. It was caught in the back of a file cabinet.'

'When you were going through your father's papers,' Joe says, 'did you find any other powers of attorney?'

'No, I didn't.'

'How about a will? Or an insurance policy?'

'No will,' I reply, 'but I did find an insurance policy.'

'Can you tell the court who was the beneficiary of his insurance, in the unfortunate circumstance of his death?'

'My sister,' I say. 'Cara.'

Her jaw drops, and I realize this is something my father never told her.

'Were you a beneficiary, too?'

'No.'

When I'd found the policy, in a file with the title to his truck and his passport, I had read it from cover to cover. I'd played the mind game, wondering if he'd taken me off the policy after I left, or if he'd only purchased the plan once I was gone.

'Were you surprised?'

'Not really.'

'Were you angry?'

I lift my chin. 'I've been making my own way for six years. I don't need his money.'

'So this whole initiative you've undertaken to become your father's guardian and make a decision about his future medical care – it isn't motivated by any pecuniary gain?'

'I won't get a cent from my father's death, if that's what you're asking.'

'Edward,' Joe says, 'what do you think your father would want to happen now?'

'Objection,' Zirconia Notch argues. 'It's a personal opinion.'

'That's true, Counselor,' the judge agrees, 'but it's also what I need to hear.'

I take a deep breath. 'I've talked to the doctors and I've asked a hundred questions. I know my father's not coming back. He used to tell me about sick wolves, which would just start starving themselves because they knew they were dragging the pack behind, and they'd stay on the outskirts until they got weak enough to lie down and die. Not because they didn't want to live, or get well again, but because, in this condition, they were putting everyone they loved at a disadvantage. My dad would be the first to tell you he thinks like a wolf. And a wolf would put the pack above everything else.'

When I'm brave enough to look at Cara, it feels like I've been run through with a sword. Her eyes are swimming, her shoulders are shaking with the effort to hold herself together. 'I'm sorry, Cara,' I say directly to her. 'I love him, too. I know you don't believe that, but it's true. And I wish I could tell you he'll get better, but he won't. He'd tell you that it's his time. That for the family to move on, he has to go.'

'That's not true,' Cara bites out. 'None of it. He wouldn't leave me behind. And you don't love him. You *never* did.'

'Ms. Notch, control your client,' the judge says.

'Cara,' her lawyer murmurs, 'we'll have our turn.'

Joe faces me. 'Your sister clearly has a different opinion. Why is that?'

'Because she feels guilty. She was in the accident, too. She's better, and he's not. I'm not saying it's her fault – just that she's too close to the situation to be able to make a decision.'

'Some might say *you* were too far away to make a decision,' Joe counters.

I nod. 'I know. But there's one thing I've realized since I've been here. You think, when you leave, that everything stops. That the world is frozen and waiting for you. But nothing stands still. Buildings get torn down. People get into accidents. Little girls grow up.' I turn to Cara. 'When you were little, you used to go to the town pool in the summer and do belly flops off the diving board. You wanted me to grade you, like they did at the Olympics. Half the time I was busy reading and I'd just make up a number, and if it was too low, you'd beg me for an instant replay. The thing is, when you get older, there are no instant replays. You either get it right or you screw it up and you have to live with what you've done. I hadn't seen my father in six years and I always thought that, eventually, we'd talk. I thought he'd say he was sorry or maybe I would, but it would be like those Hallmark movies where everything gets tied up nice and neat in the end. I can't get back those six years, yet at any moment I could have been the one to pick up the phone and call my father and say, *Hi, it's me.*' I reach into my pocket, feel that slip of fortune. 'He trusted me once, when I was fifteen. I want him to know that, no matter what, even though I left, he can still trust me. I want him to know I'm sorry things worked out the way they did between us. I may never get a chance to tell him that to his face. This is the only way I know how.'

Suddenly I remember what happened afterward in his office, when I signed the contract. The pen rolled out of my hand as if it had burned my fingers. My father picked up the whisky I'd left in my glass and drained it. *You*, he said, *are an old soul. You'll do better at this than I ever did.*

I held on to that compliment, that treasure, the way an oyster cradles a pearl, completely forgetting the pain that made it possible.

'Make no mistake,' Joe says to me, before the cross-examination begins. 'Zirconia Notch may look like she grows ganja in her herb garden and weaves sweaters out of her own hair, but she's a piranha. She used to work for Danny Boyle, and he picks his attorneys based on how fast they can draw blood.'

So as Cara's attorney walks closer to me with a smile, I grip the seat of the witness chair, preparing for battle.

'Isn't it true,' she says, 'that you're trying to convince this court that, at age fifteen, you were mature enough to be appointed by your father to make a decision about his health? Yet now you're arguing that your sister – who is seventeen and three-quarters – shouldn't be allowed to do the same thing?'

'My dad was the one who made that choice. I didn't ask for it,' I reply.

'Are you aware that Cara manages all your father's finances and pays his bills?'

'It wouldn't surprise me,' I say. 'That's what I did when I was her age.'

'You haven't seen your father in six years, correct?'

'Yes.'

'Isn't it possible that he did execute another document – perhaps naming Cara as the guardian for his health care decisions – and you're not aware of it? Or perhaps you did find one . . . and threw it away?'

Joe stands up. 'Objection! No foundation . . .'

'Withdrawn,' Zirconia Notch says, but it gets me wondering.

What if my father *did* appoint Cara, or someone else, and we just haven't found that piece of paper yet? What if he changed his mind – and I was too far away to know? I don't believe it's murder if you turn off life support in accordance with someone's wishes. But what if it turns out that's *not* what he wanted?

'Would you describe yourself as impulsive, Edward?'

'No.'

'Really? You leave home after a heated argument? That's not normal behavior.'

Joe spreads his hands. 'Your Honor? Was there a question somewhere in that value judgment?'

'Sustained,' the judge says.

Zirconia doesn't miss a beat. 'Would you describe yourself as someone who likes to be in control of things?'

'Just my own destiny,' I reply.

'What about your father's destiny?' she drills. 'You're trying to take control of that right now, aren't you?'

'He asked me to,' I say, my voice tightening. 'And he made his wishes pretty public: he signed up to be an organ donor.'

'You know this how?'

'It says so on his driver's license.'

'Are you aware that in New Hampshire, in order to be an organ donor, you don't just need a little sticker on your license? That you need to sign up with an online registry as well?'

'Well—'

'And did you know that your father did *not* sign up on that online registry?'

'No.'

'Do you think that's because maybe he changed his mind?'

'Objection,' Joe calls. 'Speculative.'

The judge frowns. 'I'll allow it. Mr. Warren, answer the question.'

I look at the lawyer. 'I think it's because he didn't know he had to take that step.'

'And you'd know how he thinks because, for the past six years, you two have been *so* close,' Zirconia says. 'Why, I bet you had long conversations into the night about all sorts of heartfelt matters. Oh, wait, that's right. *You weren't here.*'

'I'm here now,' I say.

'Right. Which is why, after talking to the doctors, you were ready to take whatever measures were necessary to end your father's life?'

'I was told by the doctors and the social worker that I should stop thinking about what I want, and think instead about what my dad would want.'

'Why didn't you discuss that with your sister?'

'I tried, but she got hysterical every time I brought up our father's condition.'

'How many times did you try to discuss this with Cara?'

'A couple.'

Zirconia Notch raises a brow. 'How many?'

'Once,' I admit.

'You realize Cara was in a massive motor vehicle accident?' she says.

'Of course.'

'You know she was seriously injured?'

'Yes.'

'You know that she'd just had major surgery?'

I sigh. 'Yes.'

'And that she was on painkillers and very fragile when you spoke with her?'

'She told me she couldn't do this anymore,' I argue. 'That she wanted it to be over.'

'And by *this* you assumed she meant your father's life? Even though she'd been vehemently opposed to turning off life support minutes before?'

'I assumed she meant the whole situation. It was too hard for her to hear, to process, all of it. That's why I told her I'd take care of everything.'

'And by "taking care of everything" you meant making a unilateral decision to terminate your father's life.'

'It's what he would want,' I insist.

'But be honest, Edward, this is really about what *you* want, isn't it?' Zirconia hammers.

'No.' I can feel a headache starting in my temples.

'Really? Because you scheduled a termination of life support for your father without telling your sister that you'd scheduled it. Moments before it happened, you *still* hadn't told your sister. And even when the hospital administration realized what you were up to and shut down the procedure,' she says, 'and even in spite of the fact that Cara was right there begging you to stop, you pushed people out of the way and did what you wanted to do all along: kill your father.'

'That's not true,' I say, getting flustered.

'Were you or were you not indicted for second-degree murder, Mr. Warren?'

'Objection!' Joe says. The judge nods. 'Sustained.'

'Is it your testimony today that you have no pecuniary interest in your father's death because you're not a beneficiary of his life insurance policy?'

'I only learned about his life insurance policy ten days ago,' I reply.

'Plenty of time to concoct a murder because you're angry that he left you off the insurance policy—' Zirconia muses.

Joe gets to his feet. 'Objection!'

'Sustained,' the judge murmurs.

Undeterred, the lawyer moves closer, her arms folded. 'Your father also has no will, which means, if he died intestate today, you'd be an heir to his estate and entitled to half of everything he owns.'

This is news to me. 'Really?'

'So theoretically, you *do* benefit from your father's demise,' she points out.

'I doubt there will be much left of my father's estate after we pay the hospital bills.'

'So you're saying that the sooner he dies, the more money there will be?'

'That's not what I meant. I didn't even know until two seconds ago that I would receive anything from his estate . . .'

'That's right. Your father's been dead to you for years, after all. So why not make it legitimate?'

Joe had warned me that Zirconia Notch would try to get me riled, would try to make me look like someone who might be able to commit murder. I take a deep breath, trying to keep so much heat from rushing to my face. 'You don't know anything about my relationship with my father.'

'On the contrary, Edward. I know that your actions here are motivated by anger and resentment—'

'No . . .'

'I know that you're angry that you were cut out of his life insurance policy. I know you're angry because your father never came after you when you left. You're angry because your sister had the relationship with your father you still secretly wish you had—'

A vein starts throbbing in my neck. 'You're wrong.'

'Admit it: you're not doing this out of love, Edward – you're doing this out of hate.'

I shake my head.

'You hate your father for turning you away when you told him you were gay. You hated him so much for that you tore apart your family—'

'*He tore it apart first,*' I burst out. 'Fine. I did hate my father. But I never even told him I was gay. I never had the chance.' I look around the gallery, until I find one frozen face. 'Because when I got to the trailer that night, I found him cheating on my mother.'

During the recess, Joe sequesters me in a conference room. He goes off to find me a glass of water I won't be able to drink because my hands are still shaking so badly. This is exactly what I *didn't* want to happen.

The door opens, and to my surprise, it's not Joe returning – but my mother. She sits down across from me. 'Edward,' she says, and that one word is a canvas for me upon which to paint a missing history.

She looks small and shaken, but I guess that's what happens when you learn that the story you've told yourself all these years isn't true. And for that, at least, I owe her an explanation. 'I went to Redmond's to come out to him, but he didn't answer when I knocked. The trailer door was open, so I went inside. The lights were on, there was a radio playing. Dad wasn't in the main room, so I headed toward the bedroom.'

It is still as vivid, six years later, as it was back then – the silver limbs in a Gordian knot, the puddles of clothing on the linoleum floor, the few seconds it took for me to realize what I was actually seeing. 'He was fucking this college intern named Sparrow or Wren or something – a girl who was two goddamned years older than me.' I look up at my mother. 'I couldn't tell you. So when you assumed that the reason I came home upset was because the conversation between us hadn't gone well, I just let you keep assuming it.'

She crosses her arms tightly, still silent.

'He owed us those two years he was gone,' I say. 'He was supposed to come back and be a father. A husband. Instead he came back thinking and acting like one of the stupid wolves he lived with. He was the alpha and we were his pack, and wolves always put family first – how many times did he tell us that? But the whole time, he was lying through his teeth. He didn't give a shit about our family. He was screwing around behind your back; he was ignoring his own kids. He wasn't a wolf. He was just a hypocrite.'

My mother's jaw looks like it is made of glass. As if turning her head, even incrementally, might make her shatter. 'Then why did you leave?'

'He begged me not to say anything to you. He said it was a one-time thing, a mistake.' I look into my lap. 'I didn't want you or Cara to get hurt. After all, you waited two years for him, like Penelope and Odysseus. And Cara – well, she always saw him as a hero, and I didn't want to be the one to rip off the rose-colored glasses. But I knew I couldn't lie for him. Eventually I'd slip up, and it would break apart our whole family.' I bury my face in my hands. 'So instead of risking that, I left.'

'I knew,' my mother murmurs.

I suck in my breath. 'What?'

'I couldn't have told you which girl it was, but I *assumed.*' She squeezes my hand. 'Things deteriorated between us, after your father came back from Canada. He moved out, staying in the trailer or with his wolves. And then he started hiring these young girls, zoology grad students, who treated him as if he was Jesus Christ. Your father, he never said anything specific, but he didn't have to. After a while, these girls stopped looking me in the eye if I happened to show up at Redmond's. I'd sit in the trailer to wait for Luke, and I'd find an extra toothbrush. A pink sweatshirt.' My mother looks up at me. 'If I'd known that was the reason you went away, I would have swum to Thailand to get you myself,' she confesses. 'I should have been the one protecting you, Edward. Not the other way around. I'm so sorry.'

There is a soft knock on the door, and Joe enters. When my mother sees him, she flies into his arms. 'It's okay, baby,' he says, stroking her back, her hair.

'It doesn't matter,' she says against his shoulder. 'It was forever ago.'

She isn't crying, but I figure that's only a matter of time. Scars are just a treasure map for pain you've buried too deep to remember.

My mother and Joe have a lovers' shorthand, an economy of gestures that comes when you are close enough to someone to speak their language. I wonder if my mother and father ever had that, or if my mother was always just trying to decipher him.

'He never deserved you,' I tell my mother. 'He never deserved any of us.'

She turns to me, still holding Joe's hand. 'Do you want him to die, Edward,' she asks, 'or do you want him dead?'

There's a difference, I realize. I can tell myself I'm here to disprove the theory of the prodigal son; I can say *I want to carry out my father's wishes* until I am blue in the face. But you can call a horse a duck, yet it won't sprout feathers and grow a bill. You can tell yourself your family is the picture of happiness, but that's because loneliness and dissatisfaction don't always show up on camera.

It turns out there's a very fine line between mercy and revenge.

So fine, in fact, that I may have lost sight of it.

Luke

The anchor I had to the human world – my family – was different. My little girl, the one who had still been afraid of the dark when I left, was now wearing braces and hugging me around the neck and showing me her new goldfish, her favorite chapter book, a picture of herself at a swim meet. She acted as if two minutes had passed, instead of two years. My wife was more reserved. She would follow me around, certain if she took her eyes off me I might disappear again. Her mouth was always pressed tightly shut, because of all the things I knew she wanted to say to me but was afraid to let loose. After our first encounter at the police station in Canada, she had been afraid to come too close, physically. Instead, she smothered me with creature comfort: the softest sweatpants in my new, reduced size; simple home-cooked foods that my stomach had to relearn; a down comforter to keep me warm. I couldn't turn around without Georgie trying to do something for me.

My son, on the other hand, was outwardly unmoved by my return. He greeted me with a handshake and few words, and sometimes I'd find him warily watching me from a doorway or a window. He was cautious and tentative and unwilling to place his trust too quickly.

He had grown up, it seemed, to be much like me.

You would think that the creature comforts would have sent me diving headlong into the human world again, but it wasn't that easy. At night, I was wide awake, and I'd roam through the house on patrol. Every noise became a threat: the first time I heard the coffeemaker spitting at the end of its cycle, I ran downstairs in my undershorts and flew into the kitchen with my teeth bared and my back arched defensively. I preferred to sit in the dark instead of beneath artificial light. The mattress was too soft beneath me; instead, I lay down on the floor beside the bed. Once, when Georgie noticed me shivering in my sleep and tried to cover me, I was up like a rocket before she even finished draping the quilt over my body, my hands wrapped around her wrists and her body rolled and pinned to the ground so that I had the physical advantage. 'I – I'm sorry,' she stammered out, but I was so caught up in instinct that I couldn't even find the words to tell her, No, I am.

There's an honesty to the wolf world that is liberating. There's no diplomacy, no decorum. You tell your enemy you hate him; you show your admiration by confessing the truth. That directness doesn't work with humans, who are masters of subterfuge. Does this dress make me look fat? Do you really love me? Did you miss me? When a person asks this, she doesn't want to know the real answer. She wants you to lie to her. After two years of living with wolves, I had forgotten how many lies it takes to build a relationship. I would think of the big beta in Quebec, which I knew would fight to the death to protect me. I trusted him implicitly because he trusted me. But here, among humans, there were so many half-truths and white lies that it was too hard to remember what was real and what wasn't. It seemed that every time I spoke the truth, Georgie burst into tears; since I no longer knew what I was supposed to say, I stopped speaking entirely.

I couldn't stand being inside, because I felt caged. Television hurt my eyes; dinner table conversation was a foreign language. Even just walking into the bathroom in the house and smelling the combined confection of shampoo and soap and deodorant made me so dizzy I had to lean against the wall. I had been in a world where there were four or five basic smells. I had reached a sensory awareness where, when the alpha began to stir in her den, thirty yards away, I knew it, simply because her stretch sent a small puff of clay earth from the underground den through its narrow opening, and that smell was like a red flag among the others of urine, pine, snow, wolf.

I couldn't go outside, either, because when I walked down the street other people's dogs began to bark in their houses or, if they were in the yard, run to confront me. I remember passing a woman riding a horse, which shied and whinnied when it spotted me. Even though I was clean-shaven now and had scrubbed two years of dirt off my skin, I still exuded something raw and natural and predatory. (To this day, I have to walk a twenty-five-yard detour around a horse before it will pass.) You can take the man out of the wild, but you can't take the wild out of the man.

So it made sense that the only place I really felt at home was at Redmond's, in the wolf enclosures. I asked Georgie to drive me over there – I still wasn't really ready to drive. The animal caretakers there treated me as if I were the Second Coming, but they weren't the ones I wanted to see. Instead,

Lone Wolf

with a relief that came close to a total breakdown, I let myself into the pen with Wazoli, Sikwla, and Kladen.

Sikwla, the beta, came at me first. When I instinctively ducked and turned my head away from him – acknowledging his dominance – he greeted me by licking all around my face. I realized how easily this nonverbal conversation came to me – so much easier, in fact, than the stilted one I'd had with Georgie on the way over here, about whether or not I'd thought about the future and what I was going to do next. I also realized how much more fluent I'd gotten in the language of the wolf. Things that I had once had to think about while in enclosures with wolves now were a natural response. When Kladen, the tester wolf, nipped at me, a throaty growl rumbled out of me. When finally, the wary Wazoli – the alpha – approached, I lay down and rolled to offer her my throat and my trust. Best of all, mucking about in the dirt like this, I started to smell like me again, instead of like Head & Shoulders and Dove soap. My hair tie got lost in our play, and my hair, which I'd cut to my shoulders, fanned over my back and became matted with mud.

These wolves were softer around the edges than my brothers and sisters in Quebec. They were still wild animals, and they still had wild animal instincts, but simply by definition a captive wolf's life is not as violent as a wild wolf's life. This would again require an adjustment for me, as I remembered that my role here was not just as a pack member but as a teacher: offering these wolves an enrichment program to make them learn what they were missing by being contained in this wire fencing.

And now that I'd lived it, who better?

I had asked one of the caretakers to bring a half of a calf from the abattoir – a celebratory meal. He did, doing only a cursory double take when he saw me crouched between Kladen and Wazoli. I wanted this food because it was a pack food, one that would remind these guys that I belonged to the family. As soon as the calf was dragged into the enclosure and the caretaker had left, the wolves descended. Wazoli went for the organ meat, Kladen the movement meat, and Sikwla the stomach contents and spine. I wedged myself in between Kladen and Sikwla, baring my teeth and curling my tongue to protect the food that was rightfully mine. I lowered my face to the carcass and began to rip off strips of raw flesh, bloodying my face and my hair and snapping at Sikwla when he came too close to my portion.

I am sure, when I came up for air, I was quite a sight: dirty and bloody, sated, delirious in the companionship of a group of animals that understood me and that I understood. I loped away from the carcass, following Sikwla to the rock where he sometimes dozed.

Until then I'd forgotten about Georgie. She was standing on the far side of the fence, staring at me with horror. Although I'd done nothing she hadn't seen before, I don't think she was reacting to my interaction with the wolves, or my meal with them. I think she just knew, at that moment, she'd lost me for good.

Georgie

Pay no attention to the man behind the curtain.

That's what the wizard says, in *The Wizard of Oz*. Keep the dog and pony show going so that the eye is drawn to the spectacle, and not to the reality. Of all the questions I get asked about Luke, the most common one is, 'What was it like to be married to someone like him?' I suppose people think, based on his television persona, that he is an animal in bed or that he eats his steak raw. The truth would have disappointed them: when Luke was with us, he was perfectly normal. He'd watch ESPN; he'd eat Fritos. He changed light-bulbs and took out the trash. He was ordinary, rather than extraordinary.

The thing is, when celebrities are born, they aren't supposed to wallow in the mundane. They are supposed to always be dressed to the nines, step out of limousines, or in Luke's case, live in the wild. Which meant that, after he returned from Quebec, Luke couldn't be the husband I needed him to be. That would have detracted from the man everyone else expected him to be.

But even those who are larger than life have people close to them – people who know that they leave the toilet seat up when they pee, or that they hate peanut butter, or that they crack their knuckles. And those of us who are close know that when the television cameras stop rolling, those legendary figures deflate into people who are simply life-size, people with zits and wrinkles, people with flaws.

I suppose that when Luke started hiring young girls to be wolf caretakers, it crossed my mind he might be sleeping with them. He wasn't, after all, sleeping with me. But what I really thought was that he needed an entourage. He needed girls who were so enamored with the man he was on camera and in the news that they believed exactly what they saw. Then, Luke could start to believe it himself.

So to all those people who want to know what it was like to be married to someone like Luke?

It was like trying to embrace a shadow.

It was coming in second place, every time.

It doesn't surprise me to find Cara stalking back and forth in front of the window of a conference room. 'It's a lie,' she says, the minute I walk in the door. 'He didn't do those things.'

Zirconia exchanges a glance with me. Of all those young women who couldn't see past their hero worship of Luke Warren, the one with the starriest eyes was his own daughter. She loved him simply because he belonged to her, which – if I heard Luke right all those years – made her relationship with him the most similar to one between wolves in a pack.

'It's possible your brother was making that up just to rattle you,' Zirconia says, 'but I don't think he's that smart, frankly.' She looks up at me. 'No offense.'

It's beginning to fall into place, like a city after an earthquake. Some buildings are still standing; some are irreparable. And of course, there are casualties. I had always wondered at Luke's vehement reaction to Edward's homosexuality – it just didn't make sense, given everything I knew about Luke – and that was because it never really happened. The only sexual exploits Edward had discussed that night had been his father's.

I sit down on the edge of a table, watching my daughter fiercely tread a line back and forth. Her sling hugs her injured arm tight against her body; the other arm is wrapped tightly over it. 'Cara,' I sigh, 'everyone makes mistakes.'

I cannot believe that I am apologizing for Luke's behavior. But – as Edward said – there is no limit to the lengths we'll go to to protect our family. We will cross oceans, we will swallow pride.

'He loved us,' Cara says. Her eyes are the color of a bruise, her mouth a wound.

'He loved *you*,' I correct. 'He still does.' I reach out a hand, trapping her as she passes by. 'I know that you ran to your dad when Joe and I were starting a family because you thought he was the safe haven; that with him, you'd be his only family, instead of just one kid out of a bunch. And I know how hard it must be for you to find out that he might not be the hero you thought he was. But whatever he did to me, Cara – that doesn't change how he feels about you.'

'Men. You can't live with them . . . and you can't legally shoot them,' Zirconia says. 'I tossed out my husband eight years ago and got a llama instead. Best decision I ever made.'

Ignoring her, I turn back to Cara. 'I guess what I'm trying to say is that it doesn't matter if your father isn't perfect. Because to him, *you* are.'

Instead of comforting her, however, those words make

Cara burst into tears. She folds herself into my arms. 'I'm sorry. I'm really sorry,' I say.

Gently, I rub her back. Luke used to talk about one of his wolves, which was afraid of storms, how the pup would crawl under his shirt for comfort. But he never took the time to know that his own daughter used to do the same thing. That on nights when lightning cracked the yolk of the moon, nights when Luke was tending to a frightened wolf, Cara would climb into bed with me and wrap her arms around my back, a mollusk riding out the tide.

'There's something else you should know,' I say. 'Edward left because he wanted to protect you. He thought if he wasn't here to tell us what he'd seen, you would never have to find out.'

Cara's good arm tightens around my neck. 'Mom,' she whispers. 'I have to—'

There is a knock on the door, a deputy sheriff announcing that court is about to reconvene. 'Cara,' Zirconia says, 'do you still want to be the legal guardian for your father?'

She pulls away from me. 'Yes.'

'Then I need you to get your head back in the game,' Zirconia says bluntly. 'I need the court to see that you're grown-up enough to love your father, no matter what. No matter if he was catting around on your mom, or if he needs to have a diaper changed every three hours, or if he spends the next decade in long-term care.'

I touch her arm. 'Is this really what you want, Cara? It could be years before he recovers. He might *never* recover. I know your father would want you to go to college, to get a job, to have a family, to be happy. You've got your whole life ahead of you.'

She lifts her chin, her eyes still too bright. 'He has a life ahead of him, too,' she says.

I have told Zirconia and Cara that I am stopping off at the restroom before heading back inside for Cara's testimony, but instead I find myself walking out the double doors of the courthouse, veering left into the parking lot. I drive the twenty minutes to Beresford Memorial Hospital and take the elevator up to the ICU.

Luke lies still, with no visible change to his condition, except a bruise around his IV site that has bloomed from purple to a mottled ocher.

I pull up a chair and stare at him.

When he came out of the wild, before the reporters showed up and drew him into an orbit of fame, I did my best to help him transition into the human world. I let him sleep for thirty hours straight; I cooked his favorite foods; I scrubbed the dirt that had become caked to his skin off his back. I figured that if I pretended life had returned to normal, maybe he would come to believe it.

To that end, I dragged him on errands. I took him to pick Cara up at school and I brought him into the bank while I used the ATM. I drove him to the post office, and to the gas station.

I started to see that women flocked to Luke. Even when he was dozing in the car, I'd come out of the dry cleaner's to find someone staring at him through the window. At Cara's school, strange ladies in vans honked until he waved. I made fun of him for it. *You're irresistible*, I told him. *Just remember me when you acquire your harem.*

I didn't realize at the time that I was being prophetic. I

thought: *Who, of all these fawning women, would put up with what I do behind closed doors?* A man who could only eat basic grains like farina and oatmeal without getting sick to his stomach, who turned the thermostat down at night until we all woke up shivering; a man whom I had actually found peeing around the perimeter of the backyard?

One day we went to the grocery store. In the produce aisle, a woman approached with two melons and asked Luke which one he thought was riper. I watched him smile and bend his head to the melons, so that his long hair fell over his face like a curtain. When he picked the fruit in her right hand, she nearly fainted.

One aisle over, a woman pushing a toddler in her grocery cart asked him to reach a box on the top shelf for her. Luke obliged, stretching to his full height and flexing his shoulders to get the item: denture cream, which I'm quite sure she had no intention of purchasing. It was, at the time, almost entertaining to see all these strangers drawn magnetically to my husband. I assumed it was some kind of reaction to his muscular build, his mane of hair, or some wolf pheromone. *They know I can protect them*, he said in all seriousness. *That's the attraction.*

But in the Bath & Body aisle, Luke had actually crumbled – he was that dazed and unnerved by the wave of scents that bled through the packaging and assaulted his senses. *It's okay*, I told him, and I pulled him upright and led him to a safer space, near the cereal.

I can't believe this, he said, burying his face in my shoulder. *I can kill a deer with my bare hands, but bubble bath is my kryptonite.*

That'll change, I promised.

Georgie, Luke said. *Promise me* you *won't.*

Now I look down at Luke, in the waxy shell of his own skin, his eyes closed and his mouth slack around the tube that is breathing for him. A god who's toppled back into mortality.

I reach for his hand. It's loose, the skin as dry as leaves. I have to fold it around my own hand, hold it up to my cheek. 'You son of a bitch,' I say.

Luke

*T*here *is only one thing that could have dragged me away from another wolf family, and that is a human. This one came in the form of a features reporter for the* Union Leader, *and was accompanied by a photographer. As visitors came to Redmond's and found me living with the pack, excitement grew – and with it, the number of tourists coming to see me for themselves. Somehow, New Hampshire's largest paper got wind of it.*

The irony didn't escape me: this was how Georgie and I had met, too. Once, I'd left the wolves for her. Now, I was going to have to leave them again because of a reporter. Every day there were more – some with television cameras – all clamoring for an interview with the man who'd lived in the wild with wolves. Kladen, Sikwla, and Wazoli were skittish and snappish – and for good reason. They could read loud and clear the signals these people sent: that they wanted something from me, that they were greedy and selfish. In the wild, any of these reporters would have been treated like a predator: brought down by the pack to save one of its members.

But that devotion to family went both ways, and I knew that I couldn't let the lives of the wolves be disrupted because of me. So I left the pen, only to be swallowed by the hail of questions and the camera flashes.

Did you really live in the wild?

What did you eat?

Were you scared?

How did you survive a Canadian winter?

What made you return?

It was that last question that sent me over the edge, because I didn't belong here, anymore. And although I would have walked into the woods in a heartbeat and tried to howl to locate my pack again, there was no guarantee that I'd ever find them or that they would take me back.

Before I'd started sleeping at Redmond's with the wolves, I had prowled the house late one night and found a light on in my son Edward's room. He looked up when I opened the door, challenging me with his eyes to ask why he was awake at 3:00 a.m. I didn't ask because, after all, so was I. Edward was propped against his pillows, reading a book. When I didn't speak, he held it up. 'The Divine Comedy,' he said. 'By Dante. I'm reading all about Hell.'

'I'm living it,' I said.

'I'm only at the first circle,' Edward told me. 'Limbo. It's not Heaven, and it's not Hell. It's the in-between.'

This was, I realized, my new address.

I couldn't be charming. I couldn't be smart. I could barely remember how to speak, much less how to put into sentences everything I had learned with the wolves. So I did what a wolf does when it finds itself in danger: I got away.

I ran to Redmond's. It was ten miles in the dark, but that meant nothing to me after Quebec, and it felt good to get my adrenaline pumping. I went up to the trailer at the top of the hill and slammed inside. I locked the door, and then went into the bedroom, and locked that door, too. I was breathing hard, sweating. I could hear the wolves howling for me.

There's no point in being able to know everything about wolves if you can't teach it to the people who need to learn.

I don't know how long I stayed in that dark, cramped room, curled in the far corner with my eyes on the door so that I'd know the minute someone was coming. But eventually, I heard muffled voices. And movement. The twitch of a key in a lock.

The scent of Georgie's shampoo, her soap.

She locked the door behind her and knelt down in front of me, moving slowly. She put her hand on the crown of my head. 'Luke,' she whispered.

Her fingers stroked my hair, and I found myself leaning into her, against her. Georgie's arms came around me. I didn't realize that I was crying until I tasted my tears on her lips. She kissed my brow, my cheeks, my neck.

It was meant as comfort but spread, the way a match intended for light might become a fire. My arms came around her and reached for the collar of her shirt. I ripped it open, rucked up her skirt. I felt her legs wrap around me, and I fumbled with my jeans. I bit her shoulder and swallowed her cry; I stood with her in my arms and pressed her back to the wall, driving into her so desperately that her spine arched, that her nails scratched into my skin. I wanted to mark her. I wanted her to be mine.

Afterward, I cradled her in my lap, tracing the line of her vertebrae. There were bruises on her, unintentional ones. I wondered if I had lost the capacity to be gentle, along with my ability to be human. I looked down to find Georgie staring up at me. 'Luke,' she said, 'let me help.'

Cara

You don't ever want to imagine your father having an affair.

In the first place, it means you have to picture him having sex, which is just disgusting. In the second place, it means that you are forced to side with your mother, who is the wronged party. And in the third place, you can't help but wonder what it was about you that wasn't compelling enough to make him think twice before driving a stake into the heart of your family.

It feels like I have a splinter in my throat after I hear this news, but it's not for the reason you'd think. I am – and I know how crazy this sounds – relieved. Now I'm not the only one who has screwed up royally.

My mother said I'm perfect in my father's eyes, but that's a lie. So maybe we can be imperfect for each other.

As soon as I sit down on the witness stand, I have a clear view of Edward. I keep thinking about what my mother said – how he was trying to protect me by leaving. If you ask me, he ought to rethink some of his altruism. Saying he was saving our family by removing himself from my life is like saying he only wants to kill my father because it's the humane thing to do.

Everyone makes mistakes, my mother had said.

I used to have a friend in elementary school whose family was so picture-perfect that they could practically be the advertisement in a photo frame. They always remembered each other's birthdays, and I swear the siblings never fought and the parents acted like they'd just fallen in love that morning. It was weird. It felt so plastic-smooth that I couldn't help but question what happened when there wasn't an audience like me for them to put on their show.

My family, on the other hand, included a father who preferred the company of wild animals, a mother who sometimes had to go to bed with a headache although we all really knew she was crying, a fifteen-year-old boy paying the bills, and me, a kid who made herself throw up the night of the Sadie Hawkins dance at school where the girls all brought their dads, just so she could stay home sick and no one would have to feel bad for her.

I wonder if what makes a family a family isn't doing everything right all the time but, instead, giving a second chance to the people you love who do things wrong.

Once again when they try to swear me in I can't really do it because my right arm is tied up tight against my body. But I still promise to tell the truth.

Zirconia begins by walking toward me. It's funny how at home she looks in a courtroom, even with her crazy fluorescent tights and yellow heels. 'Cara,' Zirconia begins, 'how old are you?'

'I'm seventeen,' I say, 'and three-quarters.'

'When is your birthday?'

'In three months.'

'At the time of your father's injury,' she asks, 'where were you living?'

'With him. I've been living with him for the past four years.'

'How would you describe your relationship with your father, Cara?'

'We do everything together,' I say, feeling my throat narrow around the words. 'I spend a lot of time with him at Redmond's, helping him with the wolves. I also took over running the household, pretty much, because he's so busy with his research. We've gone camping in the White Mountains, and he taught me orienteering. Sometimes we just hang out at home, too. We'll cook pasta – he gave me his special recipe for Bolognese sauce – and watch a DVD. But he's also the first person I want to talk to if I get a great grade on a test, or if a kid is being a jerk to me at school, or if I don't know the answer to something. Almost everything I know, I know because of him.'

I feel guilty saying this, with my mother in the courtroom, even if it's true and I can blame it on being sworn in. I think that kids are always closer to one parent than to the other. We may love both, but there's one who's your default. When I look at the spot where my mom has been sitting, though, she's gone. I wonder if she is still in the bathroom; if she's sick, if I should be worried – and then Zirconia's voice pulls me back.

'What about your father's relationship with Edward?'

'He didn't have a relationship with Edward,' I say. 'Edward left us.' But when I say this, I look at my brother. Can you really be mad at someone for doing something stupid if they truly, one hundred percent, thought they were doing what was right?

'How about *your* relationship with Edward?' Zirconia asks.

My whole life, people have said that I look like my mother and Edward is a clone of my father. But now I realize this isn't exactly true. Edward and I, we have the same color eyes. A strange, unearthly hazel that neither my mother nor my father has. 'I hardly remember him,' I murmur.

'What were your injuries in the accident?'

'I had a dislocated, fractured shoulder – the doctor says the humeral head was shattered. I also had bruised ribs and a concussion.'

'What was the treatment?'

'I had surgery,' I answer. 'I had a metal rod placed in my arm, and the shoulder is held in place with a rubber band and something like chicken wire.' I glance at the judge's white face. 'I'm not kidding.'

'Were you on any medication?'

'Painkillers. Morphine, mostly.'

'How long were you in the hospital?'

'Six days. I had an infection that had to be treated after surgery,' I say.

Zirconia frowns. 'It sounds like a very traumatic injury.'

'The worst part is that I'm right-handed. Well. I used to be, anyway.'

'You heard your brother testify about the conversation he had with you before he made the decision to terminate your father's life support. When was that?'

'My fifth night in the hospital. I was in a lot of pain, and the nurses had just given me something to help me sleep.'

'Yet your brother tried to talk to you about a matter as serious as your father's life or death?'

'My father's doctors had just come to my room to present his prognosis to me. To be honest, I got upset. I just couldn't listen to them telling me that my father wasn't going to get better – not when I didn't even feel strong enough to challenge them on what they were saying. One of the nurses made everyone else leave because I was getting agitated and she was afraid I'd tear out my staples.'

Zirconia looks at Edward. 'And that was the moment when your brother chose to have a heart-to-heart?'

'Yes. I told him I couldn't do it. I meant that I couldn't listen to the doctors talk about my father like he was already dead. But Edward apparently assumed I meant that I couldn't make a decision about my father's care.'

'Objection,' Joe says. 'Speculative.'

'Sustained,' the judge replies.

'Did you have any other conversations with your brother after that?'

'Yeah,' I say. 'When he was about to kill my father.'

'Can you describe that moment for the court?'

I don't want to, but in that second, I'm back in the hospital, hearing the hospital lawyer say that Edward told them I'd given consent. I'm running up the staircase in my bare feet to my father's room in the ICU. It's crowded, a party to which I haven't been invited. *He's a liar*, I say, and my voice throbs from a place so deep inside me that it feels primeval, foreign.

There is a moment of relief, when the lawyer calls off the procedure, and I start to sob. It's a delayed reaction, the one you feel when you realize that you've escaped death narrowly.

The last time I'd felt it was after our truck had crashed into the tree, before I—

Before.

'It was like Edward didn't even hear me,' I murmur. 'He

shoved a nurse out of the way and reached down and pulled the plug of the ventilator out of the wall.'

The judge looks at me, encouraging me to continue.

'Someone plugged the machine back in. An orderly held on to Edward until security came and took him away.'

'Cara, how is your father, after this unfortunate turn of events?'

I shake my head. 'Luckily, there hasn't been a change in his condition. Without oxygen, he could have wound up brain-dead.'

'Now, you had no idea that your brother had made this unilateral decision?'

'No. He never asked me for my input.'

'Is it what you would have wanted to happen?'

'No!' I say. 'I know if we give my dad some more time, his condition will improve.'

'Cara, you've heard Dr. Saint-Clare say it's highly improbable that your father will make a recovery, given the severity of his injuries,' Zirconia points out.

'I also heard him say that he couldn't be one hundred percent sure it wouldn't happen,' I reply. 'I'm holding out for that tiny percentage, because nobody else is.'

Zirconia tilts her head. 'Do you know your father's opinion about how he'd want to be treated in this sort of medical situation?'

I face Edward, because I want to say to him all the things he never gave me a chance to say before he pulled that plug. 'My father always says that, with wolves, if your family makes it through the day – with all the hardships of weather and starvation and predators – and survives the night, well, that's something to celebrate. I've watched him stay up all night giving a wolf pup Esbilac from a bottle; I've seen him warm a shivering newborn underneath his own shirt; I've driven with him in a blizzard to a vet to try to save a pup who can't breathe right. Even though, in the wild, any of those wolves would just die as part of natural selection, my father couldn't be that careless. He'd tell me over and over that the one gift you can't throw away is a life.'

'Then why did he pay for his girlfriend's abortion?'

My head snaps around at the sound of Edward's voice. He's standing now, red-faced, choking on his own words. 'You take care of the bills now. But back then, I did. And that's how I found out.'

Joe tugs on Edward's arm. 'Shut up,' he grits out.

'See, it wasn't just a one-time thing with another woman, even though that's what he told me. It was months, and that baby was *his*—'

'Order!' the judge yells. He smacks his gavel.

I've gone dead inside before Edward even speaks again, as Joe is calling for a recess and dragging him out of the courtroom. 'He told you all kinds of things that were lies,' Edward says to me, just to me. 'You think you know him, Cara. But really, you never knew him at all.'

Luke

*G*eorgie insisted that I see a doctor. At the hospital, I sat in the waiting room reading people. Anticipating the movements of a predator was the difference between life and death in the wild, but here it became a parlor game. I could tell seconds before a woman opened her purse that she was going to reach for a tissue. I knew that the man sitting alone in the corner was on the verge of tears, although he was smiling at his daughter. I knew that the woman rubbing her stomach had been sick for a long time; I could smell it in her blood. With great curiosity I watched the nurse at the check-in desk. Every few minutes a complete stranger approached her and she didn't even react with the good sense to back away, even though there was no way she could have known whether the person was holding a gun in his coat pocket, or was going to strike her. She assumed trust before the newcomer even showed submission – and I kept waiting the way you watch an impending train wreck: certain that any minute now tragedy would strike.

When I was called into the examination room, Georgie – who had been sitting behind me – stood up as if she planned to follow me in. 'Um,' I said. 'I thought I could do this alone.'

Embarrassed, she blushed. 'Right,' Georgie said. 'Of course.'

I followed the nurse into the exam room, where she took my pulse. Three times. 'That can't be right,' she said, and she was equally confused by my low blood pressure.

I sat alone, waiting for the doctor, my eyes on the doorknob. I listened in the hallway for the rustle of papers in my file. I closed my eyes and breathed in aftershave. 'Hello,' I said, a moment before he entered.

The doctor raised his brows. 'Good morning. I'm Dr. Stephens, and you are . . . Luke Warren, according to your chart. So you've been living in the woods with a pack of wolves for two years and you can apparently see through doors,' he said. He turned to his nurse. 'Where's the psych consult?'

'I'm not insane. I'm a wolf biologist. I followed a wild pack of gray wolves along the St. Lawrence corridor. I got them to accept me into the pack. I hunted with them, ate alongside them, slept beside them.'

I don't think he would have believed me if he hadn't seen my blood pressure numbers. He turned to his nurse. 'Clearly these are a mistake . . .'

'I took it three times,' she argued.

Dr. Stephens frowned, counting the beats of my heart himself. 'Okay,' he said. 'Your pulse is lower than the pro basketball player I treated a year ago. If I didn't know better, I'd say you were barely alive. But obviously that's not the case. So what's going on?'

'I had a . . . unique diet and exercise plan,' I explained.

The doctor's jaw dropped. 'You're telling the truth,' he said, and I nodded.

He sat down and listened while I explained how I'd become part of a pack. I told him about our meals, how we traveled, how we hunted. I explained our sleeping habits, how far we would move on patrol, how we fought predators, how we brought down prey. By the time I finished, an hour later, he was staring at me as if he'd cornered an alien, and had the opportunity to do the first full-body examination of it. 'I'd love to run some blood work,' he said, excited. 'See how your experience has affected you physically. Would you mind . . . ?'

He left me alone to order the tests, and I put my shirt back on. But instead of waiting for the phlebotomist, I walked into the hall, where I was stopped by an orderly. 'Can you show me where the nearest restroom is?' I asked.

He gave me directions – down the hall and to the left. I followed them but didn't go to the bathroom. I kept walking. I walked out the back door, down a flight of stairs, and into the bright sunlight.

There was a teenager sitting on the curb weeping. He had a pair of enormous air-traffic-controller headphones on, and he was rocking back and forth. 'Too much,' he said, over and over, as he shook his head. His voice sounded as if he was speaking from the bottom of the ocean.

I sat down next to him, and a moment later, a woman ran out of the door. It took everything in my power not to react by shrinking away. 'There you are!' she exclaimed, dragging him up by the arm.

'Is he all right?' I asked.

'His cochlear implants were activated today,' she said proudly. 'He's just getting used to them.'

I could see it, then, the silver disk in the skull, surrounded by cropped hair. 'Too much,' the teenager howled.

To this day he is the only person in this world who I think understands what it felt like for me to return.

Joe

'You know,' I say, closing the door to the conference room, 'just once I'd like you to actually tell me what you're going to say before you say it. In fact, I'd also settle for you restricting your statements to direct questions instead of spontaneous utterances.'

'I'm sorry,' Edward mutters. He buries his face in his hands. 'I didn't mean to.'

'Didn't mean to what? Throw another bomb into the courtroom? Bring your sister to tears? Completely destroy your mother?'

I look down at my phone. Georgie has vanished. I've called and I've texted, but she isn't answering. One minute she was in the courtroom, the next, Edward had confessed to his father's infidelity and she was gone. I'm trying really hard to convince myself that she hasn't become so upset by the news about her ex that she's gone into hiding. I'm trying really hard to believe that she's happy enough with me, now, to feel the sting of the revelation and then shrug it off. The only good news here, in fact, was that she wasn't in the courtroom during this latest episode of Edward's True Confessions.

I sit down, loosen my tie. 'So?'

Edward looks up at me. 'The night I caught him in the

trailer with his assistant, he was like I'd never seen him before. Freaking out. Terrified I'd tell Mom. He swore to me that it was a mistake and that it had only happened once in the heat of the moment, that it wouldn't happen again. I don't know why I bothered to believe him. But I went home, and Mom knew something was off with me. She thought it had something to do with telling my father I was gay, and because it was easier, I let her believe that. But a day later, I was paying bills, like usual, and I saw one from an abortion clinic in Concord. I only knew about it because of a junior who'd gotten pregnant that year, and who'd gone there to take care of things. Anyway, there was a Post-it note attached to the bill. It said, *Thanks for paying in full at the time of your visit – sorry our computer system was down. Please find enclosed a copy of your receipt for insurance purposes.* I was pretty surprised to find a bill from there, and I was sure it was a mix-up in the mail, until I read the patient's name: Wren McGraw. She was the college kid my father had hired to be a wolf caretaker. The one I'd found him sleeping with.' He bites down on his words, as if they are a chain between his teeth. 'The one he swore he'd never slept with before.' Edward forces a laugh. 'So I guess it's fitting that everyone always thought my father was some kind of god, since apparently he's capable of immaculate conception.'

'That's when you left,' I say.

Edward nods. 'My whole life, I felt like I was never the son he wanted me to be. But it turned out he wasn't the father I wanted him to be, either. Once you know something, you can't unknow it, and every time I saw him I knew I wouldn't be able to keep myself from getting mad at him. But I couldn't explain why I would be acting that way, not without hurting my mother or Cara. So instead, I drove to Redmond's and left the receipt for the abortion taped to his bathroom mirror. And then I took off.'

'Didn't you think it might hurt your mother if you left?'

'I was eighteen,' Edward says, an explanation. 'I wasn't thinking at all.'

'Why are you doing this, Edward? Is it some kind of karmic final bitch slap you want to give your father?'

He shakes his head. 'In fact, I think he's the one who gets the last laugh. If I didn't know better, I'd think he had this planned all along. After six years of being apart, we're all together again. We're being forced to make decisions together. Go figure,' Edward says. 'My father's finally taught us how to function like a pack.'

The good news, when we return to the courtroom, is that Georgie is there, and she seems not upset but vindicated. The bad news is that I have to cross-examine my own stepdaughter.

Cara looks like she's about to face the Inquisition. I walk toward her and lean forward. 'Cara,' I begin. 'Did you hear about the guy who fell into an upholstery machine?'

She frowns.

'Well, he's fully recovered.'

A tiny laugh bubbles out of her, and I wink. 'Cara, isn't it true that one of the wolves at your father's enclosures lost its leg?'

'Yes, to a trap,' she says. 'He chewed his own leg off to get free, and my father nursed him back to health when everyone said he was a goner.'

'But that wolf was able to use three legs to run away, correct?'

'I guess.'

'And he could still get food with three legs?'

'Yes.'

'And he could run with his pack?'

'Yes.'

'And he could communicate with other wolves in his pack?'

'Sure.'

'But that's not the case with your father, is it? His injury isn't one that would allow him to do any of those other things that would constitute a meaningful life?' I ask.

'I already told you,' Cara says stubbornly. 'To him, any life is meaningful.'

She carefully avoids looking at Edward when she says that.

'Your father's doctors have said there's virtually no chance of recovery for him, right?'

'It's not as black-and-white as they make it out to be,' she insists. 'My father is a fighter. If anyone is going to beat the odds, it's going to be him. He does things no one else can do, all the time.'

I take a deep breath, because now I'm getting to the part of the cross-examination that's going to be less than civil. I close my eyes, hoping that Cara – and Georgie – will forgive me for what I'm about to do. But my first responsibility, at this moment, is to Edward. 'Cara, do you drink alcohol?'

She blushes. 'No.'

'Have you ever drunk alcohol?'

'Yes,' she admits.

'In fact, the night of the accident, you were drinking, weren't you?'

'It was just one drink—'

'But you lied and told the police that you'd had no alcohol, right?'

'I thought I'd get in trouble,' Cara says.

'You called your father to come pick you up from a party because you didn't want to drive home with friends who'd been drinking – is that correct?'

She nods. 'My dad and I always said that if I ever got into a situation like that, he wouldn't judge me for making a bad choice to begin with as long as I called him. That way he knew he could get me home safely.'

'What did your father say to you in the car?'

She hugs her arm a little more tightly against her body. 'I don't remember,' Cara says, looking down into her lap. 'Some of the accident is just . . . missing. I know I left the party, and the next thing I remember are the EMTs.'

'Where do you live right now?' I ask.

The change in subject catches her off guard. 'I, um, with you. And my mother. But only because I still need help since I had surgery.'

'Before the accident you lived with your father?'

'Yes.'

'In the past six years since your parents' divorce, you've in fact lived with both of them, right?'

'Yes,' she says.

'Isn't it true that when you got fed up with your mother, you left her home and moved in with your father?'

'No,' Cara says. 'I didn't get fed up with my mother. I just felt—' She stops dead, realizing what she's about to say.

'Go on,' I urge softly.

'I felt like I didn't belong there, after she married you and had the twins,' Cara murmurs.

'So you left our house and moved in with your dad?'

'Well, he *is* my dad. It's not that big a deal.'

'What about when you had arguments with your father? Did you ever come back to stay with us?'

Cara bites her lower lip. 'That only happened twice. But I always went back home to him.'

'If your father does miraculously recover, where are you planning to live, Cara?'

'With him.'

'But you're going to need care for your shoulder for several months. Care that he won't be able to provide – not to mention the fact that you won't be in any shape to help with his rehabilitation . . .'

'I'll figure it out.'

'How will you pay the mortgage? Utilities?'

She thinks for a moment. 'With his life insurance policy,' she says triumphantly.

'Not if he isn't dead,' I point out. 'Which brings me to something else: you said that Edward was trying to kill your father.'

'Because he was.'

'He pulled out a ventilator plug. In that case, wouldn't your father actually have died of natural causes?'

She shakes her head. 'My brother is trying to kill my dad; I'm trying to keep him alive.'

I look at her, an apology. 'But isn't it true that if not for you and your poor judgment, your father wouldn't be in this position in the first place?'

I can see her eyes widen with surprise, with the realization that someone she trusted has just stabbed her in the back. I think of all the food I've cooked for her, the conversations we've had over the past six years. I knew the name of her first crush before Georgie did; I was the shoulder she cried on when that same guy started dating her best friend.

The judge tells Cara she can step down. Her upper lip is trembling. I start toward her, to offer a hug or a few words to cheer her up, and then realize that I can't; that in this courtroom she is the opposing party, the enemy.

Georgie folds her daughter into her embrace and looks at me coolly over Cara's head. She must have known, when she asked me to represent Edward, that it would come to this. That Cara – through no fault of her own – might lose not just one father figure but two.

Luke

When I was working with my Abenaki friends – the wolf biologists who studied the wild packs along the St. Lawrence corridor – I heard a tribal elder giving two young boys hell because they'd been caught spray-painting expletives on the back of a neighbor's barn. Blistering, the old man asked why they'd done something they knew was wrong. One of the boys said, simply, 'Grandfather, sometimes we want to be good. But sometimes we want to be bad.'

The elder said he'd have to give this some thought. There wasn't force, there wasn't violence, there wasn't even discipline. It was more like a think tank, as he treated these ten-year-olds like little adults, encouraging them to put their heads together to figure out the root of misbehavior. That night after dinner, he called the boys to him again. 'I have the answer,' he told them. 'You each have two wolves that fight inside you: a good wolf, and a bad wolf. If the bad wolf wins the fight, then you behave badly. If the good wolf wins the fight, you behave well.'

The boys looked at each other. 'Grandfather,' one said, 'how do I make sure that it's the good wolf who wins the fight?'

The old man looked from one boy to the other. 'The wolf that will win the fight is the one you feed the most.'

After I lived with the wolves, I thought a lot about that comment. When you consume a carcass, there is a spot allotted for everyone. The alpha will tell you where to stand with ear postures, turning one ear flat and the other pinned back against the head, or rotating those ears like airplane wings to direct each member of the pack to the appropriate position. A junior member of the pack is still expected to defend what's his, to growl and stand over his food. Dominance isn't about taking away the food he deserves; it's about being able to stand beside him, controlling the distance without taking any notice of his display of possessiveness.

An alpha could, of course, take any other pack member's food. But why would she? She needs those junior members, and if she starves them to death, they become useless in protecting the family.

With all due respect to the Abenaki elder, when he was teaching those boys a lesson, I think he left out this small irony. The good wolf would never let that bad wolf starve. She may test his ability to defend his food, but for the sake of the pack, she's going to make sure he survives.

Cara

When the judge calls for a two-hour lunch break so that he can eat and go to Mass, I am up and out of the courtroom like a shot, because I feel like I'm going to punch someone. After all, it's not every day that you find out your father was screwing around on your mom and that your stepfather skewers you in public. I run blindly up the stairways of the courthouse, aware that I probably have an entourage at my heels, and rattle doorknobs until I find one that's open.

Inside, I sit down on a conference table and draw my knees to my chest.

The worst part of it is that everything Joe said is true. My father wouldn't be lying in a hospital bed if it weren't for me. He never would have gone out on the roads that night. In some other, better world, he's still looking after captive packs of wolves, with his cheerful, obedient daughter by his side.

The doorknob turns, and suddenly Edward is standing in front of me. 'If you want to hide,' he says, 'you have to lock the door. Take it from me.'

'You're the last person I want to see right now.'

'Well, everyone's looking for you. Mom thinks you've

wigged out and run away again. Joe feels like crap, but he was just doing his job. And your lawyer . . . God, I don't know. I guess she's off making goat cheese or something.'

Against my will, a laugh bubbles out of me, carbonated emotion. 'Don't do that,' I say.

'Do what?'

'It's easier when I can hate you,' I admit.

'You *don't* hate me,' Edward says. 'We're on the same side, Cara. We both want to give Dad what he wants. We just each have a different idea of what that might be.'

'Why can't you just wait a month or two? And then if nothing happens, you can still do what you want to do. But it doesn't work the other way around. If you take him off life support now, we'll never know if he could have gotten better.'

He hops up on the table next to me. 'Nothing's going to be different in a month,' Edward says.

I can think of so many things that will be different. I'll be out of this sling. I'll be back at school. Maybe I will even have gotten used to having Edward back here in Beresford.

I realize that we are having the conversation Edward didn't have with me before he pulled the plug. So that's changed, too.

I look up at him. 'I'm sorry I got you arrested and put into jail.'

He grins. 'No you're not.'

I kick his foot, swinging next to mine. 'Well. Maybe just a little.'

When I was tiny, the county fair came through town. Our parents took us, and got tickets for the rides, even though I was scared to death of all of them. Edward was the one who convinced me to go on the merry-go-round. He put me

Jodi Picoult

up on one of the wooden horses and he told me the horse was magic, and might turn real right underneath me, but only if I didn't look down. So I didn't. I stared out at the pinwheeling crowd and searched for him. Even when I started to get dizzy or thought I might throw up, the circle would come around again and there he was. After a while, I stopped thinking about the horse being magic, or even how terrified I was, and instead, I made a game out of finding Edward.

I think that's what family feels like. A ride that takes you back to the same place over and over.

'Edward,' I ask. 'Could you drive me somewhere?'

If my mother and Joe are surprised to hear that Edward is the one taking me to see my father, they hide it well. It is a fifteen-mile ride, but it feels much longer. This nondescript rental car isn't Edward's old beater and I am not hauling a backpack, but we've slipped seamlessly into the same spots we used to be in when Edward drove me to school as a kid. I fiddle around with the radio station until I find one of the French Canadian FM ones. Although Edward had taken six years of French in school, he used to mock-translate for me, making up outrageous news stories about live goldfish found in public drinking fountains and a pet donkey named Mr. LeFoux who was unwittingly elected to the town selectboard. I wait for him to start translating again, but he just frowns and turns on some classic rock.

When we get to the hospital, Edward pulls up right to the front. 'Aren't you coming in?' I ask.

He shakes his head. 'I'll come back later.'

It's funny. All this time, when Edward was gone, I never

felt like I was alone. But now that he's back, as I watch him drive off, I feel lonely.

The nurses at the ICU desk all say hello to me, ask me how my shoulder feels. They tell me my dad has been a good patient, and I'm not sure if this is supposed to be some kind of joke, so I pretend to smile before I go into his room.

He is lying just the way he was the last time I visited, his arms tucked on top of the thin blanket, his head canted back on the pillow.

The pillows here suck. I know this from experience. They are too thick, and they are wrapped in plastic so your scalp sweats.

I walk toward my dad and gently reposition the pillow so it doesn't set his neck at that weird angle. 'Better, right?' I say, and I sit down on the foot of the bed.

Behind him is the weird techno-array of machines and computer monitors, like he is the star of a sci-fi movie. *How cool would that be*, I think. If he could communicate by making the little green lines jump on the screen. Twist and spell out the letters of my name.

For a moment, I watch just in case.

A nurse, an LPN, comes into the room. Her name is Rita, and she has a canary named Justin Bieber. She has a picture of the bird on her hospital ID tag. 'Cara,' she says. 'How are you doing today?' Then she pats my father on his shoulder. 'And how's my own personal Fabio?'

She calls him that because of his hair, or what's left of it where it hasn't been shaved. I guess the real Fabio is Mr. Romance Novel Cover, although I've never read one of those. I only know him as the guy who shilled I Can't Believe It's

Not Butter!, and who got hit in the face by a bird on a Disney World ride.

While Rita hangs a new IV bag, I stare at my father's hand on the blanket and try to imagine it touching a woman I cannot even picture in my memory anymore. I imagine him driving her to the clinic for her abortion. She would have been sitting in my seat.

I lean forward, as if I'm going to kiss his cheek, but really I'm doing this so Rita can't hear me. 'Dad,' I whisper. 'How about I forgive you, if you forgive me?'

And just like that, he opens his eyes.

'Oh, my God,' I cry.

Alarmed, Rita looks down at her patient. She reaches for the intercom behind the bed and pages the nurses' desk. 'Get neurology up here,' she says.

'Daddy!' I get off the bed and walk around it so that I can sit closer to him. His eyes slide to the left as I walk in that direction. 'You saw that, didn't you?' I say to Rita. 'How he followed me?' I put my hands on his cheeks. 'Can you hear me?'

His eyes are locked on mine. I've forgotten how blue they are, so bright and clear they almost hurt to look at, like the sky the morning after a snowstorm. 'I'm fighting for you,' I tell him. 'I won't give up if you don't.'

My father's head lolls to the side, and his eyes drift shut. 'Dad!' I shout. 'Daddy?'

I cry and I shake him – nothing happens. Even after Dr. Saint-Clare comes in and tries to make him react with more clinical tests, my father does not respond.

But for fifteen seconds – for fifteen glorious seconds – he did.

*   *   *

My mother is pacing in the hospital lobby when I race across it, ten minutes late for our scheduled pickup. 'You're going to be late for court,' she says, but I throw myself into her arms.

'He woke up,' I say. 'He woke up and looked at me!'

It takes a moment for my words to sink in. 'What? Just now?' She grabs my hand and starts running toward the elevator.

I stop her. 'It was only for a little bit. But there was a nurse in there who saw it, too. He looked right at me and his eyes followed me when I walked around the bed and I could see he was trying to tell me something—' I break off, hugging her tight around the neck. 'I told you so.'

My mother pulls her cell phone out of her pocket and dials a number. 'Tell Zirconia.'

Which is how, twenty minutes later, I find myself racing back into the courtroom as Judge LaPierre begins to speak. 'Ms. Notch, I understand you have something you need to say?'

'Yes, Your Honor. I need to recall my client and a new witness to the stand. Some evidence has come to light that I think the court needs to hear.'

Joe stands up. 'You rested your case,' he argues.

'Judge, a man's life or death hangs in the balance here. This happened only moments ago, or I would have given notice earlier.'

'I'll allow it.'

So once again I climb into the little wooden balcony built for a witness. 'Cara,' Zirconia asks, 'where did you go during the lunch break?'

'To visit my father in the hospital.'

'What happened when you got to his room?'

I look right at Edward, as if I am telling him the story, and not the judge. 'My dad was just lying there, like usual, like he was asleep. His eyes were closed and he wasn't moving. But this time, when I started talking to him, his eyes opened.'

Edward's jaw drops. Immediately, Joe leans toward him and whispers something in his ear.

'Can you show us?'

I close my eyes, and then as if I am a doll coming to life, I snap them open.

'What happened next?'

'I couldn't believe it,' I say. 'I got up and walked around the bed, and he kept looking at me, all the way until I sat down next to him again. He watched me the whole time.'

'And then?' Zirconia asks.

'Then his eyes closed,' I finish, 'and he went back to sleep.'

Joe is leaning back in his chair with his arms folded. I'm sure he thinks this is my Hail Mary pass, my eleventh-hour attempt to make up some crazy story that sways the judge in my favor. The thing is, it's not a story. It happened, and that has to mean something.

'Clearly Mr. Ng thinks it's incredibly convenient for you to have witnessed this,' Zirconia says. 'Is there anyone who can corroborate what you've told us?'

I point to Rita, the nurse, who has slipped into the back row of the gallery. She's still wearing her scrubs and her hospital ID tag. 'Yes,' I say. 'Her.'

Luke

*T*he hardest part about being back in the human world was relearning emotion. Everything a wolf does has a practical, simple reason. There is no cold shoulder, no saying one thing when you mean something else, no innuendo. Wolves fight for two reasons: family and territory. Humans are driven by ego; wolves have no room for it and will literally nip it out of you. For a wolf, the world is about understanding, knowledge, respect – attributes that many humans have cast off, along with an appreciation of the natural world.

The Native Americans know that wolves are mirrors for humans. What they show us are our strengths and our weaknesses. If we don't respect our territory, the wolf will invade it. If we don't keep our children close by, if we don't value the knowledge our senior population has accrued, if we leave our garbage around, the wolf will overstep its bounds to let us know we've made a mistake. The wolf is one of those creatures that links everything in the ecosystem. Where they exist in the wild, they regulate the prey populations – not just by controlling their numbers but also by assuring their parenting skills. If a wolf is in the area, there will be fewer cold-related fatalities among other animals, because domestic animals are taken inside or hidden in brush, or herded around a *youngster to keep her warm and protect her from the threat of the wolf.*

When I lived with the wolves, I was proud of the reflection of myself.

But when I came back, I always paled in comparison.

Edward

After all the hours I spent in his hospital room, by his bed, maintaining a vigil, my father opened his eyes when I wasn't there.

Story of my life.

Joe's already called a recess so that he can talk to Dr. Saint-Clare, and he's told me that I shouldn't believe everything I see, and neither should Cara. 'It's evidence, but it doesn't mean a thing until the doctors explain it,' he said.

And yet.

What if it had been me in the room when my father woke up? What would I have said to him?

What would he have said to me?

I wonder if the conversations you've never had with someone count, if you've been over them a thousand times in your mind.

Rita Czarnicki sits on the witness stand now, reciting all her medical qualifications and the number of years she's worked in the ICU. 'I was checking the IV,' she says. 'Mr. Warren's daughter was in the room, talking to him.'

'Did you assess your patient's condition when you entered the room?'

'Yes,' Rita says. 'He was unresponsive and still appeared to be in a vegetative state.'

'Then what happened?' Cara's lawyer asks.

'As his daughter was talking, Mr. Warren opened his eyes.'

'Are you saying he woke up?'

'Not like you're thinking.' The nurse hesitates. 'Most VS patients lie with their eyes open when they are awake and closed when they're asleep. But they still have no awareness of themselves or their environment and are totally unresponsive.'

'So what made this event remarkable?' the lawyer asks.

'Mr. Warren's daughter got up very quickly and moved from the foot of the bed around to the side, and his gaze seemed to follow her before his eyes closed again. That's tracking, and that doesn't happen with VS patients.'

'What did you do?'

'I immediately paged the Neurology Department, and they attempted to stimulate Mr. Warren into reactivity again by touching his toes and digging beneath his fingernails and verbally prompting him, but he didn't respond.'

'Ms. Czarnicki, you heard Cara's testimony. Did she exaggerate Mr. Warren's responsiveness in any way?'

The nurse shakes her head. 'I saw it myself.'

'Nothing further,' the attorney says.

'Mr. Ng?' the judge asks. 'Would you like to cross-examine the witness?'

'No,' Joe says, standing. 'But I do wish to recall an earlier witness to the stand. Dr. Saint-Clare?'

The neurosurgeon doesn't look happy to have been called back to court. He raps his fingers on the edge of the witness stand, as if he has somewhere else he needs to be. 'Thank you, Doctor, for making time for this,' Joe begins. 'It's been quite an afternoon.'

'Apparently,' the doctor says.

'Have you had a chance to examine Mr. Warren since you testified this morning?'

'Yes.'

'Has there been a change in his condition?'

Dr. Saint-Clare sucks in his breath. 'There's some discrepancy about that,' he says. 'Apparently Mr. Warren opened his eyes this afternoon.'

'What does that mean?'

'Unfortunately, not a lot. Patients who are in a vegetative state are unaware of themselves and their environment. They don't respond to stimuli except for reflex responses, they don't understand language, they don't have control of bladder and bowel function. They are intermittently awake, but they are not conscious. We refer to this condition as "eyes-open unconsciousness," and that's what seems to have happened today to Mr. Warren,' the doctor says. 'Like many VS patients, his eyes opened when he was stimulated by a voice, but that doesn't mean he was aware.'

'Can VS patients track moving objects with their eyes?'

'No,' Dr. Saint-Clare says. 'That finding would be evidence for awareness and would suggest the presence of a minimally conscious state.'

'How would a patient with MCS present?'

'He would exhibit an awareness of self and the environment. The patient would be able to follow simple commands, smile, cry, and follow motion with his eyes.'

'According to Ms. Czarnicki and Cara, it seems that Mr. Warren was able to do the last, isn't that right?'

Dr. Saint-Clare shakes his head. 'We think that what was construed as a movement of the eyes was actually a muscle reflex of the eyes closing. A rolling of the eyes, if you will, rather than a tracking. Since this first happened, we've tried repeatedly to get Mr. Warren to respond again, and he hasn't – not to noise or touch or any other stimuli. The injuries sustained in the crash by Mr. Warren – the brain stem lesions – suggest that there's no way he could be conscious now. Although he opened his eyes, there was no awareness attached to that movement. It was a reflexive behavior, and doesn't warrant an upgrade in diagnosis to a minimally conscious state.'

'What would you say to Cara, who would contradict your interpretation of the event?' Joe asks.

The doctor looks at my sister, and for the first time since he's taken the stand, so do I. The light has gone out of Cara's face, like a falling star at the end of its arc. 'Often in a vegetative state, patients will exhibit automatic behaviors like eye opening and closing, and a wandering gaze, or a facial grimace that family members mistake for conscious behavior. When someone you love suffers a trauma this severe, you'll grab on to any hint that he's still the same person, maybe buried beneath layers of sleep, but there nonetheless. Cara's job, as Mr. Warren's daughter, is to hope for the best. But my job, as his neurosurgeon, is to prepare her for the worst. And the bottom line is that a patient in a vegetative state like Mr. Warren's carries a very grim prognosis with a small chance of meaningful recovery, which diminishes further over time.'

'Thank you,' Joe says. 'Your witness?'

Zirconia has her arm around Cara's shoulders. She doesn't remove it, doesn't even stand up to question the neurosurgeon. 'Can you tell us beyond a reasonable doubt that Mr. Warren has no cognitive function?'

'On the contrary, I can tell you that he *does* have cognition. We can see that on an EEG. But I can also tell you that the other injuries to his brain stem prevent him from being able to access it.'

'Is there any objective scientific test you can administer to determine whether or not Mr. Warren's eye movement was purposeful? If he was trying to communicate?'

'No.'

'So, basically, you're reading minds now.'

Dr. Saint-Clare raises his brows. 'Actually, Ms. Notch,' he says, 'I'm board-certified to do just that.'

When the judge calls for a short recess before Helen Bedd, the temporary guardian, gives her testimony, I walk over to Cara. Her attorney is holding a pair of hospital socks, the kind that boost circulation, which the nurses put on my father's feet. 'This is all you could find?' Zirconia asks.

Cara nods. 'I don't know what they did with the clothes he was wearing the night of the accident.'

The lawyer bunches the socks in her fists and closes her eyes. 'I'm getting nothing,' she says.

'That's good, right?' Cara asks.

'Well, it's certainly not *bad*. It could mean that he hasn't crossed over yet. But it could also just mean that I'm better with animals than with humans.'

'Excuse me,' I interrupt. 'Could I talk to my sister?'

Both Zirconia and my mother look at Cara, letting her decide. She nods, and they retreat down the aisle, leaving us alone at the table. 'I didn't make it up,' Cara says.

'I know. I believe you.'

'And I don't care if Dr. Saint-Clare says it's medically insignificant. It was significant to me.'

I look at her. 'I've been thinking. What if it had happened when we were both here in court? I mean, if it was less than a minute, that's not a long time. What if he'd opened his eyes and you hadn't been there to see it?'

'Maybe it's happened more than once,' Cara says.

'Or maybe it hasn't.' My voice softens. 'I guess what I'm trying to say is that I'm glad you were there when it did.'

Cara looks at me for a long moment, her eyes the exact same color as mine. How have I never noticed that before? She grabs my forearm. 'Edward, what if we just agreed to do this together? If we went up to the judge and told him that we don't need him to pick between us?'

I pull away from her. 'But we still want different outcomes.'

She blinks at me. 'You mean, even after knowing Dad opened his eyes, you'd want to take him off life support?'

'You heard the doctor. He had a reflex, not a reaction. Like a hiccup. Something he couldn't control. And he wouldn't have even opened his eyes, Cara, if that machine wasn't breathing for him.' I shake my head. 'I want to believe it was more than that, too. But science trumps a gut feeling.'

She shrinks back in her chair. 'How can you do that to me?'

'Do what?'

'Make me think you're on my side and then cut me down?'

'It's my job,' I say.

'To ruin my life?'

'No. To piss you off and to get you riled up. To get under your skin. To treat you the way nobody else gets to treat you.' I stand up. 'To be your brother.'

Luke

*W*hen the Abenaki tell a story, there are several ways to start. You can say, Waji mjassaik: *in the beginning. You can say* N'dalgommek: *all my relations. Or you can begin with an apology:* Anhaldamawikw kassi palilawaliakw. *It means, I'm sorry for the wrong I might have done you this past year.*

Any of those, when I came back to the human world, would apply.

Even though I slowly got used to the sounds and smells, and I stopped diving every time a car roared around the corner or picking up my steak with my hands at the dinner table, there were still some spontaneous bleeds between my life in the wild and my life back among humans. When you live on the tightrope of survival and there's no safety net, it's hard to go back to walking on solid ground. I couldn't dull the knife edge of instinct I'd developed with the wolves. If my family went out, even just to a McDonald's, I would make sure to put myself physically between my children and anyone else in the establishment. I'd face away from them as they ate their hamburgers, because turning my back meant possibly missing a threat.

When my daughter brought home a friend from school for

a sleepover, I found myself looking through a twelve-year-old's pink duffel bag to make sure she didn't have anything with her that might harm Cara. When Edward drove to school, sometimes I followed him in my truck just to make sure he got there. When Georgie went out, I grilled her about where she was going, because I lived in fear that something bad would happen to her when I wasn't there to rescue her. I was like a veteran soldier who saw flashbacks in every situation, who knew the worst was just a breath away. I wasn't really ever happy unless we were all in the house, under lock and key.

The first Abenaki word I ever learned was Bitawbagok – *the word they use for Lake Champlain. It means, literally,* the waters between. *Since I've come back from Quebec, I have thought of my address as* Bitawkdakinna. *I don't know enough Abenaki to be sure it's a real word, but translated, it is* the world between.

I had become a bridge between the natural world and the human one. I fit into both places and belonged to neither. Half of my heart lived with the wild wolves, the other half lived with my family.

In case you cannot do the math: no one can survive with half a heart.

Helen

Your Honor.

My name is Helen Bedd.

I'm an attorney and also a guardian in the New Hampshire Office of Public Guardian. I've practiced law for twenty-five years, and for ten years before that I was a registered nurse. I've been appointed as a temporary or permanent guardian for more than 250 cases over the years.

When I received this appointment, I immediately spoke to the parties involved, given the expedited nature of the hearing. The medical team at Beresford Memorial told me in essence what Dr. Saint-Clare has reiterated today. There is little or no chance that Mr. Warren's condition will improve. Seeing her father open his eyes today must have been very compelling for Cara, but my medical background and Dr. Saint-Clare's testimony reinforce the unfortunate fact that this was probably an unconscious reflex and does not demonstrate any return to consciousness.

As part of my preparation for today, I also spoke with both Cara and Edward Warren. Both children deeply love their father, despite a disagreement about his health care needs and prognosis. Cara, at seventeen, has centered her life on her father. He's the sun in the solar system of her life.

Their relationship has been extremely close, as is often the case for children of divorce who bond particularly with one parent. I don't doubt that Cara's shouldered adult responsibilities, given her father's unique lifestyle and job. However, I've also been forced to conclude that she is operating from an emotional standpoint and not a realistic one. Due to her emotional condition at this time, and her physical condition after the accident, she is unable to accept the reality of her father's condition – whether that reality is presented by her brother, her father's doctors, or the social worker at the hospital. And while the accident was not her fault in any way, I believe there's some residual guilt that influences her vehement desire to keep her father alive at all costs. While I find her unadulterated hope for her father's recovery touching and very moving, I also see it as a function of her immaturity at seventeen, and the fact that she is unwilling to accept a truth she does not want to believe.

On the other hand, Edward is the only living relative of Mr. Warren who is past the age of majority. Although he was able to produce a signed document from his father naming him as a health care guardian, that holds less weight for me than the fact that of the two siblings, Edward is the only one who has had an actual conversation with his father about what to do in this sort of situation. However, he has been estranged from his father for six years, and some details have come to light in this court that explain further his rash decision to abandon his family when he was eighteen. I believe that it's still quite difficult for Edward to separate his anger at his father from his current actions, which led to a very rash decision that was made without consulting his sister, and an even more rash decision to take matters into his own hands when the termination of life support didn't go according to plan. In this, Edward still has a lot of growing up to do. One has to wonder, given his propensity to act on impulse, how much thought he's really given to his father's wishes.

This is a unique case. Often when probate court becomes involved in a situation of guardianship, it's because no one wants to step up to the plate and make the hard decisions. In this case, we have two very different individuals who both want the job. But we also have something that most wards do not have – a written and video testimony by Luke Warren himself. His autobiography and the countless hours of film, both televised and amateur, that show him in his element give us a very strong sense of the kind of man he was and what he would want if someone's judgment was being substituted for his own. I have been impressed by how far Luke Warren's children are willing to go for him. I have been impressed by Mr. Warren's life, and how much he's accomplished. I've been impressed by the adventurous spirit that is packed into the chapters of his book and by the colleagues on camera who never fail to mention that sense of excitement and that constant adrenaline which were part of being around Mr. Warren.

All of this points to a man who would not relish the thought of being bedridden, at best.

And yet.

The Luke Warren that was shown to the world was only one facet of the man. If you read between the lines of his book, you can just make out the shadow of another story. The hero in his autobiography isn't a hero at all. He's a failure – someone who couldn't live with the animals he came to revere, and more important, someone who couldn't manage to live by their code when he was apart from them. You've heard both Cara and Edward say it in their testimonies: to a wolf, family matters most. But Mr. Warren abandoned his family – literally, when he went into the woods of Quebec, and figuratively, when he carried on an extramarital affair that led to a terminated pregnancy.

I've never spoken directly to Mr. Warren. But I think that it probably hurt him to know that his son's instinct was to leave home when the going got tough. A wolf would have never let his offspring out of his sight.

On the other hand, Cara's idealism is based on the very foundation of a family mattering most. The odds are against Mr. Warren's survival, but the reason she is advocating for it so strongly is simply because she doesn't want to live without her father. And if Mr. Warren is lucky enough to be one of those medical anomalies who defies science, I think he'd be delighted to get a second chance. Not just at survival but at being a father.

For this reason, I think Cara's beliefs dovetail with Mr. Warren's deepest wishes. I'd urge the court to appoint her as a guardian and to allow Cara to make appropriate arrangements for her father's treatment.

Luke

*A*fter the Animal Planet series, I got a call from a biologist near Yellowstone. A hiker had been found in the woods, his body half devoured by wolves. It had raised fear in a community that had long ago accepted the release of wild wolves into the Rockies.

Some of the researchers felt that the wolves had killed for sport, but I didn't believe it. I had never seen wolves behave that way toward a fellow predator, which is how they view man. Nothing in pack behavior suggests that food should be convenient rather than carefully chosen.

So why had wolves, which I had sworn would never attack a man, done just that?

I flew out to Yellowstone.

The area where the hiker had been killed had been stripped for timber. In fact, there was hardly a forest at all anymore. Without the cover and vegetation of the natural woods, the prey animals – deer and elk, mostly – had dwindled. The wolves had started eating salmon from the rivers instead.

I went back home and followed up on my hunch with one of my captive packs. Instead of giving them meat, I only fed them fish. Unlike with a land-based animal carcass – a food that has emotional value in the chemicals that run through the muscles and internal organs – now everyone was getting the same meal.

It was socialism among wolves. They were no longer eating in hierarchy, making sure that different ranks got different types of meat. Within a few months, the pack fell apart. There was no discernible alpha or beta rank. There was no discipline. Each wolf to his own, every animal did whatever he or she wanted. Instead of a family, they had become a gang.

The reason the pack at Yellowstone went after the hiker, I think, is that the natural food supply had dwindled, and the only source left to them was one that inadvertently destroyed the ranks. They killed the poor man because there was no wolf there telling them not to.

Sometimes, it's like this for a pack. You have to reach the point of utter chaos before a new leader can emerge.

Cara

You would think that having the temporary guardian's stamp of approval would have me turning cartwheels, but the judge does something no one is expecting.

He schedules a field trip.

Which is how I come to be standing beside my brother outside the glass window of my father's ICU room, watching the judge hold a one-sided private conversation with our unconscious father.

Joe rode the elevator downstairs with my mother, who's gone home to pick the twins up from the bus stop. Zirconia is in the lounge, talking to a therapy dog.

'What do you think LaPierre is saying?' Edward asks.

'A novena?' I suggest.

'Maybe he needs to see with his own eyes what a vegetative state looks like.'

'Or maybe,' I counter, 'he's hoping to see Dad wake up again.'

'Open his eyes,' Edward corrects.

'Same difference.'

'Cara,' he says, towering over me, 'it's not.'

My mother used to talk about Edward's growth spurts. I used to think that meant Edward sprouted overnight, like the plants she kept in the kitchen. I worried he would become too big for the house, and then where would we put him?

Armand LaPierre rises from the chair beside my father's bed. He steps into the hallway just as Joe comes out of the elevator and Zirconia hurries toward us from the lounge. 'Nine a.m.,' he announces, and he walks off.

Zirconia draws me aside. 'You're in great shape. You've done everything you can at this point. Between the fact that LaPierre's Catholic, and more inclined to err on the side of life, and the endorsement of the temporary guardian, it's looking very strong, Cara.'

I hug her. 'Thanks. For everything.'

'My pleasure.' She smiles. 'You need a ride back home?'

'I'll take her,' Joe says, and I realize that he and my brother have been close enough to hear everything Zirconia said to me. I wanted to win this case. So why does that make me feel so bad?

'I'm going to stay for a while,' Edward says, nodding toward Dad's room.

'You'll call me—'

'Yes,' he says. 'If anything happens.'

'If he wakes up again—'

But Joe is already pushing me toward the elevator. The doors close behind us. The last image I have is of Edward sitting down beside my father's bed.

I watch the floor numbers fall as the elevator descends, a rocket's countdown. 'What happens if I lose?' I ask.

Joe seems surprised. 'Your lawyer thinks it's a lock.'

'Nothing's a hundred percent,' I tell him, and he grins.

'Yes,' he says. 'I remember that from today's testimony.'

I glance at him sharply. 'And I remember today's cross-exam.'

At least he has the grace to blush a little. 'How about we put that behind us?'

I hold out my hand to shake on that, but he doesn't let go. 'If you don't win,' Joe says gently, 'then Edward will be your father's guardian. He's going to schedule a time to terminate your father's life support, and to donate his organs. You can be there. And if you want, Cara, I will be right there next to you.'

My throat gets tight. 'Okay,' I say.

When the elevator doors open in the lobby, what people see is a man holding on to a girl who's crying, who looks about the right age to be his daughter. What people see is just one of hundreds of sad stories born inside the walls of this building.

When I was younger, my brother told me that he had the power to shrink me to the size of an ant. In fact, he said, he used to have another sister, but he shrank her down and stepped on her.

He also told me that when you became a grown-up, you were admitted into a private party that was full of monsters and horror movie characters. There was Chucky, drinking a cup of coffee. And the mummy on the cover of the Hardy Boys book that used to freak me out, except he was doing the twist while Jason from *Friday the 13th* played the alto sax. He told me you stayed at the party as long as you had to, making conversation with these creatures, and that was why adults were never afraid of anything.

I used to believe everything my brother told me, because he was older and I figured he knew more about the world. But as it turns out, being a grown-up doesn't mean you're fearless.

It just means you fear different things.

Luke

My Abenaki friends say that if a hunter and a bear spill each other's blood, they become the same person. No matter what, after that moment, the hunter will never be able to shoot the bear, and the bear will never be able to kill that person.

I'd like to believe it's true.

I'd like to believe that the by-product of a near-death experience is a healthy dose of mutual respect.

Edward

I was the kid who woke up in the middle of the night with a stomach-ache, certain there was a monster under the bed. I thought ghosts came to sit on my windowsill. Every gust of wind and snapping branch became a thief who was going to come through the attic to kill me. I used to wake up sobbing, and my father, who was usually just getting back from Redmond's, would be the one to calm me down. *You know*, he told me once, completely exasperated, *you've got one glass of water inside your head, with all the tears for a lifetime. If you waste them over nothing, then you won't be able to cry for real when you need to.* He told me he'd once met an eight-year-old who'd used up his whole glass of tears and who now couldn't sob, no matter what.

To this day, I hardly ever cry.

My father doesn't open his eyes, twitch, blink, or move a muscle during the three hours I sit by his bed. His IV bag empties and his catheter bag fills with urine. A nurse comes by to check his vitals. 'You should talk to him,' she tells me. 'Or read out loud. He likes *People* magazine.'

Frankly I can't imagine anything my father would like less. 'How do you know that?'

She smiles. 'Because I read him last week's issue and he didn't complain once.'

I wait until she leaves the room, and then I pull my chair up to my father's bed. It's no wonder I haven't talked much to him, but then again, I never really knew what to say. And yet, this nurse has a point. What better time to finally tell him the things I should have said ages ago than now, when he has no choice but to listen? 'I don't hate you,' I admit, the words dissolving the silence.

His response is the pump and fall of the ventilator. It almost feels wrong, an unfair fight.

'The temporary guardian, she said something today I can't get out of my head. She said you would have been hurt because I left. I guess I always figured you were thrilled. That you'd gotten rid of the son who was nothing like you. But it turns out that I'm *exactly* like you. I walked away from my family, too. I realized too late I'd made the biggest mistake of my life. I didn't belong in Thailand, and I didn't belong here. I was just . . . caught somewhere in the middle.'

Breathe in, out. In, out.

'There's something else I realized, too. You never said you wished I was more athletic or outdoorsy or straight. *I* was the one who was so sure I didn't measure up. And that's probably because there was nobody else like you. So how could I ever come close?'

I look down at him, still and slack. 'What I'm trying to say is that I blamed you, when it was me all along.'

I reach for my father's hand. The last time I held it I must have been very small, because I do not remember this at all. How weird, to start and end at the same place, to be the child hanging on to a parent for dear life. 'I'm going to take care of her. No matter what happens tomorrow,' I tell him. 'I thought you should know I'm back for good.'

My father doesn't respond. But in my mind, I can hear his voice, booming and clear.

It's about time.

Finally, I let myself cry.

By the time I return to the house, it is after midnight. Instead of falling into bed, though, or even just collapsing on the couch, I go to the attic. I haven't been up there and I have to use my phone as a flashlight, but I manage to rummage through boxes of old tax documents and moth-eaten clothing, some DVD sets of the Animal Planet shows and a bin full of my high school notebooks before I find what I'm looking for. The frames are stacked in a corner with layers of news-paper between them.

The surge of relief I feel when I realize these weren't thrown out is a shot of pure adrenaline. I carry them all downstairs.

There's one hallway in my father's house with photographs. They are all of Cara, except for two of my dad with some of his wolves, and one of them together.

Every year, my mother made us take a picture for our Christmas card. Usually it was August when she was inspired, and usually I had to wear the heaviest, itchiest sweater I owned. Since we didn't have any snow then, she'd make us pose with all the trappings of Christmas, hats and scarves and mittens, as if our relatives and friends were too dumb to tell from the scenery that it was summer in New England. Every year, she framed the photo and gave it to my father for Christmas. And every January, he hung it in the stairwell.

I sort through the pictures of me and Cara. There's one where she's so little, I'm carrying her. Then the one where her pigtails stick out like silk tufts from each side of her head. There's the one where I have braces and the one where she does. There's the last photo we took together, before I left.

It's strange to see myself six years younger. I look wiry and nervous. I'm staring at the camera, but Cara's staring at me.

I hang the photographs up along the stairwell, taking down Cara's individual school portraits. I leave up the two of my father with his wolves. Then I stand back, reading my history on the wall.

The last picture I hang is one I remember well. It was the last vacation we took as a family, before my father went to Quebec. My dad and I stand with our feet in the water on the beach at Hyannis. My mom is piggybacked on him, and Cara is piggybacked on me. Looking at us, with our tanned faces and our white teeth and our wide smiles, you'd never know that, in three years' time, my father would go off to live in the woods. You'd never know that he would have an affair. That I would leave without saying good-bye to anyone. That there would be an accident that changed everything.

This is what I like about photographs. They're proof that once, even if just for a heartbeat, everything was perfect.

The next morning I oversleep. I throw on the same shirt I was wearing the day before and my father's buffalo plaid jacket and slide into a seat beside Joe as the clerk is telling us to rise for the Honorable Armand LaPierre.

'Nice of you to show up,' Joe murmurs.

For a long, silent minute, the judge sits with his head bowed, tearing at his hair. 'In all my years of sitting on the bench,' he says finally, 'this has been one of the most difficult cases over which I've presided. It's not every day you have to make a decision about life and death. And I also realize that whatever decision I make will not be a happy decision for anyone.'

He takes a deep breath and perches his glasses on the edge of his nose. 'The fact that Cara is only seventeen is immaterial to me, given the circumstances. She lived with her father, she had a close relationship with him, she is as competent of making a decision as she will be in three months' time. Given her brother's absence for six years, I consider her on an equal par with Edward in terms of her ability to act as guardian for her father. I cannot discount the fact that the decision I make today might take away a father from a young girl who gets great reassurance out of simply knowing he's still part of her world, even if he is in a vegetative state. Furthermore, he's only been in this state for thirteen days.

'Yet I am also cognizant of the irrefutable testimony of Dr. Saint-Clare, who has stated that it is beyond a reasonable doubt that Mr. Warren will not recover from his injuries and will continue to deteriorate. When you look at the precedents set by earlier decisions like this – Cruzan and Schiavo and Quinlan – the outcome has always been death. Mr. Warren is going to die. The question is, will it be tomorrow? A month from now? A year from now? You want me to make that decision, and in order to do that, I need to determine what Luke Warren would have wanted.'

Pursing his lips, he continues. 'Ms. Bedd looked at the swath Mr. Warren cut through television and publishing media, and came to her conclusion. But to look at Mr. Warren in the public eye is not necessarily to see the man behind the celebrity. And the only concrete evidence I have of the way and manner in which Mr. Warren lived his life is a conversation he had with his son saying that if he were in this very situation, he'd want to terminate life-sustaining measures. A conversation that was reinforced on paper in a handwritten, signed advance directive.' He glances at me. 'Moreover, on Mr. Warren's driver's license, he indicated a desire to be an organ donor. We can see this as further evidence of his personal wishes.'

The judge takes off his reading glasses and turns to Cara. 'Honey, I know you don't want to lose your father,' he says. 'But yesterday, I spent an hour at his bedside, and I think you'd have to agree with me – your father's not in that hospital anymore. He's already gone.' He clears his throat. 'For all of these reasons and after great consideration, I'm awarding permanent guardianship to Edward Warren.'

It's not really the kind of verdict that you get congratulated on. A small knot of support forms around Cara, and before I can say anything to her, Joe takes me away to get the paperwork I'll need to present to the hospital, so that they will terminate my father's life support, and schedule an organ donation.

I drive myself to the hospital, and spend an hour talking to Dr. Saint-Clare and the donor coordinator. I sign my name to forms and nod as if I am taking in everything they say, going through the same motions I went through six days ago. The only difference is that this time, when I don't *have* to talk to Cara, I know I *want* to.

She's curled up on my father's bed, her face still wet with tears. When I walk in, she doesn't sit up. 'I knew I'd find you here,' I say.

'When?' she asks.

I don't pretend to misunderstand. 'Tomorrow.'

Cara closes her eyes.

I imagine her staying here all night. My mom and Joe probably gave her permission, under the circumstances. And I can't imagine any of the ICU nurses would kick her out. But if she wants to say good-bye to our father, I also know this isn't the place she needs to be.

I reach into my pocket for my wallet and pull out the photo I took from my father's billfold, the one of me as a little kid. I slip it underneath my dad's pillow, and then hold out my hand to her, an invitation.

'Cara,' I say. 'There's something I think you should hear.'

Luke

*T*o evict a wolf from a pack, you use natural suppression
and intimidation – which usually takes the form of speed
and directional control. Sometimes this is done just to test
the members of the pack to make sure everyone's up to speed
and doing his job – a beckon here, a direction to stay put, a
higher-ranking wolf keeping you from moving by cutting
you off.

At the tip of the spine, above the tail, there is a little covered
well with a gland in it that's as distinctive as a human
fingerprint. It's how wolves identify each other. In captivity,
when a wolf can't leave an enclosure, a pack member who's
being evicted will sometimes have that gland gnawed at,
gouged out by others, thus removing that wolf's individuality.
A wolf who loses its scent gland loses all status, and will often
die.

Who gets evicted? It depends. It might be a wolf that is no
longer performing to his best capabilities. It might be a young
wolf growing up with alpha characteristics, when the pack
already has a viable alpha. A wolf that's been evicted becomes
a lone wolf. In the woods, he'll eat small animals and live on
his own, howling at other packs to determine new vacancies
that suit his role. A lone wolf usually has the characteristics

of an alpha, beta, or mid-ranking wolf, and his acceptance into a new pack – which may be years later – is a happy constellation of circumstances. Not only must you be qualified to fill a certain position in the pack but there must be an opening for you.

I can tell you from experience that when wolves evict a member of the family, there is no looking back. It's not quite that easy for humans.

Then again, a wolf that has been evicted from a pack could be asked to rejoin it, in certain circumstances. Say that pack with the extra alpha wolf suddenly loses its alpha to a predator? They'll be in need of another alpha to fill his shoes.

Cara

We can't go into the enclosures. Although the wolves would most likely just keep their distance, my sling would be like a red flag; they'd try to rip it off and get at the wound to clean it. So instead we sit on the rise, outside the fence, huddled in our coats, watching the wolves watch us.

There's a cruel comfort to being here. It's better than the hospital, I guess, and lying on my father's bed listening to the beeps of machines like a time bomb ticking, knowing that when the electricity goes so will he. But I can't turn around without seeing a ghost of a memory: my father running through the enclosure with a deer's hindquarter, teaching the youngsters how to hunt. My father with Sikwla draped over his neck like a stole. My father nannying, teaching pups how to find and dive into a rendezvous hole.

Even though his wolves were in captivity, he taught them the skills to live in the wild. His goal was to get wolves rereleased into the forests of New Hampshire, the way they had been reintroduced in Yellowstone, and were now thriving. Although there had been some solo sightings of wild wolves, there were laws against their reintroduction. It had been two hundred years since they'd roamed free in the state, but that didn't stop my father from making sure that any one of his captive packs survived the way its wild counterparts would. *You know what the difference is between a dream and a goal?* he used to say to me. *A plan.*

It's funny, how he had to teach the wolves to be wild, when they taught him so much about being human.

I realize that I'm already thinking about him in the past tense.

'What's going to happen to them?' I ask.

Edward looks at me. 'I'll ask Walter to stay on. I'm not going to get rid of them, if that's what you're asking.'

'You don't know anything about wolves.'

'I'll learn.'

Now, that would be the greatest irony of all. If I'd told my dad that one day Edward would be living out his legacy with the wolves, he probably would have laughed himself into a hernia.

I stand up and walk closer, until I can curl my fingers into the chain-link fence. That was the first lesson my father taught me down here – don't ever do that. A tester wolf will turn around before you know it and will bite you.

But these wolves, they know me. Kladen rubs his silvery side up against my hand and licks me.

'You could even be the one to teach me,' Edward suggests.

I crouch down, waiting for Kladen to pace by me again. 'This place won't be the same if he's not here.'

'But he is,' Edward says. 'He's in every corner of it. He built it with his hands. He created these packs. This is who Dad was, not what you see in the hospital bed. And none of this is going away. I promise you.'

Suddenly Kladen moves to the promontory rock that, in the dark, looks like a hulking beast. I can make out the silhouettes of Sikwla and Wazoli. They tip back their throats and start to howl.

It's a rallying howl, meant for someone who's missing. I know who that is right away. It makes me start to cry again, even as all the other packs in the adjacent enclosures join in, a fugue of sorrow.

I wish, in that instant, I were a wolf. Because when someone leaves your life, there aren't words you can use to fill the space. There's just one empty, swelling minor note.

'This is why I wanted you to come here with me,' Edward says. 'Walter says that they've done it every night since the crash.'

The crash.

Edward had kept a secret, and it broke our family apart. If I confessed mine, would it put us back together?

So I turn away from the wolves, and with them still singing their dirge, I tell my brother the truth.

'Here's a hint,' my father said, furious, as he peeled away from the house in Bethlehem where already one kid was passed out and two more were having sex in a parked car. 'If you lie about having a sleepover study session at Mariah's, you should remember to *take* the fake bag you've packed.'

I was so angry I couldn't see straight, but that also could have been the grain alcohol. I had beer once, but who knew something that tasted like fruit punch could pack a wallop like this? 'I can't believe you followed me here.'

'I tracked prey for two years; believe me, teenage girls leave a much more visible trail.'

My father had just barged into the house as if I were five

years old and he'd come to pick me up at a birthday party. 'Well, thanks to you, I'm a social pariah now.'

'You're right. I should have waited until you were being date-raped, or had blood alcohol poisoning. Jesus, Cara. What the *hell* were you thinking?'

I hadn't been thinking. I'd let Mariah do the thinking for me, and it was a mistake. But I would have rather died than admit that to my father.

And I sure as hell wouldn't tell him that, actually, I was happy to leave, because it was getting a little crazy in there.

'This,' my father muttered, 'is why wolves let some of their offspring die in the wild.'

'I'm going to call Child Protection Services,' I threaten. 'I'm going to move back in with Mom.'

My father's eyes had a little green box around them from the rearview mirror reflection. 'Remind me to tell you, when you're *not* drunk, that you're grounded.'

'Remind me to tell you, when I'm not drunk, *that I hate you*,' I snapped.

At that, my father laughed. 'Cara,' he said, 'I swear, you're gonna be the death of me.'

And then suddenly there was a deer in front of the truck, and my father pulled hard to the right. Even as we struck the tree, even as frustrated with me as he was, his instinct was to throw an arm out in front of me, a last-ditch attempt at safety.

I came to because of the gas. I could smell it, seeping. My arm was useless, and I could feel the burn of the seat belt strap where it had cut a bruise like the sash of a beauty contestant. 'Daddy,' I said, and I thought I was yelling, but my mouth was filled with dust. Turning to my left, I saw him. His head was bleeding, and his eyes were locked on mine. He was trying to say something, but no words came out.

I had to get us out of there. I knew that if there was a gas leak, the whole truck could go up in flames. So I reached across him and unbuckled his seat belt. My right arm wasn't working, but with my left hand I opened the passenger door, so I could stumble out of the cab.

There was smoke pouring from under the hood, and one of the wheels was still spinning. I ran to my father's side and wrenched open his door. 'You have to help me,' I told him. With my left arm I managed to hoist him against me, part-nered in a horrible nightmare of a dance.

I was crying and there was blood in my eyes and my mouth and I tried to drag my father clear of the car but I couldn't use both arms to pull him. I wrapped one arm around his chest, but I couldn't bear his weight that way. I let go of him. I let go of him, and he slipped through my arm like sand in an hourglass. I let go of him and he fell in slow motion, smacking his head against the pavement.

After that, he didn't move anymore at all.

I swear. You're gonna be the death of me.

'I let go of him,' I tell Edward, crying so hard that I cannot catch my breath. 'Everyone was calling me a hero for saving his life, but I let go of him.'

'And that's why you can't let go, now,' he says, suddenly grasping what this has all been about.

'I'm the reason he's going to die tomorrow.'

'If you had left him in the truck, he would have died *then*,' Edward says.

'He fell down on the pavement,' I sob. 'The back of his head hit so hard I *heard* it. And that's why he won't wake up now. You heard Dr. Saint-Clare—'

'There's no way to tell which brain injuries came from the crash and which injuries came after that. Even if he hadn't fallen, Cara, he might still be like this.'

'The last words I said to him were *I hate you.*'

Edward looks at me. 'They're the last words I said to him, too,' he admits.

I wipe my eyes with the back of my hand. 'That's a pretty shitty thing for us to have in common.'

'Gotta start somewhere,' Edward says. He offers a half smile. 'Besides, he knows you didn't mean it.'

'How can you be sure?'

'Because hate's just the flip side of love. Like heads and tails on a dime. If you don't know what it feels like to love someone, how would you know what hate is? One can't exist without the other.'

Very slowly I inch my hand toward Edward's, until I can slip it beneath his. Immediately, I am eleven years old again, and crossing the street on my way to school. I never looked both ways when I was walking with Edward. I trusted him to do it for me.

He squeezes my hand. This time, I hold on tight.

When I was a kid my father used to tuck me in at night, and every time he turned off the lamp, he blew, as if there was a giant invisible candle illuminating my room. It took me years to figure out that he was flipping a switch, that he wasn't the source of all the light.

Standing in this weird déjà vu tableau, I feel as if I'm the one blowing out that invisible candle, a spark I can't see that somehow constitutes living, if not a life.

Edward is here, as are the same nurses and doctors and social worker and lawyer, and the donor coordinator. But Joe's here, too, like he promised, and my mother, because I asked.

'Are we ready?' the ICU doctor asks.

Edward looks at me, and I nod. 'Yes,' he says.

He holds my hand while the ventilator is dialed down, while morphine drips into my father's arm. Behind my father is the monitor that marks arterial pressure.

When the machine stops breathing for my father, I focus on his chest. It rises, then falls once more. It stops for a minute. Then it rises and falls again twice.

The numbers on the arterial pressure monitor fall like a stock market crash. Twenty-one minutes after we have started, my father's heart stops beating.

The next five minutes are the longest of my life. We wait to make sure he doesn't spontaneously start breathing again. That his heart doesn't restart.

My mother is crying softly behind me. Edward has tears in his eyes.

At 7:58 p.m., my father is declared dead.

'Edward, Cara,' Trina says, 'you need to say good-bye.'

Because DCD requires the organs to be harvested immediately, we can't linger. But then again, I have been saying good-bye for days. This is just a formality.

I walk up to my father and touch his cheek. It is still warm, and there's stubble like flecks of fool's gold. I put my hand over his heart, just to make sure.

It is a good thing that they whisk him to the OR for the organ donation, because I am not sure I would have been able to leave him. I might have stayed in his room forever, just sitting with his body, because once you tell the nurse that yes, it's okay to take him away, you don't ever get the chance to be with him again. To share the same space. To see his face, without it being a memory.

Joe takes my mother out into the hall, and pretty soon, it is just me and my brother, standing in the vacant spot where my father's bed used to be. It's a visual reminder of what we are missing.

The first time someone I loved left me behind, it was Edward, and I didn't know how my family would balance. We had been such a sturdy little end table, four solid legs. I was sure we would now be off-kilter, always unstable. Until one day I looked more closely, and realized that we had simply become a stool.

'Edward,' I say. 'Let's go home.'

The wolves at Redmond's howled for thirty days. People heard them as far away as Laconia and Lincoln. They made babies asleep in their cribs cry, made women search for their high school sweethearts, gave grown men nightmares. There were reports of streetlights bursting when the wolves howled, of cracks forming in the pavement. At our house, just five miles away from the enclosures, it sounded like a funeral requiem; it made the hair on the back of my neck stand on end. And then one day, abruptly, the howling ended. People stopped waiting for it when the moon hit the highest point in the sky. They no longer hummed the melody at traffic lights.

It was just as my father had said: the wolves knew when it was time to stop looking for what they'd lost, to focus instead on what was yet to come.

Luke

There is no grief among wolves. Nature has a wonderful way of making you face reality. You can sit and weep if you want, but you are likely to be killed while you're lost in your mourning, because you let your guard down.

I have seen wolves step over a pack member who dies in a hunt, and continue without looking backward. I have heard wolves call for four or five days after a member of the pack goes missing, hoping to bring her back. Death is an event. It happens, and you move on.

If an alpha is killed, the knowledge of the pack goes with it. The entire pack can crumble in a few days' time if no one steps up from the ranks or is recruited to fill the void. What follows, in that case, is anarchy. The family will disperse, be killed, or starve to death.

Whether you survive a grave injury usually depends on how valuable you are. If it's going to take too much time and energy for the pack to save you and nurse you back to health, you'll make the decision to refuse their help, to let go. Death isn't an individual choice. It all comes back to what the family needs.

Which is why, when you're a wolf, you live each day like it's the only one you have.

Epilogue

For the strength of the Pack is the Wolf, and the strength of the Wolf is the Pack.

– Rudyard Kipling

Barney

A nineteen-year-old shouldn't have a bucket list, but I did. I'd been keeping it because there isn't a lot else to do when you're hooked up to dialysis three times a week. My bucket list, though, had become a to-do list. In the eight months since my kidney transplant, I'd visited Cairo. I'd learned how to snowboard. I'd gone target shooting.

My parents were not thrilled with my new adventurous side. They were, ironically, afraid that I'd have an accident and they'd lose me, even though the years I spent in near renal failure were far more likely to have been fatal. The way I saw it, if you were given a second lease on life, what was the point of playing it safe?

Even I had to admit, though, that I might have gotten in too deep this time. I didn't know where I was – although that was the point of orienteering. But aside from the fact that I knew the sun was behind me and the lodge was some-where to the east, I was completely off track. I could have walked to Saskatchewan by now, for all I knew.

It wasn't particularly cold out, but who knew how chilly it got at night up here, and daylight was fading fast. I didn't have a GPS, just a compass and a topographical map, which looked like fingerprint ridges and was about as helpful. No one at the lodge would even have known to come after me – they all spoke French, so after breakfast this morning I'd grabbed my day pack and headed out solo into the forest.

I heard a stream running, and bushwhacked my way through the brush to find it. There was no evidence of water nearby on the topographical map, however, which meant I was SOL. I sat down at the water's edge, turning the map sideways to see if it made a difference, when I suddenly felt like I was being watched.

I turned to find a big gray wolf staring at me.

He was magnificent. His eyes were the color of honey, and his muzzle and whiskers were peppered with gray. When he tilted his head, I could swear he was trying to ask me something.

I had never seen a wolf, and this one was less than six feet away from me.

Here's the weird thing: I wasn't in the slightest bit nervous.

Here's the weirder thing: I was off the grid, but I felt like I'd been here before. Not just in this place, but in this moment.

The wolf stood and started to lope away from the stream.

After several steps, he turned back to me and sat. Then he got up and walked a distance, and sat down again.

Finally he stood and slipped into the thicker brush of the forest.

Losing sight of him felt like a punch to the gut. I scrambled to my feet, picked up my pack, and started to follow. I had never wanted anything as much as I wanted to catch up with that animal. About a hundred yards deeper into the woods, the wolf was waiting for me.

I knew, from the sun, that we were headed due west – the opposite direction from where I needed to be. I knew I was dead lost.

And yet.

I couldn't shake the feeling that I was headed home.

AUTHOR'S NOTE

For those who want to learn more about wolves, sponsor wolves, or contribute to The Wolf Centre and Foundation, where Shaun continues to work hard to understand more about wolves and wolf behavior: visit www.thewolfcentre.co.uk. I also highly recommend reading Shaun's book *The Man Who Lives with Wolves* if you want to hear from a real-life (thankfully healthy) Luke Warren.

For more information on organ donation, see www.neob.org, www.organdonor.gov, and www.donatelife.net.

You can also visit the UK organ donation site at www.uktransplant.org.uk.

ABOUT THE AUTHOR

Jodi Picoult is the bestselling author of twenty novels including *My Sister's Keeper*, *House Rules* and *Sing You Home*.

Since studying creative writing at Princeton, Picoult has worked as a technical writer for a Wall Street broker, a copywriter at an ad agency, an editor at a textbook publisher, an English teacher and as the author of five issues of the *Wonder Woman* comic book series. She is an international Number One bestseller with her novels translated into forty languages in forty countries. Three have been made into television movies and *My Sister's Keeper* was released as a major motion picture starring Cameron Diaz, Alec Baldwin and Abigail Breslin in summer 2009.

Most recently Jodi's first co-authored novel came out – she wrote *Between the Lines* with her teenage daughter Samantha van Leer.

Jodi Picoult and her husband Tim van Leer live in New Hampshire with three children, three springer spaniels, two donkeys, two geese, three ducks, six chickens, and the occasional cow.

Book Club Discussion Questions
for *Lone Wolf*

1) Because Luke was accepted as a bona fide member by several packs of wolves, some people thought he was a genius, some thought he was insane. What was your initial assessment? Did you change your mind?

2) What event makes Cara first realize why her father couldn't break free of the wolf community? Do you think you'd feel the same?

3) The author compares a wolf pack to the Mafia – different roles, different jobs to do, the 'code', family. Discuss.

4) The policemen have information about the accident. What does the reader find out about Cara? Does this change your sympathies concerning Cara?

5) Anyone who has had a loved one in hospital recognizes the medical jargon and how difficult it is to follow. How do you feel about the interchange between Edward and Dr. Saint-Clare?

6) Luke describes in detail his first experience of being in an enclosure with wolves. Do you think you could do it? (pp.62–64)

7) We learn how Luke and Georgie meet. Would you consider it romantic? Why or why not?

8) When Edward is going through his father's personal

effects, he comes across Luke's driver's license in the wallet. Luke is an organ donor. Does that help Edward in his decision?

9) Cara states that she knows why Edward left. Discuss.

10) Edward finds a handwritten statement giving him say so over Luke's medical care. At the time, Edward was only fifteen. Why was that kind of responsibility given to Edward? Should it have been?

11) Was Edward wrong to allow Cara into the wolf area? Was he being irresponsible?

12) Edward takes the wolf to his dad's hospital room. How do you feel about his actions? Discuss.

13) Edward honestly thinks he's protecting Cara and fulfilling her wishes when she bursts in to Luke's room and yells at him to stop. Is he justified in his actions? (p.177)

14) Luke realizes the wolf pack is his new family. That seems to be a huge conflict – he has a family already. Discuss.

15) 'What looks cruel and heartless from one angle might, from another, actually be the only way to protect your family.' How does this fit Edward and Georgie's thinking? (p.201)

16) Edward points out that "we people who leap without looking are not stupid. We know damn well we might be headed for a fall. But we also know that, sometimes, it's the only way out"'. Do you agree or disagree with that thinking? Have you done anything knowing you are heading for a fall?

17) The job of the alpha is to hold the family together, so that at the most crucial moment, its members all do as they're told. How are human families like this?

18) What is Cara's reasoning to justify lying to the grand jury? Seen from a seventeen year old's perspective, does it make sense?

19) Luke's real reason for walking away from the pack when he did was he knew if he didn't go then, he would stay forever. Discuss.

20) What adjustments does Luke struggle with after he's back home from the wild? At what point does Luke realize that Georgie knew she'd lost him for good? Do you blame her?

21) After Luke has returned from the wild, he comments "'when I lived with the wolves, I was proud of the reflection of myself. But when I came back, I always paled in comparison.'" Discuss. (p.405)

22) Are you surprised by Helen Bedd's suggestion to the court? Do you agree or disagree?

23) What is the significance of Edward finding and displaying the pictures in which he is included?

24) We find out what actually happened on the night of the car crash. Did that make Cara's actions more understandable?

25) What do you think Barney means when he couldn't shake the feeling that 'I was headed home'?

YOUR QUESTIONS

In the hardback edition of *Lone Wolf*, we asked readers to send us their questions for Jodi, with the chance for them to appear in the paperback edition. Below are the lucky few which were selected.

Why did you decide not to put a twist in the tale in *Lone Wolf* like your other books?   *Deirdre Wallace*

I think there are TWO twists in *Lone Wolf*: the secrets Edward and Cara are hiding, and then the last moment, when you meet Barney . . . and figure out who he is.

What do you want readers to understand through *Lone Wolf*?   *Christy Zakarias*

If we can keep people who have no hope for recovery alive artificially, should they also be allowed to die artificially? Does the potential to save someone else's life with a donated organ balance the act of hastening another's death? And when a father's life hangs in the balance, which sibling should get to decide his fate? If readers could take away anything from this book, it would be to have a conversation about your wishes for end of life care with your loved ones. That way, you take the onus of responsibility away from them when it comes to making a decision.

If you were a judge and had to decide who could have the rights to decide Luke's future, who would you have picked?
Rachael Gostick

Edward, if only because I think he's more mature and Cara is acting from a teen's perspective – very self-centered.

How do you get such amazing ideas for your stories and how do you get into the headspace of writing them? *Simaran Kaur*

Ideas come to me often, but if they stay in my head for any length of time, I find that they are the ones that I can build a novel around. Once I start to write, the characters pop up like little mushrooms and they carry the story. I know the ending of each book, which means that I can lay the trail of clues, but what happens in the middle is a mystery until it actually happens . . . As to the headspace, I am pretty disciplined. I set aside time every day to write and work to a schedule. I have a very healthy family life and don't want to miss more of it then I have to, so I treat writing like the job it is! My daughter, Samantha, who wrote *Between the Lines* with me, had a taste of this when she admitted that writing was a hard job, and not the whimsical, dreamy thing she thought it was!

As a writer, do you get lost in your writing like we (readers) do when we read your books? *Raya Hamdan*

Sure! I cry all the time when I'm writing the sad parts. But the characters make very bad choices, most of the time, and I'm very happy to let them go after nine months of writing. There are one of two who I would be happy to see again and whose lives I think need a bit of checking up on but generally speaking, like guests who stay a bit too long, I am content to say goodbye to them once the book is done and get on with my real life again!

Don't miss

JODI PICOULT'S

most powerful novel yet

SMALL GREAT THINGS

Coming November 2016
Available to pre-order now

#SmallGreatThings

Never afraid to confront the moral dilemmas of our times in the most human terms, SMALL GREAT THINGS is Jodi Picoult at her thought-provoking, life-affirming best.

Raised the daughter of a black maid in a privileged white household, Ruth Jefferson is no stranger to prejudice – though as a respected senior nurse, she feels a world away from the inequality that defined her mother's life.

Kennedy McQuarrie is a lawyer who defends those who would otherwise be helpless, and would not consider herself a racist by any means.

When a white supremacist accuses Ruth of a crime that leads to the death of his new-born baby, and costs Ruth her job, Kennedy knows it is the kind of case she became a lawyer to win.

As the trial unfolds and the efforts to establish the truth about what happened in the hospital continue, all three – accused, accuser and defender – will be forced to confront much bigger truths: the truths they tell themselves about the world they live in, the values upon which they've raised their families and the beliefs around which they've lived their lives.